Dreamwalker

J D OSWALD

PENGUIN BOOKS

PENGUIN BOOKS

Published by the Penguin Group
Penguin Books Ltd, 80 Strand, London WC2R ORL, England
Penguin Group (USA) Inc., 375 Hudson Street, New York, New York 10014, USA
Penguin Group (Canada), 90 Eglinton Avenue East, Suite 700, Toronto, Ontario, Canada M4P 2Y3
(a division of Pearson Penguin Canada Inc.)
Penguin Ireland, 25 St Stephen's Green, Dublin 2, Ireland (a division of Penguin Books Ltd)
Penguin Group (Australia), 707 Collins Street, Melbourne, Victoria 3008, Australia
(a division of Pearson Australia Group Pty Ltd)
Penguin Books India Pvt Ltd, 11 Community Centre, Panchsheel Park, New Delhi – 110 017, India
Penguin Group (NZ), 67 Apollo Drive, Rosedale, Auckland 0632, New Zealand
(a division of Pearson New Zealand Ltd)
Penguin Books (South Africa) (Pty) Ltd, Block D, Rosebank Office Park,
181 Jan Smuts Avenue, Parktown North, Gauteng 2193, South Africa

Penguin Books Ltd, Registered Offices: 80 Strand, London WC2R ORL, England

www.penguin.com

First published by DevilDog Publishing 2012
Published in Penguin Books 2013
This edition published 2014
001

Copyright © James Oswald, 2012
All rights reserved

Set in 12.5/14.75 pt Garamond MT Std
Typeset by Jouve (UK), Milton Keynes
Printed in Great Britain by Clays Ltd, St Ives plc

ISBN: 978-1-405-91765-0

www.greenpenguin.co.uk

MIX
Paper from
responsible sources
FSC www.fsc.org FSC® C018179

Penguin Books is committed to a sustainable
future for our business, our readers and our planet.
This book is made from Forest Stewardship
Council™ certified paper.

In Memory of Dot Lumley

Who saw something in the little dragon when no one else did

Prologue – Birth

When Balwen's last sits on the stolen throne,
And kitling sleeps beside the babe ne'er born,
When darkness stills the forest birds at noon,
In blood and fire Gwlad shall rise anew.
The Prophecies of Mad Goronwy

Wind ripped through the trees like war, tearing the last autumn leaves from the tortured branches and flinging them across the pathway. Rain-heavy clouds scudded across the night sky, alternately covering and uncovering patches of dark star-specked heavens. The thin glow from a shielded lantern on the front of the wagon cast insufficient light on the path. Occasional downpours crushed the ground, boiling the hard-packed earth in a short-lived frenzy and spooking the horses as they pulled wearily at their task.

Father Gideon shivered, pulling his cloak tighter around his neck with one hand, gently teasing back the reins with the other. He whispered calming noises to the horses, trying to instil a sense of peace even though his words were whipped away on the wind, never reaching the twin pairs of pointed ears twitching back and forth on the edge of fear. It was difficult to judge distance in the dark, impossible to tell how long he had been driving through the foul

1

storm, but he was fairly sure their destination was not far. A quiet sob of pain from behind him reminded him of why he was out here, braving this foul weather when he could have been back in the castle, enjoying a tankard of ale and a bowl of stew in front of the great refectory fire.

Pushing aside the dripping canvas flap, Father Gideon peered into the back of the wagon. A single hooded oil lamp lit the interior poorly with flickering shadowy yellow light, swaying back and forth to the rhythm of the wheels on the track. Lying in the middle of the wagon, surrounded with blankets and cushions, the princess slept.

She looked almost at peace, for a change, although even sleep could not hide the shrunken lines of her once-beautiful face. Even sleep could not mask the laboured effort of every breath or the regular spasms that racked her prone form from head to toe. The swelling of her belly, Prince Balch's seed, stretched out of all proportion the tiny emaciated figure that carried it. Still, Father Gideon knew it wasn't the child that was killing Princess Lleyn. Her strength of character and desire to see the pregnancy to term were perhaps the only things keeping her alive. And for all his knowledge, gleaned from a lifetime of study and travel, of administering to the sick and needy, yet he had no idea what it was that had struck his charge so low.

A snickering whinny from one of the horses brought Father Gideon back to his senses. Turning away from the princess, he saw a faint light ahead and soon the wagon was pulling across a small clearing towards the cottage he had not visited in fifteen years.

It was a curious building, much larger than its proportions suggested. Two windows, one either side of a wide doorway, looked out on to a well-cultivated vegetable patch. The structure was only one storey high, and yet the apex of the simple roof was over thirty feet off the ground. The single stone chimney leaked thin smoke into the night and a comforting glow glinted past drawn curtains.

As he approached, the swirling wind changed in direction, coming straight from the cottage. Instantly the horses tensed and stopped, throwing their heads around in uncertainty and alarm. Cursing, Father Gideon remembered where he was, to whom he was forced to turn. With a flick of the reins, he turned the wagon round on the wide path so that it stood between the cottage and the horses. They calmed noticeably and he allowed them to drop their heads to the grass, pulling on the brake to stop them straying too far.

The princess weighed next to nothing, yet Father Gideon was aware that he was no longer a young man as he carried her the last few tens of yards to the cottage. As if sensing his arrival, the door opened as he climbed the first wooden step towards the wide deck that surrounded the whole building. A vast shape blocked most of the light from escaping and an irrational fear swept over him for an instant.

'Gideon,' the figure said, its voice at once low and yet unmistakably feminine. 'I was expecting you. Bring her in.'

'Thank you, Morgwm,' Father Gideon said. He knew there was no point in asking how she had known of his journey when none back at the castle knew that he was gone, let alone that he had brought the princess with him.

Morgwm the Green had always been an enigma to him, but her knowledge of medicine was unsurpassed in the whole of Gwlad. Only the petty prejudices of men kept them from realizing what treasures of hidden knowledge were her and her kind.

Morgwm stepped back to allow him entry to the front room of the cottage, and he marvelled once more at how lithe such a big creature could be. Her tail looked to be a hindrance, yet it moved with her, missing all obstacles as if it had a mind of its own. Her taloned feet should have gouged the polished wooden floor and yet she trod with such delicate care that not a scratch could be seen.

'You're staring again, Gideon,' Morgwm said, the bright scales around her eyes flickering in the light from the fire.

'I'm sorry,' Father Gideon said, a flustered embarrassment reddening his cheeks as if he were a teenager trying to speak to a girl who had caught his notice. 'It's just, I had forgotten.'

'That I'm a dragon?' Morgwm asked, a faint chuckle in her voice. 'Would that all men could be so fair-minded. But come, place her here.' She indicated a low table close to the fire which had been spread with thick blankets. 'Let us see what is wrong with your girl.'

Father Gideon lowered his charge on to the table. She had slept throughout, although spasms of pain regularly racked her body and a sheen of grey sweat dampened her face, clagged her once-lustrous hair to the sides of her bony skull.

'She was taken ill some months ago,' he said, stepping aside so that Morgwm could get closer. 'Not long after the child first began to show. I've tried all I know, yet she grows worse with each day.'

The dragon bent low over the princess, her hands going from head to neck to the large bulge of belly, razor-sharp talons so close to delicate skin and yet never threatening. She hummed a low indistinct noise interspersed with odd clicking noises as she set about her task. Father Gideon looked away, unable to help. He was standing to one side of the fire, beside which a large cauldron of water steamed gently. On the other side a big basket sat just near enough to be warm without scorching. Something large sat inside it, wrapped in a blanket. Bread proving, he thought for a moment, except that it would have been a very large loaf, even for a dragon. Then he noticed a gap in the folded blanket showing something smooth, pale and speckled with tiny flecks of brown. A thrill passed through him as he recognized the egg, and with it came a chill fear. Morgwm surely risked a terrible punishment if discovered.

'Gallweed,' Morgwm said, and a surge of guilt flooded through Father Gideon as he remembered why he was here.

'Gallweed?' He asked. It sparked a memory but he could not place it.

'A nasty little poison. You humans have such dull senses, you cannot taste it, nor smell it. Your girl reeks of it. Someone has been administering her regular doses for months.'

'Who would do such a thing?' Father Gideon asked, although a nasty suspicion was forming in the back of his mind.

'I was thinking you might be able to tell me,' Morgwm said. 'And who is this, who attracts such a rare, potent and expensive poison?'

'You don't know her?' Father Gideon was surprised, perhaps expecting the dragon to know everything. But then it was unlikely she would ever have met any of the royal family. 'This is Princess Lleyn, heir to the Obsidian Throne.'

He watched a brief flicker of fear flash across the dragon's eyes, her hands draw back involuntarily from the prone body before her. Then her shoulders slumped a weary resignation and she turned once more to face him.

'Well, I'm afraid there's nothing I can do,' Morgwm said. 'Princess Lleyn is going to die.'

Morgwm looked at her old friend standing by the fire. He had not aged well in the years since last she had seen him, and her diagnosis seemed to knock something vital out of him. She turned once more to the princess and placed a hand on the great taut sphere of her belly. Her fingers could feel the pulse of a heart, slow and weak like that of an old man near death. Such was the way with gallweed. It would slowly suck the life out of a person. If Lleyn had really been ill for several months then she must have been a bright and vivacious person before then. Normally gallweed would kill in weeks, and that without the added burden of a pregnancy. Such a pity to struggle so hard only for the baby to be stillborn. For it surely could be no other way.

A terrible spasm wrenched the princess's body away from her touch. Morgwm reached out to try and push her back down on to the blankets, but with an almost inhuman strength Lleyn sat bolt upright. Her eyes were wide open

6

and yellow with her failing body. She reached out an arm, grabbing Morgwm's and pulling the dragon close, seemingly insensible to the nature of her nursemaid.

'My prince, O Balch, it hurts me so. Please save the child,' she whispered. Then another spasm creased her face, her grip loosened and she fell back on to the blankets. Father Gideon was at her side as Morgwm laid a scaly hand on the side of Lleyn's neck, then her forehead. The once-beautiful eyes stared unfocused at the dark recesses of the ceiling and with a tender touch Morgwm slid them closed.

'I am sorry, Gideon, truly. Even if you had come to me at the start of this I could only have made her passing easier. She was dead from the first drop of poison.'

Father Gideon looked down at the lifeless form of the princess, his eyes brimming with tears, his face drained of blood. Morgwm made to touch him, to try and comfort him, but the poor man looked like his knees would give way if a feather landed on his shoulder, so instead she busied herself with tidying up the body. In death Lleyn looked calmer, less pained, although nothing could hide her terrible emaciation. Her muscles had relaxed now, her arms fallen to the sides of the table, her naked feet splayed slightly. Only the heavy swell of her belly still seemed taut and quivering. Morgwm placed a hand on it, aware of the last ebbing warmth through the thin fabric. Not one death today, but two.

Then she felt it. A tiny kick of defiance, and behind it, so faint as to be almost undetectable, a regular pulsing rhythm. A heartbeat.

'The child. It lives still,' Morgwm said. 'I don't know

how. The poison should have killed it months ago. We must act quickly.'

Without waiting for Gideon, who was still staring forlornly at Lleyn's calm face, Morgwm pulled her bed dress up over the mound of straining belly. Although not yet twenty years, the princess had the body of an old woman. Her skin hung limply over fleshless ribs and her legs were like sticks wound in soft leather. Ignoring the poison-wrought devastation, Morgwm felt closely around the swell of belly, trying to see how things lay beneath. Finally, with one razor-sharp talon, she cut swiftly into the skin, parting it with delicate fingers and reaching within.

A short strangled squeak came from Father Gideon's mouth as Morgwm lifted the small blood-smeared baby from the cut in its mother's belly. She slit the umbilicus and tied it in a neat little knot, then hung the child up by its legs and tapped it smartly on the back. Once, twice. It coughed, clenched its tiny hands into fists and let out a great bawling wail.

'Warm water, towels, now,' Morgwm barked, and Father Gideon jumped as if he had just been stung. Soon the baby was clean and wrapped in blankets, placed on a low bench dragged up close to the fire.

'A boy,' Gideon said, looking down into the wide-eyed face. 'He has some of his father about him. That will come to haunt him in later life.' The baby gurgled contentedly, then squealed with excitement as Morgwm stooped over him.

'What am I to do with him?' Gideon asked, watching with wonder as the huge dragon cradled the tiny child. 'How shall I feed him? What shall I call him?'

8

'Calm yourself, Gideon, you'll upset the child.' Morgwm placed the bundle down on the bench again and went off to the storeroom. Herbs and spices were neatly packed in countless boxes and jars, but she didn't need to look for what she needed. Everything had a place and she knew exactly where it would be.

Taking water from the cauldron she mixed first a sticky black poultice and set it to steep by the fire. Next she took some white powder and stirred it into another bowl of water, adding cold until the temperature was just right. With the smallest spoon she could find, she once more took up the child and began to feed him.

'Mother's milk is the best feed for a newborn. It has so much in it that he needs. This powder will make a reasonable substitute, but the sooner we can find a wet nurse the better. Then we must cover our tracks.'

'How so?' Father Gideon asked. 'The princess is dead.' Morgwm could see the anguish in his eyes, hear it in his voice. Yet Gideon was a practical man who would put off his mourning if need be.

'Indeed she is,' Morgwm replied. 'And we must make it seem that the child died with her. I take it none know that you brought her here?'

Gideon nodded.

'Good. You must take her back. I will make it look like she still carries the child. I am sorry, Gideon, but you will probably be blamed for both their deaths.'

Father Gideon lowered his head, his shoulders sagging under the burden of responsibility. 'As her physician I carry that blame already,' he said. 'But what of the child? He can't go to Ystumtuen.'

'No, he cannot. He would be killed within the week. I'll take the boy to a village a few days from here. Their wise woman seeks my counsel from time to time. She'll see to it that he is well raised.'

Morgwm took up the pot of poultice from beside the fire and crossed to the dead form of the princess. With a complicated motion of her hand, she conjured a homunculus from the air and placed it where the child had so recently lain. Then she took a needle and fine thread, sewing up the gash. Finally she worked the poultice into the scar, chanting under her breath as she went.

'The poultice will take the colour of her skin.' She gently pulled the princess's bed dress back down over her nakedness. 'No one will see the scar.'

She lifted the near weightless body from the table and handed it back to Father Gideon. 'Now you must go.'

'What should we tell the child?' Gideon said. 'He's the rightful heir to the Obsidian Throne.'

'You should tell him nothing. I should tell him nothing,' Morgwm said. 'And if he's lucky he'll grow up to be a happy and healthy young man. Only then, and only if it is truly necessary, will we tell him of his birthright.'

Morgwm sat up all the night and on into the morning, pondering the events that had transpired. She knew that Gideon had seen the egg, knew also that he would never reveal her secret. Quietly, so as not to disturb the sleeping infant, she knelt beside the basket and peeled back the layers of blankets, laying a hand on the warm shell.

Her own hatchling, the first new dragon born for many decades, at least in this part of the world. Humans may have hunted dragons for thousands of years, but that wasn't the only reason their numbers were so few. Something had gone out of the heart of them millennia ago, before even she had been hatched, so that now to be a dragon was to be a pale shadow of the former glory that once had ruled the world.

Or so Sir Frynwy's stories would have it. Morgwm could not be sure that life hadn't always been the way it was, that dragons bred seldom and were more likely than not to be unsuccessful in the attempt. Maybe the tales of old were just that – imaginative diversions to alleviate the drudgery of daily existence.

The egg juddered slightly as the tiny creature inside it responded to the close proximity of its mother. It had been growing slowly stronger over the days. Hatching would be very soon. And now there was an added complication. The child would have to be taken to Pwllpeiran, and that was a good two days' forced march away, probably longer as she would have to keep well away from any roads travelled by men. The death of the princess would bring them flocking to Ystumtuen like geese to winter pastures. No, she would have to take the forest tracks, and that would take her at least a week.

Unless, of course, she used the Llinellau.

Sighing, Morgwm re-covered the egg, checked that the infant child was sleeping safely in its makeshift cot in front of the fire and went out to prepare for her journey.

Picking her way through the cabbage patch, Morgwm noticed the sky darkening and a chill descending on the clearing. She had been sure that the storm was past – the morning had been clear. Glancing up at the sun, climbing high into the late morning sky, her normal reserve dissolved and her mouth dropped open like an idiot's.

It was too early, surely. Not for another week. Or had she been so wrapped up in her work she had forgotten the passing days?

A semicircular disc was beginning to bite into the glowing yellow orb of the sun as the moon, great Rasalene himself, moved into the position of the Confluence. Dumbstruck, Morgwm stared at the darkening sky, watching as Arhelion was slowly covered. Deep in her bones she could feel the ecstasy of that great mating.

Noise burst across the clearing as all the birds flew into the trees and settled themselves down for the coming night. Never mind that only a few hours had passed since dawn, their chittering and song fell away far quicker than any evening chorus should. The wind that had been tumbling around the clearing like an unruly child died down to a scolded nothing. The cold deepened with the gloom, a strangely surreal darkness that glowed at the edges, as if the air fizzed with light somehow trapped. Inch by slow inch, the dark moon spread itself across the receptive sun until, with an almost audible pop, the cover was complete.

Morgwm stood in the near-total darkness, staring up at the perfect black circle scribed by a halo of flickering white. She was transfixed by the beauty of the sight, a deep calm washing over her as if a wrong done aeons ago had finally been put right. All the cares and worries of her long life were gone, all forgotten in that one endless perfect moment.

Then a terrible crash broke through her reverie, followed by the wailing of a healthy pair of lungs. The child! She had completely forgotten him.

Morgwm hurried back to the cottage, fearing the silence that fell once more upon the dark clearing. She swept through the door and took in everything in a single glance, astonished for the second time that day, the second time in half a lifetime.

The basket by the fire had tipped over, and even now the edge of the blanket was singeing, a charred smell of burned hair filling the room. Pieces of eggshell lay scattered over the floor, and for a terrible instant Morgwm imagined the infant, somehow able to move even though it was just hours old, knocking over the basket, spilling its priceless contents on the floor.

But there was no dead kitling on the floor, no mess of unfinished yolk. And the child still lay in its makeshift cot, gurgling in a contented way, its blankets all awry.

Confused and with her hearts in her mouth, Morgwm stepped closer, her vast feet avoiding the broken shell as if to tread on it might somehow cause harm to the dragon kit that should still have been lying within. The baby boy's eyes were open and a broad smile spread across his face as she approached. Then he squealed a happy cry and something far larger than his tiny body moved under the blankets. Morgwm pulled them away, half her mind already knowing what lay beneath.

It was a dragon, twice the size of the baby boy yet still miniscule. Perfectly formed, its skin was still smooth, the first scales no more than the faintest of dimples rippling over its chest as it breathed. It lay on its back, neck extended along the baby's side, seeking warmth and companionship to the infant's obvious delight. Tiny taloned feet worked back and forth and its wings fluttered gently, far bigger in proportion to its body than those of any adult.

Slowly, tentatively, Morgwm reached down and stroked the infant dragon's belly. Its lazy eyes opened and it looked up into the face of its mother. A grimacing smile spread across its mouth, revealing sharp fangs. Then it belched, an absurd little noise that had the baby boy alongside wriggling with amused pleasure. Morgwm cupped her hatchling in her hand and lifted it out of the cot. Its miniature hands grasped at her fingers with surprising strength, and she lifted it up to the light the better to see what she and Sir Trefaldwyn had done.

A strange sadness filled her that she had missed the hatching, but it was swept away at the realization that it must have occurred at the height of the Confluence. This then was a true child of Rasalene and Arhelion. And she could barely contain her excitement as she inspected the kitling minutely for defects, appraising her offspring with the detached professionalism of a healer. It was perfect. He was perfect.

He.

The first male dragon to be hatched in a thousand years.

I

Not much is known of the natural death of dragons, for none have been observed in advanced age. Like other beasts of the wild, it is most probable they meet violent ends when they no longer have the strength to defend themselves. No decaying dragon carcasses have ever been found, however, so it may be that, like the fabled elephants of Eirawen, they take themselves off to a secret graveyard to die. If this is the case, then whatever man finds this place will be rich beyond measure, for the ground will surely be strewn with the discarded jewels that grow within every dragon's brain.

Barrod Sheepshead, *Beasts of the Ffrydd*

Benfro hid in the bushes at the edge of the clearing, watching the cottage forty yards away. Thin smoke wafted up from the chimney and a heavy wooden chair propped open the door. Straining his senses, he tried to catch a whiff on the breeze of whatever it was that was being prepared inside.

He could smell the rich loaminess of the earth nearby, where the potatoes had been dug earlier in the day. The cabbages were a sulphur reek and all around the flowers was a riot of aromas, but they were a distraction. He had

15

to practise, to single out the least from the overwhelming mass. So he concentrated harder.

The smoke from the chimney wafted down on the lightest of winds, spreading away from him and hugging the far ground. Benfro could tell that it was beechwood burning, its distinctive lemon-acid reek was unmistakable. For an instant it dominated all his senses, but he pushed it aside and sought further inside.

There was an aroma of cedar, very delicate as if powdered. Other spices presented themselves to his nose: cloves, cinnamon, maker bark. As he identified each ingredient, Benfro could see its pot in the storeroom where it was kept. He could read the copperplate script neatly describing the contents. He knew that storeroom better than anything in his life, knew exactly where everything should be. It was essential, his mother had told him at least twenty times every day of his short life, that he know what was where. Too young yet to know what everything was for, but he could fetch anything and return it to its correct place blindfolded.

This potion was new to him and it piqued his curiosity. Breathing out a great snort to clear the myriad fragrances, Benfro clambered out of the bush and trotted across the clearing back to the house.

'I wondered how long you were going to spend in that bush,' Morgwm said as he stepped lightly through the door. Benfro smiled. He tried to keep his actions secret from his mother, but she always knew what he had been doing.

She sat at the great table by the window, mixing ingredients in a vast stone mortar. The brass scales stood beside a collection of jars, its polished silver weights shining in the sun. This must be an important potion, for nine times out of ten Morgwm would measure by eye.

'What are you making?' he asked, settling himself down on the bench to watch. Across the wooden expanse, his mother smiled at him, but her green eyes were sad, her shoulders a little slumped.

'O Benfro, you're really too young to be burdened with such things.'

Benfro sighed. For all that he was ten years old, his mother and all the villagers still treated him like an infant. He made to get up, resigned to learning nothing today, but his mother reached out her arm and touched his.

'Stay, little one,' she said. 'You shouldn't have to learn this, but I fear you will need to sooner or later.'

'What are you making?' Benfro asked, excited again.

'Vitae mortis, the reckoning powder,' Morgwm said, her eyes again downcast. 'Old Ystrad Fflur died this morning. We must perform the ceremony so that his spirit can move on to the next world.'

Benfro sat with his mouth agape. Ystrad Fflur. Dead. But he'd been talking to the old dragon just a couple of days ago. So he was slow and short-sighted, but then most of the villagers were. Did that mean they were all going to die? A lump formed in his throat at the thought of losing his friends, his family. A tear swelled in the corner of each eye and dripped down the scaly mass of his cheeks.

'Ah, to weep over someone you have known for such a short time. But then you've known him all your life while I've only known him for a fraction of mine.'

'How did he die?' Benfro asked. He didn't know how to

react. Should he be all sombre and quiet, or should he ask questions? His mother had always encouraged him to question everything but even so this didn't seem like the right time.

'He decided not to go on living,' Morgwm said, the matter-of-fact tone in her voice not quite matching the sadness in her eyes. She tipped the contents of the mortar into a small glass jar and put it in the leather bag lying alongside her on the table. 'Now run and put these away –' she indicated the pots of ingredients '– and bring me back one of the amphorae of Delyn oil.'

By the time Benfro returned with the oil, his mother was standing in the doorway, the bag slung over one shoulder, her long heavy-headed walking stick clasped in the other hand. He made to hand the heavy clay jar over to her, but she waved it away.

'No, you should carry it to the village, as a mark of respect,' she said. 'And to show the villagers that you're ready to take on some of the responsibilities of a healer.'

Benfro said nothing in reply, but as he followed his mother out of the house and across the clearing, three fast steps to one of her strides, his head felt giddy with pride.

Errol knew as he rounded the corner that it was going to be a bad afternoon. The posse was waiting for him.

'Hey, witch boy! Where d'ye think ye're going?' He didn't know who spoke the words, didn't really care. It could have been any of them. It was hard to distinguish one village boy from another at times, even though he had known them all from his first memories. They all had the same round florid faces, the same mops of straw-blonde hair cropped in the same regulation pudding-bowl style. Only the cloth and cut of their tunics and trousers gave any hint to who might be whose son, and even then everyone in Pwllpeiran was related. It was that kind of place.

'I aksed yer a question, witch boy.' Closer up, Errol could see who was being clever this time. Alderman Clusster's son, Trell. He was dressed in expensive fabrics: strong corded trousers that reached halfway down his shins and looked like he had long since grown out of them, a thick twill shirt two sizes too big and a soft leather jacket of doe-hide brown. To Errol, dressed in his much-mended sackcloth trousers and shirt, it was a display of wealth, though it didn't stop Trell from clambering up trees, through hedges and across streams with the rest of his less well dressed gang. It looked like they had taken the short cut straight from school to head him off on his way home. Errol's heart sank. If that was the case then he might as well get the torment over sooner rather than later.

'I'm going home, Trell,' he said. 'You know, Hennas's cottage up the road a ways, where your mam had to bring your sister last autumn. To get rid of that little problem she had.'

Trell looked furious. His face turned redder still and his hands clenched into fists. Now comes the bad part, Errol thought. At least the beatings were usually short. As the gang approached he thought about turning and fleeing, but bitter experience had shown him that running only prolonged the torment, and exercise seemed to increase the gang's violent tendencies. He stood his ground as they approached and was rewarded with a flicker of uncertainty in Trell's eyes. Like most bullies, the boy was a coward at heart.

'You wanted something, Trell?' Errol said, trying to keep his voice calm though it felt like his whole body was shaking. 'Only, I can ask my mam to whip up another potion if you need it.'

A shock ran through his whole body as the punch came from nowhere, collided with the side of his face. He had been expecting a kick, or at least a blow to the stomach first, but by the time Errol had thought any of this, his knees had already given up and he was on the hard-packed dry dust of the road. The gang stood around him laughing as Trell pulled back and landed a heavy kick in his stomach. Through his pain, all Errol could see was his leather satchel lying on the ground a few feet away, its contents spilled out in the dirt, kicked this way and that by the circling boys. His prize, the book he had been reading all summer, lay broken-spined, trampled as if it were worthless. A strangely lucid part of him laughed at the realization that to most of his illiterate tormentors it might have been no more than bathroom stationery. Another carelessly placed foot ripped a skein of pages in two, spilling them about the path, and Errol's laughter suddenly turned to rage.

Without thinking, without even knowing how he did it, he grabbed the nearest foot on an inward trajectory and pulled it hard towards him, rolling as he went. The laughter turned to alarm as someone yelped, and then a pile of bodies crashed to the ground all around him. Seeing Trell's face in the melee, Errol lashed out with his foot, feeling a cruel satisfaction as his soft leather heel met bony nose with a sickening crunch.

'Aaarghhh. Doo boke by dose!' Trell screamed, clutching his face as thick red blood spurted from between his fingers. He scrabbled away from the fight, shuffling on his bottom like a baby, and Errol couldn't help himself from laughing. The rest of the gang, picking themselves up off the ground, looked over at Trell's pathetic figure and joined in. Someone grabbed Errol's arm, and for a moment he thought he was going to be hit again. Instead he felt himself being pulled to his feet, his dusty shirt patted down with rough but not unkindly hands. Someone slapped him hard on the back, almost knocking him to the ground again. Turning, he saw Clun, the merchant's son, a huge grin on his face.

'Nice one, squirt,' the boy said, genuine mirth on his face. 'Perhaps ye're not such a weed after all.'

Errol was confused. He couldn't work out what had happened. He stood, staring in a daze at the sobbing figure of Trell, who was still sitting on his backside in the dirt, still clasping his bleeding face, tears mixing with the blood and dust on his cheeks. The other boys were ignoring him completely now, chattering among themselves about what they were going to do next. School was over for the week, harvest was all but finished, and two days of autumn sunshine beckoned. There was exploring to be done, adventures to be had and games to be played.

Errol realized that he was being asked to join in. Someone pushed his satchel back into his hands, the torn pages of the book roughly shoved into the top.

'Wotcher say, witch boy? Ye wanna play battle in the hayfield?' Clun asked.

'It's Errol,' Errol said, bemused at his turn of fortune. 'My name's Errol.'

'Whatever. Ye're the witches' boy. That makes ye witch boy. Ye coming?'

Errol considered his options. He had seen the games of battle played out in the fields in summers past. They were rough, usually ending in someone being hurt badly enough for Errol's mother to be called upon to heal them. Everyone involved got into serious trouble for the damage they caused. He longed to join in, indulge in some carefree rambunctiousness, but there were endless chores to be done and his mother was no longer young, if indeed she ever had been. But if he passed up this opportunity would it ever come again?

He looked down at his satchel and the mess that was his book. Then he looked across to Trell. The alderman's son had turned very pale and blood was still leaking from his nose. The green of his shirt was slicked all down the front with black, his expensive trousers speckled and the soft suede of the jacket ruined.

'I can't,' Errol said, turning reluctantly back to Clun. 'I'd better get Trell to my mam 'fore he bleeds to death, and once I get home there'll be no coming back.'

'Suit yersel,' Clun said with a small shrug. Then he slapped one of the other boys hard on the back of the head and ran off whooping, pursued by the rest of the pack.

Errol shouldered his pack and stooped to help Trell up. Something strange had just happened. It was as though their roles had reversed. How long had the alderman's son been bullying him? Years too long. And all it had taken was a kick to the face to turn it all around.

'Leabe us be,' Trell snarled, causing Errol to step back. Some of the old fear was still there, but it was just a reaction.

'At least tilt your head back a bit and put some pressure on the bridge,' Errol said, 'or you might bleed to death. Come to the cottage and my mam'll fix it up in no time.'

'Dot goink eddywhere near your sdinkink hovel,' Trell shouted, blood spittling out of the sides of his mouth as he scrabbled to his feet. 'Ye'll bay for dis, Errol Rabsbod-dob.' And with that he ran off back towards the village.

Errol noted with some satisfaction that he held his head back, one hand reaching up to the bridge of his nose as he went.

2

The knowledge and wisdom of a lifetime is stored in a dragon's jewels. Every experience, thought, action; every loss and every regret is tied up in those elegant and mesmerizing gems. And yet from the moment a dragon dies, those same memories begin to leach away, returning to the earth from which all power comes. To save those memories for eternity, to retain a remembrance of a greatness now passed, the jewels must be reckoned. And only the living flame can seal up a jewel against the ravages of time.

Healer Trefnog, *The Apothecarium*

The old dragon looked somehow larger in death than in life: freed from the shackles of existence he lay impossibly huge upon the rickety old wooden bed in his tiny cottage.

Benfro peered around his mother to stare at the dead form of Ystrad Fflur. Of all the dragons living in the village, he had been perhaps the kindest, certainly the most indulgent. Benfro remembered the room from past visits too numerous to count. He would sit by the fire listening to stories of the world outside the forest, mythical places whose very names conjured up exotic images: the Sea of Tegid, Fo Afron and the Twin Spires of Idris. Many an hour he had spent spellbound by the endless tales of legend. Benfro suspected that Ystrad Fflur was lonely and liked the company, but he had been generous too, plying him with sweetmeats and other delicacies to keep him coming back.

And now he was dead. His scales were dull and pallid, almost pulling away from his skin. His wings were crumpled sheets, callused and worn at the edges, knobbly with arthritis at the stumps. His face, scarred in some long-dead quarrel whose details Benfro had never managed to uncover, looked peaceful, no longer racked with the pain that had accompanied his every movement.

Morgwm stepped further into the room and Benfro followed her, clutching the amphora to his chest. It was heavy, but the responsibility for carrying it felt heavier still. He noticed that the fire in the grate had gone out, a chill spreading through the small room quite unlike anything he had ever experienced before. So that's what death means, Benfro thought. It's not about bodies lying motionless, or dragons giving up the will to live, it's about the fire going out and there being no more stories.

'Benfro! What are you doing in here? You shouldn't have to see this. Oh.' Benfro turned to see another dragon enter the room behind them. She carried herself with a stiff formality that he knew belied her true mischievous nature. Her face was kind and had once been beautiful. Her scales still gleamed with myriad colours, but age had begun to rob Meirionydd of some of her vigour. She stepped up to him and scratched him between his ears in her friendly way, but he could see the anguish on her face.

'I'm sorry, Morgwm. I didn't realize you were here already,' she said.

'It's all right, Meirionydd,' Morgwm said. 'Benfro's going to help me with the Fflam Gwir. It's something he has to learn.'

'True,' Meirionydd said, a note of sadness in her voice. 'I never thought he'd be so young when it came around though.'

'Ystrad Fflur has been slipping away for centuries,' Morgwm said. 'Even my most potent herbs couldn't keep the rot out of his bones.' She turned her attention to Benfro. 'Meirionydd and I have to prepare the body,' she said. 'Please take the amphora to the great hall. We'll meet you there.'

Benfro was about to protest, but he saw the look on his mother's face and decided against it. And besides the cold room was beginning to alarm him. Something about the lifeless corpse sent shivers up and down his long spine. Turning, he made to go, but Meirionydd blocked his path.

'Don't be so glum, Benfro,' she said smiling. 'This is a sad time, it's true. But Ystrad Fflur would not have wanted us to be miserable. Remember something about him that makes you happy and cling to that memory. You'll need it later on.'

Benfro nodded and ducked out of the cottage. He made his way carefully towards the large building that stood in the centre of the village where all the dragons congregated for their evening meals. As he walked he remembered Ystrad Fflur sitting in near-darkness by the fireplace, spinning a splendid yarn about his travels in the ice fields of the frozen south, sharing big chunks of crystallized ginger root which he pulled from a seemingly bottomless jar on the table beside him. The smile soon came back to his face.

'What're you so pleased with yourself about, squirt?' The voice cut through Benfro's reverie like a Yonaw-month wind. He turned to see his least favourite villager scowling at him.

'Good morning, Mistress Frecknock.' He tried to bow politely without dropping the amphora or indeed spilling any of its precious contents.

'A dragon is dead,' she snapped. 'What's so good about that? And what's that you're carrying?'

Nervously Benfro held up the amphora for inspection, although he wasn't about to hand it over. 'It's Delyn oil,' he said, 'for the reckoning.'

Frecknock made a dismissive noise as if she thought Benfro a poor liar. She had polished her scales, he noticed, tinting them with something so that they gleamed black rather than their normal iridescent bog-grey. She had done something to her wings too, forced them into what looked like a very uncomfortable position with some kind of wire frame. It contrived to make them look like they were much larger than their actual size but neatly folded away. Benfro knew that Frecknock's wings were smaller even than his, and he was only ten. The idea that she might pretend that they could lift her off the ground filled him with ill-suppressed mirth.

'What are you smirking about, horrible kitling,' she yelled. 'Give me that jar before you break it and ruin the day for everyone.'

Years of experience of Frecknock's ways meant Benfro

27

was able to dart from her grasping hands as she lunged at him. For a terrible moment he thought he was going to drop the amphora, spill its priceless contents over the grass, but he managed to keep hold of it as he ran towards the great hall.

'Come back here, you little freak!' Frecknock shouted at his back, but Benfro paid her no heed. Doubtless she would have her petty revenge on him soon enough.

The rest of the dragons of the village were gathered on the green in front of the hall when Benfro arrived moments later. They looked solemn and sad, but no more so than normal. Sliding between the patiently waiting forms, he made his way to the front, where Sir Frynwy and Ynys Môn stood in deep discussion. He wondered why they were all standing outside, although the autumn weather was quite fine, but as he approached he could see that the heavy oak doors were barred shut.

In all his short years Benfro had never seen the doors closed. The transformation to the normally welcoming building was total. Where it had always filled him with a sense of happy excitement, an anticipation of food, stories and companionship, now it seemed forbidding, a fortress facade.

'Ah Benfro, there you are.' He turned away from the terrible doors to look up into the kindly face of Sir Frynwy. The village elder looked tired and if possible slightly sadder than his usual melancholy self. Benfro smiled nervously and some of his brighter spirits lifted the old dragon's demeanour.

'I've brought the Delyn oil,' Benfro said, offering the

amphora. Sir Frynwy shook his head, motioning for Benfro to keep it.

'No, no,' he said. 'If Morgwm has chosen you to bear the oil, then I'll not take that honour from you.'

'Honour?' Benfro asked.

'The reckoning is a sad time for us all,' Ynys Môn said, 'and yet it's also a time of rejoicing. Ystrad Fflur was not the oldest of us, but he still lived a long and fruitful life. You've heard his tales; you know something of the places he has been. Now he's chosen to make his last journey, over to the other side. Before he can do that, all ties to this world must be severed. Such is the task of the reckoning, and those entrusted with it are honoured indeed.'

Benfro stared at the two old dragons and then down at the amphora, which was suddenly very heavy in his hands. He was about to ask more, but a great creaking groan announced the opening of the heavy oak doors. Turning, he saw his mother and Meirionydd standing in the opening.

'Come in, all of you,' Morgwm said. 'It is time.'

Benfro filed into the hall with all the other dragons, marvelling at how much it was changed from the day before. Then, a great table had dominated the room, with most of the villagers clustered around it. He had sat by the fireplace, unlit in this autumn warmth, listening to Sir Frynwy reciting passages from the *Histories*, the tales of Rasalene and Arhelion that he never tired of hearing. Now the table was gone, the benches pushed closer to the walls. A low stone bier had been constructed in the middle of the hall and on it lay the body of Ystrad Fflur.

He had been carefully washed, his loosening scales straightened and polished so that something of the lustre of youth was returned. He lay in the sleeping position, eyes closed and arms folded as if at peace. Benfro watched in amazement as the other dragons took up their habitual places around the body as if it were the table and they were simply meeting for the evening meal. He looked back out the doorway, across the grass and down the wide street towards Ystrad Fflur's house. It was only a few moments since he had left, and there was no way anyone could have carried the body past him without his noticing. So how had it got here? And for that matter, how had his mother and Meirionydd slipped past him too?

'Come, Benfro. I need your help now.' His bewildered musings were cut short by the gentle touch of his mother's hand on his shoulder. Benfro allowed himself to be led through the ring of villagers and up to the body. He stood staring unsure what to do next as they closed in behind him. Then Sir Frynwy cleared his throat and the hall fell silent.

'Friends, this is a sad day,' the old dragon said, his trained bardic voice ringing loud and clear, 'but it is a happy day too. We are gathered here to reckon the mortal remains of our beloved Ystrad Fflur, who has decided to embark on the final journey. His was a long life, filled with adventure and incident. And yet even a race as long-lived as us must succumb to the ravages of time. It is only fitting then that the youngest of us should be the first to help him on his way. Benfro, the oil if you please.'

Panic gripped Benfro as the eyes of all the villagers turned to him. He clutched the amphora close to his chest, unsure what he was supposed to do. His mother had told him as they had walked through the forest from the clearing to the village, but for the first time in his life he had completely forgotten what she had said. The silence was heavy with expectation. This was a sacred moment, and he was going to ruin it with his ignorance. Wildly he looked around at the impassive faces, a lump of embarrassed frustration rising in his throat. Then he saw Meirionydd miming tipping the jar, and her voice seemed to speak in his head: 'Pour it over him. All of it, from head to toe. Slowly, so that it doesn't spill on the floor.'

The oil was thick, almost like new honey freshly spun from the comb. It clung to Ystrad Fflur's face and chest, dripped between his scales and coated his tail as Benfro carefully poured it out. He had to climb on to the low stone dais to reach the top of the dead dragon's belly, and as he did so he was sure he could hear a quiet tutting in Frecknock's unmistakable nasal whine. It was a nerve-racking few minutes of concentration. All eyes were on him and he could so easily have slipped, dropped the amphora to the floor or worse knocked the dead body out of the position of perfect repose into which it had been so carefully positioned. The Delyn oil had a rich heavy smell that filled his head with strange half-images and threatened to upset his balance. He was relieved when it had finally all glooped out of the amphora and he could step away from the now-reeking corpse.

Morgwm stepped forward with the pouch of spice mix that she had prepared earlier, opening it and presenting it to him.

'Take the first handful, Benfro,' she said, 'and be the

31

last to cast it.' He reached in and clenched a fistful, feeling a strange warmth in the coarse mixture. Then Morgwm went around the ring, proffering the bag to everyone else. One by one they took some of the mixture and threw it on to the prone body. It stuck to the oil, giving off a powerful smell that reminded Benfro of the odour of freshly fallen pine needles underfoot. Finally everyone but Benfro had cast their share and Morgwm returned to his side, the bag hanging empty. Smiling, she nodded at him and he threw his handful on to the motionless chest of his old friend.

As it landed, sparks leaped over the glistening surface. The oil fluttered into flame, the palest of blue lights racing over the body. Behind him Benfro could hear the collected villagers all begin to chant in a low murmuring hum. As the noise built, so too did the flames until the whole body was swathed in dancing blue light.

Benfro watched in astonishment as Ystrad Fflur's features began to change. It was as if the years were falling off him, century by century. He seemed to grow in stature until he was fully twice the size of Ynys Môn, the biggest dragon Benfro had ever met. His wings, neatly folded by his side, which had always been small thin flaps of skin, seemed to swell in the flames, fine patterns of intricate mosaic covering them. His chest scales lost their age-dulled black sheen and took on green-tinged rainbow colours. In only a few minutes the shrunken arthritis-crippled old dragon who had told him endless tales of adventure and peril was replaced by a great warrior of a beast, surely the equal of Rasalene himself.

Then the flames changed, their blue fading to a clear

distortion of the air. It was only then that Benfro realized they carried no heat. Slowly at first, but with increasing speed, they leached the colour out of the massive corpse, turning it all white. And then like a hollow shell the form began to collapse in on itself, the flames slowly dying away until they finally guttered and disappeared, leaving a far too small pile of ashes on the dais. Wrapped up in his wonder, Benfro could not say when the chanting had stopped, only that a heavy silence filled the hall.

Sir Frynwy's measured tones cut through the emptiness after what seemed like an age. 'It is done,' he said. 'Morgwm, if you please.'

Benfro's mother stepped forward once more, plunging her hands into the pile of ashes where the old dragon's head had lain. Lifting them out again, she let the dust dribble between her fingers until all that remained in her upturned palm was a small pile of white jewels, each about an inch across.

'I shall take these to the resting place, where they can mingle with the memories of those who have gone before.' She turned from the body and walked towards the door. The dragons parted to let her through and Benfro made to follow her. A firm but friendly hand clamped his shoulder tight. He looked around into the dark eyes of Ynys Môn.

'You can't go with her, Benfro,' he said. 'Not this time at least. The resting place of our memories is a sacred and secret site. In time Morgwm may pass that knowledge on to you, but for now it's hers alone.'

'What was that she took?' Benfro asked. 'It looked like jewels.'

'And so it was,' Ynys Môn replied. 'All a dragon's memories, their experiences and knowledge are stored in their jewels. Ystrad Fflur lived a long and eventful life, that's why he had so many. The Fflam Gwir, the true flame of the reckoning, sets those memories firm so that they may live on for ever after the dragon has passed to the other side. Morgwm will lay those jewels with others who have died so that they can share their knowledge and experience. And if ever we have need to call upon their wise counsel, she can speak to them.'

They had left the hall now and were standing on the green outside. To Benfro's amazement, the vast table sat on the grass, laden with food. He watched the lone figure of his mother walking away down the street in the direction that would take her back to the cottage in its lonely clearing a few miles away. Everyone else was helping themselves to the feast, and for a moment Benfro felt a pang of dreadful loneliness that his mother could not join in. Then Meirionydd pushed a plate filled with meats covered in rich-smelling gravy into his hands.

'That was a wonderful thing you did back there, Benfro,' she said. 'Ystrad Fflur will be delighted to know that you cast the flame for him. Now we must remember him with happiness and laughter. Feast!'

Errol sat in the shade of the great chestnut tree, watching the other young boys at play in the hay field. Stacks of newly cut grass stood like sentinels, arranged in a grid and large enough to hide behind. It was a good game they played, if you liked battle and were big and strong. Errol knew that he was none of these things. He was small and thin, with a raggedy appearance quite unlike that of the other villagers. Where their faces were round and full, his was sharp, his features almost chiselled. His skin was softer, darker than that of his peers, his hair an unruly dark red where everyone else's was either blonde or black.

Errol rubbed at his chin, still sore from where Trell had punched him over a week ago. Life had changed a great deal since that one small incident. In the main the other boys in the village left him alone now, though Clun still tried to get him to join in with their mindless games from time to time. Only Trell himself was still hostile, unsurprisingly given the shape and size of his purple-bruised nose. At least Trell's father had the intelligence to understand how the fight had started and who was really to blame. Or maybe he was just aware of how much Hennas did for the villagers, his own daughter not least. Errol found it very difficult to care what Trell thought any more. Without the backing of the other boys, he was a slightly pathetic comical figure. Besides, the small world of Pwllpeiran and its petty narrow-minded inhabitants was no longer enough for Errol. Not since he had found the book.

The other boys continued with their mindless play and Errol switched his focus away from them on to the field, the hedge at its border and the small clumpy bushes nearer to where he sat. Narrowing his eyes, he tried to concentrate on the gaps in between them, to see the Grym, the flow of life energy that pulsed from one to the next, linking all living things together in one vast web.

He screwed his eyes up against the late afternoon sun, tried closing them, squeezing his thumbs into his eyeballs and then opening them again. That produced only stars and strange swirling patterns that faded quickly away. He could see nothing of the lines in the bright sunshine and began to wonder whether it wasn't all a big joke.

He had found the book, *An Introduction to the Order of the High Ffrydd* by someone called Father Castlemilk, covered in a thick layer of dust and printed in an archaic typeface, on the single classroom bookshelf which the village counted as a library. Errol could see both that the book was very old and that it had not been consulted in years. It referred to many magics that might be performed, while never telling how they might be made to work, just warning of the terrible dangers that came from their misuse. Only the reference to the Grym, the vast all-encompassing power of the world, and the invisible strands that linked every living thing together, gave any hint as to something that could be achieved. And then it was only how to see the lines, not how to use them. Nevertheless, since first finding and reading the book early in the summer Errol had spent every day trying to hone his senses to the point where he could see the lines.

And still he failed.

He picked up the book, which was lying on the thin grass beside him. He had tried to repair it, but the fight had damaged it very badly. Its spine was broken, the thick leather cover scraped and torn in places. Most of the pages were hanging by loose threads and many of them were ripped. A handful were missing. It didn't matter to Errol that he could no longer read it. He could recite the whole thing from beginning to end. But Father Kewick would be incandescent with rage when he found out. If he found out.

Hastily, Errol shoved the book back into his bag and wondered if he dare pretend he had never seen it. The thought of such dishonesty was almost inconceivable to him. And yet there was no good reason why he should own up and get into trouble. It was very unlikely the fat predicant would miss the book. He would only know it was damaged if Errol returned it. Not many in the village could read, let alone well enough to decipher the tiny script in most of the ancient tomes. The subject matter of most was another deterrent to their being handled; treatises on man management and obscure theological tracts were hardly enticing, so they sat gathering dust and slowly mouldering away.

Only the histories and the tales of travels to far-off lands held any interest for youngsters trying to grapple with the intricacies of letters and words. These had been Errol's favourites as he learned to read with old Father Drebble. His replacement, Father Kewick, was a different teacher altogether, and not long after he took over the histories and journals had been removed from the library. As censorship went it had been quite counterproductive, since it had forced Errol to seek out something else to satisfy his burning inquisitiveness. As a predicant of the Order of the Candle, Kewick probably had no idea what fascinating things were written in Father Castlemilk's introduction to the rival Order of the High Ffrydd.

Something rustled in the branches over his head, rousing Errol from his musing. Hurriedly he finished cramming the broken book back into his bag, shoving the whole thing behind his back.

Dead twigs and dry leaves tumbled down from above, shortly followed by a foot, a leg and then a slight figure. It seemed to drop like a stone, but then caught the lowest branch, falling lightly to the ground with the grace of a cat. A small girl with an impish grin under an unkempt mop of black hair brushed tree canopy detritus from her oft-mended tunic and stared at him with her slightly unsettling green eyes. Errol had seen her around the village but didn't know her name. Most of the girls stayed at home with their mothers, helping with the household chores. They might be seen at Suldith prayers, all dressed up in their best clothes, staring at the boys and giggling, but Errol hadn't been to prayers since Father Drebble had died. In the main he was happy to ignore any girls he might meet, and they seemed happy to reciprocate.

This one was different – confident and bold. The few times he had seen her, she had been wandering around on her own but purposefully as if on important business, not dashing nervously from house to house. And she wore clothing more appropriate for a boy, rough and ready cloth cut for hard wearing rather than style. She had never spoken to him, never even seemed to glance in his direction before. Now she fixed him with a curious smile.

'Hello, Errol Ramsbottom,' she said, flopping down on the ground beside him. 'Mind if I join you?'

Errol shrugged. 'If I say yes, will you go away?' He glanced nervously towards the field, where battle was continuing. If Clun and the other boys saw her with him

38

he would never hear the end of it. Shaded by the great leafy canopy he was fairly sure he couldn't be seen.

'Prob'ly not,' the girl replied, leaning her back into the curve of the great trunk.

'You might as well stay then,' Errol said with a shrug.

'What you been doing?' the girl asked.

'What do you mean?'

'I been watching you, Errol Ramsbottom,' she said. 'You been sitting here fer an hour now, just starin' at nothin'. You looking for the grym lines or somethin'?'

'The grym lines? How would you know about a thing like that?' Errol looked at the girl. She was dressed in a pair of short trousers, loose tatters of fraying cloth showing where they had been hacked down from an earlier life. A stout rope held the spare folds of cloth around her middle. Her knees were dirty and flecked with small scabs, as were her bare forearms, clasped around her drawn-up legs.

'The grym lines connect everythin'. They're everywhere. My uncle Arlo says that if ye stare long enough and hard enough ye can see 'em.'

'And can you?' Errol asked, his curiosity piqued. He had thought the secret all his own, yet this strange little girl seemed to know all about it.

'Oh aye,' the girl said. 'An' it's Martha, by the by.'

'What?'

'Martha,' she said. 'My name. Ye forgot ter ask.'

'Why would I be interested?' Errol asked, slightly irritated to be having a conversation with a girl.

'Cos I know things,' Martha said, a slight smirk on her

dirty face. 'I've seen you around the place, always sneakin' off ter be alone, never playin' them rough games with the other boys. I saw you stand up ter Trell last week. He's not happy about that but Clun's da's sweet on your ma so he'll stand up fer ye now. I know ye're old Hennas's boy, but nobody knows who yer da was. I know ye've been studying for the novitiate and your ma don't want you to go.'

'You know a lot about me,' Errol interrupted, his annoyance coming back. He knew that most of the villagers talked about him and his mother behind their backs, and Clun's father had been visiting their cottage in the woods quite a lot since his wife had died, but he had thought the man was looking for some potion to help with the grieving, not eyeing up his mother as a replacement. 'Who's your father then, the village alderman?'

Martha laughed. 'Old Ned Clusster?' The idea seemed to cause her great mirth. 'No, Tom Tydfil's my da,' she said, chest swelling with pride.

'The smith?' Errol asked. 'I didn't even know he had a wife, let alone a daughter.' He had never much mixed with village life; his mother's cottage was a good half a mile away on the forest edge, and he only ever came down for schooling. Some of the villagers he knew by name but not well enough to do more than say hello. They didn't exactly invite him in, nor his mother unless they were sick.

'My ma died when I was little,' Martha said, a cloud of sadness passing over her face.

'I'm sorry,' Errol said and was surprised to find he genuinely meant it. Martha smiled at his concern for her.

'Anyway,' she said, as if getting back to the topic of

interest to her. 'If ye want to see the grym lines, ye're best tryin' over by the river, at Jagged Leap.'

Errol knew the place well. It was another of his favoured haunts when he could get away from his schooling or the never-ending round of chores his mother would have him do. But he didn't want to give this slight girl the satisfaction of knowing she was right about him.

'And why would I be interested in these grym lines,' he said with as much disdain in his voice as he could muster. Martha looked at him as if he were an idiot.

'Ye've been readin' that old book all summer. If ye want to be a priest, ye've got to know about the lines,' she said as if explaining something to a baby. 'Hain't old Father Kewick taught ye nothin'?'

'He teaches reading, writing and the importance of making sure you are never to blame,' Errol said, reflecting his frustration at lessons these days. Most of the other boys still struggled with their reading and, besides himself, only Clun even knew how to hold a pen. Errol had mastered both before even starting school. Most days now he sat at the back, copying dry texts about the importance of good organizational structure and a clear chain of command. Only when the old priest's back was turned, or he was called away on urgent village business, could he turn to the few books remaining in the library that were worth reading.

'He's a Candle all right,' Martha said. 'Not like old Drebble. He was a Ram. Da says he went all over he world. Saw everythin'. Even went as far as the Sea of Tegid.'

'I want to join the Order of the High Ffrydd,' Errol

said, wondering why he was telling this girl something he had not yet admitted to anyone else. 'I'm going to master the ways of magic and become an inquisitor.'

Martha laughed, but it wasn't an unkind gesture, more an appreciation of enthusiasm. 'Ye've gotta get through the choosin' first, Errol Ramsbottom,' she said. 'Then ye've gotta survive the novitiate before ye can even be a warrior priest. It takes years to get to be even captain of one of the troops.'

'How d'you know so much about these things?' Errol asked, amazed that such a rich source of information was so close and he had never known.

'Uncle Arlo told me,' Martha said. 'He's a sergeant in the army. He's always goin' on about the warrior priests an' how they all look down on the ordinary soldiers. Sometimes he comes to visit when he gets leave. Da says he drinks too much, but he tells the best stories when he's drunk.'

'He sounds interesting,' Errol said. 'I'd like to meet him some time.'

Martha laughed again and he grinned at her infectious mirth. It was nice to be able to talk to someone who wasn't trying to teach him a lesson.

'Ye'd do well to keep away from him, Errol Ramsbottom,' she said. 'You look too much like the enemy.'

'I what?' Errol asked, brought up short by the statement. Martha merely shrugged and got to her feet.

'Yer da, I guess. Must a been, cos yer ma's from the south.'

'What do you mean, enemy?' Errol asked, confused. He'd lived with taunts about his looks all his life but had always assumed they had to do with his mother's profession. Witch boy. That was what they called him.

'Yer a Llanwennog, Errol,' Martha said. ''Least yer da was one. Anyway, yer friends are comin' back. I'd better scram.'

Errol looked down at the field, where Clun and the rest of the gang, bored of playing battle, were making their way up the slope towards the chestnut tree. And when he turned back, she was gone.

3

There is a common myth that has grown up around King Divitie XXIII's abolition of the timeless tradition of the aurddraig. It is said that in his time of greatest need the king was aided by a dragon. So grateful was he to the creature that he immediately granted it and all its kind the freedom of the Twin Kingdoms and his own personal guarantee of protection from persecution. The truth is rather more prosaic.

Few dragons still lived at the time of Divitie's reign, and the Order of the High Ffrydd had developed sophisticated techniques for tracking them down. The warrior priests were only called into action once a dragon had been located. Then they would be dispatched to use their skill in magic to execute the creature and recover its precious jewels. The warrior priests were few in number, the most adept magicians in the Twin Kingdoms.

Divitie reigned during a time of heightened threat from the barbarian Llanwennogs to the north. He saw in the Order of the High Ffrydd, with its highly trained and skilled warrior priests, an army in the making. Along with Inquisitor Hardy he set about changing the focus of the order. The warrior priests were elevated in importance, their numbers increased tenfold. The quaisters, who had previously been the dominant rank within the order, were reduced to the position of teachers and administrators. The lifting of the aurddraig was no more than a small part of the rewriting of the order's charter to emphasize its new role as defender of the realm.

It is likely that Divitie himself ordered the story of his narrow escape to be circulated. A canny politician, he knew well how to manipulate his people, and in particular the noble houses who had always provided the king's army in the past.

Barrod Sheepshead,
A History of the House of Balwen

The old king sat on the edge of his huge black throne like some shrivelled piece of pig meat left in the sun for the flies to lay their eggs in. He was dressed in robes of state which looked as if they had been made for a man twice his size. Even the slim golden crown slipped down his head, held in place only by his protuberant ears. His face was sallow; bloodshot eyes focusing on a point not far from the end of a pointed nose mottled red with broken veins; thin lips stained with endless wine cracked open to reveal a few rotting yellow-brown teeth in the fetid hole behind; cheeks hollow, their skin blotched with liver spots and ragged with gristly white stubble; lank greasy hair a shade less healthy than urine in colour, hanging limply from his balding pate to his weedy drooping shoulders. One trembling hand held a tall golden goblet half-filled with dark red wine, the other grasped the thick carved arm of the throne as if to stop the weight of his drink from toppling him over into the dark depths of the great chair. He sat like a little child, huddled up to one massive armrest.

Approaching her father across the great expanse of the Neuadd, Princess Beulah of the House of Balwen could hardly suppress the disgust and contempt the pathetic figure of King Diseverin IX roused in her. Shuddering, she climbed the low stone steps up to the throne, glancing from side to side at the expanse of bare stone floor and the odd stained-glass windows, broken long ago in the Brumal Wars and repaired without any regard for the images they had once sported. Things would change once the old man died. Once it was her sitting on the Obsidian Throne. Things would change, but not yet.

Kneeling at her father's feet, Beulah took his free hand, seeing the crease of concern fly across Diseverin's face as his balance was upset. She pulled the rank-smelling thing towards her, gagging at the odour of rotting meat that hung around her father, and kissed the large ring of state that rattled around one bony finger. A spark of life leaped from her lips and into the polished ruby, flowing through the king's hand and up into his body, rousing him from his stupor like a puppet master taking up his strings. Duty performed, Beulah backed quickly away.

'Eh? Is that you, Lleyn?' the king asked, his cataract-clouded eyes flickering around even though there was scant hope of them ever again focusing on anything.

'Lleyn is dead,' Beulah said. 'It's me, Beulah.'

'What? Beulah? My little girl? So like your mother.' The king attempted a smile and a waft of foulest garbage rose into the air. Beulah tried not to retch, putting a scented handkerchief over her mouth and nose to ward off the stench.

'How are you feeling today, father?' she asked from behind her mask.

'Tired, my little one. Affairs of state weigh heavy on me,' the king said. Then, as if only just remembering it was there, he lifted the goblet to his lips and took a long draught. Most of the wine went down his chin and soaked into the ermine ruff of his robes of state. They were pink with repeated soakings, the fur matted and claggy.

'You should go, little one,' the king said, holding out his now-empty goblet for a page to fill. 'I have a busy schedule today. Same as every day. Sometimes I wonder that Padraig doesn't go out of his way to make work for me.'

Beulah bowed. It was enough of a dismissal. It didn't matter that her father's day would be spent in a soft-drunken stupor as an endless stream of courtiers petitioned him for favours or simply tried to flatter him. Seneschal Padraig and his cronies in the Order of the Candle carried on the day-to-day running of the state. The king had long since been reduced to a ceremonial role. That too would change when she came to power, Beulah vowed. But she was not yet old enough to ascend the throne. If her father died now, Padraig would be made regent. Even if it was only for a year her power would be eroded. She could not claim the Obsidian Throne in her own right until she turned twenty-one. So the old man needed to stay alive. At least for now.

Beulah was no stranger to leaching the life force out of her enemies. Her tutor, Inquisitor Melyn, had taught her the magic of the lines well, and his knowledge of poisons had been indispensable in the removal of her elder sister. Even without her bizarre liaison with the Llanwennog hostage, Lleyn would have had to go. Her pregnancy had just been the perfect cover. Now Beulah found herself having to do a very different task, keeping her ailing father alive. Were it not for her frequent administrations, King Diseverin IX would surely have died years ago. Still, that which could be taken away could as easily be given, even if the old man was doing his best to kill himself all the while.

Bowing slightly, Beulah turned and left the great hall, heading first to the kitchens to add vital powders to the king's wine and food, then to her personal quarters and the tub of hot rose-scented water that she so desperately yearned for.

Creeping silently through the undergrowth, Benfro tried to keep his focus on the white-speckled russet-brown camouflage of the roe deer. It was grazing on the moss clinging to the side of an enormous oak tree that had fallen in some long-ago storm, leaving a scar in the canopy that leaked sunlight into the gloom. Somewhere out there Ynys Môn was working his way around behind the deer, but for all the noise he was making he could have been miles away.

Benfro thought he was quite adept at stalking. He leaped at every opportunity to head out into the deep forest with the dour old dragon. Away from the other villagers, out there in the wild, Ynys Môn was a fount of information, a skilled hunter and far more indulgent of Benfro's failures and shortcomings than his mother ever was. Sometimes their trips went on for several days, like this one, and in the evenings they would make camp around a small fire. Benfro would prepare whatever they had managed to catch during the day and Ynys Môn would tell tales of distant times when dragons had been great creatures, masters of the earth and sky. A time when men were no more than simple creatures raising flocks of sheep and scratching in the ground for food.

The roe deer looked up suddenly, its mouth working away still as its ears swivelled this way and that trying to determine what had changed. Benfro froze, his breath held. The birds were still twittering in the high branches and overhead a buzzard wheeled and screamed. There was nothing in the scene to suggest that two dragons were within pouncing distance. He willed the beast to relax, to put its head back down and resume feeding. Slowly, as if it could feel and react to his thoughts, the deer settled. Letting out his breath silently, Benfro stepped forward.

The crack was like thunder, sending a flock of pigeons out of their roost in an explosion of feathers. Benfro looked down to see the dry stick under his foot and cursed himself for being distracted. That was the mistake of a rank amateur and his pride was hurt almost as much as his sole. Spooked, the deer looked up, froze momentarily, then took off into the trees. With a cry of frustrated rage, Benfro set off after it.

Now it was down to the chase. There was no room for subtlety, only speed and the ability to keep an eye on his quarry as it darted this way and that through the trees. As he ran, Benfro was acutely aware that they were at least two days' walk from the village and heading in the wrong direction. He also knew that without a kill they would be eating roots for supper. And Ynys Môn would never let him forget the elementary mistake he had made, especially if he had no meat. So he crashed on through the thinning trees.

The deer began to tire, designed more for quick flight than any sustained chase. Benfro could sense its weariness in the way it hesitated for a fraction before deciding which way to jump. He was definitely gaining on it, and the widening spaces between the trees helped him even more. His hearts hammered in his chest and his legs felt like they were on fire, but he was determined to fell the creature.

Closer and closer he came to the deer, jinking left and right, back and forth but always keeping to much the same direction. He began to see the pattern in its flight and so how to put an end to it. With a great forward lunge he leaped at the space the deer was surely going to spring into next. Even as he did so, he realized the potential for humiliating and painful injury, but the spooked animal jumped as predicted and Benfro crashed into it, knocking them both to the ground. As they fell he grabbed its head and neatly broke its neck, so that by the time he had rolled to a halt the creature was dead.

'Bravo, a splendid chase,' said Ynys Môn, trotting up through the trees. 'And a good-sized beast too. It looks like we won't be starving tonight after all, though I can't help thinking you would have been better off using your b——.'

Somewhere in the back of his mind Benfro registered that the old dragon had caught up with him. He was also aware that he had caught and killed the deer with his bare hands and that, strapped to his back, was a hunting bow that would have made the whole chase much quicker and simpler. But what was taking up most of his available attention was the sight his chase had brought them to.

The trees thinned almost to nothing. He was crouching at the top of a steep incline that stretched around in an almost perfect circle half a mile across, forming a crater perhaps a half hundred yards deep. A few massive trees, ancient and glorious, grew within the great cauldron and in its centre rose a building the likes of which he had never seen before.

It was made from stone, for a start. All the houses in the village had stone foundations, but in the main they were constructed of wood, great beams of oak blackened and twisted with age. This structure was built of vast blocks, carefully shaped. It was also on a scale that beggared belief. Benfro could count four rows of windows in the main body of the building, but towers rose from that, with the tallest at least the same height again. Instead of thick reed thatch, the roof was covered in dark slate.

A cluster of smaller buildings surrounded the great palace, for that was surely what this must be, but the whole settlement seemed to be deserted. No smoke rose from the myriad chimneys, nothing moved along the overgrown path that wound its way from one side of the crater to the other, climbing out of the depression at each end through cuttings hewn into the rise. Benfro could also see that some of the smaller buildings were in a poor state of repair. Some had roofs that had fallen in to reveal skeletal wooden beams beneath. Others had no roof structure at all, their walls beginning to crumble where small trees had taken hold. Indeed the whole crater was slowly reverting back to forest, what must once have been well-tended pastures now speckled with small shrubs and saplings.

'Ystumtuen. Well, well,' Ynys Môn said quietly, standing by Benfro's side. 'I must be getting old. I had no idea we'd come so far.'

'What is it?' Benfro asked.

'Now it's a sad ruin. Years ago this was King Divitie's hunting lodge,' Ynys Môn said. 'It's not far from here that he was trapped by a particularly nasty boar. The same boar, as it happens, that gave me this.' He pointed to the scar and line of missing scales on his flank. 'He would have died there if I hadn't been out hunting that day myself.'

'What happened? And who's King Divitie?' Benfro asked, bemused.

'Goodness, has your mother told you nothing of men?' The old dragon seemed shocked as much as surprised.

'Only that they're not to be trusted. That they'll try and kill me if they find me.'

Ynys Môn sighed, resting his hand on Benfro's shoulder. 'That's true,' he said. 'They live such short lives and you can't expect one to honour the word of another. But Morgwm is very remiss not to have told you more. What if you'd blundered in there before I caught up with you?'

'There's nobody there,' Benfro said. 'It looks like it's been deserted for ages.'

'You've better eyes than me, young Benfro,' Ynys Môn said. 'And you're right. Ystumtuen has been abandoned nearly ten years now. Not long after you were hatched. When Princess Lleyn died.'

'Princess Lleyn?' Benfro asked, his mind filling with

questions. He longed to ask Ynys Môn everything, but even more he wanted to go down to that great palace and explore its ruined halls. And yet it shivered him with a deep-seated fear. This was a place of men yet only a few days' walk from the village.

'You're wondering how it is that we can live so close to them, how your mother can have dealings with them if they want only to kill us,' Ynys Môn said, correctly anticipating Benfro's worry. 'It wasn't always that way,' he continued. 'In fact it's only been a hundred and fifty years or so since the aurddraig was stopped.'

'Aurddraig?' Benfro asked.

'A bounty, paid by the Royal House of Balwen, for the head of any dragon presented at court.'

'That's monstrous,' Benfro said, a shiver running down his spine to the tip of his tail.

'Quite so,' Ynys Môn said, his voice calm with the resignation of centuries. 'But we were powerless to stop them then and we still are today. They wield the power of the earth and killing is in their blood. It's what they do. But we're not without resources ourselves, you know. And not all men hate us. Remember that, Benfro. There are some who simply fear what they don't understand, and others who fight their own kind, kill them even, just to protect us. Up here in the forest we've largely been left alone. That's why we all live in the village. It's protected by magics that even the most powerful of men can't penetrate.'

'So why did they stop. Killing us, that is,' Benfro asked. 'Have they stopped? Mother is always telling me all the terrible things they'd do to me if they caught me.'

Ynys Môn pulled out his flask, considered it for a moment and then put it back again without drinking. He seemed to be weighing something up in his mind and Benfro's hearts sank. He was going to be told to ask his mother.

'I suppose you could say it was all down to me,' the old dragon said finally. Benfro looked up, his excitement burning bright once more.

'As I said, it was a hundred and fifty years ago. Possibly a bit more. In the time of King Divitie. Actually I think he was King Divitie the twenty-third or something – they're not very imaginative with their names, the royal House of Balwen. The men are all Balwen, Divitie or Diseverin, the women usually Beulah or Lleyn. But I digress.

'King Divitie – this King Divitie – well, he was the great-grandfather of the current King Diseverin and he loved to hunt. Not dragons, strangely enough. He had always thought our persecution monstrous and unnecessary. He preferred smaller, faster prey. He also preferred not to kill things that could talk. Civilized, for a man, was King Divitie. So he went after deer and wild boar, things like that. He built Ystumtuen. Oh there's been a settlement here for millennia, but he developed it into the great palace you can see now. And he spent most of his time there.

'It was a time of great anxiety for those of us already living in the village, being so close to so many men. Before he came this part of the Ffrydd was almost forgotten, just a few small villages out on the forest edge. But having the royal court move close by was terrifying. That's when your mother arrived. She set some kind of protective ward around us, but for it to work she needed to be outside its influence. That's why you live away from us all, you know. We built her that house, cleared that clearing, and in return she became our protector. She could have been a great mage, your mother, but she turned to healing instead.'

Benfro looked at the old dragon with a mixture of surprise and excitement. No one had ever spoken to him about his mother before. He had never really considered what had gone on before he was hatched, but she must have had a life. And if Ynys Môn knew about Morgwm, then he would surely know about the other unanswered question that bothered Benfro most days.

'So you would have known my father,' he said, then wished he hadn't as the old dragon stiffened visibly. Benfro cursed himself for being so impetuous. If there was one good way to have his inquisitiveness snubbed it was to bring up this subject.

'I met your father once, yes,' Ynys Môn said gravely. Benfro wasn't sure what it was he could hear in the old dragon's voice. Was it regret or disapproval? There was a story there to be told, but he bit his lip, suppressing the urge to ask further.

'He came along much later, though,' Ynys Môn continued. 'I . . . We . . . Well, he's dead now, so let's leave it at that, eh.'

Though he longed to know more about his father, bitter experience had taught Benfro not to push the matter.

'What became of the king?' he asked in a small voice, hoping to re-create the earlier mood. It seemed to work, or maybe Ynys Môn was looking for a subject, any subject to talk about other than Benfro's father.

'Divitie, yes.' He cleared his throat. 'Well, one day the king was out hunting, not far from here, when he got separated from his followers chasing a great big vicious tusker. I've already told you how it gouged me. Well it killed Divitie's horse and would've finished him off too if I hadn't been hunting it through the same part of the forest. I don't know why I helped him. Maybe I was so angry at that boar for the injury it'd caused me, I just wanted to kill it myself before someone else robbed me of my revenge. Maybe your mother's magic had lulled me into believing the threat from men was over.'

Benfro started at the words. His mother's magic. He had said she could have been a powerful mage too. Suddenly he began to see her in a different light, one that he longed to explore further. But he knew too well what would happen if he interrupted Ynys Môn now. With a supreme effort he choked down the question before it could burst from his lips. Oblivious to his internal battle, the old dragon continued with his tale.

'Between the two of us we managed to kill the beast, though not without injury. The king was wounded in the leg and could hardly stand, let alone walk. He said he would grant me a boon if I would help him. I asked that he abolish the aurddraig, and he laughed, saying he was going to do that anyway. He was a good man, Divitie.

'I helped him back here. That caused a bit of a stir, a whole troop of warrior priests surrounding me with their blades of light held high. You can imagine how I felt. Pretty foolish for allowing a man to get me to trust him, for one thing. But he was good to his word. There in front of them all he declared an end to the aurddraig and said that henceforth anyone found persecuting our kind would be put to the sword. He even went as far as to say we would be welcome in his court.

'For a few years, while Divitie still lived, there was a peace of sorts between the men and us. Some of them came to see what they could learn from us and left amazed that they could have been ignorant for so long. Others continued to distrust and hate us, though there were few actual killings. The Order of the High Ffrydd, the warrior priests, were the worst. They were set up to eliminate dragonkind from the world. It's written into their holy charter. But Divitie held them in check. He even executed a few inquisitors, though I suspect that was more because they challenged his power than because they persecuted us.

'The problem with men, or the blessing, I suppose, is that they live such short lives. I'm not that old in dragon terms, Benfro, but I've lived ten men's lives and hope to live at least fifty more. King Divitie died at a ripe old age for a man. He was eighty-eight, I'm told. His son took the throne and his son after him, as is their way. None of them undid his proclamation, but with each passing generation we were forced to be more and more accountable to the royal court. First we had to be counted, then we had to pay homage to the king, taxes to the treasury. And, worst indignity of all, all of our kitlings had to be presented to the king's master of dragons before they reached three years of age.

'The current king is Diseverin and he is a weak man, overfond of strong drink. Under his reign things have begun to slip back to the old ways. When he took the throne he introduced a law requiring us to seek his permission to have hatchlings. We don't breed often, as you know, but long ago we decided this was an imposition too far. So Morgwm reworked the protective spell on the village. Men cannot find it, no matter how hard they try. If they follow the paths or hack their way through the trees, they will always end up in the clearing where you and your mother live.'

'But I've never seen a man,' Benfro said. 'Let alone been presented to any master of dragons.'

'Your mother's a skilled mage, Benfro. Even if she doesn't show it off,' Ynys Môn said. 'She can sense when men are coming. That's why she sends you away to stay with us.'

'So they're at my home now?' Benfro asked, a sudden flurry of panic spurring him to his feet.

'What do you think you're doing, young dragon?' Ynys Môn said.

'We've got to get back. We've got to help her. They could be killing her.'

'Sit down, Benfro,' Yns Môn said.

'But . . .' Benfro protested.

'What can you do?' Ynys Môn asked. 'You can barely hunt a deer without making a mess of it. How are you going to defend your mother against a troop of warrior priests? I won't lie to you, Benfro. Morgwm is in danger every time a man comes to her clearing. They might decide to kill her on a whim. Men are like that.'

4

Perhaps the first spell a young kitling might be encouraged to learn is that of concealment. Any dragon skilled in the subtle arts will easily see through it, but the mental exercise is a good grounding for later workings, and a novice can safely be left to practise unsupervised. It is also of great use in hunting, and in avoiding the unexpected attention of men.

Aderyn, *Educational Notes for the Young*

The rock jutted out over the stream, creating permanent shade in one corner of the deep pool where huge old salmon hid, lazily waiting for the next great spate. Errol had sat for many an hour here in his childhood, staring at the water and trying to glimpse those elusive fish. The villagers occasionally tried to catch them using nets or lines. But ever since old Ben Coulter had been found face down in the pool, his net still clutched in one hand and a gaping wound on the side of his face seeping dark blood into the calm waters, the villagers had shunned the place as haunted and evil. It had taken Errol less than five minutes to piece together what had really happened. It was obvious that the man had slipped while trying to sweep his net around the base of the great rock, banged his head and fallen unconscious into the water. The current eddied around the deepest part of the pool in a continuous slow circle which could have kept the dead body in place for days if there was no rain.

Errol kept his deductions to himself, happy for the villagers to treat Jagged Leap as if it were cursed. It was a strange place anyway, though he had never felt afraid there. There were stories of people hearing voices. Some told tall tales of dragons coming down out of the woods to drink from the waters, though Errol had never experienced either. He liked the place for its aura of peace and calm. Even when storm winds shook the nearby trees and threw dead leaves and branches across the ground, the flat space on top of the rock always seemed sheltered. He had never known it to be cold there either.

He sat there now, perched on the edge above a twelve-foot drop into the black water below, his legs dangling as he watched the sunlight sparkle on the surface. Evening was fast fading and the birds were a riot of noise in the trees, competing with the rush and babble as the stream scrambled over rocks and gurgled its never-ending downward journey. It wasn't a dangerous pool really, he mused. It was deep where the rock jutted out over it, but a little further downstream it shallowed, and a bank of sand formed a small beach. If only old Ben had kept his wits he would probably have survived his fall and hauled himself out there, but he must have been knocked senseless.

'Wotcher thinkin' about, Errol Ramsbottom?' The voice startled him for an instant. He had heard no one approaching, but by the time he turned to see who spoke he already knew.

Martha seemed to be stalking him these days. And she had the irritating ability to move around as if invisible. She would turn up in the most unexpected of places, always with her curious questioning and her oddly formal way of addressing him by his full name. He never knew when she would appear. Sometimes a week or two would go by without him hearing her voice; sometimes she would pop up two or three times a day. He hadn't seen her for several days now and was surprised to find his spirits lifted by her arrival.

'You seen the lines prop'ly yet?' she asked not unkindly, though the question sent a small shudder of resentment through him. Try as he might, Errol couldn't see anything that the book had promised would appear to the diligent student. In recent weeks he had become ever more despondent at his failure, to the point where he had all but given up trying. And yet he was still drawn to this place by the possibility.

Ignoring his silence, Martha sat herself down beside him, swinging her legs over the drop. Errol was all too aware of how close she was and couldn't make up his mind whether her familiarity was pleasant or unsettling. Deciding on the latter, he tried to inch away, but she just leaned closer, resting the weight of her head against his shoulder so that he had to support her or let her fall over.

'You hain't seen 'em yet, have you?' she said.

'No,' Errol conceded, 'I haven't. Sometimes I think they're nothing but figments of someone's imagination.'

Martha looked up at him, mercifully leaning away as she did. She seemed to be studying his features in the decaying light and he wondered if he should look back at her, deciding it was easier to concentrate on the scrubby trees that dotted the far bank of the river.

'That's why you don't see 'em, Errol Ramsbottom,' she said eventually with a little triumphant flourish in her voice. 'There's a part of you don't want 'em to exist. So they don't.'

'What're you saying? I have to believe in these lines to see them?'

'That'd help.' Martha pointed at the trees, picking out one far upstream first and then going to the next and the next in succession. 'I can see the Grym flowing between each of those trees. That one there –' she pointed to one almost directly across from where they sat '– that one's dying. The Grym's all weak around it, kind of broken up. It's only still alive cos of the nexus.'

'The nexus?' Errol asked despite himself. He always found his curiosity at Martha's seemingly endless knowledge was greater than his irritation at her.

'Ain't you never wondered 'bout this place – what makes it so special?' she asked without expecting an answer. 'It's a junction between two powerful lines of the Grym. That's why I said you'd see 'em here. They're so bright, I thought you'd see 'em easy.'

'I can't see anything,' Errol said sadly. 'There must be something wrong with me.'

'Only in your thinkin',' Martha said, suddenly grabbing his hand and pointing it into the darkening distance. Her grip was warm and comforting in a manner that both alarmed and exhilarated him. 'Look over there, towards that big oak. The west line goes straight through it, over the ground to where we're sitting. An' there.' She pulled his hand round so that he was forced to turn and face her, to smell her dark hair and the subtle aroma that rose from her skin. 'The north line comes in through that gap in the shrub cover and follows the line of the river downstream. Follow it now.' She pushed his arm round, leaning out dangerously over the drop to the water below until she reached around him, her small body pressed closer still to his. 'All the way down the slope with the river until the bend. It carries on straight. I don't know where, same as I don't know where it comes from. Someday, when I'm a bit older, I'm goin' to find out.'

Errol strained his eyes in the darkness, trying to make out anything while trying not to think about how much he was enjoying Martha's close company. He could see the water, white as it splashed across the rocks below the pool and tumbled down towards the bend about fifty yards away. It was difficult to make out anything as night fell. Overhead was cloudy, only the dullest reflection of the retreating sun lending any light to the scene at all.

For a moment he thought he could see something. A tiny sliver of doubt tried to tell him that it was just the water running over rocks, but it was too still, too perfectly straight to be foam. And the more he looked at it, the more it seemed to carry on past the bend in the river and on into the forest beyond it.

'You can see it now, can't you?' Martha said, her voice a soft breathy whisper in his ear.

'I can see something,' Errol said, turning to face her,

clinging to her hand still as if it were the solution to the problem he had been fighting with for over a year. He pointed upstream and traced the faintly glowing path of what he thought he could make out above the dark fast-flowing stream. 'It comes from there, all the way to here, where we're sitting.' He looked quickly back across the water. 'And yes, I can see it swelling up from the roots of the oak. That must be why the tree's so big. It's feeding on the Grym!'

With surprising reluctance Errol let go of Martha's hand and turned to see where the line went behind them after its intersection at the rock. With each passing second it was growing stronger in his sight so that everything around it seemed cast in shadow. Even so he could feel something wrong about the scene, as if an easily over-looked detail had been removed. Or something was there that shouldn't have been.

At the same instant as Martha gasped in alarm, Errol heard an all-too-familiar voice say, 'Told ye I'd get even, witch boy,' and a heavy object caught him a glancing blow across the side of his head.

Benfro and Ynys Môn walked through the evening and on into the glowering darkness, their path lit by the stars and a sliver of crescent moon in a clear autumn sky. For a while Benfro thought they were going to walk all night, but eventually they came upon a clearing and, with a the-atrical creaking of hips, the old dragon suggested they stop for the night. Benfro dropped the deer carcass and set about making a fire. It was late and all he really wanted to do was sleep, but he knew his teacher would expect a meal.

'Don't bother,' Ynys Môn said once the flames were crackling. Benfro had picked up the carcass and extended a single talon to begin butchering it, but now he put it down away from the heat. The old dragon reached into his pack. His hand stayed there for long moments, as if he were searching for something, though the bag was not that big. Finally he smiled and drew out a cloth-wrapped bundle which turned out to be cheese and cold meat. He handed over half before settling himself down in front of the crackling flames. Benfro sat in the warmth and began to eat, wondering how his teacher had managed to hide a satchel full of food from him for the whole of their trip. His curiosity was momentarily curbed by the realization of just how hungry he was, and soon the meal was devoured.

'Why do men hate us so?' Benfro asked once Ynys Môn had finished eating and was sipping from a flask which he seemed disinclined to share.

'Ah, now there's a question that gets to the heart of it all.' The old dragon stoppered his flask and set it by his side. The flames of the fire lit his face with flickering orange, highlighting the scars and chipped scales on his weathered face, arms and chest, but there was a gleam in his eye as he began to speak again.

'Some say it goes back to the legendary times, to great Gog and Magog and their disastrous battling over Ammorgwm the Fair.' Ynys Môn must have seen the blank look on Benfro's face. 'Don't tell me you don't know that story,' he said incredulously. 'What has your mother been teaching you all these years?'

'Herbs and potions mostly,' Benfro said. 'Sometimes she tells me stories about Rasalene and Arhelion. And she told me the one about Palisander and Angharad, but Sir Frynwy tells it better.'

'Hmm, well. I've no doubt the bard could tell you about Gog and Magog too, but since he's not here, I'll have to do my best. A short version of it anyway, since it's as good an explanation as any other as to why men hate us so.' He cleared his throat, making a fair if exaggerated impression of Sir Frynwy before one of his special tellings.

'Gog and Magog were twin brothers, both hatched under the Confluence back in the times of legend, when dragons were masters of Gwlad. They were wise and magnificent and there was nothing they couldn't do if they set their minds to it. But like all great mages, they had a fatal flaw, for both were insufferably arrogant. And they both fell in love with the most beautiful dragon who ever lived, Ammorgwm the Fair.

'She was without compare. More beautiful even than Palisander's great paramour Angharad. Her smile could melt the coldest of hearts and none could meet her without coming away from that meeting a better dragon. Gog and Magog both knew they were destined to wed her and both wooed her with a single-mindedness that bordered on obsession. But Ammorgwm cared for no one in particular; she loved everyone the same, in her innocent unworldly way.

'Now whether it was Gog who first grew suspicious of Magog or the other way, it doesn't really matter. The brothers fell out over who'd have Ammorgwm, and their argument soon turned into battle. Before long their warring shook Gwlad. The sky burned. The earth broke open. In their arrogance they cared nothing for the rest of dragonkind, only for what they wanted.

'It was Palisander himself who went to Ammorgwm, so the tale has it, and asked her to intervene. He was very old by then, and respected by most. He knew that no one but Ammorgwm could make the brothers stop their terrible fighting. And if they didn't, then soon Gwlad would be destroyed. But Ammorgwm was a simple soul, as naive as she was beautiful. She understood nothing of violence. She wanted only for everyone to be happy, and so she walked out to meet Gog and Magog on their field of battle. The brothers were using terrible, powerful spells to try and overcome each other, and poor Ammorgwm was struck down by a rebounding mystical blast.

'At her death the whole of Gwlad stood still for an instant, shocking even Gog and Magog out of their dreadful rage. When they saw what had happened, what they had done, they were distraught beyond measure. Neither would admit fault, each blaming the other, but equally they could see the danger in their warring. So without a further word they went their separate ways, vowing never more to speak to one another.

'But Magog went a stage further. He hated his brother so much he couldn't bear to breathe the same air or fly in the same skies any more. He worked a great magic, both wondrous and terrible, that split Gwlad into two spheres. Gog and his followers were banished to one while Magog and his clan lived in the other.

'The world was riven, families rent apart. There was no time to say goodbye, no time to retrieve favoured possessions. It all happened in an instant, for Magog had planned it that way, knowing his brother would try to twist his working if he but had a chance. And Magog was right to be so wary, because it is said that Gog gave a parting gift to his brother.

'He opened up men's eyes to the subtle arts. And at the same time he gave them his own hatred of Magog and his cronies. Over the centuries this hatred grew along with their power, and as it grew so they stopped discriminating between followers of Magog and the thousands of neutral dragons who'd remained in his sphere. All were fair game. We dragons might live long lives, but there are few enough of us. Men live only a few tens of years, but they multiply with each new generation. And they're vicious, violent. They love to hunt and kill just for the sport of it.'

The old dragon paused, taking a sip from his flask. 'I don't know if there's even a grain of truth in the legends. They say Gog and Magog lived more than three thousand years ago, and even old Sir Frynwy's only fifteen hundred. If it happened at all, it was long before any of us were hatched. Maybe it's just a tale told to teach us the folly of pride. Whatever the truth of it, men hate us. They're powerful in magic and they're numerous beyond counting. If they weren't too busy killing each other most of the time, we dragons would have been hunted to extinction long ago.'

Silence filled the clearing for a while, underscored by the crackling of the fire, the occasional shriek and hoot of

68

night animals as Benfro imagined the two warring brothers, the beautiful Ammorgwm and brave Palisander. It was a good tale, every bit the equal of Sir Frynwy's tellings, and with added atmosphere given the setting, but it left so many questions unanswered.

'But you saved their king,' Benfro said. 'So why did they go back on his word?'

'Because that's how they are, Benfro. Divitie may have been a friend to us, but simply abolishing a law can't undo the blind fear and hatred behind it. Men are very slow to change their minds and some have their power only because of the way things were. The Order of the High Ffrydd was set up to hunt dragons. Do you suppose they're going to welcome us with open arms?'

Benfro stared down at the fire, feeling small and helpless. 'Must I hide from them all my life?'

'By the moon, no! There are places in Gwlad where men are few and far between, places where dragons are at least tolerated rather than actively persecuted. We live here because we made that choice. Our village is protected, hidden away as long as we respect its magic. You've yet to make your choice, Benfro. You might settle with us, or you might take the long road like your father. You might even seek out those few other dragons spread out across the land. But first you have to grow up. You need to learn about the subtle arts, about your heritage. Until then we will do everything we can to protect you.'

'I want to learn magic, but mother won't let me.'

'Of course not. A dragon cannot begin his apprenticeship until he turns fourteen, Benfro. You know that.'

'But if men are so dangerous, shouldn't I learn sooner? At least enough to sense them coming, or to hide from them?'

Ynys Môn put away his flask, took up a long stick and began poking the fire, banking it up for the night. Benfro knew it was time to sleep – the conversation was over – and he settled himself down with a weary resignation.

'Perhaps you're right,' the old dragon said. 'Perhaps we shouldn't leave you so helpless.'

'What do you mean?' Benfro asked.

'Morgwm will hate me for it,' Ynys Môn said, 'and I'll get a stern talk from Sir Frynwy, but tomorrow I'll show you a simple spell. One that won't get you into trouble and may well help you at times.

'Tomorrow, young Benfro, I'll show you how to hide.'

5

Dragons set great store by their jewels, which they believe hold their collected wisdom and memories even after death. In their ceremony of reckoning the body of the dead is burned with special oils until nothing is left but ash. Then the healer, generally one of the more senior members of their society, takes the revealed jewels to a secret place, where those from other dead dragons are stored. In this way the creatures, who are great solitary wanderers in life, find a camaraderie in death. The persistent myths of dragons having great hoards of treasure most probably stem from this practice, but in truth the beasts set little store by what men might consider valuable.

There is one exception to this practice, however. When one whom the dragons consider to be a great mage dies, then his jewels are placed in a solitary place, away from the others. Usually these places are considered naturally powerful by dragons, and in times of great stress they will go to them, presumably to pray to the memories of their dead leaders for guidance.

Father Charmoise, Dragons' Tales

He was too close to Martha, their arms linked. And they were both of them too close to the edge. Stars flashed in Errol's eyes as his sense of balance flipped through ninety degrees. For a flickering moment he thought he could see Trell's face turning from smiling glee to horrified concern as he realized his enemy was not alone. But it was too dark to see such details, surely. Then, with a lurch, his head snapped back upright and he realized he was going to fall. Scrabbling, he tried to push Martha away from him, back on to the top of the rock, but she grabbed at him instinctively, clinging to him as they both went over the edge.

It seemed to take for ever to fall to the water, and all the while Errol could see the great yellow pulsing lines of the Grym spearing away from him. On the bank he could see the thinner lines connecting the smaller shrubs, the sickly-looking and palest strands faltering around the base of the dying tree that Martha had pointed out earlier. Beyond that he could see a finer web covering the ground like a woven sheet, following every bump and contour as it linked individual blades of grass. And he could see tiny flickering lights of a different shade or colour, moving freely over the Grym like ants on a boulder. Then, as he realized that they were ants, and other insects and small animals, each bright with the life force of the world, he hit the water.

It drove the air out of his lungs like a punch to the stomach. Cold wet hands grabbed at him, pulling him down to the blackened deeps. He could feel Martha panicking, thrashing around to free herself from their tangled embrace. He was a strong swimmer himself, but judging by her frenzy Martha was not. He tried to relax, to orient himself and regain the surface. It wasn't far to the edge where the sandy beach ran down into the water. They could get out there easily, if he could just calm her down enough to float.

A burning sensation in Errol's chest reminded him that he needed to breathe more urgently than anything else. Panic flirted with his mind, threatening to overwhelm him. He fought it down, realizing as he did just how easy it would be to die now. And for Martha to die too. Struggling against the cold that sapped his strength and the intense pain in his chest, he reached out for the thrashing figure above him, hoping his touch would calm her enough to save them both. Then something hard and sharp and boot-like connected with his head and everything changed.

The dark was warm, which was odd. Errol could remember being in the water, the cold chill tugging at his legs, sucking his clothes to his puckering skin. He could remember being spun slowly by the lazy, powerful current, pulling him downwards with exactly the same force as his body wanted to rise. Yet now he was sitting in the warm and dark, calm.

'How?' he asked himself, and his voice rang out loud and clear. But it was like listening to a memory of his speech, the words forming directly in his mind.

'I brought you here, Errol Ramsbottom,' came a reply that he had not been expecting. It was not a man's voice, although it was undoubtedly masculine. It was larger somehow, more measured and authoritative. A voice used to being taken seriously.

'Who?' Errol asked, unsure as to whether he spoke the word or merely thought it, unsure as to where he really was.

'You know who I am, Errol,' the voice said, and Errol realized that he did.

'Dragon?' he said. He had seen pictures in one of old Father Drebble's bestiaries of forest dragons. They were sad-looking things with drab hides and pathetic vestigial wings.

'My descendants are a pale shadow of their true selves,' the voice said. 'That has been their choice. But once, when I walked this earth, we were great, the masters of all. Since I died I have watched them shrink into obscurity.'

'Died?' Errol said, and his voice rang out the question in his head.

'Yes, Errol. I died. Many thousands of years ago. And my jewels were laid to rest at this nexus in the Llinellau Grym. Since then I have watched countless generations come and go, both dragon and men, never amounting to very much. But we are reaching a critical point, your kind and mine, and you will have a key part to play in that change.'

'Me?' Errol said. 'But I'm no one. I mean, I'm not special.'

'If that is what you truly believe, that is how it will be,' the dragon voice said. 'But I think you are made of greater stuff than you realize. You have already taken the first step on the path to becoming a mage. I've watched you these past few years, growing up, learning far faster than your peers, trying so hard to understand the world around you. It will come in time, but have you the patience to learn? And are you prepared to accept help from wherever it is offered?'

'What do you mean?' Errol had a creeping feeling of

unease. Like he had walked into a room and couldn't remember why.

'Your destiny is your own, Errol Ramsbottom. You can be as much or as little as you want. All you need to do is make the right decisions. But remember this: you can have power or you can have happiness. Sometimes it may seem that you can have both at the same time, but that can never last. In the end it is either one or the other.'

'I don't understand,' Errol said, but there was water in his mouth and the warm protective darkness had turned to a cold wet clinging fear. Gasping and choking, he lunged up, his head breaking free of the surface of the pool in a short-lived ecstasy of relief. The night was almost total now, the looming shape of the rock a darker shade of black against the cloud. Thrashing this way and that, Errol tried to see where Martha had got to, but she was nowhere to be seen.

Panic gripped him and he thrust his head under the surface in a useless attempt to see where she might have sunk. Even in the daylight he wouldn't have been able to see more than a couple of inches; with no moon or stars to light his way he stood no chance. She would drown, dragged down by that deceptive lazy current. And it would be his fault.

No. It would be Trell's fault. Hot rage flushed through Errol at the memory of that leering face coming out of the darkness. Then the fall and the oddly fascinating beauty of the Grym encompassing all living things, grasses, trees and shrubs set within their grid, insects and other animals bright sparks against the background glow.

Martha would be a glow too, Errol realized. And there

had been so much life in her. There was so much life in her still, surely, that she would stand out like a beacon atop a dark hill. Treading water, he tried to recapture the frame of mind that had allowed him to see so much of the Grym before. A sense of terrible urgency and dread spread through him as he realized that time was slipping away from him. Martha could be underwater or merely trapped against rocks with her head immersed. Either way she would soon be dead.

Trying to suppress the panic, he fixed his attention on the major lines. He knew they were there. He had seen them. He was sure of them. He believed in them. Even so, all he could conjure up was the faintest of trails. Frustrated and shivering, he swam swiftly towards the beach, standing up out of the water to get a better look. His clothes hung soaking from him and the wind did its best to get into his bones. Still he wouldn't give up. She had to be here somewhere.

'Damn it, Martha! Where are you?' he shouted at the night, but no reply came. Hurrying, Errol sprinted to the top of the rock. There was no sign of Trell anywhere, so like him to run off when he could have been useful. From his earlier vantage point Errol could see down into the pool below, but it was as black as pitch, just the faintest of glimmerings showing where the lines deflected through the water to meet under his feet.

'Dragon, help, please,' Benfro said quietly, desperately. Almost instantly he could feel the presence in his mind like a blast of fire. He forgot the chill and the wet, forgot his panic. The Grym appeared to him in all its multi-hued magnificence, the lines pulsing their slow cycle of plant life and the myriad small specks an uncountable mass of insects and small nocturnal animals. He could see the solid life-glow of the old fish as they poked around at the base of the rock, and there, unmoving among their slow spiral, pale and weakening, a shape at once utterly alien and deeply familiar.

He didn't wait to think about it, didn't consider his own safety; Errol just jumped. This time he hit the water in no time, plunging beneath the surface with his lungs full. Swift strokes took him to the bottom of the pool and the cold still form of Martha. He took her in his arms and pushed off, swimming as strongly as he could for the shallows and the beach.

By the time he had dragged Martha's motionless body up on to the dry sand, Errol's anger-fuelled energy was beginning to wane. He could feel his arms and legs stiffening with the cold and knew that he would collapse soon. But Martha was unmoving, pale in the darkness. Bending close, he tried to hear her breathing. There was something he should be doing; his mother had schooled him in how to deal with emergencies, but faced with the real thing, he could only stare stupidly.

'Don't be an idiot,' the dragon voice said to him, shocking his mind from the stupor it was falling into. 'Her lungs are full of water. You've got to get that out. Roll her over and pump her arms up and down.'

Bemused, Errol did as he was told, marvelling at the pints of water that spewed from Martha's mouth.

'Now you've got to get some air into her,' the voice said, and as it did, Errol remembered what he was meant to do. Working as quickly as his cold muscles would let him, he bent over Martha's head, lifting it back slightly. Then he pinched her nose closed, opened her mouth and breathed deep into her. Like ice, her lips burned his, and she lay so still he was convinced that she was dead. He was too late.

'Don't stop now,' the dragon voice said to him. 'Check if she has a pulse.'

Errol had seen his mother take pulses before; that much he could do without instruction. Martha's was weak and fluttering, but it was there. Now all he had to do was make her breathe. Taking her head in his hands once more, he put his mouth to hers and blew. Her chest rose then fell again, staying down. He was about to try once more when, with a great racking cough, Martha spewed up even more water, rolled on to her side and started taking in ragged, gasping breaths.

'Thank the Shepherd,' Errol said quietly, pulling Martha up to him and hugging her tight, trying to give her some of the warmth he could ill afford to spare.

'I don't think he had anything to do with it, actually,' the dragon voice said in his head, 'but I'll allow you such platitudes, given the circumstances.'

Martha opened her eyes at the words.

'You met Sir Radnor then,' she said, her voice hoarse and deep, almost adult. And then a bizarre smile spread across her face. 'Hey, you kissed me, Errol Ramsbottom. Does that mean you're my boyfriend?'

Errol was going to protest, but instead he just laughed as they shivered there on the damp sandy beach. Then a shout from the trees behind them broke the moment. Turning, Errol could see torches coming up the path at speed, the flames flickering with promised warmth. Tom

Tydfil the smith was at the head of the line, his face creased with anguish. Godric Defaid and his son Clun were not far behind, with Trell reluctantly following his father, bringing up the rear.

'Where is she?' Tom shouted at the top of his voice, then spotted Errol on the beach. 'What have you done to my daughter, witch boy? By the Shepherd, I'll flay you alive if she's hurt!'

Errol tried to protest, but he was too tired and Tom too strong. The smith pushed him roughly aside and pulled Martha up into his arms. She seemed to be fighting him off, but she too was weak and cold, collapsing into his arms eventually with a sob and a sorry glance in Errol's direction.

'He was darin' her to stand on the edge – I saw 'em both,' Trell shouted in a high-pitched weedy voice of desperation.

'Is this true?' the smith demanded, threat in his voice.

Errol looked at the three men who made up the village council. Only Godric had some glimmer of sympathy in his eyes.

'We were near the edge, yes,' Errol said, a shiver quavering his voice. 'But we wouldn't have fallen in if Trell hadn't clouted me with that great stick.' He pointed up at the flat base of the rock where a stout branch, cudgel-shaped and cleaned of twigs, lay discarded.

'That's preposterous,' Alderman Clusster said, bristling at the accusation to his good name. 'How dare you accuse my son after he tried to save you!'

'Save me.' Errol laughed. 'He wanted to kill me. He only got scared when he realized Martha was here as well.'

'And just what were ye doin' wit' my daughter, witch boy? How dare ye bring her here, of all places?'

Errol frowned at the smith. He hadn't brought Martha to the Jagged Leap; she had come of her own accord. And the accusation that he had been doing anything with the smith's daughter was laughable too. He was innocent in that regard. Or at least he had been until they had fallen in the pool. Now it felt oddly wrong protesting that innocence. To Errol's eternal gratitude, Clun's father stepped in to stop the interrogation.

'Now's not the time, Tom,' Godric said. 'Look, they're both soaked through, and the night's only going to get colder. I'll take Errol back to his ma and we can sort this all out in the morning.'

'Any excuse to go and visit the old witch, eh Godric,' Alderman Clusster said with barely concealed distaste. Ignoring him, the councillor helped Errol to his feet.

'Give him yer coat, Clun. The poor boy's freezin',' he said. Clun quickly pulled the garment off and handed it over without a word. Errol wrapped it around his shoulders. It was several sizes too big for him but he didn't care. The warmth enveloped him like an oven.

'Can ye make it back to the cottage, Errol, or shall we go down to the village?' Godric asked him, ignoring the other two councillors.

'I can make it home, thank you,' Errol said. Once he got moving he was sure he would warm up, and his mother would have plenty of potions to restore him. She would also have endless questions and would no doubt berate him for his foolishness, but he would far rather get that over and done with than spend an evening in some stranger's house.

'Tomorrow then, Tom, Ned,' Godric said, and holding up his flaming torch beckoned Errol and Clun ahead of him up the path.

'Well, ye're a bit of a dark horse, Errol,' Clun said after they had been walking for several minutes at a fast pace. 'Who'd 'a' thought it, Tom Tydfil's daughter an' the witch boy.' He sniggered quietly to himself.

'It's not like that,' Errol protested half-heartedly. He knew it was pointless trying to change Clun's mind, and besides a part of him wanted it to be like that.

'Sure, I understand,' Clun said, the chuckle still in his voice. 'You an' her jes up there on Jagged Leap watchin' the grass grow.'

'Her name's Martha,' Errol said, realizing as he did that it was not the right thing to say.

'Martha is it,' Clun guffawed. 'When's the weddin' then?'

Errol kept his mouth shut and endured a long series of jokes from Clun as they made their way along the wide track into the forest. Godric said nothing, simply holding his torch aloft for them to see the way. Soon they were passing along familiar paths, and before too long they had entered the small clearing where his mother's cottage stood.

The door was open, spilling light over the grass and the silhouetted shadow of Hennas. Errol could tell by the way she was standing that he was in trouble. It was hours after he should have been home. He should have been tending to the animals, digging over the vegetable patch and any number of other mindless tasks his mother found to fill his time. Yet looking at her standing there, awaiting their arrival, he couldn't help thinking that she knew exactly what had happened already.

'Good evening, Mistress Hennas,' Godric said, having overtaken the two boys. 'There's been an incident with yer boy, Errol. I thought it best to bring him straight home.'

'I know full well what my son has been up to, Godric,' Hennas said, her smile for the councillor turning to an all-too-familiar grimace of disapproval as she swept her gaze across to Errol. 'You'd think that Ben Coulter's death at Jagged Leap would be enough to keep him away from that place.' Her face softened then, and Errol let out a sigh of relief. 'But he's headstrong and wilful, like all boys of his age, I've no doubt. He thinks he can do anything. Hopefully this experience will prove to him that he can't.' She stepped out of the doorway and motioned for them to come into the house.

Inside it was warm, a cheery fire crackling in the hearth. Errol went straight to it, peeling off Clun's moist coat and holding his hands out to the flames. Now he was home and safe the cold and exhaustion swept over him as if only sheer force of will had been holding it back.

'Go change, Errol,' Hennas said not unkindly. 'You'll catch a chill standing there in those wet clothes. Clun, you go with him. I'll hang your coat up to dry a while before you leave.'

Reluctantly Errol took a candle from the mantel and trudged out of the room into the back of the cottage. Clun hesitated for a moment, then followed, leaving the adults alone.

'So this is where ye live,' Clun said as they entered the small room. Errol felt uneasy, waiting for the snide comment to come. Instead, Clun just looked around at the small bed in the corner, the wooden chest full of clothes and the big table set under the window covered in scraps of parchment, books and quill pens. 'It's not bad, really,' he said. 'Better than I was expectin'.'

'Where'd you think I lived, a pigsty?' Errol asked, slightly more bitterly than he felt. He peeled off his clothes, still soaked but no longer dripping wet, and rubbed his cold skin with a rough towel before pulling on clean trousers and a heavy cotton shirt. He was still cold and wanted to get back to the warm living room at the front of the house, but Clun stopped him.

'Give 'em a bit longer,' he said.

'Why?' Errol asked, then the realization hit him. 'Oh.'

'Yeah.' Clun smiled. 'It's kind of weird really. We could be stepbrothers soon.'

'Is that why you started being nice to me?' Errol asked.

'Partly, I guess,' Clun replied. 'Mostly cos ye stood up for yersel. I was getting that sick of Trell, goin' on like his dad was king or summat when he's really jes 'a self-righteous little shit. Clusster goes on about yer mam bein' a witch and all, but ye know what happened when he got his own daughter up the duff. Came running up here like a scalded cat, beggin' fer help.'

Errol remembered the visit well. He had kept to his room, but the cottage wasn't so big that he couldn't hear every word of the heated conversation, even over the hysterical sobbing of Trell's sister Maggs. Hennas had refused to even countenance what the alderman had asked, insisting it was Maggs's choice to make and not something she could be browbeaten into by her father. Errol had feared for his mother's safety, such was the alderman's rage at her. He had learned a few words that weren't in the big dictionary in the school library that evening, but finally Maggs had pulled herself together enough to order her father out of the room. After that things had gone very quiet, but nine months later there were no new Clussters. On her sixteenth birthday, not half a year ago, Maggs had left the village and gone to stay with her aunt in Candlehall. Or at least that was what the gossip said.

'Wait a minute,' Errol said, Clun's words finally sinking in. 'Alderman Clusster was the father? His own daughter? That's . . . That's . . .'

''T ain't as uncommon as ye might think,' Clun said. 'Ye never wondered why half a the villagers look the same?'

Errol had, on many occasions. He nodded.

'Yeah, well, that's why most of them don't like ye. Ye're different.'

'Martha said I looked like a Llanwennog,' Errol said, recalling the incident with a clarity that surprised him.

'Couldn't say,' Clun said. 'Never met one. But it's not just yer looks, Errol. Ye're smart – ye can read an' write, ye speak proper like. And yer mam's got a power over everyone. It's weird. She helps 'em, heals 'em, gets rid a their little problems, and they hate her fer it. Well, some a them, anyway.'

Errol wondered what Clun was going on about. Was this just a delaying tactic to give his father more time to press his suit? He'd never had such a long conversation with anyone other than his mother before. Except with Martha, of course. But that was different, somehow.

'I can't wait to get out a this place,' Clun said after a while. 'This whole village. It's too small. Everyone's in each other's business the whole time. What d'ye reckon my chances are inna choosin' this year?'

Errol was taken aback by the question, coming as it did out of nowhere.

'The choosing? Are you old enough?' he asked.

'More 'n old enough. Ye've gotta be fourteen but there weren't no choosin' last year. I'll be fifteen next week,' Clun replied.

'What does Kewick think?' Errol asked.

'He don't know. Nobody knows, not even da. Anyway, Kewick'd want me to go for the Candles. I don't want to end up like him.'

'What then, be a Ram like old Father Drebble?' Errol tried to imagine Clun travelling the long road, teaching the words of the Shepherd and healing the sick. It wasn't an easy task. That left only one real option.

'Nah. I wanna be a warrior priest, join the High Ffrydd an' fight,' Clun said. Errol choked back a laugh but couldn't help the smile from spreading across his face.

'What's so funny?' Clun asked angrily. 'You think I couldn't make the grade?'

'No, that's not it,' Errol said. 'Well, maybe, but there's still a few months to go before it comes around. I can help you with the tests, if you want.'

'You, help me?' Clun asked, incredulity on his face. 'What would you know about it?'

Errol reached over to the table and picked up An Introduction to the Order of the High Ffrydd. He had made a half-hearted attempt to repair it but lacked both the materials and the skills.

'It got a bit damaged in that fight when I broke Trell's nose,' he said, handing it over to Clun. The older boy took the book, opened it at random and peered at the tiny archaic letters as Errol held up the fluttering candle for light. After a very short moment Clun snapped the book shut, inspected the scuffed, scratched cover and threw it down on the bed.

'I can't make any sense of it,' he said. 'An' there's pages missing.'

'It doesn't matter.' Errol tapped his head with a finger. 'I've got it all up here. I could recite the whole thing if I wanted. And Father Kewick never even realized it was in the library.'

'Ye'd teach me, help me,' Clun said. 'Why?'

'Why not?' Errol said, wondering the same thing as he said it. 'Like you said, we might well be stepbrothers soon. And I'll be fourteen in time for the choosing next year. I can join you then.'

6

In the earliest days of the Twin Kingdoms King Brynceri was constantly under threat from marauding dragons. Perhaps the fiercest of these was Maddau, who lived in the mountains at the edge of the Graith Fawr. As was his way, Brynceri sought out Maddau and challenged the beast to combat. It was a fierce battle, and in the heat of the fray the dragon bit off the king's ring finger, swallowing it whole.

Now Brynceri was a powerful magician and skilled warrior, but he also drew power from the ring, which had been passed down the line of kings from Balwen himself. It was said that the Shepherd had given it to Balwen when he had gifted him with the knowledge of magic, and without it Brynceri was momentarily weakened.

The dragon Maddau might have bested him had not the wandering monk Ruthin chanced upon the scene. Focusing the essence of the Grym into a pure blade of fire, Ruthin rushed to his king's aid, and together they slew the dragon. Brynceri took his sword and slit open the belly of the beast, retrieving his ring and severed finger. These he gave to Ruthin, making him inquisitor and charging him with exterminating every dragon in Gwlad.

Thus was born the Order of the High Ffrydd,
and its sacred mission continues to this day.

Father Castlemilk, *An Introduction*
to the Order of the High Ffrydd

Spring turned to summer and then on towards autumn, time marching its unstoppable course marked out in the changing colours, smells and sounds of the land. Father Kewick was grooming some of his more capable students for the approaching choosing, leaning heavily on his own areas of expertise in bureaucracy. Too young to be included in this elite group, Errol spent most of his class time reading and rereading the ever-decreasing number of books in the library. He suspected the fat predicant was slowly working his way through them, cataloguing what was there and removing anything he thought unsuitable, which was almost everything that wasn't directly relevant to the history or organization of the Order of the Candle.

Alderman Clusster had gone very quiet following the incident at Jagged Leap, and Trell's position as Father Kewick's favourite, picked for special attention and extra tuition, meant he had little time to bother Errol. Tom Tydfil glowered at him every time Errol passed by the smithy, but Martha must have told her father what had really happened that night as no more was said of the incident. Martha herself disappeared, and it wasn't until a month of frustrated looking had passed that Errol found out she had been sent away to stay with her aunt for the summer.

And so Errol spent most of his free time with Clun, much to Godric's delight since it gave him plenty of opportunity to walk up to Hennas's cottage in the forest and pay his respects. For her part, Errol's mother seemed to be slowly succumbing to the man's persistence and more than once Errol heard her whistling a simple tune to herself as she went about preparing her healing herbs or cleaning the house. She tended to shout at him less often for neglecting his chores and would often just tell him to go out and play.

An Introduction to the Order of the High Ffrydd did not say anything specific about the choosing, and the two boys would spend long hours debating exactly what form the tests might take. Clun was of the opinion that they would be physical.

'They're a fighting order,' he said one afternoon as they sat on the banks of the river some way downstream of Jagged Leap. 'They're bound to want to know how good ye're inna scrap. Yer'll have to beef up a bit 'fore yer choosin' or they'll laugh yer out a the first test.'

'There's more to fighting than brute strength,' Errol said, flicking a stone into the water. 'You need an appreciation of tactics, good intelligence. And besides, you have to be able to use the Grym. That's all to do with sharpness of mind, not the size of your muscles.'

'So ye keep on saying,' the older boy said. 'But I can't see any use a this Grym of yours. It's jes lines onna ground.'

'At least you can see them now,' Errol said. 'That's got to count for something when the inquisitor comes.' Having spent so long trying to see the lines himself, Errol was amazed and a little jealous at how easily his new friend had acquired the skill.

'I guess,' Clun said, his usual cheery demeanour dropping away suddenly. 'Then again it might all be a waste a time.'

'What do you mean?' Errol asked.

'Da say's there ain't gonna be no warrior priest this year, no coenobite neither. Just a predicant from the Order of the Candle. Kewick's fixed it so only his own order's represented. He's been coachin' Trell and Wendell and the others to be good little bookkeepers, jes like himself.'

'They'll come,' Errol said, not knowing how he knew it was true, but certain nonetheless. 'You'll get your chance, Clun. And you'll be the first to make the order from this village in over thirty years.'

Clun smiled then, but it was a weak thing, smothered in self-doubt.

'I've gotta go,' he said, scrambling to his feet and brushing the dirt from his trousers. 'Da's got a shipment comin' in from Candlehall this afternoon and he'll want help with unloading. Yer wanna come?'

Errol considered for all of three seconds. A hot sunny afternoon spent hefting wooden crates off the back of a wagon and into the gloomy storeroom at the back of Godric's shop was not his idea of time profitably spent, even if he would earn a coin or two in the process.

'No thanks,' he said. 'I think I'll just lie here in the sun and meditate.'

'Suit yersel,' Clun said, and with no more than a backward glance he trotted off down the hill towards the village. Errol watched him go for a while and then settled back against the warm rock, his bare feet dangling into the cool water. It was almost perfect, he thought, as he closed his eyes and let the sun warm his face. There was just one thing missing.

'Errol!' The voice was loud. As if it was right inside his head.

'Martha?' He opened his eyes, tried to leap to his feet, and only then remembered where he was sitting. Scrabbling for a foothold, or something to catch with his hand, Errol plunged once more into the cold waters of the river.

Inquisitor Melyn strode through the long stone corridors of the monastery in a terrible rage. Novitiates darted into alcoves and side rooms at his approach, and even battle-hardened warrior priests flattened themselves against the walls, their heavy leather boots cracking against the polished tiles as they came swiftly to attention. He ignored them all, too annoyed even to take out his anger on his subordinates.

It was always this way when he returned from Candlehall, Melyn fumed. Having to deal with the soft city bureaucrats and their endless meetings wore him down to the point where he needed to lash out at things, and the long tiring ride back to Emmass Fawr didn't help. He longed to drag old Padraig up here, to the roof of the world, the border with Llanwennog. No more than a day's hard trek from the monastery to the outer watchtowers and the senile old seneschal would be able to see for himself the steadily growing population on the Caenant plains. But the stupid old man insisted on pursuing his diplomatic insanity. Could he not see that there was no future in it? The only way to be properly rid of the Llanwennog menace was invasion. And if they left it much longer old Ballah would have his forces ready for them, ready to make his own foray through the uncharted rim mountains, deep into the Ffrydd and on down into the Hafod and Hendry. Then they'd sit up and listen to him, with violent death at their doors.

'Fetch Usel, the medic,' Melyn ordered one of the guards who stood at his door. The man nodded a hasty salute and dashed away on his errand as the inquisitor pushed through into his personal quarters.

It was a sparse room, austere like the man who occupied it. The furniture was old, simple and utilitarian: a couple of hard wooden chairs beside the open unlit fireplace, a wide desk placed to get maximum light from the two windows at the expense of the view out over the top of the monastery to the rugged mountains beyond, a small table pushed up against one wall with a pewter jug and two goblets sitting on top of it. A curtained-off alcove held his bed. Melyn did not agree with the inquisitors of old, who had pampered themselves with large suites of rooms. He bathed in the communal baths, ate in the great dining hall where his subordinates could see him. All he needed to run the Order of the High Ffrydd was in this one small room, most of it in his head.

He went to the table and poured himself a goblet of rich dark wine. He took a long swig and then, with a thought, released the spell he had cast on himself days before. He sat himself down in one of the chairs by the fireplace, stretched his legs out uncomfortably, grimacing at the pain in his right knee, not wanting to look at the damage. A knock at the door was the perfect distraction.

'Come.'

The door creaked open and a tall slim fellow stepped in. His face was smooth and he had a mop of sandy hair that seemed out of place in a monastery where all the novitiates' and warrior priests' heads were cropped severely short.

'You wanted to see me, Inquisitor,' the man said. 'Is there a problem?'

'Yes, Usel. It's my knee. I wrenched it a couple of days ago.'

The medic crossed the room and knelt down beside the inquisitor without a word. Melyn felt a spark of anger at his disrespectful manner; most members of the order would have at least bowed to their inquisitor or offered to kiss his ring of office. Usel treated him as no more or less than any other patient. If the man hadn't been such a good battle surgeon, Melyn thought, he'd have had him flogged for insubordination years ago. As it was, he tolerated the medic's eccentricities, for now.

'I'll need to see it, sir,' Usel said, indicating that Melyn would have to remove his breeches. Trying not to show how much it pained him, the inquisitor complied, seeing for the first time the livid purple swollen mess where his knee should have been, a sharp contrast to the pale white wiry muscle and flesh of the rest of his legs.

'You should have rested this as soon as it happened.'

'I've been healing it myself as best I could. It doesn't seem to be responding as well to the Grym as I'd hoped.'

'There are some injuries that no amount of magic will heal, especially if you keep stressing them by . . . oh . . . riding a horse all day and late into the night.'

'I was in a hurry to get back.'

'Well, you'd better not be in a hurry to go away again. I'll make up a poultice and strap this up, but it's going to take weeks to heal, even for an adept as skilled as yourself. May I be blunt with you, Inquisitor?'

Melyn looked at Usel with an instant of surprise.

'You mean you haven't been up to now?'

'You're not as young as you once were, sir. I don't mean to say you're not still far more capable than any of us. And most men your age would be happy to be able to clamber on to a horse, let alone ride into battle. But your body is beginning to show signs of that age. You need to treat it with just a little bit more respect than you've been used to.'

Melyn looked at the medic. He hated the man, it was true. His first instinct was to conjure a blade of light and strike him down where he knelt for daring to even think the things he was saying. But there was a grain of truth in Usel's words that couldn't be denied. Perhaps that was why he hated him: because he was right, and because every time he had to consult him, it was a reminder of the passing of years, the frailty of old age.

'I'll bear that in mind,' Melyn said through clenched teeth. 'Now go. I must pray to the Shepherd for a speedy recovery.'

'I'll bring the poultice later tonight,' Usel said, standing to leave. 'It's best applied before you sleep. You do sleep, don't you?'

Melyn stared at the door as it closed, then looked down

at his swollen knee. He reached down and prodded it, then wished he hadn't as a jab of pain shot up his leg and into his groin. Slowly, he stood again, pulling up his breeches and fastening his belt. He was about to leave the room and head to the chapel when another knock came at the door.

'What is it now!?' Melyn could feel the rage building in him as a surging power, ready to be tapped, controlled, used. The door creaked open and a stooped figure came in. There were several thousand novitiates, quaisters and warrior priests based in and around the monastery complex, any of whom he would happily hang in the dungeons for a week without food and water if the mood so took him, but this wasn't one of them.

'What is it, Andro?' He let the untapped power of his anger seep out into the surrounding walls. If Usel thought that Melyn was starting to get old, then what would the medic think of the master librarian? His face was skeletal and those once-piercing blue eyes were now starting to cloud. Blood spots disfigured his dry leathery skin and his hair was as white as the snow that capped the nearby peaks all year long. But then Andro had been old when Melyn had been just a novitiate. It was a miracle he still lived at all, or at least it was a testament to the old man's skill at magic.

'Walk while you tell me,' the inquisitor said, guiding his old friend out the door and limping slowly along the corridor. 'I must get to the chapel and pray.'

'The choosing, Inquisitor,' Andro said, struggling to keep up with even the reduced pace. Melyn slowed further, secretly grateful.

'Is it that time already?' Melyn asked, genuinely surprised. 'How the years get faster as we grow old, eh?'

'Indeed, Inquisitor.' Andro smiled, displaying a complete set of teeth still strong though yellowing with age. 'And it's true that Seneschal Padraig will ever play his games. I've been over the lists and he's cut us out of yet more towns this year.'

Melyn let out a short laugh, more of a bark than any sign of humour.

'Ha! Is that all, old friend? You know as well as I do that we could recruit more than we can train even without the choosing. We don't need it, and he knows as much. Padraig only does it to provoke a response.'

'Of course, Inquisitor,' Andro conceded. 'You yourself were not picked at any choosing. But knowing your interest in such matters, I thought I should bring to your attention the, ah, geography of the situation.'

Melyn stopped and faced his old tutor. 'What exactly are you trying to say, Andro?'

'There are a number of villages on the edge of the forest close to the old hunting lodge at Ystumtuen,' the old man said. 'Predicants have been given sole responsibility for all of them this year.'

'And do you think this a coincidence?' Melyn asked after a short silence.

'No, Inquisitor, I don't,' Andro said. 'It's not just the choosing. Padraig has put his predicants in every village from Candlehall to the edges of the Ffrydd itself. He's a canny operator. He's taken years over it, but every time a village priest dies his replacement is drawn from the Order of the Candle. I dare say old Cassters of the Ram should

96

be more concerned, but he's always been happy for his lot to do pretty much as they please.'

'The Rams are wanderers and healers,' Melyn said. 'They make good enough teachers, but by the time they settle down in one place they're almost all near gathering. Padraig's probably putting his people in as much to cut down on the paperwork as anything else.'

'So you'd consider it of no importance, then?' For an instant Melyn was transported back to his childhood classroom. One of a hundred novitiates desperate to make their mark, to be noticed, to succeed. That questioning tone, just waiting for him to make a tactical mistake, waiting for him to leave a small opening, was unmistakable.

'Ah, no.' Melyn smiled, stopping at the door of his private chapel. 'Archimandrite Cassters might not mind the Candle taking over his order, but I'm not so forgiving. No. I'm minded to visit these small villages myself this year. It's been too long since I attended a good choosing. Arrange it for me, will you, Andro.'

'Of course, Inquisitor,' the old man said. He bowed slightly, then turned and shuffled away down the corridor.

The water was cold but not deep, and after the heat of the day it was rather refreshing. Errol picked himself up and waded to the bank, clambering back on to the rock. He pulled off his boots and emptied them into the river, then looked around to see who had startled him. No doubt they were hiding behind a nearby tree, doubled over with laughter right now. Or more likely running back to the village to tell everyone. It didn't matter; it wouldn't be the first time he'd been the butt of a joke. Smiling, Errol pulled off his trousers, squeezed the water out of them and laid them on the warm rock to dry. Then he settled himself against the nearest tree, away from the water's edge this time, and once more closed his eyes.

'Errol.' The voice was quiet this time, almost a whisper, yet somehow louder than the rushing of the water and the rustling of an autumn breeze in the drying leaves. Errol's eyes snapped open and he looked around, startled.

'Clun? Is that you?' No reply came, and he could see no one nearby. Nor was there anywhere for someone to hide close enough. It was too warm to worry about such things anyway, the solitude too enjoyable. Settling once more against the rock, Errol let his mind wander again, noting with slight interest the pattern of the Grym as it spread away from where he lay, as if he were the spider in the middle of a web that spread over the whole world.

'Errol!' The voice was more insistent now, and louder. It spoke directly to his mind, the wind and the river mere backdrops. And it was a voice that he recognized.

'Sir Radnor?' Errol said. 'Dragon?'

'Ah, at last,' the voice said. 'I was beginning to think you would never hear.'

'I . . .' Errol found he was lost for words

'You thought I was no more than a figment of your imagination? Well, there's gratitude for you, I suppose.'

'I . . .'

'Never mind,' the voice said. 'Your summer has not been wasted. I can sense that you have been sharpening your skill at perceiving the Grym. This is good. For only when you have mastered its perception can you ever hope to use it to your benefit.'

'Use it?' Errol said, finally managing to find his voice. The image that he held in his mind, of himself at the centre of a web of Grym, had changed subtly, almost imperceptibly. Now he was still in a web, still near its centre, but he was no longer the spider.

'The Grym is in us all, surrounds us all, links us all together. But we need not be passive to it. Cows are passive, and sheep. It is enough for them simply to exist. Dragons are much more. We can take control of our lives and we can manipulate the Grym to our own ends.'

'But I'm not a dragon,' Errol said.

'You are so sure of that,' the voice said. 'But there is much of the dragon about you, young Errol. Like Martha you have an insatiable curiosity about the world. And unlike most of your kind you do not have a thirst for power, only knowledge. You have been touched by dragons, Errol Ramsbottom. We have marked you as one of our own.'

Distracted by the thoughts of Martha that cascaded unbidden into his mind at the mention of her name, Errol almost missed the rest of what Sir Radnor was saying. Only as he was sinking into the memory of her scent as she sat close to him atop Jagged Leap did the full import of what had been said sink in.

'Touched by dragons?' Errol asked, a curious rush of excitement pulsing through his chest. 'But I've never met a dragon. I mean, when? How?'

'That is something you will learn in time,' Sir Radnor said, his bodiless voice clear and strong. As he listened to it reverberate around his skull, Errol realized that it wasn't completely formless. It had a power about it that filled him with strength, and it had a direction that called him towards it. Instinctively turning his head to try and pinpoint the location, he laughed at himself for being so stupid. The voice was inside his head, not out there in the warm afternoon. And he knew anyway where the last resting place of Sir Radnor was to be found.

'Good, Errol,' the voice said. 'Come to me.'

Errol looked upstream. Jagged Leap was a good mile away, obscured by trees and the folds in the hill that marked the river's passage, yet he could picture the place in his mind with perfect clarity. He could see the rock jutting out over the pool, the dark waters moving slowly but strongly past it, swirling around in that deadly eddy. He could see the low sand beach where he had breathed life back into Martha's cold, wet, still body. And he could see the lines criss-crossing everything, defining it all like some artist's sketch beneath the finished picture.

One line in particular caught his attention. It should have been impossible to see it travel all the way from the rock to the point where he stood, but somehow he could. It was a line but it was also two points with nothing between them, the distance no more than thought. The crossing was no more difficult than an idea. It seemed the most natural thing simply to step from one place to the other.

It was like swimming in warm water, yet staying dry. There was no sense of motion but suddenly he was off balance, as if he stood on the back of a moving cart that had stopped without warning. Dizzy, Errol collapsed to the ground, cracking his knees painfully on hard stone and grazing his outstretched palms.

'Excellent,' the voice said. 'You're a natural, Errol.'

He looked up, taking long moments to comprehend what he was seeing. He was kneeling on the rock at Jagged Leap, transported there in an instant by something his brain wasn't quite ready to comprehend. But it wasn't his miraculous journey that took his breath away. His mouth hung open in wonder at the creature which stood before him.

It was a dragon, but quite unlike any of the crude illustrations Errol had seen in books. Those had been sorry-looking creatures with lustreless scales and flaccid wings no bigger than a half-door, certainly not big enough to lift their bulk. Dragon's wings, the books had told him, were not for flying at all, but were simply there to allow them to catch the sun, to warm their blood so that they could function. Much like lizards.

This dragon was different.

It was huge, for one thing. Errol had imagined the creatures as about the size of a large horse. This one towered over him almost as big as a house. Its long tail was curled around in a loop, surrounding him like a tapering wall. Its scales were polished and as shiny as mirrors, scattering the afternoon light in a magical rainbow of colours. As he looked up, craning his neck to see that huge head, the dragon flexed open its wings and two great sails spread across the sky. They were massive powerful things that could have no other purpose than to allow the magnificent beast complete mastery over the air.

Errol knew he should have been scared. Confronted by any other creature even half as big, with great pointed fangs, razor-sharp claws and talons, those oval piercing green eyes, he would have run a mile. Or more likely been frozen to the spot in abject terror and died helpless, paralysed. Yet here, in front of the dragon, he felt safer than he had ever felt. Safer even than his earliest memories of his mother soothing him after something bad had happened.

'Welcome, Errol,' the dragon said, its voice strong and deep but not so loud as to be uncomfortable. 'It's been a long time since last I had an apprentice, longer still since one showed so much promise.'

'Apprentice?' Errol asked, confusion taking over from his initial surprise.

'Do you not wish to learn from me?' Sir Radnor asked, a gentle mocking in his voice.

'Of course,' Errol blurted out, lest the chance be taken away from him.

'Good,' the dragon said. 'Then let us begin.'

It was only then that Errol realized his trousers were still lying on a rock a mile downstream.

Melyn limped into his private chapel, bolting the door behind him. Fresh mountain air blew in through the unglazed narrow slits of two windows, chilling the small room. He turned towards the heavy black slate altar which sat on a dais raised above the rest of the flagstone floor. Hanging from the wall above it, the image of the Shepherd, arms outstretched and crook held high as he did battle against the Running Wolves, glowed as if it were alive, lit from below by two stubby tallow candles.

On the altar the reliquary stood closed, its ancient wood smooth with the touch of millennia. Trembling slightly, Melyn reached up and unclipped the plain bronze clasp, opening the box to reveal the desiccated finger still wearing its simple gold band set with a lone crimson stone. Balwen's ring, gifted to him by the Shepherd himself and passed down through generations of the royal house, until Brynceri had lost his finger in his fight with the dragon Maddau. It glowed with an inner fire that filled Melyn with the strength of his convictions. This was his direct link to the Shepherd, the gift of his god.

He was at peace in this place, calm and collected. Even the pain in his knee seemed less. Countless inquisitors before him had made the private chapel their own, adding heavy woollen drapes to the smooth stone walls, filling the massive oak chest at the far end of the room with other relics gathered from all four corners of Gwlad, decorating the floor with bizarre sigils and runes which had become scuffed and indistinct over the centuries. Melyn was loath to remove any of this, although he felt much that had been added to the room was unnecessary. He could feel the Shepherd all around him. His presence was as solid as a man standing by his side. And he knew that his god would be there for him if he truly needed his advice. His god was always there, always with him of course. But here, in the chapel, high in the mountains of the Rim, the Shepherd would speak to him.

Melyn settled into the twin dips in the floor that marked the spot where every inquisitor had prayed since Ruthin had first been charged with founding the order. It was not a comfortable position, especially with his stiff and swollen knee, but then no man should dare to approach his god in comfort.

Hours passed, or maybe it was minutes. Isolated from the hubbub of the monastery and shielded by thick oak and solid stone, the chapel was a point of perfect stillness in the midst of chaos. Melyn let the silence wash over him, as he had done countless times before, trying to suppress the hope in his heart. If the Shepherd wished to speak with him then he would appear. If not, well who was he to question the reasoning of his god?

'You are troubled, my faithful servant.' The familiar voice filled Melyn with the same ecstatic thrill that it ever had. He did not look up, did not dare, but knew that perfect bliss of being in the presence of his maker. All his aches and pains were washed away, as if they had never been. He could feel the swelling in his knee shrinking away, the pain soothed as the wrenched muscles and cartilage mended themselves.

'I have received news that concerns me, my lord,' Melyn said, not knowing quite how to voice his anxieties.

'You fear that Padraig seeks to take control of the lower Ffrydd,' the voice of God said. 'You worry that you will not be able to keep an eye on the last of the dragons that live there.'

'That they live at all is an affront to me,' Melyn said, a flush of anger reddening his neck before cold embarrassment washed over him. Such emotion had no place in the presence of God.

'They serve a purpose in my great plan. For now at least. But do not fear, my inquisitor. The time will come soon enough when you can fulfil the obligation placed upon your Order. King Divitie's amity towards dragon-kind will not outlive his great-grandson.'

'I live only to serve you, my lord,' Melyn said. 'But I am weak. I fear for my people. Your people. Our enemies harry us along our borders, yet the king is grown old and senile and his most trusted adviser seeks to appease them at every turn. I fear that we will soon be overrun and still Padraig claims to speak with your authority.'

'As he does in many things, Melyn. Were not each of the three orders cut from the same cloth? Do you think because I deign to speak directly to you that your order somehow has an exclusive hold on the truth? I have good reasons why Padraig should pursue his diplomatic route with the heathen Llanwennogs, as I have good reasons why you should keep your army of warrior priests ever at the ready. It is not the place of any man to question those reasons.'

Melyn felt the displeasure as an echo of unbelievable pain. It was a light punishment, he knew, yet within it was the promise of eternal damnation, of perfect wretched-ness and torment. He knew that his god could be a cruel god, and in that moment he caught a glimpse of just how cruel that god could be.

'I could never hope to understand your great plan, lord. Please forgive me for my pride,' he said.

'Do not immolate yourself just yet, my faithful servant. I have need of your pride, and your strength. That is why I chose you in the first place. But I need you to have patience still. There will be no Llanwennog attack while Diseverin sits on the Obsidian Throne, and I have every confidence that young Beulah will keep her father alive until such time as she can take up the mantle of power herself. Then you can have your war, Melyn son of Arall.

Then you can spread the word of truth over the whole world.'

Melyn's heart soared at the prospect, his mind full of the possibilities. He would lead a mighty army of warrior priests out of the Ffrydd and into Llanwennog. He would burn the word of God into the unbelievers and bring the glory of the Shepherd to the ignorant. And he would know, without a doubt if ever one had troubled him before, that he was doing the bidding of his god. He could not fail. He burned with righteousness, alive in a perfect moment of holy bliss.

7

The subtle arts are so named because, like the Grym they attempt to manipulate, they are interwoven and complex. There are simple spells, wards and other glamours which the novice should be able to master with relative ease, but as you seek to combine the effects of different workings to achieve some greater end, so the complexity multiplies. Great care should always be taken when employing the arts to understand both what it is you are trying to achieve and what other workings may already be in progress around you. Unexpected effects are commonplace, and quite often one spell will negate another entirely.

Corwen teul Maddau,
On the Application of the Subtle Arts

Benfro hated collecting herbs. It was monotonous, repetitive work and yet he couldn't let his mind wander. If he mixed up his devil's bane with ground sedge at best he would get an earful from his mother and have to do the whole thing again. At worst he wouldn't find out until he was preparing poultices and his hands began to itch.

It wasn't even as if his mother needed half of the potions she stored. The villagers, though old, were in the main healthy. Sir Frynwy needed a steady supply of galan root for his arthritis and there were a few staples like wood sorrel and dandelion leaf that went into the cooking, but most of the more exotic potions seemed to sit untouched in store from the day they were made until the day Morgwm decided they had lost their potency and needed to be replaced. Then it was up to Benfro to scour the forest for ingredients. And as if that weren't bad enough, most of the recipes required leaves to be picked during certain times of the day and phases of the moon. Some could only be picked in darkness, others only when in full sunlight. The variations were endless and yet somehow he was supposed to remember them all.

It was an impossible task. And still his mother expected him not only to master it, but master it now. For his part Benfro couldn't see what the rush was. There were far more enjoyable ways to spend the days. Hunting with Ynys Môn, for instance, or sitting with old Sir Frynwy and listening to tales of ancient times. Meirionydd had promised that she would show him something of the magic that filled the world around them, if Morgwm would let her. As yet Benfro's mother had shown little sign of giving this permission and he sometimes wondered if she weren't using it as a cynical ploy to get him to do his chores. But ever since his hunting trip into the deep woods with Ynys Môn, when he had first heard the story of Gog and Magog, Benfro had been desperate to learn more. So he went along with his mother's demands in the hope that, sooner rather than later, she would let him learn what he really wanted to learn. And in the meantime he could practise the concealment spell that Ynys Môn had taught him, even if there were only forest creatures to creep up on unseen.

The part of the forest in which he now hunted for bird's-foot trefoil, wild garlic and other hard-to-find plants was a place Benfro didn't often visit. Half a day's walk from home, it was a dank place where the river broke over a series of rocky escarpments before tumbling through rapids cut deep into the softer rock as it splashed down towards the village. There were paths through this difficult country, but more often than not they led only to areas of deep muddy bog cleverly disguised as firm ground. Springs welled up from rocky areas bringing with them a strange metallic smell that reminded Benfro of the Delyn oil he had poured over the remains of Ystrad Fflur.

Benfro paused in his journey across the latest in a seemingly endless sequence of rock-strewn bogs. The escarpments climbed away from him, one by one, like a staircase built for some inconceivably large beast. From where he was now he could just make out the edge of the next one and beyond it the next. There were few trees, and he could see, far distant, the green-clad slopes of the Rim mountains rising out of the forest at the edge of the Graith Fawr. Their size made him shiver, their distance impossible to comprehend. All his short life Benfro had lived in the forest, his existence defined by proximity to trees. They acted as a frame, something in which to set things. He could cope with a clearing as big as that in which the village sat, which was perhaps no more than two thousand paces from end to end along the track, half that across. Those mountains, hazy and unclear in the afternoon sun, were too distant to understand. They frightened him.

A buzzard screaming overhead brought Benfro back to his senses. This was the reason he tended not to come to this place often: it was too exposed, too wild. Downstream, where the river separated into deep fish-filled pools and short stretches of white water overhung with the close canopy of the forest, he was more at ease. Still, there was a job to do and here was the only place he knew that it could be done.

The plants he sought clung to the face of the escarpment, seeming to root themselves into the very rock. Their leaves were thick, bulbous and shone with a waxy outer skin that darkened them to such a degree they were almost red. Benfro couldn't remember what potion it was that they contributed to, but Morgwm had shaken out the dusty powder from the cracked jar in the storeroom the night before and announced that he would have to fetch more supplies. Of course he had complained – he was supposed to be fishing with Ynys Môn today – but it had been a half-hearted protest. He knew there was no point trying to change his mother's mind.

Benfro pulled a handful of the dark plants out of the rock face and shoved them into his leather satchel. There weren't as many of them on this part of the escarpment as he had thought when he had viewed it from further away. Most of the greenery was moss and long strands of spiky grass. A few clumps higher up the face looked promising. Since he was going to have to get up to the next level anyway and he didn't fancy clambering back over the rocky flats to the forest edge where the slope was easier, he decided it would be more fun to climb.

The cliff was not quite vertical and riddled with cracks and fissures. Water trickled through most of these, making the stone slippery with moss and lichen, but Benfro was a skilled climber. He managed to gather a couple more handfuls of thick squelching leaves before he reached the top and was about to haul himself over when he heard a familiar voice.

'Merciful Arhelion, hear my prayer. Show me the ways and the paths to the world.'

Peering over the edge of the cliff, Benfro looked across the flat boulder-strewn space between him and the next escarpment. It was much like the one he had crossed earlier, like some giant had crushed great rocks and spilled the boulders like gravel over his staircase. This terrace was perhaps a little less ragged than the one below, with more pools of water and fewer rocks. In the middle of it one particularly large slab stood, flat-topped and surrounded by its own still moat. And atop this sat the one dragon Benfro had no desire to meet. Frecknock.

'Great Rasalene, hear my supplication. Lend power to my voice that I may be heard throughout Gwlad.'

Benfro shifted his weight, his feet stuck hard into two cracks in the cliff, his arms tensed, ready to drop his head down should his tormentor turn towards him. But Frecknock was not looking at anything. Her eyes were tight shut, her head turned resolutely towards the east. On the rock beside her Benfro could see a thick leather-bound book, a heavy gourd of the type his mother used to keep spiced wine in and a small pottery bowl in which a pale blue flame struggled to stay alight. As he watched, Frecknock seemed to swell up, puffing out her scaly chest and holding her hands with palms raised away from her body as if holding a pair of invisible weights. Was it his imagination, or could he see a faint colourless glow surrounding her like a second skin?

'Hear my voice, all who walk the long road. I am Frecknock and I would call you to me.'

Benfro nearly fell from the cliff, such was the power of that voice. Yet Frecknock had not shouted. He had not even heard her words, he realized. They had been in his head. And they carried with them something that he couldn't quite understand. It was a feeling akin to helplessness, and yet it made him want to go to her side, to comfort her. He could feel the muscles in his arms and legs tensing to pull him over the lip of the cliff. He should go to her side, be with her. She would be good for him, would nurture him and care for him.

But this was Frecknock. She was the bane of his life. Her every action was designed to get him into trouble or to punish him regardless of any deed he may have committed. This was Frecknock, who had shown him nothing but scorn since he could remember. Shaking his head, he threw off the strange feeling like he might shake rain from his ears. As he did so, he thought he could see faint lines crossing the terrace to the rock and into the sitting dragon. She was so still that for a moment he thought her dead, but that strange, clinging, invisible second skin still hung around her and something told him that it was her life force.

'Beautiful Frecknock,' a voice thundered in Benfro's head and again he nearly fell from his perch. Frecknock herself went rigid, her arms spreading wider and her head lifting, questing from side to side as if looking for the source of the voice. Still she kept her eyes closed.

'At last, an answer!' she cried. 'Who is it who heeds my call?'

'I am Sir Felyn,' the voice said. 'Long have I travelled the hard road, looking for more of my kind. Yours is a voice of salvation, a spring of sweet water to the sun-parched throat. But I fear the distance between us is too great. I would come to you but I cannot see where you are.'

Listening in, Benfro felt a twinge of guilt. This was a personal matter, and however much he might dislike Frecknock, she was still entitled to her privacy. And yet he was fascinated too. Here was actual magic being performed, something his mother would never let him see.

'Tell me of your travels, good Sir Felyn,' Frecknock said, her voice tinged with that same strange allure she had emitted before. Benfro had to suppress the urge to shout out his life story, but the other voice, wherever it was coming from, was made of sterner stuff.

'Ah, sweet Frecknock,' it said, 'if I were to waste my time telling you of all the places I have seen, I would never find my way to your side.'

Benfro could feel cramp beginning to take hold in his legs where they were splayed awkwardly to reach the two footholds. He realized that he was still tensed on the verge of clambering over the cliff edge and rushing to Frecknock's side. Her need was such a palpable thing. It reached out from her straight to him like a line. And as he thought it, so he could see it. A thick cord that hugged the ground as it speared from the rock where she sat seemed to pass straight through his head. Almost imperceptible pulses of light flowed along the line towards him, and with each one the desire to join the dragon he most detested grew. With a conscious effort he shifted his weight, edging sideways a fraction so that he could move his head out of the flow. Instantly the feeling was lessened. Across the clearing he could see Frecknock's mouth moving but he could hear no words over the trickle and splash of water through the rocks. Neither could he now see the line, though he was sure he had not imagined it. Slowly, as if he expected to be stung or burned, Benfro shifted back to his original position.

'. . . a terrible mistake. They mean well, but they are so old, so set in their ways.' Frecknock's voice came back strong and clear, and with it the line swam again into Benfro's vision. Once more he could feel the longing, the desperate loneliness and deep desire to be loved pouring out from her like the musk of a roe deer in the spring. The image sprang unbidden into Benfro's mind and with it the realization of what Frecknock was doing. Embarrassment burned the tips of his ears and he was about to slink away, to return to his herb collecting, when Sir Felyn spoke again.

'Yours is a tragic tale indeed, beautiful Frecknock,' he said, and it seemed to Benfro that the voice came from beneath him, as if the other dragon were standing at the foot of the cliff. He looked down, but there was no one there, just that same pale line, following the lie of the land

and spearing away into the distant trees. Somehow that line was connecting Frecknock with her would-be suitor across some immeasurable distance. But how had she known what to do? And what chance was there of her finding another dragon out here? Sir Frynwy had always led him to believe that the villagers were the only dragons left in the Ffrydd, but he had also told Benfro many tales of far-distant lands. Were there other villages out there in the wider world? And other dragons living in them? And who was this Sir Felyn? What was this hard road he had travelled?

Without knowing quite what he was doing, Benfro tried to get closer to the strange dragon whose voice in his head was now praising Frecknock's strength of character and nobility. He leaned out from the cliff at first, then realized the folly of moving himself physically as the voice faded away almost to nothing. Swinging back into his original position, Benfro strained his ears, as he would when out hunting with Ynys Môn and he wanted to locate new prey. The roar of the forest came to him with all its jumbled cacophony, drowning out Frecknock's reply to Sir Felyn's latest outrageous flattery. Shaking his head, Benfro tried once more to focus on the words forming in his head and ignore the world outside.

'But sweet Frecknock, I must come to you quickly,' Sir Felyn said. 'Though the distance between us be half the world, I will make that journey. If only you will tell me where you are.'

Something nagged at the back of Benfro's mind. There was something wrong, yet he couldn't put his finger on it. He listened closely to Sir Felyn's voice, trying hard to imagine what the traveling dragon might look like. Certainly he was well spoken, if a little overzealous in his praise of Frecknock. Benfro had little to go on by way of comparison but he had never considered her to be a great beauty, certainly not in the same league as Ammorgwm the Fair or even Wise Maddau from Sir Frynwy's tales.

An image swam into Benfro's mind then which made no sense to him. It was a small room with walls of dark stone, cut square. Heavy tapestries, their pictures obscured by years of dust, hung all around; a couple of chairs, too small for any dragon to fit in, sat on either side of a small fireplace, which was unlit even though a shiver of cold ran through him. He appeared to be sitting at a wooden desk, upon which stood a half-empty goblet and a wooden platter with the remains of a small meal on it. A window opened out on to a bright vista, and as Benfro concentrated, he could see mountain tops covered in a heavy coating of white, etched sharply against a sky so blue it was almost black.

'That's right, my pretty one,' Benfro heard the voice of Sir Felyn say, and it was as if he was saying it. He could almost feel his lips moving. 'Come closer to me. Give yourself to me. Let me see where you are hiding.'

Benfro was thirsty. He had tramped all morning through the forest and spent several hours on the escarpment in the full glare of the sun. Now, without thinking, he reached out for the goblet. It seemed the most natural thing to do at first, but then he remembered where he was. He could see the cliff face close by, feel the rough stone under his fingers. But at the same time he saw his hand stretch out for the goblet. Only it wasn't his hand. It was a stubby fleshy thing. Pink and with flat-ended clear talons fixed in place, it was an alien thing. Revolting.

In that instant the link snapped, and Benfro found himself clinging to the rock, bewildered. What had he just seen? Was that Sir Felyn? If so, he was no dragon and Frecknock was being deceived. Part of him laughed inwardly at the thought that vain, foolish Frecknock would once more be thwarted. But there was something more worrying about the situation.

'Are you alone, sweet Frecknock?' The voice came back as Benfro moved his head back into the line.

'Of course, Sir Felyn,' Frecknock replied, a touch of her normal waspish self behind her words, as if the question annoyed her.

'Only I thought for a moment I felt another –'

'Do you think me so foolish?' Frecknock asked. 'You know as well as do I the dangers in using the Llinellau. I've taken every precaution to ensure I'm heard by none but my own kind.'

'And you are a skilled mage, brave Frecknock,' Sir Felyn said. 'One I should very much like to meet. So tell me where you have chosen to perform this rite. It must surely be a place of ancient power.'

Benfro's muscles ached with hanging from the cliff top. He wanted to shift his weight around, but doing so meant he lost contact with this fascinating conversation. He was also convinced that Sir Felyn, whoever he was, meant no good. The voice seemed overly interested in where Frecknock was, and not at all concerned with who she was. And that hand had been so alien, so wrong.

'You will come to me soon?' Frecknock asked.

'Like the wind,' Sir Felyn replied. 'Just tell me where I should fly.'

'I live in a small village, deep in the forest of the Ffrydd,' Frecknock began at the same time as Benfro's grip on the cliff edge gave way. Desperately scrabbling for another hold, he flung himself up and over the ledge. It was a narrow strip of rock holding back a shallow pool, and in his desperation not to fall he rolled over and into the water with a great splash.

'By the Wolf! I was so close!'

Melyn picked up his goblet, considered it for a moment and then threw it across the room. It clattered dully against an old tapestry, spilling what remained of the wine down a faded picture of King Brynceri slaying the beast Maddau. It was millennia since the truly powerful dragons had all been killed, but there were still plenty of their kind out there. It galled him that he could do virtually nothing about the ones living in far-off lands, pained him even more that for the past one hundred and fifty years his order had been prevented by King Divitie's edict from performing its sacred duty. But even if the old king had put an end to the persecution of dragons, that didn't mean he had been foolish enough to grant them free licence. They were closely monitored, prevented from breeding and forbidden above all else to practise the subtle arts.

And yet here, just this afternoon as he sat in quiet contemplation, he had heard one of them make a calling. A sad, pathetic female desperately searching for a mate, she had been so poor at her scrying that she had been unable to see his true nature. No great threat to the order then, but something far older and far more potent had prevented him from locating her and that worried him. She had said she lived in a village in the forest of the Ffrydd, but as far as he knew there were no dragon settlements any more. They lived alone, what few remained.

So either she had lied, desperate to lure a mate with promises of more of her kind, or some power he could not overcome protected and hid a group of dragons not a fortnight's march from where he sat. Not without justification, Inquisitor Melyn considered himself the foremost practitioner of magic in the Twin Kingdoms of the Hafod and Hendry. To be met with an obstacle even his skill could not surmount was both a blow to his pride and more importantly a threat to the security of the throne he served.

Steadying himself, Melyn settled back in his chair and sought the place where he could tap into the power that was all around him. It was a basic skill, one that a novitiate was expected to master in his first few months of training, and yet lately he had been finding it difficult sometimes to get that perfect focus. Was he grown so old now that his mind was slipping away? It was unlikely. More probably he was just distracted by the endless round of petty politics played by the bureaucrats of the Candle. Day by day Padraig was building his power base in the hope that he would be able to steer young Beulah when finally she took the Obsidian Throne. Little did the old seneschal know that the princess was Melyn's, body and soul.

Focus, Melyn thought. Let the power flow. Here in the great monastery complex high on the edge of the Rim mountains there was no need to concern himself with city matters. Here he was Inquisitor of the Order of the High

Ffrydd. He must use his skill to find this Frecknock. And if she truly was one of a group, hiding in the forest against the laws of the Twin Kingdoms, then he would not flinch in delivering swift justice to her and all her kind.

Hours passed, and the light in the room began to dim, but Melyn did not notice, so intent was he on his task. He tried to rebuild the feel in his mind of the calling, the timbre of that voice and the strange way he had suddenly felt thirsty, reached for his goblet and . . . What? If he didn't know better he would have said that another mind had touched his own, undetected. But that was not possible. No one had got the better of him like that since he was a novitiate. Even Andro had never been able to truly walk his mind undetected. Yet now he was uncertain.

Focus. Forget what had happened. Try to find Frecknock. Melyn knew the paths he had travelled to get back to her. He retraced his route carefully time and time again, always with the same result. A dead end, a twist in the web would send him spinning back to where he had started. Again and again he tried, and with each failed attempt the cold fury that fed his questing grew warmer, the task harder, until he was no more than floating angrily in his own thoughts.

A light knock at the door interrupted his seething irritation.

'Who is it?' he asked, flicking the candles into life with a mental command. At least he could take satisfaction in still being able to perform that small piece of magic.

Instead of an answer the latch rose and the door swung open. For an instant Melyn was about to strike out at the interloper. Who dared enter his private chambers unannounced? He was on his feet, a blade of light already conjured from his hand ready to deal a fatal blow, before he recognized the slight figure of Princess Beulah.

'Princess,' Melyn said, lowering his weapon but keeping it alight. 'You should not come here unannounced. I might have taken your head off.'

Beulah simply smiled, shrugging off her travelling cloak and throwing it to the floor. She was dressed for the road, long leather boots, soft suede trousers and a balloon-sleeved jacket over a heavy cotton shirt laced loosely to the neck. With her straw-blonde hair cut short, she could have been mistaken for a slender boy not yet troubled by the need to shave. Only the speckling across the tops of her cheeks might make a man look twice. She took in the room with a slow turn of her head, then crossed to where the empty goblet lay on the floor, picked it up and filled it from the flagon sitting on the table.

'That's better,' she said after taking a long draught. 'I swear the Calling Road gets dustier every time I ride it. Now tell me, Melyn, what could put my high inquisitor in such a state that he throws his cup against the wall and would cut the head off the first novitiate unfortunate enough to cross his path?'

Melyn sighed, hefting the blade and feeling the power course along its length for a few moments before extinguishing it with a thought.

'Dragons, my lady,' he said. 'I have reason to believe there is a settlement of them somewhere in the forest of the Ffrydd.'

'Really?' Beulah said. 'Well how splendid.'

'Not splendid at all, ' Melyn said picking up his chair,

which had fallen over in his hasty rise, and offering it to his guest. When she had sat down he pulled up another and settled himself into it.

'Dragons are dangerous creatures,' he said. 'They're innately magical, and if not kept in check they're terribly destructive. Why do you think King Brynceri founded this order and established the aurddraig?'

'But I've seen dragons, Melyn,' the princess said. 'Back when grandpa was king they used to come to Ystumtuen occasionally to pay him their respects. I always thought they looked kind of sad and pathetic with those droopy wings and saggy scales.'

'You see only the outward appearance they choose to display to the world, my lady. Look here.' He pointed at the darkened and stained tapestry, now with a fresh red wine smear. 'See how the beast really is. That is Maddau, cornered in her lair not far from this monastery. Alone, she nearly killed King Brynceri. If Ruthin hadn't been close by, our history would be very different – the House of Balwen wouldn't exist for one thing. To this day, thousands of years later, nothing will grow on the spot where she was finally slain.'

'You don't think that time has exaggerated the tale,' Beulah said.

'Princess, don't mock me,' Melyn said. 'I've studied these creatures all my life. I've seen their true form and I know their deceptions. They're beasts of the Wolf, an affront to the natural order of things, an accident waiting to happen.'

'Calm yourself, Melyn,' Beulah said. 'I'm just teasing. You know I've no love of dragons. And if what you say is true, then they must be dealt with most severely. But you know I can't do anything until the Obsidian Throne is mine. Have patience for just one more year. Then you can take up arms against your hated dragons. Which brings me to why I'm here. Not that any excuse to get out of Candlehall and the stench of daddy dearest isn't welcome.'

'You bear your burden with fortitude, my princess,' Melyn said, noting the rancour with which Beulah spoke of her father. 'But is it wise to leave the king so long without his protection?'

'He'll be fine,' Beulah said. 'He's been better lately. He can go a month without my aid. Perhaps even longer if necessary. A slight lapse about now'd be a good thing anyway. It would show the court that the old man's health is on the final downturn. There are many at Candlehall who already believe he's only hanging on heroically to avoid a regency anyway. They see it as a show of faith in me.'

'And I've no doubt you've encouraged this talk at every available opportunity,' Melyn said.

'Of course,' Beulah said. 'You taught me the art of statecraft, after all, old friend. And it's a matter of statecraft that brings me here.'

'Go on,' Melyn said. Rising, he refilled Beulah's goblet before retrieving one for himself from an oak dresser beside the door.

'I'll reach my majority in less than a year,' Beulah said. 'I see no point hanging around waiting for my father to die. He'll see the sunset on my twenty-first birthday, but that will be his last. My mourning will, of course, be so much the greater for losing him on such an auspicious date, but it's vitally important that the small faction that will speak out against me find no popular support. So I need to get out of Candlehall and into the countryside, much as I hate it.'

'You want your people to get to know you,' Melyn said.

'Exactly. And now's the perfect opportunity. The choosing is upon us again. I know Padraig's tried to exclude your warrior priests from wide areas of the countryside, but I assume you're not taking that lying down.'

'Indeed not, my lady,' Melyn said, surprised and delighted at how accurate her intelligence was. She knew perfectly well what he had planned or she wouldn't have made the long journey up from the lower lands of the Hendry.

'So when are you leaving?'

'Tomorrow at dawn,' Melyn said, looking over to the window. It was pitch-black outside. What had happened to the afternoon and evening? 'I was planning on an early night.'

'At dawn then,' the princess said, smiling that predatory smile of hers. 'And who knows? We might even have a chance to hunt down these unruly dragons of yours.'

8

There is no more worthy calling for a young man than to become a novitiate in one of the three great orders. To dedicate oneself to serving the Shepherd, the king and the Twin Kingdoms is the noblest of all lives. But first you must be chosen, and that is no easy thing.

How then can you hope to succeed at the choosing? There is no practice or set of exercises that can guarantee your success. When the representatives of the orders come on their annual rounds they will test you rigorously on your physical stamina and your mental agility, but they will be looking for a great deal more than that.

To become a novitiate in the Order of the High Ffrydd you must show a tenacity of spirit, a zeal and an innate ability that few possess. Many are the years that the quaisters return empty-handed to the monastery at Emmass Fawr.

Father Castlemilk, *An Introduction
to the Order of the High Ffrydd*

At first Benfro thought that the scream was in his head, so loudly did it reverberate around his skull. But as he pushed himself choking and spluttering out of the cold water he realized that he was hearing Frecknock through the normal means. And, as normal, she was extremely angry with him. For a moment he considered trying out Ynys Môn's concealment spell, but he abandoned the idea as soon as he heard Frecknock's voice.

'You stupid little worm! What in Rasalene's name do you think you're doing here?'

Benfro shook water out of his ears and looked up. Frecknock was standing now, staring at him with terrible wrath writ large across her face. The book, candle pot and gourd were nowhere to be seen, although a heavy leather bag hung over the older dragon's shoulder, bulging squarely.

'I was collecting herbs for my mother,' Benfro said, holding up his own soggy leather satchel.

'Some story,' Frecknock said. 'You were up to no good. Spying on me.'

'Why would I want to do that?' Benfro asked with what he hoped was an innocent voice. Bitter experience told him that it was unlikely to work. That Frecknock hated him and always would was one of the few certainties in his life.

'Who knows what sick little fantasies go on in your tiny brain,' Frecknock screamed. Yet Benfro could see she was worried. It occurred to him that she didn't know how long he had been there, nor what he had seen. Perhaps he could use that to his advantage.

'I was just climbing the cliff. You know, trying to make a bit of fun out of a boring chore,' he said. 'This is the only place where I can get this stuff from.' He delved into his satchel and pulled out a handful of the sticky weed.

Frecknock watched him with narrowed eyes but she said nothing and didn't move from her rock.

'There wasn't as much down there as I thought so I had to come up here for some more. I lost my grip at the top.'

'And how long were you hanging there spying on me?' Frecknock asked.

'Spying? Me?' Benfro tried to put on his best innocent face. It never worked on his mother but Frecknock was not so wise, he was fairly sure. 'I didn't even know you were here until you started shouting at me. What're you doing here anyway?'

'None of your business,' Frecknock said. She shouldered her bag and leaped down from the rock, wading across the shallow pool towards him. He would have backed away, but he couldn't. 'And if you tell anyone you saw me here, I'll make you regret it. Understand?'

'I wouldn't dream of it,' Benfro said, worried. Sitting in a pool of water, bedraggled and still a bit confused, he was easy game. His only course of action was to try and appease her. 'I'm sorry if I startled you.'

'You will be,' Frecknock said, towering over him. Her eyes seemed to glow as if there were lit candles within, and Benfro could feel his head tightening like some great beast had gripped it in a huge talon.

'You've no idea what trouble you're in. Now look at me, squirt.'

The summer lasted long into autumn, one hot sunny day following another in a seemingly endless procession. A bumper harvest had been cut and stored and now the hedgerows were filled with an abundance of berries. Food was plentiful and everyone was at ease.

After a few months of keen learning, Clun had decided that there was more to being chosen by the Order of the High Ffrydd than simply books and coloured patterns in the grass. He had taken to staging mock battles, sometimes just between Errol and himself, sometimes involving all the village boys. Only Kewick's elite, Trell and a few others, were excluded from these events, although Errol would try to slip away when the games descended into anarchy.

It was increasingly difficult to get time to himself, he had found. And that meant the short afternoons and evenings when he could make his way up to Jagged Leap were all too few. It was nice to see his mother happy. Hennas had let down some of her barriers and was a changed woman, Errol admitted. But it also meant that Godric was never far from the house, Clun his constant companion. After twelve years of being an outcast, it was nice to have a friend, but Errol had also grown used to his own company.

Jagged Leap became his sanctuary and Errol would head there whenever he could. Sir Radnor would query him about the goings-on in the village, demanding studious attention to detail and constantly goading him for yet more. Errol found himself remembering things he had not realized he had noticed. Only when the old dragon's spirit was satisfied would he answer Errol's own questions, and then only obliquely. More often than not he would instead begin the telling of some ancient dragon history so that, over the months, Errol became something of an expert on the exploits of Rasalene and Arhelion, the Seven Quests of Palisander and the tragic tale of Ammorgwm the Fair. What he had not learned was much in the way of magic, or so it seemed to him.

'Sir Radnor,' Errol asked one evening as the sun was settling red in the treetops to the west, 'that night you called me, when I was sitting on the riverbank downstream. I came to you, but I can't remember how. One moment I was standing there, the next I was here. I don't remember walking up the path.'

'That's because you didn't walk up the path,' the dragon said.

'So how did I get here?'

'Did Palisander fly to Angharad's side when he had completed all seven of his tasks? Did he walk there?'

'No,' Errol said, recalling the story. 'He came to her side in a single step. At least, that's how you told it.'

'I do not make up these tales for your amusement, young Errol. Indeed I do not make up these tales at all. They happened, and every detail is as important as the next. Once he had slain the boar of Caer Idris, Palisander knew that he had won his lady's heart. He could not bear to be apart from her any longer and so, though half the world separated them, he was at her side in one step. You too took only one step from the riverbank a mile downstream to this rock. It is not something men have been able to do before. I know of only one other of your kind who has ever done such a thing, and she is more dragon in her spirit than even she knows.'

'But how did I do it?' Errol asked, excitement making him impatient though he knew from experience that there was no profit in trying to hurry a dragon.

'That is something that you must remember for yourself,' Sir Radnor said. 'You have done it once, so surely you will do it again. I cannot show you how to do something that is so intrinsic to your own self, only try to open your mind to the possibilities. But beware, Errol, for the world is a vast place and most of it is hostile.'

'I . . .' Errol started, then fell silent as he began to digest the words of the dragon. 'Who else has done this? You said "she".'

'Do you still wish to join the Order of the High Ffrydd, Errol? To become a warrior priest for your king?'

'I don't really know,' Errol said. 'I used to. It was all me and Clun used to talk about. But there's so much more to the world. I want to see Caer Idris and the Deepening Pools. I'd like to meet live dragons and learn more of magic.'

'You could do all of that in the order,' Sir Radnor said.

'But I'd have to fight and kill other men just because I was told to,' Errol said. It was the first time he had voiced the doubts that had been growing in him since he had begun to understand something of dragons. The order no longer hunted them, that much was true, but the romance of being a great warrior had begun to wear off in the light of Sir Radnor's tales. There was little that was great about the battlefield from his perspective.

'There is more to the order than just killing,' the dragon said, and Errol wondered what his tutor was trying to do. It was almost as if the long-dead spirit wanted him to join the group that had been responsible for the slaughter of most of dragonkind. 'There is learning and the chance to master the ways of the Grym.'

'And there's the opportunity to be bullied by bigger boys, the chance to be taught yet more biased history, to learn how to use the power of the world for violent ends. To become a too-powerful weapon in the hands of a weak-minded king.' Errol was surprised at the strength of his feelings on the matter. He had not really thought about it in great depth until now and yet Sir Radnor had drawn him out and forced him to consider the matter. It reminded him of the way old Father Drebble had encouraged him to read.

'Drebble was a kind-hearted man, as many who serve the Ram are,' Sir Radnor said. 'He used to come and talk to me from time to time.'

There was an almost wistful tone in the spirit dragon's voice, and Errol felt the terrible crushing loneliness behind it at the same time as he realized just how easily his thoughts leaked out.

'Yes, that is another thing you will have to learn to do,' the dragon's voice said. 'But I think you have done enough for one evening, Errol. It's getting late and you will be missed. I do not think you would wish to be caught out here again.'

Errol realized then how dark it had become. Sometimes he thought he could see Sir Radnor, impossibly vast and regal, towering over the rock. Most days, and this was one of them, he could only hear the voice, booming in his head. Then he would retreat inside himself too, building worlds in his imagination so that the day could pass and night fall without his noticing. A few stars had begun twinkling in the indigo sky and a smear of red like distant fire silhouetted the treetops.

He did not want to go, but he knew when he was being dismissed. Thanking Sir Radnor, he jumped down from the rock and made his way along the path into the trees. He would have happily stayed out all night. The chances were that Godric would be at the cottage when he returned, sharing a meal and then most likely staying the night. That meant Clun would once more be sharing Errol's room, and at the moment he really wanted to be alone. Clun's undiminished enthusiasm for the Order of the High Ffrydd had become increasingly difficult to reciprocate and now he began to understand why.

A strange sensation running down Errol's spine put him on edge. He didn't know how he knew, but he was convinced that he was no longer alone. It was almost as if someone had just popped into existence nearby, and the faint echo of a memory tickled at his thoughts, like a delicate scent taking him back to an earlier experience he could remember only as feelings.

'Who's there?' he asked the darkness, turning slowly to try and catch any movement. Something flitted across his vision a few yards further down the path, where a gap in the trees lit a small clearing with rising moonlight. For an instant he was afraid, then realization dawned and with it a great, exciting joy filled him. 'Martha?'

She stepped into the light like some ghostly spectre and for a terrible instant Errol thought he had been mistaken. The figure before him seemed taller than he remembered, and slimmer though she had never been fat. Her hair was no longer a short-cropped unruly mop, but hung over her shoulder in a loose ponytail. She was dressed in a pair of trousers that made her legs look longer and a white cotton blouse that seemed almost to glow in the moonlight. A long cloak was clasped at her throat, and though the moon washed it of all colour, he was sure it was dark green, to match her eyes. Could a person really change so much in a year?

'You've been sitting up on Jagged Leap, Errol Ramsbottom,' she said, and at once Errol was certain, though there was a change to her accent, her words better pronounced, her speech less like the clipped brogue of the villagers. 'You've been talking to old dragon Radnor.'

'When did you get back?' Errol asked, stepping closer and suddenly not sure what he should do. The last time he had seen her, Martha had been bedraggled, weak and cold. He had just pulled her from the river and breathed life back into her. True, she had annoyed him at times with her seemingly inane comments and awkward habit of turning up unannounced in the most unlikely of places. Yet he couldn't deny that he had missed her company every single day since she had been sent away.

'You've grown, Errol Ramsbottom,' Martha said, and before he could say anything she had grabbed him in a fierce hug. She was warm and smelled of exotic far-off places. Her hair was clean and soft against his cheek and for a flustered moment Errol couldn't think where to put his hands. All too soon though the embrace was over, and she stepped away.

'Where've you been, Martha? When did you get back?' Errol had a thousand more questions but these ones were the first to push their way to his mouth.

'Been with my aunt in Candlehall,' Martha said. 'Went to see the king in his stolen hall.'

'Candlehall,' Errol said, his curiosity piqued. 'What's it like? Is it as big as they say? Are the streets really paved with gold?'

Martha laughed. 'No, silly. Gold'd wear away under all those feet.' She took his hand in the dark. 'Walk with me,' she said as if he had a choice in the matter. 'Tell me what you've been doing since . . .' She looked over her shoulder into the darkness and back up the path towards Jagged Leap.

'Not a lot,' Errol said. 'You know what this place is like.' Still he told her of his mother's now open relationship with Godric, of how Clun had befriended him and how he had been teaching the older boy about the lines.

'Why'd he want to know about that?' Martha asked, her astonishment stopping her in mid-stride.

'He wants to be chosen for the Order of the High Ffrydd,' Errol said.

'Dragon slayers!' Martha said, dropping his hand. 'How could you help them?'

'I'm not . . . They're not . . .' Errol said. 'They don't kill dragons any more. They protect the Twin Kingdoms from invasion.'

Martha's face was stern in the moonlight, but it softened as she looked at him. She held her hand out once more and Errol took it with perhaps a little too much haste.

'I visited the old king in the Neuadd,' she said as they resumed walking through the dark trees. 'Dragons built that hall. They built most of the palace more'n a thousand years ago. They built the Obsidian Throne. It's far too big for a man, makes the king look silly. But the men there have broken it all. They smashed the carvings and broke up the windows so you couldn't see the pictures any more. Only I could see their ghosts. They talked to me, told me all about it.'

'All about what?' Errol asked.

'All about the trickery King Diseverin used to defeat the great dragon Magog. How they hunted down the others, one by one. How they cracked open their skulls and pulled out their jewels.' Martha stopped once more, turning to face Errol, her features serious, sad and angry.

They stood in the middle of a leaf-strewn clearing about thirty paces across, the shedding trees strangely well defined in the monochrome light. At that moment he felt the first signs of the end of autumn, the first cold breath of winter on the way.

'Errol, they've got dungeons filled with the jewels of slain dragons,' she said. Her distress was so intense that he didn't even notice her omission of his surname.

'But Sir Radnor says most dragons like their jewels to be laid together with those of their friends,' he said.

'Not unreckoned,' Martha said. 'These jewels are raw, not set. They bleed into one another, constantly in pain. The ghosts are in torment far worse than any hell.'

'I . . .' Errol began, but he truly didn't understand what Martha was saying.

'Promise me you won't go to the choosing, Errol,' she said and this time he did notice.

'I'm too young,' he said. 'I'd have to wait another year anyway.'

'But you won't go. Not even next year.'

'No,' Errol said, realizing as he did that any desire he

had once harboured to be a warrior priest, or for that matter a coenobite of the Ram, had disappeared. He had never known anything but contempt for the Order of the Candle since Father Kewick had begun to strip the library of all its interesting books. 'No, I don't want anything to do with any of the orders.'

Martha smiled a great beaming flash of white in the moonlit darkness. Then Errol felt her pull him towards her. Before he knew what was happening she had grabbed his head in both hands and was kissing him full on the lips.

Errol was not totally naive. At thirteen and having grown up the son of the village healer, he knew plenty about the facts of life. He had not, as yet, been in any particular hurry to investigate them further, partly because there was so much else to learn about, partly because of the steady stream of young women who came to his mother's cottage in search of certain preparations. And so he was quite unprepared for the heady pleasure of that long slow kiss. Neither was he prepared for the longing that began the instant it was over.

'Da'll be looking for me,' Martha said as she broke away from their embrace. 'I must go home.'

'Me too, I suppose,' Errol said. 'Though it's not as if mother will miss me. She's too wrapped up with Godric these days to notice if I'm there or not.'

'Meet me here tomorrow at midday,' Martha said. 'We'll go and see old Sir Radnor together.'

'Won't your father be angry?' Errol asked.

'Not if he doesn't know,' Martha said, smiling in that mischievous way that made Errol's heart skip. 'Go now, quick.'

'Tomorrow then,' Errol said. He turned away, walking toward the trees with an uncharacteristic lightness of step, heading in the direction he knew would take him home. After no more than half a dozen paces, he stopped. He had to say something, to tell Martha how much he had missed her and how good it was now she was back. But when he turned she was nowhere to be seen.

9

Perhaps the most powerful of all the books on the subtle arts is the *Llyfr Draconius*. The name of the mage who first began this work is lost in the mists of time, but whoever it was they were possessed of uncanny ability and foresight. For while the book itself never changes, it has absorbed the knowledge of all who have used it down countless millennia. It is dense with the power of the Grym.

But there is a dark side to the *Llyfr Draconius*, and a danger too. It is all too easy for an unskilled reader to find themselves drawn into the book; their whole life sucked into its enchanted pages. Rather than taking what knowledge they might need from it, and giving that which they have themselves learned in return, the unwary may lose their mind just trying to read the ancient runes. It is even said that in the depths of night the book can be heard wailing with the screams of apprentice mages who foolishly thought themselves ready to seek its advice.

More dangerous, perhaps, is the novice who has learned to read the book but not yet understood fully what it contains. There are temptations within its pages that few have the strength of will to resist.

Corwen teul Maddau,
On the Application of the Subtle Arts

Benfro knew as soon as he stepped into the cottage that he was in trouble. His mother stood with her back to the fireplace, arms folded across her chest and a stern look on her face that left no room for a more cheerful interpretation. It might have been merely that he was considerably later getting home than he should have been, though evening was only now descending into night and he knew the forest for miles around like he knew his own tail. It couldn't have been that he had failed in his search for herbs, since his satchel fairly bulged with the day's gathering. Whatever it was must have been serious though, for old Sir Frynwy sat silent at the table.

'Come in, Benfro,' Morgwm said as he hesitated on the threshold. 'Sir Frynwy would like a word.'

Benfro stepped inside, dropping the satchel to the floor, where it landed with a soft damp slap.

'What's happening?' he asked.

'Sit down, Benfro,' Sir Frynwy said, pointing to the bench opposite him. The tabletop, usually covered with the makings of potions, bunches of herbs for sorting and tying and other paraphernalia of Morgwm's trade, was empty and scrubbed clean. It made the room look somehow threatening, as if it were somebody else's house, not the warm comfortable room where he had lived these last thirteen years. With a dreadful sense of impending punishment, Benfro slid on to the wide bench across from the old dragon. He caught those wise eyes looking straight at him and lowered his own to the rough wooden surface of the table.

'Look at me, please, Benfro,' Sir Frynwy said. His tone was not accusatory, not angry, but neither was it the normal bright and cheerful voice the village elder normally used when addressing him.

'Meirionydd tells me that you're very interested in magic,' the old dragon said. 'You're constantly asking her to teach you about it, are you not?'

'I don't see why I shouldn't . . .' Benfro began, but Sir Frynwy lifted a hand to silence him.

'There's nothing wrong with a healthy curiosity, Benfro,' he said. 'I'm not here to castigate you for being curious. But tell me, what has Meirionydd said to your repeated requests?'

'She says that she'll teach me when mother says I'm old enough to learn,' Benfro said.

'And do you not think your mother's wisdom in such matters is greater than yours?'

'But I'm not a kitling any more,' Benfro said. 'I'm thirteen!'

'And I'm very nearly eighteen hundred years old, Benfro. Can you even begin to comprehend how long that is?'

'I'm not a kitling any more,' Benfro repeated, realizing as he said it that he did sound very much like one.

'No, you're not,' Sir Frynwy said. 'But take some advice from one who's lived a bit longer than you. Don't be in such a rush to grow up. When it comes, you'll wish it hadn't happened so quickly. Which brings me to why I'm here. Something of mine has gone missing, something both valuable and dangerous. I am confident that none of the villagers would meddle with it, since they know well what it can do. You, on the other hand, Benfro, don't have our experience.'

'What are you talking about?' Benfro asked. 'I haven't taken anything.'

'Come now, young Benfro,' Sir Frynwy said. 'I've already told you I don't want to discourage your curiosity. A willingness to learn is the greatest of gifts. But the *Llyfr Draconius* is too dangerous for your young mind. Trust me on this, and when the time is right I myself will introduce you to its mysteries.'

'I haven't . . . I don't . . . How could I have taken something when I don't even know what it is?'

Sir Frynwy sighed the same exasperated sound that Benfro's mother always made when he was slow to identify his herbs or when he inadvertently mixed the wrong ingredients and filled the cottage with the smell of rotting eggs.

'I'm not going to punish you, Benfro,' Sir Frynwy said, then looked up at Morgwm, who still stood motionless by the fire, the light of the flames casting her face and expression in inscrutable shadow. 'And neither is your mother. This is too important for that. But I must insist that you give the book back. It will do you no good, even if you can read it. And it could cause us all great harm.'

A book, Benfro thought. Sir Frynwy's talking about a book. But he hadn't taken anything from the old dragon. He had never taken anything from any of the villagers that they hadn't explicitly told him he could, nor had it ever occurred to him to do so. The only books he had ever so much as touched were the ones his mother kept on the long shelves at the back of this room. His eyes darted towards them and their familiar dark leather spines:

Healer Trefnog's *The Apothecarium*, Aderyn's *Educational Notes for the Young* and his favourite, Sir Cadrigal's *Beast of Gwlad* with its bizarre pictures of creatures that couldn't possibly exist. There were dozens, maybe even a hundred, and he had read them all, though most were dry descriptions of plants and potions.

'I haven't taken anything from you, Sir Frynwy,' Benfro said. 'Honestly.'

The old dragon stared hard at him, straight into Benfro's eyes so that he felt trapped and could not look away. Stuck there, motionless for long moments that felt like hours, Benfro couldn't help but notice how old Sir Frynwy looked. His face was pocked with missing scales, his eyes slightly misty as if time had faded their black pupils like a badly cured skin. He had lost one fang at some time in the past, but the dimple where it had pushed down from his jaw still held its shape, showing a gash of black-streaked pink gum. The other fang still held, but the end had been chipped off, leaving a cracked and yellowing stump. Thin white hairs sprouted from Sir Frynwy's nostrils and ears in tiny clumps, and his whole face looked shrunken and withered like the last apple at winter's end.

'I'm sorry, Benfro,' he said finally, the words breaking the spell. Slightly dizzy, Benfro took in a deep breath, the first he could remember for a long while.

'It would have been easier if it was you,' the old dragon continued. 'But I can see now that you're innocent of this charge. I must look elsewhere.' He stood up, an action which did not come easily, Benfro noticed.

'Please, Sir Frynwy,' Morgwm said, finally moving from her place by the fire. 'You'll stay for some supper at least.'

'No, Morgwm, thank you,' Sir Frynwy said. 'I must get back to the village. If there's a chance I've simply mislaid the book —'

'Then you wouldn't have come here with your accusations,' Morgwm said.

'I didn't mean to insult Benfro,' Sir Frynwy said, 'nor you, Morgwm. But you of all people know how dangerous the *Llyfr Draconius* could be if it fell into the hands of someone . . . inexperienced.'

'Which is why I recommended you destroy it years ago, Sir Frynwy,' Morgwm said.

'And you know that I couldn't do such a thing,' the old dragon said. Forgotten, Benfro listened to the conversation with growing intrigue. This was obviously an argument his mother and the village elder had been conducting for a long time now, but its subject was fascinating to him. He loved books, particularly those with pictures of exotic lands and strange creatures in them. Even some of the books of herbs his mother had used to teach him to read were fascinating in their own way. But the idea that a book could be dangerous was something that had never occurred to Benfro. He longed to know more, to understand how a collection of words on parchment could be so perilous that his mother, who would scream at him for getting a single page smudged with dirty fingers, could argue for it to be destroyed.

'What does it look like, this book?' he asked.

'It's not something you need concern yourself with, Benfro,' Sir Frynwy said. 'I'm sorry that I ever suspected you. You've been brought up to respect your elders and tell the truth at all times. I can see that now.'

'I could help you find it,' Benfro said, trying to think where he had seen a book recently. Meirionydd had hundreds in her study, though he had never been allowed to even touch them and Ynys Môn kept a few bestiaries and tales of hunting exotic game.

'Don't worry yourself,' Sir Frynwy said. He had crossed the room and now held the door open. 'I'll convene a meeting of the whole village tomorrow afternoon. You can come too, if you like, Benfro. If your mother will release you from your chores.'

'Can I go?' Benfro asked his mother, excited at the prospect of a meeting in the great hall. There had been none he had attended yet which hadn't ended with a feast.

Morgwm smiled at him.

'Let me see how well you did gathering today,' she said. 'Then if you can make a start on the potions before lunchtime we'll see about letting you have the afternoon off.'

'Well, I'll head back to the village then,' Sir Frynwy said, nodding towards Morgwm by way of a goodbye. 'Tomorrow, Benfro,' he said with a smile and a wink. Then he turned and left.

'Your satchel, young dragon,' Morgwm said as Benfro made to settle down at the table. It had been a long day and he was hungry, a state which was not helped by the anticipation of a feast tomorrow. Still, if he got started with sorting and washing the plants tonight, then surely his mother would have to let him go to the meeting.

Sliding off the bench, Benfro picked up the leather bag and showed it to his mother. She took it from him, opening it and pulling out some of the soft fronds, sniffing them and squeezing the rubbery leaves between her fingers before hefting the satchel to gauge how much was in it. Finally, after much frowning and poking around at the contents, she smiled.

'Not a bad day's haul,' she said. 'And you went all the way up to the falling pools. I'm impressed. Did you see anyone up there?'

'No,' Benfro said. 'I haven't seen anyone all day. Why?'

'Oh, no reason,' Morgwm answered. 'Meirionydd mentioned that Frecknock was going there to practise some of her charms. She wouldn't have liked it much if you'd disturbed her.'

A worry niggled at the back of Benfro's mind, as if he had forgotten something important. But, since he had forgotten it, he had no idea what it could have been. With a shrug, he set the plates and cups on the table in anticipation of food.

Errol would remember those few short weeks as the happiest of his life. Clun was wrapped up in his battle games, having found a book in the library about the strategy of war. Errol had read it and could only assume that Father Kewick had left it behind because of the chapters on the organization of supply trails and the importance of good bookkeeping. Whatever the reason, he was grateful, as it meant that his soon-to-be stepbrother left him alone for most of the day. Hennas had accepted Godric's proposal of marriage and spent most of her time planning their wedding feast. For his part, Godric was immersed in preparations for the choosing, along with Alderman Clusster and Tom Tydfil. Father Kewick had abandoned lessons for all but his select few students. All of which meant that Errol was left to his own devices.

He would meet Martha in the woods close to Jagged Leap every morning, and together they would spend the day listening to Sir Radnor's tales of ancient times or just walk through the ever-more-skeletal trees, holding hands and enjoying each other's company. As the days passed, the temperature dropped steadily but the first rains of winter held off, and so they spent the days in heated discussion or comfortable silence away from the hustle of the village and the prying eyes of the villagers. Every evening, as the sun left only its orange echo across the darkening sky, they would return to the same clearing and part, Errol for the cottage in the woods which he expected would not be his home for much longer, Martha for the smithy and her overprotective father.

'It's not as if I can't look after myself,' she said one frosty morning as Errol stood, rubbing his hands together and blowing on them, wishing he had brought some mittens. He whirled around at her voice, wondering again why he had not heard her footfalls crunching on the frozen leaves.

'I lasted in Candlehall for over a year, after all,' Martha continued. Errol had grown accustomed to her seemingly random thoughts. It was part of her charm that she was constantly saying things out of all context. Only with long and laboured consideration could he occasionally work out the tortured twist of logic that had led from something said perhaps hours or days before to what she said now. Yesterday she had complained that her father was always keeping an eye on her, never letting her out. Errol could only assume that she was simply picking up the thread of that conversation.

'It can't be all that bad,' he said, reaching out and taking her hand. She wore no mittens either and yet her skin was warm like newly laid eggs.

'He locks me in the house,' she said. 'Every morning after breakfast. He goes off to his meetings or to the forge and he locks the door. Then he doesn't come home till late. It's a good thing I can cook or I might starve.'

'How do you get out here then?' Errol asked. 'Climb out a window?'

'Don't be silly.' Martha laughed. 'Someone'd see me and follow. Or tell da. 'Sides, there's much easier ways.'

'How then?' Errol asked, genuinely interested.

'I thought old Radnor had taught you about the lines,' Martha said. 'Didn't he tell you how to walk them?'

'Yes,' Errol said. 'He did. I even managed it once. But I haven't tried again. Or rather I have, but it was too strange. I couldn't see what I was doing.'

Martha laughed, not unkindly. 'You think too much about things, Errol,' she said, dropping his hand. 'You should just do.'

Errol gasped. She had been right beside him in the middle of the clearing, yet now Martha stood a good twenty paces away.

'How . . . ?' He began, but he knew the answer already. He could see the lines crossing the clearing and the brighter points where they met. Martha stood squarely over one. All he needed to do was take that small step, forget the distance between them and let himself flow along the line. In theory it was easy, but as he looked at the shifting, pulsing grid his attention was pulled this way and that. A tree off to one side was ailing, its life force pale and stuttering. One of the lines speared off in the direction of home, and for a moment Errol wondered what was going on there.

'Over here, Errol.' Martha's voice pulled him back and he staggered from the force of what felt like stepping into his own skin. He had been doing it, he realized with a thrill. But he had allowed his concentration to wander and had lost his target among all the other infinite possibilities. He shook his head and concentrated once more on the point where Martha stood, seeing her patient happy smile. He felt he was closer to her than to anyone he had ever known. Even his mother was a stranger to him in many ways, more so now that she had abandoned the solitary life they had shared for Godric Defaid's bed. But Martha understood him. She shared his thirst for knowledge, his insatiable desire to know things not just accept what he was told. She made no demands of him that he didn't make of himself. Quite simply, when she was about he was happy; when she wasn't he felt sad and unfocused. He wanted her always to be around.

'See? Not so difficult, is it,' she said, her voice suddenly very close. The next instant Errol realized he was standing right beside her, almost touching her. His knees felt a little unsteady, his head fuzzy as if it were trying to catch up with the rest of him, and before he could do anything he had fallen into her ready embrace.

*

Benfro hurried along the path to the village, scarcely noticing the fallen leaves that carpeted the ground and deadened his footfalls. Autumn was always a short season in the foothills, and it wouldn't be long before frost set in. Hunting would soon be sparse, the fish in the river sluggish and unwilling to take bait. But all this mattered little to him at the moment; there was a meeting to attend and afterwards there would be a feast.

He had spent the morning trying not to hurry. Too many times before he had made that mistake when preparing medicinal potions with his mother. Benfro knew that if he made a mistake he would have to start again from the beginning and he would never be finished in time. So he had held his burning anticipation in check and applied himself as best he could to the task.

Now he was free. The odd-smelling poultice was packed into earthen jars sealed with wax-dipped corks. The labels were all neatly written, fixed to the jars with paste, and the whole morning's work had been stored carefully away. Benfro had even begun clearing up the mess, but his mother had finally relented at that point, letting him go before he broke something in his haste.

'Don't be too late back,' she had said as he had run out the door. 'And don't upset the meeting. Sir Frynwy's doing you a great honour allowing you there at all.'

The track climbed a short hill, narrowing near the top where it passed through a cutting, as if countless thousands of passing feet had slowly worn a groove through the earth. The trees hung over the road here, their shedding branches meeting and twining in the middle so that the way was always dark and cold. As a kitling, Benfro had been afraid to walk these few tens of yards alone, but he had long since grown out of such foolish nonsense. Still, he slowed to a walk as he entered the tunnel.

'Well, hello there, squirt. And where do you think you're going this afternoon?'

Benfro's hearts nearly stopped. He stood motionless for long moments as his mind caught up with his imagination. He knew the voice. There was only one dragon who would ever address him in such a manner. But still she had managed to shock him. And on this errand she was the last dragon he wanted to see.

Frecknock stepped from the trees on to the leaf-strewn path. She was between him and the village, Benfro noted with dismay. He would have to deal with her before he could get to the meeting.

'I asked you a question, squirt,' Frecknock said.

'I'm going to the meeting,' he replied.

'You? And what makes you think you'd be welcome at a meeting of the village elders? You're only ten years old.'

'Thirteen, actually,' Benfro said. He was always wary of Frecknock. She was bigger than him and he knew from experience she could catch him a nasty blow if he wasn't careful to keep out of her reach.

'Sir Frynwy invited me,' he said. 'He values my opinion.'

'So you know what this meeting is about?' Frecknock said, her voice suddenly less harsh, more interested. Benfro's suspicions grew.

'Yes, I do,' he said.

'Well tell me then, Benfro,' Frecknock said, her voice almost laughing.

'I think that Sir Frynwy should do that himself,' Benfro said.

'Oh dear,' Frecknock said. 'It's about his precious *Llyfr Draconius*, isn't it. And you saw me with a book up at the falling pools. Now you're going to tell the whole council about it, and they're going to ask me what I was doing.'

'I don't know what you're talking about,' Benfro said, backing away, but as Frecknock uttered the words, memories bubbled up in his mind like marsh gas.

'Come now, squirt,' she said, advancing as he retreated. 'You are not a good liar at all. The tip of your tail twitches and you keep rubbing your hands together. Take it from one who knows. You need to practise more.'

'I don't . . . I didn't . . . What did you do to me?' Benfro asked. 'You were there doing that . . . thing. I saw you, but I couldn't remember. Not till now.'

'So it actually worked,' Frecknock said. 'How splendid.' She was smiling at him in an odd way, still approaching as he retreated up the path in the direction he had just come from. Benfro wondered if he should turn and flee. He knew other ways to the village through the trees, and even if he missed the meeting he could explain to Sir Frynwy what had happened. He could explain everything now that his memory had returned. They would still let him come to the feast, surely. He tried to turn his head the better to make his escape, only to find that he couldn't drag his eyes away from Frecknock's.

'Stop now, squirt,' she said, and to his surprise Benfro did. He didn't want to, but somehow his legs weren't obeying him any more.

'Good, that's right,' Frecknock said. 'A little respect for

your elders and betters.' Benfro was still fixated on her eyes. They burned like dying embers and seemed to grow until all he could see was a terrible glow surrounding him, drowning him.

'You're too nosey for your own good, you know that, squirt?' Frecknock's voice was enormous, drowning out his thoughts like a thunderstorm. Benfro found it difficult to concentrate on anything but that sound and the swirling sickening light.

'I can see that even you are wilful enough to throw off my memory hex. It was a hasty ill-planned thing anyway. Still, it's served its purpose. Now we'll have to see about a more permanent solution to your nosiness.'

'What are you talking about?' Benfro asked, struggling as if he were sinking in wet mud. 'What do you want?'

'Such bravado,' Frecknock said. 'You wouldn't be so cocky if you knew what I could do to you. Now tell me what you saw yesterday up at the rock pools.'

Something in Benfro's mind clicked, and he remembered everything with total clarity: the rock, Frecknock sitting so still, the gourd and the book, the voice of Sir Felyn and the soft alien hands.

'You took it,' he said. 'You took the book.'

'Yes, I did,' Frecknock said. 'But you won't tell anyone about it. Or about my little assignation.'

'You can't stop me,' Benfro said, hearing the wavering uncertainty in his own voice. 'I'll tell everyone. You're putting us all in danger.'

'No, I'm not,' Frecknock said, her words becoming

solid in the air around him, battering his senses like a gale against loose shutters. 'And you won't tell anyone.'

Benfro struggled against the voice that pressed in on him like a suffocating weight. He was losing all sense of who he was. It was as if he was being crushed by Frecknock's terrible presence. As if everything he had ever known and been was smothered by her. Then, as quickly as it had come, the feeling evaporated. His head was once more his own and the noises of the forest, absent for too long, filtered back to his ears.

'Tell me now,' Frecknock asked him, her eyes perfectly normal so that he began to doubt what he had seen before. 'Have you seen a heavy leather book recently?'

Benfro stared around, shocked. The light was gone, the terrible overpowering sense of suppression was gone. He lifted a leg off the ground and it came as it ever had. He moved his head from side to side without difficulty.

'I asked you a question, squirt. Have you seen a heavy leather book recently?'

Of course I have, Benfro thought. You know I have. You had it. You stole it from Sir Frynwy.

'No, I haven't,' he said.

'No, I haven't,' he said again. But that wasn't what he had meant to say.

'No, I haven't.' It came out a third time, even though he was trying to scream that he knew what she had done.

'That's good,' Frecknock said at last, a little smile spreading across her face. 'I wasn't sure that it would work. Not without melting your pathetic little brain, at least.'

She stepped to one side of the track to let Benfro past.

He could only stare at her with a frustrated rage surging through him. What had she done to him? Why couldn't he say what he wanted to say?

'Well don't just stand there, squirt,' Frecknock said eventually. 'Sir Frynwy invited you to his meeting. Don't you think it a bit rude to be late?' And she clouted him hard across the back of the head repeatedly until he ran from her towards the village.

10

It is written that in the earliest days, when he still walked among his chosen, the Shepherd directed King Balwen towards fair Myfanwy and filled his heart with love for her as he filled her with devotion for him. His blessing upon that union was the foundation of our people, the beginning of the Twin Kingdoms.

Our lord no longer walks among his flock, but he watches over us at all times. From our first breath he is there, even until we depart this life and make that final journey to the safe pastures. He is our guide through life, our protector from the Running Wolves. His compassion knows no bounds, his wisdom is infinite, and nowhere is his generosity more amply demonstrated than in his blessing of the union of man and woman. For if we search our hearts, we can see that he has brought together [name of groom] and [name of spouse], just as he has brought together every man and woman since the beginning of time.

From 'The Marriage Service', *The Authorized Prayer Book of the Order of the Candle*

The wedding ceremony itself was something of an anti-climax, Errol thought. After the weeks of preparation, the panics and long arguments over seating, after the frightening transformation of his mother from a strong-willed, capable and slightly scary woman into something not much better than the giggling girls who sat and whispered at the back of the church during Suldith prayers, the actual marriage was frighteningly short. One moment he was ushering villagers into their seats, amused at the way they all spoke to him as if they were his best friend. Then almost before he had settled himself into the unfamiliar pew at the front of the church, Father Kewick in his grandest cassock was uttering the Shepherd's Blessing: 'Keep watch over your flock and protect us from the Running Wolves,' and the whole thing was over.

Errol had never been overly concerned about material wealth. His mother had raised him to appreciate what they had, and their cottage out in the woods had always seemed more than adequate. He wanted for little, apart from books, and even they could be returned once he had read them. Clothes were necessary to keep him warm, food for sustenance, but neither was something he gave very much thought to. Godric on the other hand was possibly the richest man in the village and seemed determined to let everyone know. So Errol was dressed in the finest clothes he had ever seen.

It was nice to wear a pair of boots that fit properly and kept out the creeping autumn cold. The trousers were soft, supple leather, far warmer than his old ripped and mended rough cloth rags, but the cotton shirt was stiff around the collar and made him itch. The jacket was apparently the latest fashion from Candlehall, but Errol thought it made him look like a cockerel strutting around the yard after the hens. As he stood at the entrance of the village hall, next to an equally embarrassed-looking Clun, shaking hands and exchanging pleasantries with people who had only ever cursed him before in his life, he longed to escape back to the cottage, his old clothes, his old life.

Perhaps it was the people. The whole village had turned out for the marriage of Godric Defaid, expecting to be well fed and entertained. Hennas had no relatives, but Godric's extended family had all made the journey, swelling the congregation even more. Errol was not used to the company of so many, preferring the solitude of the woods or the company of just his mother. Or Martha. The milling faces made his head swim, each new person's false smile adding to the sea of people until he felt he must surely drown.

'Ye've come up a bit in the world, boy.' Errol started out of his daydreaming at the voice, looking up from the massive, powerful hand that clasped his and into the wide face of the smith, Tom Tydfil. 'Still, I never thought I'd see Godric so happy. Not since Molly died, anyway. I guess I've ter thank yer mam for that.' It was a strange, almost grudging compliment. Then Errol remembered that Tom too had lost his wife. Only where Godric had sought out and found a new partner, Tom Tydfil had turned to the bottle for solace.

'Ye'll mind me daughter, Martha,' the smith said. Errol looked across from the smith to the figure who stood beside him, almost hidden by his bulk, and nearly fell over.

She was wearing a long dress, the first time Errol could

recall not seeing her in trousers. Autumn-leaf green, it was embroidered on the bodice with twining patterns that might have been simply pleasing shapes or might have been two dragons climbing into the sky with great wings, their curling tails hanging down in mirrored curves that crossed at a point at the base of her stomach, their heads rising with the cut of the dress to emphasize the slight swell of her breasts. Her shoulders were bare, covered with a loose shawl of fine green silk, and she wore long gloves of the same material which came two thirds of the way up her arms. She had taken her jet-black hair out of its normal ponytail and tied it up around her head in a swirl that made her seem both older and taller than her thirteen years. Smiling that mischievous grin he knew so well, she raised one hand for him to take.

'Errol, we meet again,' Martha said. 'And not so wet this time.'

Errol was confused, both by this unsettling vision of beauty before him and by her words. He had been with her just yesterday, after all. They had been discussing the endless preparations for the wedding, and then Sir Radnor had recited to them a passage from Sir Rhudian's Marriage of Gwynhyfyr, one of the oldest dragon tales. Errol had even managed to walk the lines for a short distance in the afternoon, though the effort still left him dizzy and he needed Martha's presence to anchor him from the infinite distractions of the Grym. Martha had told him she would see him at the wedding, then disappeared in front of his eyes. Yet now she was acting as if she hadn't seen him for years.

Martha's eyes flicked away from Errol's face to her

father's and back as he stood there holding her hand like it was a wet fish. Then it dawned on Errol that Tom Tydfil really knew nothing of their daily meetings.

'There's to be dancing later on,' Martha said, breaking the uneasy silence.

'Martha, don't be so forward,' her father said, taking her by the elbow and making to steer her along the line to where Clun was watching with interest.

'I hope you'll do me the honour,' Errol said, letting go of her hand reluctantly. Martha smiled back, giving him a little wink before allowing herself to be introduced to Clun, who bowed deeply, took her hand and planted a chaste kiss on her fingers. Errol felt a curious pang of jealousy and animosity towards his stepbrother.

'The likes a her aren't fer the likes a yer, boy.' Errol turned back to the line, now finally nearing its end. Alderman Clusster looked at him with barely concealed distaste and did not offer his hand to be shaken. Beside him Trell glared sullenly. He was wearing a black outfit not unlike that of a predicant of the Order of the Candle, and next to him his sister Maggs looked on nervously. Errol smiled at her in what he hoped was a reassuring manner. It must have been four years now since she had been dragged up to his mother's cottage, in tears and terrified. She would be eighteen now, he thought. She looked a lot older, but before he could say anything they had moved on.

Errol was beginning to feel hungry. He could smell the roasting meat of a whole cow which had been slaughtered for the occasion, and it reminded him that breakfast had been a long time ago, lunch an opportunity missed in the hectic round of last-minute panics. The line had almost finished, just a few close friends of Godric taking their time to gossip about trivial matters while they tried to ingratiate themselves with his new wife. He wondered if he could slip away and find Martha before the feast began. Then he noticed the doors swing open. Two strangers, a man and a woman, entered the room. By their clothes he could tell they had been travelling for most of the day, perhaps more. They stood in the entrance, looking back and forth, then, noticing his stare, the man beckoned him over.

As he approached, Errol could see that the man was old, at least sixty and probably more. His face was lined and leathery, his hair white but full. He stood over six feet in his riding boots and radiated a quiet sense of power and authority. The woman was considerably younger, perhaps in her early twenties, and stood as tall as the man. Her riding cloak was as fine as any Errol had ever seen and embroidered with sigils he recognized but couldn't quite place. Her face was not beautiful but neither was it ugly, marred only by a band of brown freckles that spread across her upper cheeks and nose like a muddy splash. She looked straight at him, her eyes seeming to bore into his, with what he could only think of as an expression of fascinated horror.

'Inquisitor Melyn! Your Highness!' Errol was thrust aside by the bustling figure of Father Kewick, who crossed the distance between him and the door in a couple of frantic bounds before crashing to one knee. The old man allowed his hand to be taken and the priest kissed the single large ring as if his continued existence depended on it.

'I am Father Kewick,' he said. 'Of the Order of the Candle. No one told me –'

'Enough, Kewick,' the old man said. 'Our visit was not announced. You need feel no shame. But tell me, what is this celebration? Surely the choosing is not until tomorrow.'

'The choosing, yes.' Father Kewick seemed flustered. 'We are celebrating a marriage, Your Grace. Goodman Godric Defaid and Hennas Ramsbottom, the village healer.' He pointed to the happy couple, who were still oblivious to the new arrivals.

'Then we've arrived at an auspicious time,' the old man said. 'For both the happy couple and ourselves, since it looks like we'll be well fed. Come, Kewick, introduce us.' He pulled his cloak off, revealing the simple cloth garb of a warrior priest, and handed it to the flustered Kewick, who took it as if it might explode or transmute into some wild beast. All the while he bobbed up and down, dipping his head in obeisance then snatching nervous glances at each of the newcomers.

Errol watched them walk across the room towards his mother and stepfather. The young woman kept her cloak on and stared around the room as if looking for something. Only then did it all fall into place. Kewick had called the old man Inquisitor Melyn. He was Inquisitor of the Order of the High Ffrydd, come for tomorrow's choosing. So Clun would get his chance after all. But Kewick had called the woman Your Highness, and Errol had recognized the sigils on her cloak. She must surely be the heir to the Obsidian Throne, Princess Beulah of the Speckled Face. He had never seen her before, which was hardly surprising given his background and upbringing. She could never have seen him before. So why was she staring at him as if he had just thrown a glass of wine in her face?

'Thank you all for coming at such short notice,' Sir Frynwy said, his voice as serious as Benfro had ever heard it. The great hall in the centre of the village was packed; he hadn't seen it so full since they had all come to see the reckoning of Ystrad Fflur. That time he had stood at the front, the centre of attention. This time, delayed by his strange encounter with Frecknock, Benfro had to content himself with squeezing in at the back where he could see little through the crush of bodies.

'It has been many hundreds of years since the first of us came to this village,' Sir Frynwy continued. 'Since then we have lived as the mother expected, as we agreed when we took the choice. We have seen old friends depart and new friends arrive. We have had hatchings – too few, I must admit – but the latest gives us cause to hope. You all know that young Benfro is the first male dragon to be born in living memory.'

Was he? Benfro felt a chill shiver run through him as those dragons closest to him, who had registered his late arrival, turned to look at him. He knew them all. He had known them all his life. Yet now they seemed almost like strangers.

'You also know that he is curious and impatient to learn all manner of things, most especially with regard to the subtle arts. So be aware that I have already spoken with him and know him to be innocent in this matter,' Sir Frynwy said. 'For someone has been into my house and

162

taken from it my copy, the last remaining copy, of the *Llyfr Draconius*.'

Ripples of shocked murmuring bounced around the hall. Meirionydd, who stood near the back and had seen Benfro come in, pushed her way through the throng to his side.

'You knew of this, Benfro?' she asked.

'Sir Frynwy came to our house last night,' he said. 'I didn't take it. I don't even know what it is.' He wanted to say, 'But I think Frecknock has it. I saw her with a book and she was doing some kind of spell,' but all that came out of his frustrated mouth was 'I didn't take it.'

'I believe you, Benfro,' Meirionydd said. 'And if Sir Frynwy's convinced of your innocence then there's no argument about it. But it would have been easier for all of us if this were just a case of your curiosity getting the better of you. The *Llyfr Draconius* is a dangerous thing in the hands of one not trained in its use. And if the warrior priests should find it . . .' She did not finish the sentence.

'But what is it?' Benfro asked, his ignorance made unbearable by his burning need to tell anyone what he had seen. Yet he was unable to say anything about Frecknock and his encounters with her today and the day before. It felt like he was trapped inside his own head and he searched frantically for a way out.

'Why would someone take it?' he asked again, trying to work around the block in his mind.

'I don't know,' Meirionydd said. 'We're happy here. We all chose to be here. And we know what would happen if the men found our village. Messing around with the subtle arts is just too risky.'

'But the men don't hunt us any more,' Benfro said.

'No, not as they once did. Their king doesn't pay them in gold for our heads any more. But they still hate us and try to control us. We're not allowed to use what they call magic; we can't breed without their licence; we're not meant to live in groups of more than four; we have to pay a tithe to their treasury every year.'

'But the village is four dozen strong,' Benfro said, looking at the collection of dragons around him, all in heated discussion. 'At least that.'

'We are forty-seven, your mother and yourself included,' Meirionydd said. 'And men know nothing of our existence.'

'But they come here from time to time. That's why Ynys Môn takes me on long hunting trips. He said so.'

'Not here, Benfro,' Meirionydd said. 'They come to your mother's house. They think she lives alone. And if someone comes to her with ill intent, the road will lead them nowhere. Such is the power that protects us all.'

Benfro wanted to ask more, but Sir Frynwy's strong voice cut through the hubbub like a rumble of thunder.

'My friends, please,' he said. 'I know this is difficult. I don't want to accuse any of you, and it may well be that none of you is guilty. But you must understand how serious this is. Anyone dabbling in the subtle arts risks harming us all. Even Meirionydd, who is by far the most skilled mage among us, would not risk the delicate balance that keeps us hidden. So please, be patient. Think back over the last few weeks and try to remember anything that you might have seen. I will come to each of you in turn. We will find the book before the day is finished. Then we'll put all of this behind us and come together for a feast.'

Meirionydd left him then, and Benfro found a place to sit where he could watch as she and Sir Frynwy went from dragon to dragon, talking quietly. Each conversation was the same, a shake of the head or a short suggestion soon dismissed. Benfro wanted to shout out that he knew where the book was, that he knew it had already been used. But whatever it was Frecknock had done to him, it stopped him from saying anything on the matter.

Neither was Frecknock at the meeting, he noticed. Surely that would be suspicious. Hope surged through Benfro then. If Frecknock was confronted by Sir Frynwy then surely she must admit to what she had done. She might even lift whatever strange compulsion she had put on him.

The small door at the corner of the hall which led to the kitchen and stores opened almost unnoticed. Benfro's hearts dropped as he saw his tormentor slip into the room. She had nothing with her, and the look of terrible defiance she gave him on seeing his stare convinced him that there was no chance of her ever admitting to her deeds. Still, Sir Frynwy and Meirionydd were both old and wise in the subtle arts. Perhaps they would be able to see the duplicity in her. They must surely ask her why she was late to such an important meeting. With a terrible sinking feeling, Benfro watched as Frecknock made her way across the hall towards him.

'Hello there, squirt,' she said. 'Are you enjoying the inquisition?'

'Where have you been?' Benfro asked, unable to voice

the question he really wanted to ask: 'What have you done to me?'

'Hah! As if I'd tell you what I was doing,' Frecknock said. 'You're a nosey little squit of a thing who'll probably be the ruin of us all. The less you know about anything the better, as far as I'm concerned. Better you just wander off into the forest and let the rest of us get back to our old lives.'

'Now, Frecknock, there's no reason to be rude.' Sir Frynwy said from behind her. Benfro had watched his approach with a delighted sense of triumph.

'Sir Frynwy,' Frecknock said, turning and nodding her head to her senior.

'I have been around everyone now, save you, Frecknock,' he said. 'You were late for the meeting, I noticed. Do you know why I called it?'

'You have lost your book, Sir Frynwy,' Frecknock said. For an instant the old dragon's eyes seemed to light up with relief. 'At least that's what Benfro told me this morning. I was heading into the forest to collect some special herbs,' she added. Benfro watched the conversation intently. As Frecknock mentioned herbs, Sir Frynwy's eye twitched slightly and he dropped his head a fraction as if embarrassed by something.

'Well, you're here now,' he said finally. 'And you of all of us should know how important it is that we find the book. You've studied it with Meirionydd for some years now, after all.'

'As you say, I know it well,' Frecknock said. Benfro could tell from her posture that she considered this high praise indeed. He saw too just how vain she was. The safety of

166

the village, the lives of the other villagers, were of less worth to her than that she was considered important.

'But have you seen the book?' Benfro asked, knowing full well the answer but unable to voice it. Frecknock stared at him with the closest thing to true hatred he had ever seen – a cold murderous look that lasted only a second but chilled him to the core. Then in an instant it was gone, replaced by a sickly false smile.

'Of course not, Benfro,' she said. 'At least not since last week, when Meirionydd and I went through the Aleydine Codex. You wouldn't know what that is though.'

'What would someone want the book for, Sir Frynwy?' Benfro asked, ignoring Frecknock's taunt. He couldn't tell the old dragon directly what he had seen, but he might be able to make him think around the problem.

'Almost anything, Benfro,' Sir Frynwy said. 'It contains the fundamental knowledge of the subtle arts. When you're older, and provided your mother approves, Meirionydd and I will introduce you to its mysteries. But we must find it first. And since none of us has seen it since last week, I'll have to arrange a search of the village. I'd hoped it wouldn't come to this, but there's no option. It's too dangerous not to know where it lies.'

Sir Frynwy turned away from Benfro and Frecknock, climbing once more on to the raised dais at the end of the hall. The voices of the villagers dwindled to almost nothing, expectant in their hush.

'Friends, we are all here, save Morgwm of course, and I have spoken with her already. None has seen the book, yet it can't have gone far. So we will have to search the village, house by house. Some of us are not as good at remembering things as we once were, so it may have quite innocently been forgotten. Since I'm charged with looking after the book, we'll start at my house. Benfro, you and Frecknock will accompany me and aid in the search.'

Too swept up by the events to be astonished, Benfro bustled out of the hall after Sir Frynwy and Frecknock, almost running to keep up. The village was not large, and as elder, the old dragon's house was close to the hall. It stood in its own yard surrounded by an abundance of wild flowers and, after the hall, was probably the biggest building in the village, though Sir Frynwy lived alone. Benfro had been inside many times before, but only into the front hall and, once, into the library. He glanced up at the wisteria-hung oak-frame front, two storeys high with great glass-filled windows like eyes, big enough for him to climb in. The door was not locked and Sir Frynwy pushed it open before motioning for Frecknock to step over the threshold. A small crowd of dragons had clustered around the gate, peering over the fence to see what would happen next. Benfro took a last glance at them and stepped inside.

The hallway was dark, panelled in ancient oak. It smelled of Sir Frynwy – there was no other way to describe it – an old slightly musky odour part wood, part tobacco smoke, part patrician authority that put Benfro instantly on his guard. Ahead of him the great wide staircase climbed away to the upper floor, and he felt a thrill of excitement that he was going to see the whole of this house. But first there was the library, the obvious place to look for a book.

Frecknock opened the door and stepped in without waiting to be asked. Benfro was shocked at her boldness, but then she had been studying with Sir Frynwy and Meirionydd for some years now, so perhaps she felt such familiar ease was acceptable. If it annoyed Sir Frynwy, he did not show it, instead motioning Benfro to go inside too.

'Come along now, Benfro,' he said. 'The quicker we can get this whole place searched, the quicker we can eat.'

'I . . .' Benfro was desperately trying to say that he knew who had taken the book and that she was standing in front of them. But 'I don't know where to look' was all that came out, and Frecknock's evil grin showed that she knew what turmoil he was in.

The library was nearly as dark as the hall, the light from the huge window almost totally obscured by hanging creepers and ivy on the wall outside. It was a big room, lined on all walls with bookcases. An unlit fireplace broke the pattern on one wall with two comfortable-looking armchairs pulled up close to its dead mouth. The only other furniture in the room was a large writing desk strewn with parchments. A couple of sconces attached to the desk dripped wax from the stubs of candles.

'Where was it you used to keep the book, Sir Frynwy?' Frecknock asked, crossing the room to a shelf close to the fireplace. 'Here, wasn't it?'

'I've searched this whole room a dozen times,' the old dragon said. 'You won't find it in here, really.'

'Nevertheless, we have to look, don't we?' Frecknock said. 'After all, others will be searching each of our houses in turn, won't they? Each and every one from top to bottom until the book is found.'

'It is only fair,' Sir Frynwy said, although he didn't sound too happy about it.

'Well don't just stand there like a dead sheep, Benfro,' Frecknock said. 'Get started on those books over there.' She pointed to a stack by the writing desk, haphazardly piled as if Sir Frynwy had been consulting them as he wrote.

'I don't know what I'm looking for,' Benfro said. It was a lie: he knew exactly the size, shape and colour of the book Frecknock had been using, but he wasn't about to make life any easier for her.

'It's a leather-bound book, Benfro,' Sir Frynwy said, coming over to where he stood by the stack. 'It's very old, older than me, in fact. The cover is a deep brown and the title is tooled into the spine in gold lettering.' He began to pick up the books from the stack, one by one, his long fingers stroking them as if they were beloved pets. 'It is much heavier than any book its size should be, something to do with the weight of knowledge it contains. And it has a very distinctive feel to it . . . Oh.'

Benfro watched as Sir Frynwy's expression changed in an instant. It was as if someone had stuck him with a pin and all the air had flowed out of him.

'What is it?' Benfro asked, noting the way the old dragon clasped the last book he had picked up tight to his scaly chest, almost as if he were trying to hide it.

'This,' Sir Frynwy said after a long pause. He held out the book for Benfro to take. Its cover felt strange, almost warm, and as he took it Benfro thought he could hear whispering voices, like an urgent conversation in the next room. Then as Sir Frynwy let it slip fully from his grasp, Benfro nearly dropped the book. It was as heavy as if it had been made of stone. Astonished, he looked up at the old dragon's distraught face.

'Ah me, what a fool I am,' he said. 'It's the *Llyfr Draco-nius*. It was here all along.'

Benfro held the magic book tightly in his grasp, wishing it would wash away the spell that Frecknock had cast on him that morning. He wanted to shout that she had taken it, that she must have sneaked in as the meeting began and put it where it would be found. His mouth stayed shut, clamped by a force he couldn't overcome. All he could do was seethe as Frecknock looked on at his frustration and Sir Frynwy's mortification with an air of malicious glee.

Proud sheep in the house of hazel and thorns,
Fey white-foot exiled from the ruined hall,
The blood of the north and the blood of the south,
Mixed will turn both to dust.

The Prophecies of Mad Goronwy

Darkness had almost completely fallen by the time Benfro made his way home. The trees silhouetted against the grey-black sky were like the skin-stripped skeletons of mythical beasts. As the wind pulled them back and forth, it seemed like they still lived, tethered cruelly to the earth, thrashing to break free. Trapped by Frecknock's spell, desperate to explode with the truth yet shackled and bound by forces he could not see let alone understand, he could well imagine the torment they might feel.

It had been a poor feast after all the anticipation. There was general relief among the villagers that the book had been found, but Sir Frynwy himself, after apologizing in person to each of the villagers in turn, had retreated to his house. With no telling of the great histories to look forward to, the party soon broke up. And even before then it had been a sombre affair. Ynys Môn had tried to lessen some of Sir Frynwy's shame by telling all who would listen of the time he had managed to become entangled in one of his own traps, hanging from a tree for three days before he was rescued, but on the whole it had been a quite miserable evening. Only Frecknock seemed happy, telling all who would listen how she thought it was time someone else took over the guardianship of the book, someone young and with all their faculties about them. Benfro had avoided her as best he could, going from dragon to dragon, trying to tell them what he had seen and what she had done to him. Each time the result was the same. He could talk around the subject, but as soon as he tried to say exactly what had happened, he seemed to lose the ability to form words. After a final embarrassed conversation with Meirionydd, he had made his excuses and left.

No moon shone and clouds obscured the stars so that the darkness was almost total. He had chosen to walk through the forest, still unsettled by his encounter with Frecknock on the path that morning, but he could have made the journey home blindfolded. He knew the woods around the village better than anything, each tree and bush, animal track, spring and grotto. The ground underfoot was soft with dead leaves, and each footfall brought a whiff of autumn decay to his nose. Winter would soon be here.

The smell of burning wood was the first sign that he was nearing home. Then he caught a glimpse of light through the thinning undergrowth and minutes later he was stepping quietly through the almost empty vegetable patch. There would be a lot of work to do preparing the beds for the winter crops and digging in last year's compost. It struck Benfro as he walked that none of the villagers grew any of their own vegetables. As far as he was aware, only Ynys Môn hunted regularly. And yet they always had food, and exotic food at that. Even that evening's sombre feast had seen a good spread of mutton and beef, venison and turkey. And there had been flatbreads flavoured with roasted nuts and garlic, steamed asparagus tips as thick as his thumb and yet still tender and sweet, platters of fruits that he had eaten a thousand times before and yet never seen growing in the forest around the village. The other dragons had drunk mead and wine, though none would let him try any. Benfro had no idea where they got it from. But what bothered him more was that it had never occurred to him before.

'So Sir Frynwy had the book all along,' Morgwm said to him as he stepped into the house. She was sitting in her favourite chair by the fire, a steaming bowl of tea on the table beside her. Benfro had been about to ask about the food, but as ever she had said the one thing that could knock him off his train of thought. He fell back on his earlier trouble with Frecknock. As far as he was concerned, she was the villain of the piece, not Sir Frynwy. She had stolen the book, then hidden it in his study, where he would be most embarrassed by its recovery. She wanted it for herself so that she could spend her days looking for a mate.

But 'How did you know?' was all Benfro was able to say. Something of his internal conflict must have shown on his face, as his mother looked at him with her penetrating stare which could be either kindly or cruel depending on what he had done.

'Sit, Benfro,' she said, pouring some tea into a second bowl and handing it to him. He could smell the sweet mixture of chamomile and honey bark, a gentle sleeping draught best used to aid the rest of those too exhausted or unsettled to relax. He took the bowl, letting the heat of the brew warm his hands, and sat down beside the fire.

'How do the other villagers get their food, for the feasts and stuff?' he asked. It was the first of many questions that were swimming around in his head and he eyed the tea with suspicion. Was his mother trying to make him sleep and forget?

'Ah, so you're beginning to turn your curiosity to good use,' Morgwm said. 'Why do you suppose that we grow all our own vegetables and eat meat only when you or Ynys Môn are successful at the hunt?'

'I don't know,' Benfro said. It was all part of the same puzzle, he realized. But he could make no sense of it.

'As to how I knew about Sir Frynwy,' Morgwm said. 'You're home too early for there to have been a telling. Sir Frynwy is a trained bard – he lives for the tale. If he has not made one this night, then he is deeply troubled. I can only imagine that he is more than a little embarrassed at calling a village meeting, accusing all his friends of theft and then discovering that no crime had occurred in the first place.'

Benfro couldn't help thinking that there was more to it than this simple piece of logic. He might have come home early for any number of reasons, although right then he could think of none.

'I think someone really did take the book,' he said, surprised that the words had come out exactly as he had intended.

'You do?' Morgwm's gaze caught his eyes, looking deep into him as she always did when she wanted to know whether or not he was telling the truth. 'Who?'

Benfro tried to say Frecknock. Her sneering face was at

175

the front of his mind and he could hear the mocking tone of her voice. But he could not speak her name.

'I . . . I don't know,' he said, frustration boiling to anger inside him. 'Why would sh . . . someone want to take it anyway? What does it do? I held it. It was heavier than it should have been. I heard voices. What is it?' The questions came boiling out of him in a cascade. His mother just sat and stared at him with her calm, piercing eyes, waiting patiently for him to finish. When finally he fell silent she took a long sip of her tea. Without thinking, Benfro did the same, the hot sweet liquid soothing him in an instant.

'I suppose you'll need to know sooner rather than later,' Morgwm said at last. 'Though it'll be a good few years yet before you're ready to read the book yourself. You've touched it and felt something of its power. It's spoken to you too, if what you say is true. It sees potential in you.

'The book is an artefact as much as a source of knowledge. It contains the wisdom and skill of countless dragons. But it's not like the books you're used to. Reading it is not a simple task undertaken lightly. If you were to try, you would understand nothing and likely lose your mind before you had finished. Try to read it unprepared and it will read you.'

'I don't understand,' Benfro said. 'If it's so dangerous, why keep it at all?'

'Because it's a little part of what we once were. And because it's a source of great power. You asked where the villagers get their food from, why we have to grow our own and they seem to be able to pluck theirs out of thin air. Well, the knowledge contained in the *Llyfr Draconius* allows those with the skill to reach out and bring things to them from far away. The beef you ate this evening was probably raised somewhere in the lower Hendry. The slaughterhouse where it came from will put the loss of a carcass down to fairies. Men are much happier making up complicated explanations for things than facing the truth.'

'Men? Men give us food?' Benfro asked.

'Not give, no,' Morgwm answered. 'We take. In time you'll learn that it is not unnatural or inexplicable. You'll probably master the skill yourself. But not tonight.' She smiled.

'If you can just take food,' Benfro asked, certain that whatever any of the villagers might do his mother could also, 'then why do we dig the field outside every year? Why do I have to hunt for deer and boar in the forest?'

'That's the heart of it, Benfro,' his mother said, smiling again. 'And it all has to do with men. I know Ynys Môn has told you something of them, and Meirionydd too. You've seen the ruins of Ystumtuen too. You know that once, not long ago, we were hunted and killed for our jewels. The king paid aurddraig – dragon gold for any dragon's head presented to him at court. Do you know why men stopped killing us?'

'Ynys Môn told me he saved their king from being killed by a great tusker,' Benfro said, enthusiasm getting the better of him before he realized he might be getting his old friend into trouble for telling him too much.

'He simplifies things, as ever,' Morgwm said. 'But that's essentially true. King Divitie never had much enthusiasm for the aurddraig anyway. He was tutored by the Order of the Ram, the travelling monks, and they've always been more open to foreign ideas than the other orders of men. Some of them used to come to me for advice on healing.

'There's something you must know about men, Benfro, though I hope you never meet any. They're duplicitous, scheming, always seeking more power. And they're quite ruthless. They kill their own kind with scarcely a thought, so it's not difficult to see how they would treat something as different to them as a dragon. They've a basic skill for the subtle arts too, but like everything else they do it's a brutalized and violent skill. No dragon could conjure a blade of fire. Using the power of every living thing to maim and kill is an affront to the natural order. Yet this is one of the first skills they teach their novitiates in the Order of the High Ffrydd.'

'Order?' Benfro asked, not wanting to break the flow of information, but desperate to understand it as best he could.

'Men worship a god they call the Shepherd,' Morgwm said. 'Don't ask me why, they just do. In the Twin Kingdoms there are three religious houses or orders, the Order of the High Ffrydd are warrior priests. They were charged with the extermination of all dragons, but over time they've become little more than a powerful army for the king. I've told you of the Order of the Ram. They're travellers, learning and teaching as they go from place to place. Of all the men I have met, they're the most open. Then there's the Order of the Candle. These are the bureaucrats, the petty-minded little men who make rules to keep the people in line. When Divitie stopped the warrior priests from killing our kind, the Order of the Candle stepped in, making rules to define how we were to be allowed to live. Dragons can't use the subtle arts; we must not live together in groups of more than four; we must not breed save with a licence from the king, and our kitlings must be presented to the court in Candlehall within a year of their hatching. And we must pay a tithe to their treasury every year.'

'But –' Benfro started.

'Yes, I know,' Morgwm said, smiling again. 'We pay no heed to their laws. And why should we? But we do have to be careful. If they knew how we flouted them, then they'd hunt us down again. I fear that soon they will do so anyway. King Divitie is long dead, his son after him. King Diseverin is a weak-minded fool not long for this world, and his daughter, Princess Beulah, poisoned her own sister so that she might gain the throne for herself. And she is a creature of Inquisitor Melyn, head of the Order of the High Ffrydd. When she comes to the throne it is likely her first decree will be the reinstating of the aurddraig.

'So we come back to the village. If men knew it existed they would destroy it. But as long as it exists then the dragons who live there are free to live their lives unhindered. Each of them has chosen to settle there and they are protected by an ancient and powerful spell. For that spell to work, one must live outside the wards – to act as a gatekeeper, if you like. That's my role. Men searching the forest will always end up on the track that leads here. They'll find a cottage where a lone dragon healer lives, with her vegetables and herbs and wise advice for any who would seek it. As long as I live here, the village is safe.'

Benfro took a sip from his bowl and realized that it was empty. He could feel the warmth of the draught in his belly, working its way up to his head, where it would soothe him to a gentle sleep. But for now his mind was buzzing with all that he had learned.

'And the *Llyfr Draconius*?' He asked. 'How does that fit in with . . . with everything?'

'It's only what it could do, should it fall into the wrong hands,' Morgwm said. 'Someone with little skill attempting to perform some of the spells within its pages might easily draw attention to themselves. And that might break the spell that protects the village. That's why you must promise me, Benfro, by great Rasalene himself, that you'll never try to read the book alone.'

'I promise, of course,' Benfro said, fascinated and horrified in equal measure. He still longed to know the secrets contained within the *Llyfr Draconius*, but something of his mother's innate caution had rubbed off on him. He could wait a while longer, knowing that he would find out in time. But Frecknock was meddling with magic now. And while she had been learning from Sir Frynwy and Meirionydd, Benfro couldn't help thinking that she was not as skilled as she would like to think. He longed to tell his mother about her, but her one successful spell had locked that terrible secret inside him like a maggot in an apple.

'No doubt the boy's mother tumbled with a Llanwennog she met on the road.'

Melyn watched as the gathering of rough villagers massacred a dance that had been popular in Candlehall high society some twenty years earlier. 'Or it could have been one of Balch's servants. We're not that far from Ystumtuen, you know, and by all accounts the woman Hennas was a travelling healer before she settled here.'

'He's the spitting image of Prince Balch,' Beulah said. 'And look at him. He's thin and spindly where his mother's heavy. He's still just a boy yet he's a good handspan taller than her. I don't think he's her son at all.'

'Beulah, you see plots and intrigue at every turn. The boy has Llanwennog blood but there's no more to it than that. Prince Balch died not two months after your sister. You know as well as I do that he couldn't have fathered another.'

'But he's thirteen, Melyn,' Beulah said. 'That's exactly how old Lleyn's child would have been, had it survived.'

'Which it didn't,' Melyn said calmly. The boy in question was wheeling inexpertly around the dance floor with a very pretty young woman in a long green dress. She aroused his interest far more than he did. Had she been a boy he would have selected her for his order in an instant. He could see the potential in her like a glowing flame. The poor girl probably heard voices in the night and had strange premonitions that often came true. Perhaps she even managed to make things happen just because she wanted to. In a backward place like this she would inevitably be accused of being a witch. If she was lucky she might be able to scratch a living out on the forest fringe, away from people. But she would soon go mad with the voices. If she was unlucky she would be stoned to death or burned at the stake before she reached twenty. It was a terrible waste of a talent, but the Order of the High Ffrydd was an exclusively male domain. On the other hand, there was always a place for a willing domestic. And who knew what she might do in exchange for a little knowledge and power.

'How can you be sure?' Beulah's voice cut across his idle musing.

'Because I inspected the dead body,' he said. 'Your sister hadn't even managed to give birth. The child was dead inside her.'

'I still don't like it,' Beulah said.

'If it makes you any happier, I'm going to probe his mother about him anyway, just as soon as she's had a few more drinks,' Melyn said. 'There are only two candidates here worthy of choosing and he's one of them.'

'But he's only thirteen,' Beulah said.

'So much the better,' Melyn said. 'I can keep him apart until he's old enough. By the time he turns fourteen he'll belong to me. And with those looks he'll make an excellent spy.'

'Very well,' Beulah said. She looked out across the party. 'And the other one?'

'The boy Clun has potential, even if he is a bit old,' Melyn said. 'And he's bold. He came and asked me about the choosing. I'll take him too, before Padraig gets his hands on him.'

Beulah laughed, a little unpleasant snort.

'What?' The inquisitor asked.

'These peasants,' Beulah said, casting her arm across at the dancing people. 'They can't believe their luck. There are few enough nobles who can say their marriage was attended by one of the royal house, or even an inquisitor. Godric and Hennas will for ever be the couple whose union was witnessed by the heir to the Obsidian Throne.

It's funny they should see us as blessing their union when in truth we come to steal their sons.'

Errol would look back upon it as both the happiest and the worst evening of his life. Once the speeches had been made and the formal dances performed, he was free from his duties and could get away from the crush of people to a quiet corner of the room. The arrival of Inquisitor Melyn and Princess Beulah had caused complete chaos, although it was universally agreed that their presence was a good omen for the marriage. Errol had heard a number of hushed conversations where the words 'blessing' and 'miracle' were used.

For his part he was not so sure. The princess had stared at him throughout the formal dances, even when Godric had plucked up the courage to ask her to join in. For a terrible moment Errol thought he was going to end up partnering her through one of the progressive dances. He was uncomfortable with the whole celebration, awkward in the company of others and not quite sure he knew how to dance properly, though his mother had done her best over the last two weeks to teach him. Fortunately the princess had thanked the goodman and left the floor, returning to the bridal throne which she had claimed for her own, as soon as the music finished.

The inquisitor had refused to join in the celebrations, sitting instead with a flagon of mead by his side and watching everything with sharp, curious eyes. Errol had caught his gaze a couple of times, feeling the dangerous power behind it, like a man barely in control of a violent rage. He had felt stripped by that stare as if his every secret was being pulled out into the open, examined and discarded as unimportant. He wasn't the only one caught in that penetrating gaze either.

'What you thinkin' 'bout, Errol?' Martha dropped herself unceremoniously into the chair beside him before he could stand and offer it to her. Her face was flushed with the exertion of dancing, a bright excited sparkle in her eyes. It was difficult for him not to stare. But then why not?

'The princess,' Errol said. 'Every time she sees me she looks like someone's put vinegar in her wine. I've never met her before but you'd think we'd been enemies since birth.'

'That's cos you look like her enemy,' Martha said. 'I told you the first time we talked. You've got Llanwennog blood in you, Errol Ramsbottom. It shows.'

'My dad, I guess,' Errol said. 'Mother never talks about him.'

'Well, you've got a new da now,' Martha said.

'Yeah.' Errol smiled. 'I guess I have at that.'

'You want to get some air?' Martha asked, looking up at the doors to the hall that opened on to the night outside.

'Won't your dad . . . ?' Errol started to ask, but a quick glance at the trestle tables across the hall behind which the great barrels of beer had been stacked made the question redundant. The big burly form of the smith was already slumped in a chair, head back, eyes closed and mouth open. An empty tankard hung from one limp hand; the other clasped his belly as if trying to hold in its tumescence.

'He's not a violent drunk,' Martha said, as if apologizing for something. 'He's never hit anyone, as far as I can remember. He jes likes to drink till he fergets. This . . .'

She swept her green-gloved hand across the room. 'It's hard for him.'

Errol stood, offering his arm to Martha, unsure what to say. He had never known his father and so felt no sense of loss. Godric Defaid had lost his wife after fifteen years together, but he had managed to rebuild his life and now he was embarking on another great adventure. Tom Tydfil had never even tried to lift himself out of his own despair. He wondered what it must have been like for Martha, growing up without a mother and with a father so wrapped up in his grief.

'You'd be young Master Ramsbottom then.' Errol looked up into the face of Inquisitor Melyn, startled by how close he was. Judging by the way Martha clutched at his arm, she too had been surprised by his sudden appearance. The music was loud enough to cover the noise of an approach.

'Your Grace,' Errol said, hastily remembering his manners and bowing. 'We are honoured by your presence. May I introduce Miss Tydfil.'

'The smith's daughter, yes,' Melyn said, nodding his head in Martha's direction but not offering to take her hand. Errol noted the way the old priest's eyes flickered over her face and body almost greedily and felt a prickle of resentment run across the skin on the back of his neck.

'You make a lovely couple,' the inquisitor said.

'We're not . . . That is . . . we're just friends,' Errol said.

'Oh you're much more than that, Errol,' the inquisitor said. 'Though I doubt even you realize it. But you're young still. There's time to learn these things. So tell me, have you ever considered joining one of the religious orders?'

Errol felt Martha's grip on his arm tighten again. He was tempted to look at her, but the inquisitor's eyes held his gaze. They were two bottomless black pits that threatened to swallow him whole. He knew that they were just eyes, yet they were vast, bigger than anything he could imagine. And he was falling into them, endlessly plunging, helpless and doomed.

But he wasn't helpless, neither was he doomed. This was a man. Powerful, yes, but a man nonetheless. It must be some magic trick that he was playing, trying to overwhelm him. Was it a test? And if so, would he fail by succumbing or pass?

As he thought, Errol realized that he could see the lines glowing all around him. He had never noticed them inside a building before, where there wasn't much alive save people. But the web was there and the inquisitor was tapping into it somehow. His whole body was suffused with a tenuous glow and a thin tendril reached out to bridge the gap between them.

Without knowing quite how he was doing it, Errol focused on that tendril, squeezing it with his mind until it broke. Perhaps it was a natural revulsion at being in any way connected to the old priest, but however it was done, he instantly felt himself released. The noise of the room came back to his ears, and he realized that for what might have been minutes but was probably no more than a single heartbeat he had been fighting a duel. Now he felt exhilarated at having won, but at the same time he was shaking and a cold sweat prickled his back underneath the itchy cotton of his shirt. Finally he remembered the question that had heralded the attack.

'I'm too young for the choosing this year,' Errol said. 'I'm only thirteen.'

If the inquisitor was startled at how easily Errol had shaken off the attack, he showed no sign of it.

'Fourteen is the youngest a boy can become a novitiate,' he said, 'but we've taken children into the Order of the High Ffrydd at younger ages. Especially those that show great promise. You can learn a great deal in the months before your next birthday.'

'I . . . I still have much to learn here,' Errol said, knowing as he did how stupid it sounded. Beside him Martha was tense and silent as if she too were fighting some internal battle.

'Nonsense,' the inquisitor said with a short cruel laugh. 'That's the boy in you talking. It's safe here, and boring. But you long for more. I've spoken with that ass Kewick about you. He says you've read every book this place has. Think about it, Errol. The order's not just about warring and violence. We've been at peace with Llanwennog for decades and no one hunts dragons any more. We're all about learning, about unravelling the mysteries that the Shepherd has laid on this earth for us to uncover.'

Errol had the indefinable sense that he was being lied to. There was something the inquisitor was not telling him. It did not matter though. He had made up his mind months ago that he wanted nothing to do with the religious orders, and he had promised Martha he would never join the Order of the High Ffrydd. Still, there was the small problem of how to turn down what was supposed to be the highest honour he could ever be given.

'You need to think about it,' Melyn said, a smile coming

slowly to his face as if uncertain how to sit there. 'And besides, this is a time for enjoying yourself. Talk to your stepbrother about it. He's already accepted my offer.' He turned and walked away.

'I think we should go outside,' Martha said quietly. Errol was happy to be steered towards the door. Outside it was cold with oncoming winter, the night sky awash with uncountable stars. Two dozen horses grazed on the village green and a huddle of men sat around a makeshift fire that would surely ruin the grass.

'Who are . . . ?' Errol began before realizing that it was unlikely Princess Beulah would travel alone. This was her bodyguard, and he would do well to keep away from them. Quickly he steered Martha into the shadows and away down the space between the hall and the church next door. It would take them out on to the open fields that climbed towards the forest.

'We have to run away,' Martha said. 'Tonight.'

'What?' Errol said.

'You must've felt it, surely?' Martha said. She was shivering slightly in the cold and Errol took his jacket off, draping it over her shoulders. 'He's chosen you.'

'But I'm too young,' Errol said.

'He don't care,' Martha said. 'He wants you close. He sees you as a threat, or maybe an opportunity.'

'How do you know this?' Errol asked.

'He was concentratin' on you,' Martha said. 'Didn't think I was worth worryin' 'bout. He's not a nice man.'

'You can read people's thoughts?'

'Not like that, no,' Martha said. 'I can . . . sense things. You can too, it's jes you ain't never tried. But that don't matter. Nothin' matters but we've gotta get away from here. Away from him.'

'How?' Errol asked. 'Where can we go?'

'I don't know,' Martha said. It was the first time he had seen her look anything other than completely in control.

'I'll speak to my ma,' Errol said. 'She'll know what to do. And she's travelled a lot.'

'All right,' Martha said. 'But don't take long. I'm goin' to go home and change. I'll pack a bag and meet you up in the forest in an hour. You know the place.' She pulled him into a hug that he wished would go on for ever, finally releasing him and stepping back into the shadows.

'Go now,' she said, then disappeared.

Errol shivered, realizing that she still had his jacket. He hurried back up the narrow alley towards the village green. He would speak to his mother. She would know what to do. He just hoped that he wouldn't get anyone into trouble by running away.

Some of the men who had been sitting around the campfire had moved, Errol noticed as he stepped into the square. He had just enough time to register that people were close by, then a gruff voice said, 'That's him,' something connected with the back of his head, and the last thing he saw was the ground rushing up to swallow him in blackness.

12

In times of great need a mage might wish to consult with the collected memories of his ancestors, stored in their jewels and brought together after reckoning. There is much to be gained from seeking this counsel, but a note of caution need be sounded.

Memories mean no harm, but they are dead things and long for the spark that exists in the living. With no concept of hunger, no need for sleep, they will slowly drain the life out of an unwary visitor, even while they engage in impassioned debate or expound on subtle arts long forgotten. The jewels of a single dragon are a powerful thing, hypnotic and beguiling. Infinitely more potent are the gathered memories of an entire dynasty.

Corwen teul Maddau,
On the Application of the Subtle Arts

A rough shaking woke Benfro. His head fuzzy, it took a while for him to realize that it was still dark

'Wake up, Benfro,' his mother said. 'Hurry.'

'What?' he asked, rubbing his eyes in an attempt to make things clearer. He was still half in a dream where he had been flying over the treetops, watching his shadow skim across the whizzing green canopy below. He often dreamed of flying, and the cruel truth of waking up hit him hard every time.

'Quickly, Benfro,' Morgwm said, and as he came more to his senses he could feel her agitation

'What is it?'

'Men coming,' she said. 'By the moon, I should have seen them earlier. I must be getting old.'

'Men?' Benfro asked, excitement and fear spreading through him in equal measure. 'How do you know?'

'There's no time for that now,' Morgwm said, pulling Benfro out of his bed and thrusting his leather satchel into his hands. It was heavy and full. 'You have to get away from here as quickly as possible. You know what will happen if they find you.'

'But . . .' Benfro started to say. Morgwm lifted her hand to silence him.

'No more questions,' she said. 'Just do as I say. You can't go to the village; they haven't had time to prepare for this. You'll just have to head out into the forest. Far away. Don't stop walking until at least midday. And don't come back until the evening after tomorrow.'

Benfro was about to say something, he wasn't sure what, but the look on his mother's face silenced him. Pausing only to take a long drink from the water butt and splash some of the cold liquid over his face, he hugged his mother and left.

Outside, the moon shone full through ragged clouds. There was a gentle breeze but it bore the cold wind of winter, rippling his scales and numbing the tips of his ears in short order. He strode across the vegetable patch to the forest edge, heading north and into the deep forest. At the edge of the trees he paused, turning back to look at his mother, but she had gone back inside.

Benfro was no stranger to the woods around the village and his mother's cottage. He had ranged far and wide on his own and in the company of other dragons, usually Ynys Môn. He had often hunted with the old dragon at night as well, but this time the trees seemed strangely alien. Maybe it was the sharp transition from sleep to wakefulness, or perhaps the way the moonlight wavered as the clouds scrambled across its face. Months had passed since his mother had told him about the magic that protected the villagers from being discovered, about the rules of men and the terrifying power that they could wield. Yet his mother's words still rang in his ears as if they had just been spoken.

'There's no reasoning with men, Benfro. They have a terrible power and they will kill you as soon as look at you.'

Dawn saw Benfro at the escarpments where he had seen Frecknock make her calling. Time had not lessened his inability to tell anyone about that episode, and as the days had passed, so his resentment for her had grown. Punishment he understood. Sometimes he might even have grudgingly admitted to deserving it. Like the time he had carefully collected a wasps' nest from an old oak tree near the village and put it in the outhouse around the back of Ynys Bir's house just to see what might happen. His mistake that time was to have used the carved stick given to him by Ystrad Fflur the year before on his hatchday and to have left it with the nest in the outhouse. His punishment had been swift and painful, involving the removal of the now quite angry wasps from the outhouse. Once it was over, and he had apologized to the elderly dragon, things had returned to normal.

What Frecknock had done to him was not punishment in any way he could understand. He was used to her rages at him, even when he had done no wrong, but to have this terrible secret gnawing at his insides was a torture out of all proportion to any wrong he could conceivably have caused her. Fretting about it didn't help. If anything it only made his resentment and frustration grow. Still, they were the best company he could manage as he went deeper and deeper into the forest of the Ffrydd.

Benfro reached the top of the escarpments at midday. His mother had provisioned him well, stuffing his satchel with enough food to last a week. Gnawing on a haunch of venison, he looked out to the south and wondered what Morgwm was doing right now.

He could not see the village from his vantage point, only the path of the river marked out like a scar by taller trees. All had lost their leaves to winter, save the conifers, which clumped together in odd patches, black in the weak sun. The slope of the hill dropped away from him in gentle undulations. Followed ever downwards, they would lead to the villages of men on the forest fringe and then into the Twin Kingdoms of the Hafod and Hendry. So much he knew from Sir Frynwy's lessons, but he could no more imagine it all than he could understand the subtle arts.

As he looked out over the land Benfro felt an upwelling of anger quite out of keeping with his normal demeanour. How could it be fair that the world was denied to him this way? He didn't want to spend his life in fear of creatures he had never met. He didn't want to know about distant lands only as descriptions in books. He wanted to get away from this small corner of the world. He wanted to see things first hand, to make up his own mind about the tranquillity of the Sea of Tegid and the magnificent splendour of the Twin Spires of Idris. But most of all he wanted to fight back against the tyranny of men. To avenge the wrongs that they had visited on dragonkind over countless millennia.

A buzzard screaming overhead seemed to echo the rage that surged through him at that moment. Benfro looked up at it, soaring through the air, and his anger turned to despair. He remembered his dreams of flying over the treetops, the sun warm on his back, his shadow a scout covering the ground ahead of him. He stretched his useless wings out, flapping the two thin scraps of skin against the cold air for a moment before folding them away again. They had seemed big when he was just a kitling, but while he had grown they had stayed resolutely the same size. There was no way now that they would ever lift him off the ground.

The afternoon soon bled its light into evening as he climbed ever upwards. It didn't take long for Benfro to go beyond the furthest point he could easily recall and on into rarely visited territory. The river was now little more than a babbling stream, but he kept it close by for reference and because his pack contained no water skin. There were few animals about – most of the birds had flown south for the winter and he caught only glimpses of fleeing deer and saw occasional wild boar scrapings at the bases of trees. It was as well he had plenty of food, he thought, and he was grateful too that Ynys Môn was not there to chide him for his sloppy forest craft.

Darkness had begun to fall and he was beginning to resign himself to a night under the cold stars when he stumbled across the cave. It was almost as if he had been drawn to it, though it was well hidden. Inside it was as black as pitch, but warmer than out. Benfro felt around in his satchel for his tinder box and soon had a small flame going. As he built it up, the fire illuminated a large cavern with a flat sandy floor that sloped gently up towards the back. There was evidence of fires having been built in the cave before, though not for many months. It looked like another dragon had spent time there, making a comfortable bed of heather which had dried completely but still gave off a pleasant aroma. The fire did not cast enough light to see how far the cave went, so Benfro took up a brand and set off to explore.

A tunnel wound its way into the hillside from the entrance. Looking at the walls, Benfro could not tell whether it was natural or had been hewn. However it had been formed, it twisted and turned so that he lost all sense of direction after only a few minutes. The brand he held burned lower, threatening to go out and plunge him into total darkness, yet he felt no anxiety. The place was oddly warm and welcoming. He felt safe, as if his mother was watching over him. More than that, he felt as if old friends long forgotten had returned to ease his troubles.

When he finally made it to the end of the tunnel, Benfro was not surprised by what he found. The realization of where he was had been growing unnoticed at the back of his mind as he walked. Nevertheless he was awed. The tunnel widened out into a cavern, and though Benfro's makeshift torch had all but extinguished itself, he no longer needed it to see. The whole space was lit by the living glow of hundreds of white jewels piled high on the floor.

'Master Defaid, might I have the honour of a dance?'

Melyn watched as Beulah shrugged off her boredom like it was a heavy travel cloak. He knew that she would rather leave this place at once and ride straight for home, but she was ever the professional. Godric and Hennas had shown no inclination to be parted yet and he needed time alone with the healer. The princess had finally decided that she would have to make the trader an offer he couldn't refuse. As the awestruck man made his way on to the dance floor, more led than leading, the inquisitor stepped into the space he had left.

'You should be careful with your new husband, mistress. My lady is not to be trusted with a handsome man,' Melyn said, fixing the healer with a stare and trying to remember how to smile. He need not have worried. Hennas was intoxicated, partly by alcohol, partly by amazement at her good fortune. Her mind was an open book, ready to be read and rewritten.

'Your Grace,' she said, trying to leap to her feet and curtsy at the same time.

'Please, don't stand on my account,' Melyn said, settling himself into the seat beside her. 'This is your celebration, not mine. And besides, I wanted to have a word.'

'Oh,' Hennas said, and as he peered into her thoughts he could see a glimmer of defiance. It was a small thing now, battered by too many events. He could easily over-come it.

'Your son, Errol,' Melyn said, searching her mind for an image of the boy's father. 'He's not like the other villagers. I take it his father was from the north-east.'

A frown spread over Hennas's face, the lightest of creases around her eyes. Melyn sent calming thoughts to her, an image of trustworthiness. She relaxed as if a great weight had been taken from her shoulders.

'It was a silly thing, a wild romance. He was so kind, so different, so wise,' she said. 'But we couldn't settle. Everywhere we went there was hatred. They hated that I could heal, even though they needed my help. But most of all they hated him for being born a Llanwennog. They're not all bad, Inquisitor. You must know that. Mordecai was a good man.'

Melyn could see an image of a man, an older version of Errol. Similar in many ways to Prince Balch, yet different enough to be another person. Probably a bastard cast-off of the royal house; that would explain the boy's aptitude for magic. He made a mental note to look up the name when he returned to the monastery.

'What happened?' Melyn asked, smoothing away the healer's distrust of him and his order as he bolstered her confidence.

'We stayed too long at Dina,' Hennas said, her face slackening with the memory. 'There was an argument in a tavern. Someone had a knife. I tried to save him, but there was so much blood. He died in my arms. Errol came just eight months later.'

'You've raised him well,' Melyn said. 'But you know as well as I do that this place is too backward for him.'

'What?'

Melyn could feel her resolve building again, her instinctive hatred of everything that was authority. He didn't doubt that Mordecai's death had gone unpunished. Quite probably without any investigation at all. He put a suggestion of a similar fate befalling Errol into her troubled mind.

'Errol's a bright boy, far brighter than his peers,' Melyn said, aware in another part of his mind that the music of the dance was coming to an end. 'He needs to be nurtured. He needs tutoring and access to libraries. I can give him all of these things.'

'What are you saying?' Hennas asked. 'You can't mean . . .'

Melyn quashed the growing fear in the healer's mind, replacing it with a warm feeling of pride, a sense that she could undo some of the wrong of Mordecai's death by letting her son fulfil his potential and become a novitiate in the Order of the High Ffrydd. It was, he realized, almost too easy.

'Yes, Hennas,' Melyn said. 'I've chosen Errol for the novitiate. Clun too, if you can persuade Godric to let us take both his sons.'

The regular, rhythmic motion swayed Errol back from black unconsciousness to an uneasy half-sleep. His head hurt like someone had been using it for kicking practice, and his mouth was full of a sickly sweet taste like fruit gone sour. He could smell stale wine and an earthy straw aroma that made his stomach churn in time with the movement. Trapped between slumber and wakefulness, it was all he could do to lie, lurching and miserable, as he tried to work out where he was.

He could remember the wedding, with its curious promises and formality. Then there had been the line, where all the villagers who had shunned him for all of his life suddenly pretended they were his best friends. Errol had most respect for those few who had still shunned him, like Alderman Clusster with his dark little secret, and the burly smith, Tom Tydfil.

Errol saw a vision of beauty in a green dress, smiling at him and no one else. He had danced with her. He remembered her confidence and the way she corrected his mistakes, the warm feel of her hands and her body close to his. Then, as if he dreamed, the scene changed, and he was dancing with Maggs Clusster, her face strained, older than it should have been, her eyes always darting away from him to the dark corner of the room where her father sat with angry, glowering eyes.

But that wasn't right, Errol thought. He hadn't danced with Maggs. He had danced with . . . He couldn't remember. And as he tried to grasp the image of the girl in the green dress, so it slipped away like water through cold fingers.

Other faces swam through his mind. He saw two travellers, an old man and a young woman. Father Kewick bustling over to them like an anxious dog. He remembered the whole party stopping to welcome the newcomers, astonished by their presence. He recalled being introduced to Princess Beulah, heir to the Obsidian Throne, and he wondered why it was she looked at him as if he were something she regretted having trodden in.

And then there was the old man, Inquisitor Melyn. He had come to Errol later in the evening, offered to take him into the Order of the High Ffrydd even though he was too young for the choosing. He remembered his mother saying what an honour it was and how he couldn't possibly decline. He remembered accepting.

Errol sat up in a hurry, then wished he hadn't. The pain in his head made everything dim and blurred. His stomach lurched and heaved, and he crashed back down to his resting place on a pallet of straw.

'Ah, so yer 'wake now,' a voice said. Errol found that if he half-opened one eye the pain was almost bearable. At least for short periods. He squinted up at a ceiling of brown canvas drawn tight over ash hoops and a familiar face peering down at him, frowning. His stepbrother. Clun.

'Where are we?' Errol asked. His voice was hoarse and croaky as if he had been shouting for hours. His throat burned. 'What happened to me?'

'Ye don't remember?' Clun said, a grin splitting his face wide. 'Ye got drunk, Errol. Rip-roarin' drunk. I've never seen anythin' quite like it. Ye must've drunk two skinfuls of wine at least.'

'What're you talking about?' Errol said. 'I'm not allowed wine. I'm too young.'

He slowly inched his way up to a slumped sitting position, wishing all the while that his pallet would stop swaying from side to side. As he moved, the smell of stale wine grew stronger. He looked down at his clothes and saw his new shirt stained with red as if someone had slit his throat while he slept. His trousers were soiled and torn around the knees and he couldn't remember what had happened to his jacket. He was sitting on a bed of straw in the back of a moving wagon. Barrels and sacks were lashed down all around and Clun was perched on a small chest alongside him. Everything stank of sour grapes.

'I guess ye broke the rules then,' his stepbrother said, still grinning at Errol's discomfort.

'Where are we?' Errol asked again.

'On our way to Emmass Fawr,' Clun said. 'We did it, Errol, both of us. We've bin chosen.'

Errol found it difficult to share his stepbrother's enthusiasm. It wasn't just that his head hurt like a thunderstorm was raging in it. He could remember a time when he had wanted nothing more than to be a warrior priest of the High Ffrydd, but that was a different Errol. Something had changed – he had changed, but he couldn't remember when or why. It was all a muddle, but he knew one thing over all. He no longer wanted anything to do with the Order of the High Ffrydd.

Slowly, trying not to move his head too much, Errol rolled on to all fours and crawled along the bed of the wagon to its end. The canvas flap was tied shut, but there was enough of a gap for him to see out. A troop of warrior priests rode behind the wagon in formation, and they were travelling along a wide stone-paved road with thick forest on either side.

'So, you're awake now,' a gruff voice said. Looking sideways with a wince, Errol saw the figure of Inquisitor Melyn astride his horse. It was a fine beast with a mottled grey coat and wide soup-plate feet. The inquisitor looked small on it, out of proportion as if he were a child riding a large pony. Nevertheless he was in complete control of the animal. With barely a touch on the reins, it moved closer to the wagon.

'Judging by your face, you've received punishment enough for your drunkenness. I hope you'll learn your lesson from the experience. Lesser candidates have been expelled from the monastery for such behaviour.'

'Your Grace, I'm sorry,' Errol said. 'I don't remember drinking.'

'Alcohol has that effect, boy,' Melyn said, leaning forward in his saddle. 'I'm guessing you can't remember much from last night. Not your mother's distress at your behaviour in front of the princess, not your boastful announcement to the whole of your village that you would return some day as inquisitor?'

'I didn't ... Did I say that?' Errol flushed with embarrassment. He could remember nothing of the sort, but there were large gaps in his memory. The inquisitor turned to the nearest of the troop, the head of his personal guard.

'Captain Osgal,' he said, 'do you recall the young lad's exact words before he passed out last night?'

The captain looked distinctly uncomfortable, Errol thought, as if he feared the inquisitor. His eyes flicked between Errol and the old priest rapidly as he came to a decision.

'His exact words were difficult to make out, your Grace,' he said eventually. 'But the gist of it was that he was going to be the most famous inquisitor the order had ever known. When the princess asked him if he meant to be greater even than Ruthin, who drove the dragons out of

Emmass Fawr and claimed it for himself, he said that he would happily perform any task she might set him.'

Errol stared at the warrior priest in disbelief. Why would he do such a thing? It made no sense at all.

'Princess Beulah wasn't looking for a champion,' Melyn said, 'but it seems she's got one. You'll have to work very hard indeed, young Ramsbottom, if you want to come even close to being selected for the Royal Guard.'

'I . . . I'm sorry,' Errol said, not sure what else he could say. 'The princess, is she . . . ?'

'She's returned to Candlehall,' the inquisitor said. 'King Diseverin's not well. She needs to be close to her father at this difficult time.'

'Can I get a message to her?' Errol realized as he asked the question just how stupid it sounded. 'I must apologize. I have to—'

'You have much to learn about royalty. You'd do well not to remind her that you exist. Besides, you've more pressing things to worry about. Get some rest. Take this chance to sleep off your hangover. You won't find me so forgiving once we arrive at Emmass Fawr.'

The inquisitor spurred his horse into a trot that took it ahead of the wagon, effectively ending the conversation. Errol peered out the back of the wagon wondering what he had got himself into. Surrounded by strangers, he suddenly felt a pang of longing for home, his mother and the simple life of the village.

'You've got the Shepherd's luck,' Captain Osgal said. Errol looked up at the warrior priest. He was tall and thin, with a narrow face and straggly hair, younger than Errol had at first thought.

'I've seen His Grace kill men for less than you did last night,' he continued. 'You be very careful around him, boy. He's got you marked for something.'

'Benfro, welcome. What a pleasant surprise.' The voice was in his head, but there was no mistaking the dragon who spoke.

'Ystrad Fflur?' Benfro asked, bewildered. 'Where are you? Aren't you—'

'Dead?' the voice said. 'Of course I am. You were at my reckoning, weren't you? Or was that some other young dragon performing the ceremony?'

'But how?' Benfro asked.

'Dear me, youngling. Do they not teach you anything? This is our nest, where all our jewels are laid to rest in peaceful companionship. We sit on a nexus in the Grym and observe the world.'

'We?' Benfro asked. 'Grym?'

'My fellow departed,' the voice of Ystrad Fflur said. 'I may have lived a long time but these are not all my jewels. No, dragons have been nested in this spot for many thousands of years. But you should know all this, Benfro. Else why are you here?'

'Mother sent me away from the house,' Benfro explained. 'She said men were coming and I had to hide in the forest for a couple of days.'

'And you came here,' Ystrad Fflur said. 'How interesting. But men, you say. Strange. We didn't see them coming. Well, Morgwm always was much more sensitive to these things, and she's still alive, which helps.'

Benfro found himself transported back to Ystrad

Fflur's dark and cosy study, where he had spent many a happy afternoon listening to the old dragon's stories and eating pieces of candied ginger from a seemingly endless supply. He understood now that it had been purloined by magic from some far-distant place.

'The merchants of Talarddeg always had the best ginger,' Ystrad Fflur said, seemingly able to read Benfro's thoughts. 'Time was when I could walk the streets, going from shop to shop, sampling the wares and haggling over the price. I always felt bad, helping myself without paying, but the long road was too dangerous, our numbers too few. The choice was no choice at all. In the end.'

'I don't understand,' Benfro said. 'You travelled to this place, Talarddeg?'

'Oh, I travelled all over Gwlad, young Benfro. There's not many places Ystrad Fflur hasn't been. But I've always had a soft spot for Talarddeg. It's the only city in the whole world where men and dragons coexisted from the beginning. It was built for both of us and we lived happily side by side. Until those terrible priests started arriving, spouting nonsense about some invisible god they call the Shepherd. No room for dragons in their new world. Dragons were beasts of the Wolf, we were driven out of our homes, slaughtered if we tried to resist.'

Benfro stood in the cavern staring at the glowing pile of jewels. It was the same eerie light as the line that had connected him with Frecknock and Sir Felyn. He wondered if here, in this magic place, he might be able to throw off the compulsion and tell Ystrad Fflur what he had seen. The images were in his head, he could think about what Frecknock had done, and the old dragon had seemed able to read his thoughts. The silence hung heavy as he struggled to say the words he wanted to say. But nothing would come out.

'You seem troubled, Benfro,' Ystrad Fflur's voice came back after a while. 'Is there something you want to ask?'

'Can't you read my mind?' Benfro asked.

'Not as you might understand it, no,' the old dragon said. 'I can see something of your thoughts, especially those you are actively pursuing, but your mind is safe, believe me. And even if I could, I wouldn't rummage around in another dragon's thoughts. It would be impolite.'

'Is there a spell that can stop m . . . a dragon from saying something, even though he can think it?' Benfro asked.

'Dear me, Benfro. When I was alive I wouldn't discuss that sort of thing with you. What makes you think I will now?'

'I don't want to know how it's done, honest,' Benfro said. 'I just want to know if it's possible.'

There was a long pause, as if the old dragon were considering the question. Deep in the back of his mind Benfro thought he could hear the whispering of many voices, but when he tried to focus his attention on them they slipped away like eels in a spring spate.

'It's possible to use the Grym to influence the minds of others,' Ystrad Fflur said. 'It's something I've heard the warrior priests do. But it's inconceivable that a dragon would do such a thing.'

'But it can be done,' Benfro said, hoping that the dead dragon would ask him why he wanted to know, would maybe even look deeper into his mind and see the block that stopped him from telling all.

'Yes, Benfro, it can be done.'

'And what about speaking to other dragons over vast distances?' Benfro asked, searching for another way to try and solve his dilemma. 'Can that be done?'

'You're certainly full of questions, young Benfro,' Ystrad Fflur said. 'But I suppose a little curiosity is a healthy thing. Yes, indeed, the Grym can be used to talk to others over great distances. It's the power that flows through all living things, after all, and it links everything to everything else.'

'So you'd hear if someone tried to do it?'

'Not necessarily, no,' Ystrad Fflur said. 'A calling can be made to all who will hear, but it's unwise to send your message to your enemies.'

'Enemies?'

'Men, Benfro, men. They're quite skilled in many aspects of the Grym, though blind to even more. Some of them have learned to listen with more than their ears. When first they began to slaughter us, they would lure us into traps by pretending to be dragons. But anyone who's heard their thoughts can recognize them for the alien things that they are. No dragon has fallen for that trick in many hundreds of years.'

But Frecknock was young and she was headstrong. Would it occur to her that Sir Felyn was anything other than an amorous wandering dragon?

'You must go, Benfro,' Ystrad Fflur said. 'You can't stay in this place. Especially if no one knows you're here.'

'What? But I want to stay. There's so much to say. I miss your stories Ystrad Fflur.'

'And I miss your company too. But this is not a safe

place for a novice in the ways of the Grym. Even though our jewels are reckoned, still they yearn for experience. Tarry here too long and they'll suck the will to live out of you.'

'But I'm fine,' Benfro said.

'No, you are not.' This time it was not Ystrad Fflur's voice. The dragon who spoke was female, with a rich commanding tone. 'Even now you make excuses to stay. Your mind is too young to comprehend what is happening to it. Ystrad Fflur has warned you. Now I warn you too. Leave now, Benfro son of Trefaldwyn. You are no longer welcome in this place.'

The push, when it came, was at once feather-light and as firm as an autumn gale. The pressure built over every part of Benfro's body, so that he had to step back to stop from falling over. As soon as he moved, the force strengthened, pushing him towards the black entrance to the cavern. Looking up at his makeshift torch, Benfro saw that it was now no more than a charred stump of stick. He couldn't pick it up even if he wanted to. The wind whipped him along too fast and soon he was tumbling over his feet in the total darkness of the twisting treacherous tunnel.

13

To be chosen to join the Order of the High Ffrydd is the highest of accolades, but with the honour comes a great responsibility. On initiation, the novitiate must renounce the family that has raised him and deliver himself into the bosom of the order. He must swear to uphold its laws and traditions, to work tirelessly in furthering its aims. He must agree to obey his quaisters, the warrior priests and the inquisitor no matter what they demand of him, without hesitation or question. He must apply himself to his studies and excel in all things. He must seek perfection.

At initiation each novitiate takes ownership of a stout candle. It is lit at evening worship and may not be extinguished by any save the novitiate to whom it has been given, and only once he has made his morning prayers. Boys fond of their sleep and their beds will soon find their candles growing short, and should the flame burn out before a novitiate has completed his basic training, he will be expelled from the order.

Father Castlemilk. *An Introduction
to the Order of the High Ffrydd*

Two more days passed before Errol could face the thought of food. His head hurt constantly and the jarring motion of the wagon didn't help his mood. Worse still, his memories were a jumble of half-recognized images, contradictions and blank holes. And when he tried to piece things together, to rebuild the confusion of his past, the pain in his head doubled. All his young life he had relied on his wits to keep him one step ahead. Now, when he needed them most, they had deserted him.

The journey was uneventful. They stopped in several other villages, but none of the hopeful young lads put forward came anywhere near Melyn's high expectations. Errol and Clun were not allowed to see much as they travelled, confined to the back of the wagon except for evening and morning meals. Even Clun's irrepressible enthusiasm began to wear off after ten days, and by the time they had been on the road for three weeks almost every topic of conversation had been exhausted. They would spend all day lying around in the wagon, dozing or just staring at the canvas, then lie awake all night listening to the snores of the warrior priests and the occasional whickering neighs of the horses. And so it was a welcome relief when one morning in the fourth week of their progress the canvas was hurriedly pulled aside.

'Right, you two, out,' Captain Osgal said. 'You've got legs, you can help.'

Errol leaped out on to the track. They were at the base of a steep hill and flanked on both sides by tall trees. He could see the track cutting a zigzag path up the slope, but it disappeared into low cloud before he could make out where it went. Before he had time to see more, the wagon lurched away, the horses struggling to pull its weight up the hill.

'Come on,' Osgal shouted. 'Put your backs into it. I don't fancy a night out on the hill. If we get a move on we can reach Emmass Fawr by nightfall.'

The rest of the day was misery compounded. Errol was sure Osgal was simply torturing them for the hell of it. There was no real need to push the wagon; once they'd got it moving, the horses were more than capable of pulling it at a good speed. But if they didn't work hard, the captain would order one of his warrior priests to beat them with a whippy piece of stick. Clun was fit and set to the task with gusto, but even he was struggling after an hour and a half. Errol had been sick once by then, and his back was sore through his rough canvas shirt from repeated beatings.

They stopped for the briefest of lunches and then the torment began again. Yet even as he struggled in the ever-thinning air, Errol could feel some force stronger than the promise of a beating compelling him along. As if the road itself were calling him to its end. It didn't give him strength, but as his arms and legs turned to jelly, his lungs burned and his stomach clenched, it kept him going.

And then suddenly they were through the cloud, and the road levelled off. They had reached the top.

For the briefest of moments Errol saw a magical vista spread out around him. Tall mountain peaks poked out of a flat white blanket like stones in a sea of milk. But before he could take in more than a blink, a rough hand grabbed him and he was lifted bodily into the back of the wagon. Too weary to do anything else, he fell heavily, winded, and by the time he had recovered, the straps were being tied down, sealing him in. Clun was not with him.

'What's going on?' he asked.

'You're not fourteen yet,' Osgal's voice replied. 'Can't let you see the ceremony.'

'What ceremony?' Errol asked, but there was no reply and soon the wagon was moving again. Too exhausted to be curious, he rolled himself up in a blanket and fell asleep.

Benfro soared through low clouds, feeling their damp coldness on his outstretched wings. The wind ruffled his ears and whipped his tail. It stroked his scaly belly like autumn grass, holding his weight with gentle pressure. He was in total control, climbing and banking with a simple thought while below him the forest galloped past in a blur, shades of black picked out in the clear light of the full moon.

Looking around, he could see for miles, an endless stretch of trees arrayed in their winter finery. The forest sloped away from him, dropping in a series of undulations towards the low country, the Hendry. To either side, far distant, the Rim mountains climbed out of the trees, great walls of stone breached by the cataclysm that had made the Graith Fawr. To his left the ridge was topped with white snow. Something caught his attention, impossibly small over the vast distance, invisible in the bright darkness. Banking without a thought, he headed in its direction.

Too soon the mountains began to rise in front of him. Benfro swept his powerful wings up and down, tips almost touching rock at the bottom of each slow stroke. Effortlessly he climbed, matching the slope as he went, until with one final great sweep he burst over the ridge.

The sky was clear here, a deep indigo blue that sparkled with innumerable stars, the reflected light of the glittering snow. A wide track followed the contour of the mountain, snaking back and forth with single-minded purpose. Something about the road was appealing, alluring. Benfro found himself following its loops as he flew, rather than crossing the deep chasms and gulleys. The endless turns were as effortless as thinking, and he took a simple perfect pleasure in their ease so that it didn't occur to him to try to shorten the journey. Neither was he concerned as to where he was going. It was enough just to fly, to explore the world, to be free of the constraints that tied him to the old dragons in the village.

The narrow ridge opened into a plateau, so high up that clouds scudded along beneath it, their tops picked out in silver moonlight. Snow lay over the ground, almost hiding the small huddle of houses that clustered around the track. Thin wisps of smoke rose from low chimneys and light escaped from some of the windows, casting oddly angular and yellow shapes on the ground. Benfro banked, circling the small settlement and wondering who lived there. It was difficult to tell from so high, but the houses seemed small to him, their single storeys inadequate.

Not so the great arch that climbed over the road. It was as magnificent as it was ridiculous, so out of proportion with the houses that he had not noticed at first that it was there. Now he saw it, Benfro could not understand how he could have missed it. Carved from pale stone, it rose from the ground, straddling the path high enough and wide enough for a creature five times his size to pass through without stooping. To either side, it dropped into a low wall that cut the houses off from whatever lay beyond. His curiosity piqued, Benfro flapped his great wings together and sped off above the path, leaving the vast gateway behind.

The plateau narrowed again, the track constrained to a thin ridge with sheer drops into uncharted darkness below. Again Benfro felt the urge to follow the twists and turns as he flew ever closer to what must surely be his journey's end, for the road seemed to enter the curiously square mountain top.

Only it wasn't a mountain top. It was a building.

The sheer scale of it was impossible to comprehend. He recalled the great tower and buildings at Ystumtuen, but the whole circular depression in which that hunting lodge sat would have fitted inside one wing of this massive structure. It squatted on the top of the mountain like some angular fungus, growing tendrils down into the depths, thrusting spore-towers towards the sky.

Benfro circled the great palace, gazing down on its intricate and random pattern of wings and courtyards. Pinpricks of light shone out from some windows, but hundreds, thousands more were dark. Even though the wind on his face spoke to him of great speed, it took long minutes to complete a full circuit of the structure, and all the while Benfro sank in the air so that the great sheer walls rose above him like some giant of stone waking, standing and reaching out a huge hand to crush him like a fly.

The wonder and awe turned to fear. In all his short life Benfro had known little real horror. Heights scarcely worried him despite or maybe because of the number of times he had fallen out of trees and off high rocks into the river. There were no animals in the forest that could do him harm, though Sir Frynwy had told him of snakes that could kill a dragon with a single bite of their venomous fangs. The only thing he had been raised to dread was men, and that was an abstract threat. He had never woken sweating in the darkness from a nightmare where men had trapped him, so at first Benfro did not understand the feeling that swept over him. It was as if the weather had worsened, the temperature dropping until his joints ached with the cold. Even though the moon hung full overhead, a bright orb in a night sky studded with steadfast stars, still it seemed darker somehow. The great rising mass of the fortress was a threatening thing, a promise of harm, and all of a sudden he wanted to get away from it.

Wheeling about, Benfro swung his wings in heavy, panicky sweeps. He could see the great arch over the track not half a mile away, and yet it could have been the other side of Gwlad for all that the distance shrank. However he flew, pitching from side to side in great spiralling turns, he always came back to the monstrous building. And with each turn he lost more height, coming closer and closer to the track and the great gawping maw where it disappeared inside. The endless ranks of dead windows were no longer secrets to be unearthed, but the myriad facets of a giant spider's eye. A beast of such mythical proportions, it would not fit into one of Ynys Môn's bestiaries.

Benfro could hear the building calling to him. It sang a song of wonders, but he could see that it was just a distraction. There was nothing inside but hurt, pain, death. He had to get away, but his wings were so heavy now, his whole body tired as if he had not slept for weeks. He couldn't keep in the air any more. He had to land. But to land on that path was to give in to it, to be sucked in and chewed up.

To land was surely to die.

A rough hand at his shoulder dragged Errol from sleep.

'Wake up, boy. Now's no time for dozing.'

He didn't recognize the voice, nor could he see who spoke in the darkness. Shaking his head, he threw off the blanket and clambered out of the wagon. He was in a large hall lit by too few guttering torches hanging from iron sconces on the walls. The floor was smooth stone flags, glistening with slippery moisture, and over in a far corner he could just make out what he assumed was a pile of manure, judging by the smell.

'Help me here, won't you,' the voice said. Errol turned to see who spoke. It was an elderly man, back bent out of shape by years of hard labour. His hair was thinning on top, but it made up for the loss by spilling out of his chin in all directions in a great thick beard.

'Who are you?' Errol asked.

'You c'n call me Danno,' the man said. 'Now give me a hand wi' these horses. Can't leave them here in a cold sweat.'

Errol shivered as he realized it was cold. His canvas shirt was no protection, and he longed for something more substantial like a cloak. But he had only his blanket. Wrapping it around him, he set to helping the old man unhitch the horses and led them into a stable. There had been few horses in Pwllpeiran, and Errol knew very little about how to look after them. These great beasts seemed content enough to get their heads down and eat. Danno took a handful of straw and began to rub down the flanks of one animal, so Errol copied him and attended to the other.

'Umm, is this Emmass Fawr?' he asked after a while.

Danno laughed. 'Where'd you think you were. Tynhelyg?'

'I don't know. I was expecting . . .' But he couldn't finish the sentence because he hadn't known what to expect.

'You're too young, aren't you?' Danno said. 'To be a novitiate.'

'Yes,' Errol said. 'But Inquisitor Melyn said that I could learn lots before my birthday.'

'Well, you've just learned how to wipe down a horse,' Danno said. 'And now you're going to learn how to push a wagon into the corner of the courtyard. Then we'll see about learning how to clean the leather tack, and maybe how to fetch water for the drinking troughs and muck out the stables.'

Errol's heart fell. It wasn't that he hated manual work, but he had assumed his learning would be more bookwork than animal husbandry. He followed Danno out of the stable and back across the open hall to the wagon. Together they manoeuvred it into the corner close to the midden.

'Why are there no windows in here?' Errol asked when they had finished and the old man was leaning against the wall to get his breath back.

'Cos we're underground is why,' he said. 'No point havin' windows underground, is there.'

'Well, can you show me how to get outside?' Errol asked. 'Once I've finished helping you here, of course,' he added.

'No, he cannot,' a voice said from across the hall. 'No one who has not been through the ceremony of the novitiate can be allowed to see the light of day in Emmass Fawr.'

Straining his eyes in the semi-darkness, Errol made out a tall thin man with white hair.

At the sight of him, Danno dropped to his knees and bowed his head. 'Master Andro.'

'I'm sorry, Danno,' the man said, 'but Errol's not for you.'

'You know my name?' Errol said.

'Oh I know a great deal more than that about you, Errol Ramsbottom. Come. Follow me. The library awaits us.'

14

When using magic to influence your enemy's thoughts, it is imperative always to complete the task before withdrawing. The spell should never be attempted if circumstances are likely to lead to distraction. At best, such an interruption will unravel any earlier workings you have made. At worst, it will leave your mind open to your enemy should he wish to retaliate.

Father Andro, *Magic and the Mind*

'Benfro, you must wake up!' The voice was familiar, welcoming. But it was the voice of death. It brought to his mind an empty carcass being consumed by flames that gave off no heat. He ignored it, trying to fight the pull of gravity with his pathetic, insufficient wings.

'Come back to us, Benfro. It's not safe.' Again the voice spoke to him. It was reassuring, it tasted of sweet ginger, but it was flat, the emotion behind it long gone. Behind it a chorus of other voices chattered like the squabbling of crows over a piece of meat. He was that meat, being pecked back and forth, pulled ever closer to the road, surrounded by a clinging darkness that froze him to the bones.

'Benfro. Wake up!' This time the voice was different, and as it spoke to him he felt a hand on his shoulder, shaking him. For an instant he was confused. How could someone shake him? He was flying, his wings outstretched as they tried to catch the last dying breaths of wind before he landed on that terrible road.

Then the smell of dry heather filled his nose. The track and the building disappeared in a confusing whirl of images and it felt like he was being pulled backwards at incredible speed, past the great arch, past the dark tiny cottages, along the ridge, down into the forest where the bare branches whipped past him yet somehow never connected. Faster and faster he flew, out of control, without his wings, backwards along the river as it dwindled uphill into a series of rocky pools climbing in great steps. Helpless, he rushed through the grove of leafless oaks towards the cliff and the cave and the jewels of all the dead villagers. And then with a lurch he came to a halt, his eyes flicking open even though he had been seeing perfectly well before. He was lying on the bed of heather, his fire burned down to almost nothing in the cold cavern, and another dragon was there with him. She swept him up into her arms and hugged him close.

'O Benfro, thank the moon!' Morgwm said, squeezing him with all her strength. Benfro held his mother tight, confused, tired but aware in the back of his mind that he had just escaped some terrible fate.

They started out from the cave before dawn had even blushed the eastern sky, making swift progress along tracks that Benfro had never seen before and yet which his mother seemed to know like her wings. They had spent no more than five minutes in the cave from the moment he had woken to find Morgwm at his side, and the whole episode had about it the same dreamlike quality as his flight over the forest. Walking swiftly through the dark silent trees was just an extension of the chilling fear that had dragged him down towards that terrible road, the gaping maw of that impossibly large building.

It wasn't until weak light was bleeding into the day that Morgwm led him out of the trees, through some dark shrubs still clinging to their shiny bulbous leaves and on to the top of the first escarpment. The narrow stream, the sound of which they had followed from the cave, trickled over the edge, falling to the rocky plateau in the first of many steps that would see it emerge hundreds of feet below as a river. From their vantage point they could see down the valley for several miles, and all of it was trees, some dark green with needles, most stripped of leaves, their branches stretching to the sky like naked limbs, twisted and bent. The air was clear, the sky slate-grey. Wisps of cloud clung to some of the upper slopes as if the trees themselves were breathing out great foggy gasps into the cold. Benfro's own breath steamed from his nostrils in sympathy, bringing to mind the tales Sir Frynwy had told him of the oldest times, when dragons were no better than beasts, breathing fire and killing one another for sport.

'Let's stop a while, Benfro,' Morgwm said finally. She had been carrying his leather bag and now set it down on the rocks. She settled herself down beside it and began to take things out, arranging them on a stone slab as if it were the table back home. As if nothing untoward had happened.

'Have they gone, the men?' Benfro asked. It wasn't the

question he wanted to ask, but his mother's silence since leaving the cave, and the swiftness of their departure, made him wary of prying too deeply into that subject even though he longed to know more.

'It was only one man, and an old friend at that,' Morgwm said. 'I haven't seen him since the day you were hatched.'

'He knows about me?' Benfro asked, a surge of panic running through him at the thought that his secret might be discovered.

'I don't think so,' Morgwm said. 'But if there's any man I'd trust with that secret then it's Gideon. He loves knowledge far more than the prejudices of his kind. But he's getting old now.'

'What did he come to see you about?'

'He wanted to know about something I did for him years ago. A favour.'

'What favour?' Benfro asked, the cavern and his dreams momentarily forgotten. His mother sat quietly for a while, studying him as if trying to decide whether he was ready to know. It was a different look to the one she had given him in the past, and for a brief moment he thought he might have passed some unspoken test, that the secrets of the world might finally be given to him.

'It's best you know nothing about it,' Morgwm said finally. She held out a slab of bread and some cheese. 'Here, eat something.'

'Why?' Benfro asked. 'What's the point? It's not as if I'm good for anything around here. I'm just in the way. You won't tell me anything about the world out there. You won't tell me anything about the subtle arts even though they seem to touch everything around me. Am I just going to live in the village all my life? Thousands of years of drudgery? Will you always control what I can and can't do?' He fell silent as much out of embarrassment as running out of breath. Morgwm still held out the bread and cheese, still looked at him with that half-smile and those knowing eyes, only where once they had comforted and reassured him, now they merely annoyed.

'You still need to eat,' Morgwm said. 'Even if I've done much to earn that outburst. But, Benfro, you have to understand that you can't learn everything at once. You can't learn everything at all. There's always more.'

'So why won't you even begin to teach me?' Benfro asked.

'And what do you think I have been doing for the last thirteen years?' Morgwm asked. 'Were you hatched knowing your letters? Have you always been able to identify the seven variants of spottle fungus and know which ailments to use which for? I don't think you always knew how to catch fish and hunt deer.'

Benfro eyed the bread and cheese, not wanting to meet his mother's eyes. She was right, as ever, but she was also missing the point. His resentment still bubbled under the surface. There was so much more that he was being denied.

'I know you've taught me everything I know,' he said. 'You and the other dragons in the village. But it's all such a waste of time. No one ever gets sick, so why endlessly prepare potions that just lose their efficacy and have to be replaced? And why hunt for meat when you can just steal it?'

Morgwm emitted a gentle chuckle and threw the food to Benfro. Startled, he caught it.

'You're so young, Benfro,' she said. 'No, don't fly off in a rage again. You are young. You were hatched only thirteen years ago. Even Frecknock's seen over a hundred more. She apprenticed with me for seventy of those years and all the while she raged about how useless it was. But what if no one bothered to learn about healing? Who'd make Sir Frynwy his liniment? Who'd have known how to set Ynys Môn's wing the time he broke half the bones in it falling down that cliff? Who'd have performed Ystrad Fflur's reckoning?'

Benfro considered his bread and cheese for a moment before taking a bite. He had heard this line before, many times, though it was news to him that Frecknock had once studied under his mother's tutelage. Had she lived with Morgwm in the cottage in the clearing? Slept in his bed, in his room? Thinking of her only stoked his anger, but the food dulled it as much. He hadn't eaten since they had left the cave; it was well after his normal breakfast time, and he had spent half the night marching through the forest. That first bite reminded him of how empty his stomach felt. The rest went in quick gulps, scarcely chewed, and all the while his mother looked on with her half-smile and knowing eyes. By the time he had finished, he had regained some measure of composure, although the curiosity still burned at him impatiently.

'At least tell me what happened last night,' Benfro said once he had finished his meal. 'I dreamed of flying, and then it was real.'

'No, Benfro, it wasn't real,' Morgwm said. 'You didn't leave the cave. At least your body didn't. But your mind flew. Tell me where you went.'

Benfro told her about the trees, the mountains rising out of them like islands in an impossible sea, the great arch across the road and the enormous building smothering the mountain top.

'You went to Emmass Fawr, the fortress of the Order of the High Ffrydd,' Morgwm said. 'In all my years I've never seen it, but others have described it to me. By the moon, Benfro, why would you go to such a place?'

'I don't know. I was just flying and then it caught my attention. But how did I get there if I was still in the cave?'

'I'm not sure,' Morgwm said. 'That's to say, I know how it's done. I've done similar in the past, but it takes enormous skill and endless practice. Even then it shouldn't be possible to sense all that you did, nor in such detail. You couldn't have experienced things the way you say you did.'

'I'm not lying,' Benfro said. 'It was exactly as I described. It's not the first time I've dreamed of flying either. But it was the first time I've flown anywhere other than over the trees.'

'I know you're not lying, Benfro,' Morgwm said. 'It's not in your nature. I'm just at a loss as to how you could've seen what you saw. I need to talk to Sir Frynwy about this. He knows far more than I do. Meirionydd too.'

'Ystrad Fflur called me back,' Benfro said. 'Or at least he tried to. His voice was all wrong though.'

'You heard Ystrad Fflur? In your dream?' Morgwm asked.

'And the others. I couldn't quite make out what they were saying though. How many dragons are there in the cave?'

Morgwm placed her food carefully back down on the stone, fixing Benfro with that stare that made him squirm. It was not an unkind stare, but it felt like she was looking right into his thoughts, as if there was no part of him that could hide from her, and whatever he had done wrong, she would surely know.

'You're a strange creature, Benfro,' she said. 'You shouldn't have been able to find the cave at all, yet you walked through the wards laid around it as if they weren't there. And without training of any kind, you managed to talk to Ystrad Fflur's spirit. Perhaps it's time after all to begin teaching you about these things. Before your curiosity gets you into even more trouble.'

Benfro's hearts leaped. Was he finally going to learn some of the secrets he longed to know? There was so much he wanted to ask – about the line he had seen when Frecknock had made her calling, about the calling itself. And just how did the villagers get their food? Could he soon learn to do that himself? Not that he didn't enjoy hunting and fishing with Ynys Môn, but it would be nice to just reach out and have whatever he wanted. Perhaps he could even get hold of some of the sweetened ginger root Ystrad Fflur had always given him, from faraway Talarddeg. Better still he might not have to spend endless days scouring the forest for herbs and endless nights transcribing ancient potions and recipes.

'Sweet Benfro, your youth shows all too clearly,' Morgwm said, picking up the remains of their meal and putting it back in the bag before slinging it over her shoulder. 'The subtle arts are not easily learned, even if you do show great potential. And even if Meirionydd and Sir

Frynwy accept that you need to learn, that doesn't mean you can skip your lessons with me.'

They made their way back to the trees and a path that followed the hill down to the plateau where Frecknock had made her calling. The rock was deserted now, standing in its pool of water like a small castle surrounded by a moat. Morgwm stopped to take a drink and Benfro joined her at the water's edge, desperate to speak of the events that had occurred yet still unable to make the words come out.

'This is a powerful place,' Morgwm said after she had drunk enough. 'Many major strands in the Grym connect here. It would be a good place to lay a mage's jewels.'

'Would they not be better added to the pile up in the cavern?' Benfro asked.

'Ah no, Benfro,' Morgwm said. 'The nest is the final resting place for most dragons, it's true. But mages are traditionally placed alone at points where the master lines, the Llinellau Feistr, intersect, there to watch over the world. It's important you understand this, since you seem determined to take up that mantle. True mages are solitary creatures both in life and in the eternity after death.'

'Is Frecknock training to be a mage?' Benfro asked. It was the only thing he could think of that might bring the young dragon into the conversation.

'Goodness, no,' Morgwm said. 'Frecknock doesn't have the skill or the application to come even close. No, she studies the art like all of us did when we were young. She'll master some basic skills in time, I've no doubt. At the moment she seems too preoccupied with her appearance to get very far. What made you think of her?'

'I . . .' Benfro wanted to say that he had seen her sitting on that very rock with the *Llyfr Draconius*, calling to any dragon mate she could find, but the words wouldn't come out.

'Well, never mind,' Morgwm said. 'We can't hang around here all day anyway; it's a long way home.' She stepped back up to the path. Benfro took one last look at the rock and the pool, still fighting the compulsion that would not let him speak of what had happened there. It would not budge, and he gave up in disgust, clambering up where his mother had gone and running to catch up with her as she passed through the endless winter trees.

Errol lay on his bunk staring at the rough slats that supported the thin mattress of the bunk above him. The vast dormitory was dark and so he had to assume it was night. As he had not seen sunlight since the day before entering the great stone expanse of Emmass Fawr, he could not be sure.

After his initial surprise introduction to Danno and the stables, Errol had quickly settled into a routine in the monastery. He would spend a couple of hours in the morning helping out with the horses and then the rest of the day in the library. Or at least he assumed it was morning when he was woken.

For uncounted weeks now he had been happy in a melancholic sort of way. Danno was a simple-minded man, not much given to conversation. Nonetheless, the exercise kept Errol focused and he had learned a great deal about horses. But it was once the stable work was done that he really came alive.

Surrounded by books, writings, maps and pictures, it felt like he had died and gone to the gathering fields. There was so much knowledge to be gleaned here that he could have easily spent ten lifetimes and only scratched the surface. And that was only the books written in Saesneg. There were dozens of other languages whose words he could only guess at, though he was beginning to learn. Andro, the head librarian, had seen to that from day one, as soon as the old man realized that Errol could read and understand the ancient scripts from the early centuries of the House of Balwen.

Errol liked Andro. He was impossibly old, his skin and hair white with a lifetime spent in the dark vaults. But he was full of knowledge, both mundane and obscure. He knew about distant lands, about foreign people, about magic and about dragons. And he seemed happy, delighted even, to answer Errol's endless questions even as he taught him the ways and rules of the library.

Errol had learned about the different filing systems used. He had recited the rules until they tripped around his skull like meaningless sounds. 'You will never carry an unguarded flame beyond the first portal. Covered lanterns may be used in the second and third portals. Only adepts of the fifth order may enter the higher portals. The punishment for any transgression of these rules is to be cast from the Elden Tower into the Faaeren Chasm.' Errol had no idea where either of these places was, but he didn't doubt the fall would be fatal. It seemed a harsh punishment until he saw, and smelled, the endless racks of dusty dry parchment that filled the racks. A stray spark could start a fire that would likely burn for decades.

Every day was hard work: lifting and carrying tomes that weighed almost as much as he did, deciphering spidery hands, compiling indexes and trying to catalogue subjects that had no meaning to him. And all the while his only light was a hooded lantern. By the time Andro released him from his duties, presumably at the end of a day, all Errol could think of was getting a quick meal from the librarians' refectory and then crawling into his bed in the cold dormitory.

No one else slept here. He had to himself a room big enough to house a hundred or more. There was a great fireplace at one end of the room, though he had never seen a flame burn in it. Like all the other rooms he had seen so far in the vastness of Emmass Fawr, this one had no windows, and its walls were formed from huge square blocks, perfectly cut and set. The ceiling was higher than many of the ancient trees Errol knew from home, its vaulted arches cast in strange shadows by the one torch he was allowed. The floor was stone, smoothed by the tread of uncounted feet. Everything was cold with the constant chill of a cave.

For the first few nights he had lain awake shivering in misery, huddling into the one inadequate blanket that had been given to him. Searching the room had yielded nothing, so he had slept in his rough cassock. Then after a day hugging the heat of a single lantern while he struggled with a book written in a very ancient form of Saesneg, barely recognizable as the same language he spoke every day, he had finally summoned up the courage to speak to Andro about his miserable nights. The old man had simply smiled at him and said, 'You wouldn't have been chosen to be here if you didn't know how to cope with a little cold. Think about it, Errol. You've dealt with it before.'

So he had thought about it, endlessly, for several more days, until it had finally dawned on him. The lines. Thinking about them had troubled him. His memories told him that fat Father Kewick had taught him about them, but he knew that could not be the case. Still, he had summoned up all his scant energy and searched for them, trying to recall the exact way he had felt when he had managed to see them before. They had appeared faint at first, like gossamer threads of a spider's web seen out of the corner of his eye. Looking straight at them only made them disappear. But at least he knew they were there, and finally he had been able to connect with one, how he was not sure, and pull the warming energy of it into him.

Since then life had been easier. It was still cold, but it was as if he sat indoors beside a fire while the frost deepened outside. And the loneliness he had felt since he had seen Clun being led away eased slightly as each night bought the whispering of many thousands of voices to his mind.

And so he lay, staring in the near-total darkness at the slats above him, drawing warmth from the line that passed directly under this bunk and trying to make some sense of the myriad murmuring sounds of the great fortress monastery.

A noise from outside his head woke Errol from the semi-slumber that he had drifted into. A crack of light grew around the massive door as it was pushed open, and a tall figure stepped in.

'Errol Ramsbottom?'

Errol scrambled out of his bed and pulled on his boots, walking the short distance to the door. As the light fell on the face of the man who had called him, Errol could see it was Captain Osgal. The warrior priest looked him up and down quickly, as if selecting a lamb for slaughter.

'Come with me,' he said, turning and heading out the door.

'Where are we going?' Errol asked, struggling to keep up with the tall man's stride.

'Don't ask questions,' Osgal said, then fell silent again. Errol followed him along corridors, up great flights of stairs and through enormous halls until his feet began to hurt. Still they carried on, always climbing, and as they progressed so he saw more people, most in the dull brown cassock uniform of the order, some in the garb of common people. Finally they reached a courtyard, and for the first time in what seemed like years Errol saw the sky.

It was only a small patch, high above him and framed by the rising height of tall buildings on all sides, but it was the sky. It was night and clear, stars winking in the blue-black, and it was the most magical sight Errol had ever seen. He even recognized the loping form of the Wolf Running, which meant that he was looking north. It was a small thing, but to get his bearings even slightly was a joy, like finding out he had been given the keys to his own palace.

'Stop dawdling, Ramsbottom. You're late, and he don't like it when people are late.' Osgal's voice was further away than it should have been, and Errol realized he had stopped. Running, he crossed the courtyard and entered the building on the other side.

It was a stark contrast from the parts of the monastery he had already seen. For a start the doorway seemed tiny. He ducked involuntarily as he stepped through, even though the lintel was several feet above his head. The corridor they entered was claustrophobic after the great vaulted tunnels in the other buildings of the complex. The stonework here looked almost shoddy, the blocks large but manageable, with mortar showing in finger-wide joints. Errol stubbed the toe of his boot on the uneven flagstones trying to keep up with Captain Osgal, who marched down the middle of the corridor brushing aside any who didn't see him soon enough to get out of his way.

They reached the end of the corridor and climbed a stone spiral staircase. Errol had barely slept after a long day in the library and now he had been jogging to keep up with the captain for what seemed like hours. His legs creaked and burned as he pushed himself ever onwards and upwards, and the thin air rasped in his lungs as if it were laced with sand. He could feel himself getting weaker with each step.

Finally, when he thought he could go no further and was about to beg the captain to stop, they reached the top of the stairs and a short corridor. There were only a few doors and no people. Captain Osgal stopped at the far end and knocked. There was an indistinct noise, then he opened the door, motioning for Errol to step in.

'Ah, Errol, there you are. I'm glad you could make it.'

Inquisitor Melyn sat in a large leather-faced seat behind an even larger desk. Two windows behind him were dark eyes, and Errol had to work hard to stop himself from staring out, trying to catch a glimpse of the night sky.

'Thank you, Captain,' the inquisitor said. 'You may go.' Osgal closed the door, leaving Errol standing in the brightly lit room. A fire burned in a large fireplace set into one wall of the room, and he wondered if he might be able to sit by it for a while. His exertions had kept him warm, but now the sweat on his skin was cooling and making him shiver. Instinctively, he reached out for the lines, seeking a warming connection. To his surprise he could see none in the room. A shiver of panic ran through him. He was so used to seeing them now, their absence was as if he had been struck blind.

'I can see I was right to choose you, in spite of your youth, Errol,' the inquisitor said. The old man stood and walked over to the fireplace. A heavy pewter jug sat on a trivet close to the flames. As he poured a steaming dark red liquid from it into two goblets, Errol smelled a heady aroma of cinnamon, cloves and other spices. It put him in mind of his mother and the wonderful-smelling salves she used to make.

'Come, have a seat. Drink some mulled wine,' Melyn said. Errol hurried towards the fireplace, accepting the proffered mug but waiting for the inquisitor to settle into his own chair before perching himself on the edge of his, as close to the fire as he could get.

'Andro tells me that you're a promising student,' Melyn said, fixing Errol with a stare that held him as securely as ropes. 'Tell me, Errol, do you enjoy working in the library?'

'Yes, sir.' Errol replied, the truth easy, slipping out of his mouth like rainwater from a storm-filled barrel.

'Has Andro shown you beyond the third portal yet?' the inquisitor asked, lifting his goblet to his lips. Errol did the same, but the smell brought back memories of confusion, hangover and misery in a lurching wagon. He needed his wits about him, so he merely swirled the dark heady liquid against his closed lips and swallowed air. Watching Melyn he had the impression that the old man was doing the same.

'Not even novitiates are allowed beyond the third portal,' Errol said, the rules and the terrible punishment that went with them fixed firmly in his mind.

'Ah, but you're not yet a novitiate, Errol,' Melyn said. 'And still you've mastered both the sight and rudiments of manipulating the lines. You've the skills of one twice your age. How is this possible? Who taught you these things?'

Those eyes burrowed into Errol. They were like yellow lights, flickering and whirling, growing ever larger. Or maybe it was just that the room was darkening and shrinking around him so that all he could see was that stare.

'Drink, Errol, drink,' Melyn said, and without any conscious thought Errol felt the goblet once more at his lips, tilting. Something of his will remained, for he still did no more than sip, a little of the mulled wine spilling around his mouth, down his chin and on to his clothes.

All unbidden an image sprang into his mind of the party after his mother's wedding to Godric. He was being introduced to the inquisitor, staring into those intense eyes as he did now. They tunnelled into him like worms, seeking the centre of his being. And yet something anchored him, gave him the strength to fight off the invasion. His hand was warm, clenched around something. Another hand. There was a smell of garden flowers and fresh hay, a feeling of green.

A frown spread across the inquisitor's face and Errol realized he was back in the old man's study, sitting on the edge of a chair beside the fire, a goblet of mulled wine in his hand. Melyn still stared at him, but those eyes were no longer the only thing in the room. Errol held them in his gaze still. Somehow he knew that he must do that or risk being discovered. But discovered at what?

'Drink,' a voice said deep in his head, almost silent. 'Drink, but drink slowly. Let him think he is in charge.' Errol nearly jumped, but he managed to raise his goblet to his mouth and let a thin trickle of the wine into his mouth. It was cooling fast and no longer filled his head with alcoholic fumes.

The inquisitor said nothing, still fixing him with his stare. Errol found his mind wandering. He was back at the party again, dancing energetically with Maggs. He was sitting in the cold classroom listening to fat Father Kewick telling the rapt class stories of dragons – how their mindless aggression had almost led to the destruction of the world and how brave King Brynceri had waged war upon them, founding the Order of the High Ffrydd to protect the realm and carry out the work of the Shepherd. He was sitting on a bank overlooking the river, discussing with Clun how he would be chosen for the Order of the High Ffrydd and become a warrior priest. He was watching the sunset from the rock at Jagged Leap with Maggs Clusster by his side, holding his hand. All these images and more tumbled through Errol's mind, and he watched them pass as a spectator might watch a parade. It didn't take long for him to realize that they weren't his memories, or at least they weren't his true memories. Somehow the inquisitor had taken what he remembered and twisted it, editing out crucial details, putting people in wrong places and times, doing things they couldn't possibly have done. But, taken as a whole, it added up to a plausible version of the truth.

More images flickered through his head, reinforcing the inquisitor's version of the truth. It was a bit like a dream, Errol realized. Only in this dream he was aware he was dreaming. A part of him watched from a distance, noting the inconsistencies and pondering on the gaps that still blotted his memory.

'Well, it's been nice having this little chat, Errol,' Inquisitor Melyn said, and with those words Errol was properly back in his head. He could feel the edge of the chair hard against his legs, the solid heavy weight of the goblet in his hands. And he was free to move his eyes away from the inquisitor's piercing stare. His mouth felt dry and he instinctively raised the goblet to his lips once more, drinking deeply.

'It'll be your birthday soon,' Melyn said. 'Then you can be initiated into the order. Once you've performed the ceremony you will be able to join the other novitiates in their training.'

'Soon?' Errol said. 'But . . . it can't be. I mean it was just last week I . . . How long have I been here?'

'Nearly six months, Errol. You've been with us half a year.'

15

The Obsidian Throne, in the Neuadd at Candlehall, is a powerful magical artefact. Some say that it stood on the top of the Hill of Kings, open to the elements, for millennia before King Brynceri built the hall that still surrounds it to this day. Inquisitor Ruthin insisted that it had been put there by the Shepherd himself, so that Balwen might have somewhere to rest after he had driven the godless across the Gwahanfa ranges into Llanwennog. Whatever its true history, there is no denying the power it contains. But that power, while it has guarded the Twin Kingdoms for many centuries, can also be brutally destructive.

King Weddelm II was crowned when he was only nineteen, after his father had been killed in a hunting accident. Within six months of his coronation, he had been driven insane by the power of the throne, plunging the land into a decade of terrible war. Diseverin II, who was only eighteen when he came to power, wasted half of the manhood of the kingdom on his futile attempts to drive an army through the Wrthol pass. Other young kings have threatened the stability of the Twin Kingdoms down the years, all through the corrupting influence of the throne.

After almost a century of bloody warring, King Diseverin IV finally enacted the royal edict that stands to this day. No heir of Balwen may assume the throne until after his twenty-first birthday. Should a king die before his eldest son reaches that age, then the senior among the leaders of the three orders, the Candle, the Ram and the High Ffrydd, shall act as regent until the heir comes of age. In the four hundred years since Diseverin's reign only once has a regent ruled over the Twin Kingdoms, and that for only six months.

Barrod Sheepshead,
A History of the House of Balwen

Benfro sat at the table, staring out of the window at the endless rain. He was bored. He hated winter with its storms and wind, its short days and long dark nights. The cold didn't bother him much, though he preferred to bask in the heat of the sun. What was worst about the whole wretched season was that there was so little to do.

There were plenty of chores: firewood to be collected and stacked; water to be carted from the stream; dishes to be washed; floors to be cleaned. And on top of that his mother had set him the task of making copies of several of her books on herbs. But the bad weather meant no trips to the village, no hunting in the woods, no climbing trees in search of nests to raid, no exploring. So he sat at the table with several sheets of parchment, a bottle of ink and a long quill pen, scratching out the letters one by one in precise, neat script, just as he had been taught. He had long since given up reading the words, preferring to stare out the window and lose himself in his thoughts.

Weeks had passed since he had woken in the cave from his strange dream. He could still remember the fear and helplessness, but these emotions were fading now, outshone by the wondrous feeling of flight. He longed for more dreams, to the point where he often went to his bed early and lay for what seemed like hours staring at the dark ceiling, waiting for sleep to come yet trying to keep hold of his consciousness. Always he woke the next morning early, with no memory of anything but the wooden beams overhead. It puzzled him since he had always dreamed and always been able to remember dreaming. Now it was as if someone had put a fence around his sleeping mind.

Despite his mother's promises, Benfro had learned nothing of the subtle arts since his misadventure. She had spoken to Sir Frynwy and Meirionydd, as she had promised, but the answer had come back from both of them the same. He could not begin until his fourteenth hatchday had passed. He had only Ynys Môn's spell of hiding to practise, and that seemed more of a sleight of hand than a proper spell.

The constant patter of rain on the roof almost masked the sound of a footfall on the wooden floor of the veranda outside the front door. Lost in his distracted musings, it took Benfro a moment to register the noise. Even then he thought he might have imagined it but for the feeling that there was something outside, someone outside. It was almost as if there was a silent hole in the background roar.

Quietly, Benfro rose to his feet and crossed to the door. His mother was out in the forest somewhere. She was not far, he knew; she never went any great distance without either taking him with her or sending him to the village. Whoever, whatever, stood outside was no dragon, however. He could tell without knowing how he knew. Or perhaps it was that the tread had been so light that it could only have been made by something much smaller even than him. Benfro reached for the latch and was surprised to find that his arm was trembling slightly. Taking a deep breath, he swung open the door.

The figure standing on the threshold was unlike any he had ever seen before, but Benfro knew instantly that it was a man. No witless beast would come near a house such as this, nor would it clothe itself in what appeared to be dark brown cloth, similar to that with which Frecknock occasionally bedecked herself. Benfro had heard of clothes, but with his thick hide and close-lapping scales they were not something he had ever entertained the thought of wearing. The man, on the other hand, seemed to be almost completely enveloped in them.

He was surprisingly short and slight, much smaller than Benfro had imagined the creatures who inspired such fear in his mother and the villagers would be. Yet there was an otherness about him that sent a shiver down Benfro's spine to the very tip of his tail. The man was obviously as startled to see him, for he took a step backwards, gabbling something incomprehensible.

'Who are you?' Benfro asked. 'What do you want?'

The man stopped gabbling, lifted pale pink hands from the folds of his cloak and reached up to pull back his hood. With a start, Benfro realized he had seen such hands before.

'You do not speak our tongue?' the man said, and Benfro's attention snapped back to his head. It was strange, fleshy-pink and round, with a thinning mop of grey hair settled on the top a bit like a crow's nest in a tall tree. Two small eyes looked up at him not unkindly.

'You are Morgwm's hatchling,' the man said. 'I was not sure. I did not think even she would do something so bold.'

'What do you mean?' Benfro asked.

'Forgive me, please,' the man said. 'It is a long time since I have heard the ancient language, longer still ere last I tried to speak it. I came here in search for Morgwm the Green. My name is Gideon.'

'My mother has mentioned you,' Benfro said, remembering the name. 'She said that she trusted you.'

'She does me a very great honour then,' Gideon said. He was still standing outside, and although the veranda was covered, water dripped from his cloak to the wooden boards. Benfro looked around the clearing, hoping that his mother might be somewhere near, but she was nowhere to be seen.

'Would you like to come in?' he asked eventually, unsure what else he could do but offer the hospitality any dragon would give to a weary traveller. For a moment Gideon looked uncertain, but then he stepped through the open doorway, dwarfed by its size.

The man went straight to the fireplace, warming his pink hands in front of the flames for a while before pulling off his damp cloak. Underneath it he wore more clothes, Benfro noticed. They were the same dark material but followed his shape more closely. Aware he was staring, Benfro looked for something else to do.

'Can I get you something to drink?' he asked. Gideon returned his stare for perhaps longer than was necessary, as if he was trying to understand what had been said. Benfro resisted the urge to lift a hand to his lips and mimic the action of drinking.

'Thank you, some chamomile tea perhaps,' Gideon said after a while. Benfro set the kettle on the fire and went through to the storeroom for the herb. He lingered longer in the dark room than was polite. Certainly it was only the work of a moment to locate the pot which held the dried flowers. All the while he listened out for his mother's return. Although everything he had been taught since he was a kit told him he should flee, he didn't feel any fear at the presence of this man. And yet his normally burning curiosity was quenched by an overwhelming sense of awkwardness. Were it another dragon who had come to visit he would have known what to do, what to talk about. But this was so completely beyond anything he had ever experienced that he could only stand, indecisive and fretful in the dark.

Finally the whistle of the kettle meant he could linger no longer. He went back into the main room, took down the smallest of the drinking bowls and sprinkled a handful of the herbs into it before adding boiling water. The smell of the flowers reminded him of autumn, sunshine and dry-baked earth. It was a welcome distraction from the endless rain.

'My humblest thanks to you,' Gideon said as Benfro

handed him the bowl. His speech was formal, like the old dragons in Sir Frynwy's tales, and it occurred to Benfro that the man must have learned it from books. He had never thought about such things before, but now it made sense that men and dragons would have different ways of speaking.

'Pray tell me, what is your name, good sir dragon?' Gideon asked. Benfro tried not to smirk at the overblown question.

'Benfro,' he said. 'My name's Benfro.'

'Well, Sir Benfro,' Gideon said, 'this is a fine bowl of chamomile tea.'

Benfro was about to respond when he heard a heavy thump on the wooden deck, closely followed by the door crashing open. Morgwm stood there, dripping with rain, her eyes darting swiftly about the room as she took in the situation. For an instant she looked so terrifying, so feral and monstrous that both he and Gideon cringed, ready for the killing blow. Then in an instant it was gone.

'Gideon, by the moon!' Morgwm said. Then she slipped into the same gibberish that the man had spoken when first he had arrived.

'I am sorry, Morgwm,' Gideon said in that same stilted and formal speech that Benfro could understand. 'It was never my intention to come unannounced. Always in the past you have known of my arrival e'en ere I was a league from your door.'

Morgwm looked silently at the man for a long moment, then across at Benfro before understanding lit up her face with a happy grin.

'You speak our language well,' she said. 'If a little archaically. I never knew that you had learned it.'

'Twas a folly of my youth,' Gideon said. 'Or so didst seem at the time. Seldom has the opportunity presented itself for me to practise. And never before have I been honoured with a true speaker with whom to converse.'

'But you've visited me countless times, Gideon,' Morgwm said. 'Did it never occur to you to speak the Draigiaith then?'

'In truth our visits were ever too short, their business too urgent. And your command of the Saesneg made it more sensible to use my native tongue.'

'Well, as you've no doubt discovered, Benfro speaks only Draigiaith. He'll learn other languages in time but he's only thirteen years old. There's plenty of time for such learning.'

'I would that it were so, good Morgwm,' Gideon said, 'for I come with ill tidings. The boy has been chosen to become one of the warrior priests.'

'That cannot be,' Morgwm said. 'Hennas would never allow such a thing.'

'Her mind has been turned since last you visited her,' Gideon said. 'And by a practitioner far more skilled than I. She believes her son has been granted the greatest of honours.'

'Her son, you say,' Morgwm said. 'That's something then. The persuasion she made me put on her when she agreed to take the boy is still holding. His true identity may not yet have been discovered.'

'I hope that is so,' Gideon said. 'But even if it is, forces conspire against his continued good fortune. The villagers of Pwllpeiran told me that Princess Beulah attended the choosing this year, and that she showed great interest in the boy. I can only think that she saw something in his appearance that aroused her suspicions. That he was chosen at all is unusual, for he is not yet old enough to become a novitiate.'

'I'm sorry, indeed,' Morgwm said, 'but I've done everything I can for the boy. I don't see how I can help any more.'

'Neither would I presume to ask,' Gideon said. 'Even as we speak, others strive to protect him. We are not without our allies in the Order of the High Ffrydd. Not all of them are Melyn's men.'

'Melyn!' The word escaped Benfro's mouth like a shout of alarm. He had been sitting quietly, listening to the conversation with fascination even though he understood very little of what it concerned. The mention of the name had shocked him out of his musing. Melyn. Could this be Sir Felyn's true identity? It had to be. If this man, Gideon, could speak like a dragon, then surely others could too.

'Is there something you wish to say, Benfro?' Morgwm asked. There was indeed, yet he was still bound by Frecknock's compulsion which held his mouth shut on the matter.

'No, mother,' Benfro said. 'I just recognized the name. Melyn.'

'Inquisitor Melyn is not someone you would ever want to meet, Sir Benfro,' Gideon said. 'He is strong in the subtle arts, ruthless in his quest for power and he would see every dragon on the face of Gwlad dead, their unreckoned jewels hoarded in the caverns beneath Emmass Fawr for his personal pleasure.' The man turned back to Morgwm.

'And that is why I have come here, to warn you,' he said. 'Melyn is wise and cunning like a fox. Beulah belongs to him body and soul. She will soon take the Obsidian Throne, for only her personal intervention is keeping the king alive. As soon as she reaches her majority, she will simply let him die. If she suspects a dragon has helped to save her sister's son then she will not hesitate to reinstate the aurddraig. She may well do so anyway, without that excuse to prompt her.'

'And when is her birthday?' Morgwm asked.

'The same day I brought the boy's mother to you,' Gideon said. 'The day Princess Lleyn died.'

'The day that Benfro was hatched,' Morgwm said.

Princess Beulah sat in her chambers watching the dull pink glow of morning rise over the rooftops of Candlehall. The city was as quiet at this early hour as it would ever be, the only noise the clanking of wagons bringing produce from the countryside to feed the insatiable urban appetite. Occasional cries and crashes broke through the morning chorus of birds feeding in the trees outside the palace. An aroma of new-baked bread wafted up on the cool breeze, making promises of breakfast.

Beulah rose from her chair and dressed herself in the plain clothes she had chosen for this morning. No handmaidens attended her, which was how she preferred it. She had long since dismissed all the tiresome ladies-in-waiting her father had insisted serve her. Their endless gossip was irritating and trite, their sole interest which of the noblemen who fawned upon the king might make the best husband. Beulah was not interested in such trivial nonsense; Melyn had opened her eyes to much greater possibilities. And today she might even begin to pursue some of those plans, for today she turned twenty-one. Today, should her ailing father have the decency to die, she could take the Obsidian Throne for herself and not have to defer to some power-hungry regent.

The palace was quiet as she walked down the long corridors that led from her quarters to the rooms of state where her father lived. Sleepy-looking guards stood to attention at her approach, opening the doors for her. She gave them not a glance, sweeping through and into the king's apartments without a sound.

Seneschal Padraig was waiting for her in the outer chamber. His face was wrinkled and old, heavy bags under his eyes, his hair thin and yellowing, his hands long and claw-like, bent with arthritis. The windows were shuttered against the morning chill, and he sat at a desk lit by several thick candles, their flames flickering in the draught of her arrival and sending the shadows dancing around the room.

'Good morning, my lady,' Padraig said, rising from his chair. 'And may I be the first to wish you a happy birthday.'

'Thank you, Seneschal,' Beulah said. 'But that honour should belong to my father, the king.' She stepped towards the doors to the sleeping chamber, unsurprised to see the old man move to head her off.

'King Diseverin doesn't normally rise for another hour,' he said. 'He's an old man who needs his sleep.'

'Ha! You're an old man, Padraig, and you sleep less than two hours a night.'

'I must confess to being in better health than the king,' Padraig said. 'As you well know, he's fond of his wine. Perhaps it would be better if you didn't disturb him until he has awoken.'

'I've no intention of disturbing him, Seneschal. I will sit and watch him until he wakes. I will be the first person he sees on this special day. It's my gift to him on my birthday.' Beulah smiled, though she felt no amity towards the obdurate priest. He had built himself too comfortable a position running the Twin Kingdoms for her father. His input was valuable, but he needed to be reminded who wielded the true power.

'It's a bit dark in here, isn't it,' she said, raising her hand and holding it in front of the seneschal. A tiny ball of light appeared, hovering in the air a few inches above her palm. It was pure white, almost too bright to look at, and it chased the shadows away from the corners of the room, exposing the tatty furnishings, the dirty, torn tapestries and dusty paintings of illustrious Balwens long dead. Padraig shrunk back from the light as if it might burn him, a haunted fear in his eyes. Beulah closed her hand around the orb, extinguishing it with a thought and stepping past the seneschal towards the doors to the king's sleeping chamber.

'You've always been a loyal servant to my father, Padraig,' Beulah said. 'But as you said, he's an old man. He'll not live for ever. One day I will sit on the Obsidian Throne.'

'My lady, I live to serve the Twin Kingdoms and the

House of Balwen,' Padraig said bowing, 'whoever sits upon the throne.'

Beulah turned her back on the seneschal, pushing open the doors to her father's bedroom. Inside it was almost completely dark, just the light from the outer chamber picking out the great bed, the armchairs and sofa, the shapes of the large shuttered windows and the doors that led to dressing and bathing rooms. Beulah knew it well from her childhood, when her mother had still lived. She had often come here in the mornings to bounce around on the massive soft bed and play hide and seek with her sisters. The memory almost made her laugh out loud. How stupid she had been back then, how naive to find happiness in such simple things.

Then the room had smelled of the fine rose-water perfumes her mother had worn; now her nose wrinkled at the all-too-familiar odour of stale wine, unwashed bodies and rot. It might have been fun to scare the seneschal with her conjuring, but she felt no need to bring more light to this horrible place. She knew that the furniture was torn and dirty, the massive bed soiled by drunken incontinence and the dissolute habits of her father. He was a sot not worthy of the name he carried.

There, in the dark stench of his sleep, she hated her father more than anything. More than she had when her mother had died because he had been too drunk to call for help. She hated him far more than she had when he had washed his hands of all his daughters: putting Lleyn under the tutelage of Cassters of the Ram, sending poor Iolwen to study with Padraig and thence into the hands of the enemy, handing herself over to Inquisitor Melyn. At least that had turned out all right for her, though it had been a cruel blow for a grieving six-year-old. She could taste the pain, the confusion and terror at the break-up of a happy family in that foul-smelling room, and for a moment Beulah considered how easy it would be to kill her father there and then. She was old enough; she could take the throne and no one would stand in her way.

But that was not her way. King Diseverin would not die in his bed, unconscious from too much drinking. He had done enough harm to the standing of the House of Balwen without adding such an ignominious end to his list of failings. No, she needed him awake and sober for this of all days. She needed him to declare to the Twin Kingdoms that she had reached her majority. She needed him to acknowledge her as his heir.

Beulah closed the doors, momentarily plunging the room into total darkness. With the stench and the sonorous snores of her sleeping father, it could have been a bear's den, the beast asleep, surrounded by the fetid bones of its victims. She knew better, using her well-trained senses to navigate across the room to the windows, which she unshuttered one by one, pulling back their heavy velvet curtains to reveal the light of morning. Startled by the brightness, the king let out a great snort, rolled over and buried his head in his pillows.

Reaching out a hand, Beulah touched her father's neck where it was exposed to the light, trying not to retch at the feel of his clammy skin. This was the hard part, she realized. Manipulating the forces around people was easy – she did it every day – but this particular person filled her with such hatred and revulsion that she could scarcely bring herself to be in the same room as him, let alone touch him. To feel his feeble mind was worse still. And yet she had a job to do.

The palace in Candlehall was well placed for drawing down power from the lines. Beulah concentrated for a moment then let the energy flow from her into her father's degenerating body. She washed away the drunkenness from him, soothed the beginnings of his hangover and filled him with more strength than he had possessed in many a year. She swept away some of the cloudiness from his thoughts, noticing how pathetically he still clung to the image of his wife, her mother, dead these sixteen years, and left him with that thought, building on his sense of guilt.

It was delicate work, subtle and intricate, but Beulah had been taught by the best. When she was finished, she took a moment to replenish her own energy from the buzz that filled the whole city around her. She could feel her rejuvenated father beginning to wake, his mind more alive than the previous night's drinking should have allowed, but not so clear that he might be able to think for himself. She didn't want him to do anything unpredictable to ruin her big day. Then she rose from the bed, crossing the room to the sofa that stood in the great bay window overlooking the grass courtyard and the Neuadd. As she settled into its dusty embrace, her father rolled over, eyes screwed up against the growing light of dawn.

'Eh? What's going on? Who opened the shutters?' King Diseverin IX said, sitting up and rubbing at his stubbly face.

'I did, father,' Beulah said, putting a bright and cheery tone into her voice.

'Who? Oh, Beulah. What are you doing here?' the king asked. She waited for a count of ten, knowing that she had put the knowledge in his head, confident that it would take exactly that long for her father's muddled mind to access it.

'Ah yes,' the king said, right on cue. 'Happy birthday.'

16

The Processional, or Kingmaker's Dance, was first introduced in the reign of King Weddelm III, the Foolish. It is derived from the old progressive dances favoured at that time, in which each dancing couple must complete a complex turn about the floor before the man can release his partner and move on to the next woman in line. Weddelm, who was fond of dancing, developed the Processional to denote the ranking of his nobles and sons, arranging the dance so that he would take each of their partners in turn, starting with the lowest and ending with the wife or betrothed of the heir to the Obsidian Throne.

When his only son and heir, Prince Lonk, disappeared on his fool's quest for the lost treasure of Cenobus, Weddelm used the Processional to signal his favoured heir, bringing to a close the unbroken tradition of male rule when he ended his dance in the arms of his eldest daughter, Iolwen, spurning the wife of his cousin Dafydd.

Duke Baggot, Iolwen's husband, used the old king's folly as justification for his own claim on the throne, which subsequently plunged the Twin Kingdoms into the terror of the Brumal Wars.

Barrod Sheepshead,
A History of the House of Balwen

Benfro sat in the fork of the tree, watching the road. It was a place he sometimes came when he wanted to think or just get away from the turmoil of life. He had been coming here a lot of late.

Ever since Gideon's visit, with his confusing news about the workings of men, the terrible scheming Princess Beulah and her mentor, Inquisitor Melyn, Benfro had been struggling against the compulsion that Frecknock had placed on him. There was rarely a waking moment when he didn't think about his encounter up on the escarpments. Time had only confirmed in his mind that Inquisitor Melyn and Sir Felyn were one and the same. Even the realization that dragons and men spoke radically different languages had not altered his convictions. If Gideon could make himself understood, how much better might Melyn be at this? Benfro burned with the need to tell anyone who would listen about the danger they were all in, about how close the village was to discovery. But he could not say a word, however hard he tried, whoever he approached. Some of the villagers were no doubt beginning to wonder if he was completely sane, the way he had been engaging them in conversation and then breaking off when once more he found he was prevented from saying what so desperately needed to be said.

At least some good had come of Gideon's visit, Benfro mused as the wind twisted the top branches of his tree, gently rocking his perch from side to side. In the weeks since the man had departed Morgwm had become much more open about the threat his kind presented, and she had also begun to teach Benfro something of their language. She had produced several books written in it, and as he studied them he could see that it had the same roots as his own tongue, though the alphabet was strange to his eye, the pronunciation stranger still. His mother had taken to asking him questions in Saesneg, as it was called, without warning, sometimes engaging him in long conversations until he no longer knew what he was saying or hearing. But with each passing day he had improved, and it was fascinating to see the world from an entirely new perspective.

It had occurred to Benfro, as the weeks went past and the year turned, that he might be able to break Frecknock's spell by telling of his experiences in this new language. Magic, however, was not so easily fooled, and his attempt had only ended in another episode of deep embarrassment and frustration. And so it was that he sat in his favourite tree, overlooking the path to the village, as the wind swung him back and forth.

A movement in the corner of Benfro's eye caught his attention. Someone was moving along the track, but keeping to the shadows even though the afternoon sky was darkening and heavy with clouds. It was Frecknock, and the sight of her filled him with a terrible anger. Bad enough that she had made his life an impossible torment these past months, but her vanity and selfish obsession was putting everyone at risk. And here she was, trotting along the path towards Morgwm's cottage, no doubt looking to replenish her stock of scale polish and other unguents, preening herself that she might be a more tempting lure for the attentions of the bold and gallant Sir Felyn.

He had to tell her, Benfro realized. There was no one

else he could warn, but he must surely be able to tell Frecknock what he suspected – no, what he knew to be true. She might not believe him, she might even try to punish him for his temerity, but she would have to listen to him. And maybe the next time she made her selfish, foolish calling, she would be a bit more circumspect.

Hauling himself out of his seat, Benfro dropped down to the leaf-mulched ground and trotted through the skeletal trees to the edge of the path. Frecknock had already passed but she was not far away.

'Frecknock!' he called. She froze in her tracks, seeming to huddle down into herself as if she could become invisible. He walked towards her slowly, hesitant to open himself to her wrath but at the same time convinced this was the only way to resolve his dilemma. As he approached her, he wondered why he had not thought to do so before. But then she was the architect of his misfortune, the dragon who had dedicated her life to making his miserable. It was hardly surprising that he had taken so long to come to her.

'Frecknock,' he said again. 'Please, it's only me.'

Frecknock turned slowly to face him, her stare as hostile and penetrating as ever. She looked him over like she might a piece of meat waiting to be cooked, her eyes darting back and forth before lingering on his feet. Benfro glanced down to see mud and dead leaves clinging to his talons.

'Been spying on me again, squirt?' Frecknock said.

'No!' Benfro said. 'I was just sitting and thinking when you came past.'

'Hah! Likely story,' Frecknock said. She pulled herself

back up to her normal height and Benfro realized that he had grown. She no longer towered over him the way she had before. Or maybe it was that she had done her worst to him and he had survived.

'What do you want, squirt? Some of us have better things to do with our lives than mooning around in the forest, you know.'

'I need to talk to you about . . .' Benfro began. Then the familiar feeling crept up on him. His tongue tied and the words so prominent in his mind would not come out. 'That is, I think . . .'

'Spit it out, squirt. What are you trying to say?' Frecknock asked. She looked at him with her normal nose-in-the-air disdain, as if he were something she would rather not have to see at all. Benfro's anger grew. It was her stupid pride and arrogance that was putting everyone in danger. He latched on to his rage, using it to push the words he wanted to say to the front of his mind.

'You stupid cow. Can't you see what you've done . . .' was all that came out, and as he heard what he had said, Benfro's hearts almost stopped. For an instant terrible outrage flickered across Frecknock's face. Her eyes widened in shock, then narrowed into a deep scowl; her nostrils flared, almost steaming in the cold winter air; her ears flicked back, hugging the side of her head as she leaned forward closer and closer to Benfro's own face. In turn he shrank back, aware that he had not so much crossed a line as trampled his way over it and on into the next country. He tensed himself for the blows, both physical and mental, that he knew would come, but Frecknock just stared at him, her black eyes limpid and calm. Then she let out a great barking snort of laughter.

'You can't say it, can you, squirt,' she said, chuckling to herself. Benfro relaxed a little, realizing that he would not be punished. His anger was still hot within him.

'You . . . I can't . . .' he said. Frecknock just laughed more deeply.

'Of course you can't, kitling,' Frecknock said. 'I made it so.'

'But . . . but . . . I need . . .' Benfro battled against the compulsion that choked the words off in his mouth even as he tried to say them.

'You need to mind your own business, squirt,' Frecknock said, her face lit up with glee at his discomfort. 'Now I suggest you go and climb a tree or something. I'm busy and I don't want to have you following me around like some lovesick puppy.'

For an instant Benfro thought he was going to hit her. He had never been prone to violence – it was not in his nature. His mother was always kind, patient and accepting. The villagers were in the main good-natured and tolerant of his constant questioning. He had grown up with their peaceful ways, and they had formed him into the unassuming and easy-going dragon that he was. Faced by Frecknock's mocking laughter, her casual abuse of a power he could not understand, he wanted to lash out with his claws, kick with his talons and throw the sort of tantrum a kitling would be ashamed of. But he knew even as the possibility filled him with energy that physical violence would gain him very little and cost him immeasurably more. He took a little solace from the knowledge that he was a fast learner. Had it not taken him only a few weeks to learn the language of men? Tomorrow was his hatchday, and then he could start to learn magic. Soon he would be able to throw off whatever dark spell it was that Frecknock had cast on him. He could warn the others about her folly and put a stop to it. He could save them all – if it wasn't too late.

'You really don't know how stupid you're being,' he said finally, taking some small satisfaction from the look of annoyance that spread over Frecknock's face as she digested his words. Then before she could say anything, or worse cast another glamour over him, he turned on his heels and strode off down the path towards the village.

Halfway through her party Princess Beulah realized she had enjoyed herself more at the little village wedding where she and Melyn had discovered the Llanwennog boy. What was his name? Errol something? At least there the people had been determined to enjoy themselves. Here, in the great hall of the Neuadd, everyone was too nervous, too anxious to show themselves off in the best light. It was a parade of the shallow and insecure, and Beulah was bored with it all.

She understood the importance of show. The various noble houses that owed their existence to the House of Balwen needed constant reminding that the royal household was still in control, lest they start to get ideas. The Brumal Wars were not so far in the past that they could be easily forgotten, and her father's reign had not been so glorious that she could take every duke and earl's support for granted. Even so, it would be a brave man who tried anything direct, given her well known connections to the Order of the High Ffrydd.

So all the nobility of the twin kingdoms was here in the great Neuadd of Candlehall to congratulate her on successfully reaching her twenty-first birthday, as if that were some great achievement. The wiser among them could already see the balance of power sliding from Seneschal Padraig and his acolytes of the Candle to her and Inquisitor Melyn. The boldest among the wise had pampered and preened their unmarried sons and even now were presenting them like show-cockerels to the king as suitable consorts for his daughter.

Beulah felt like a prize heifer at some backwoods agricultural fair. This was supposed to be her celebration, and yet it was more like she was on display before an auction. Soon the wealthy and influential would begin to place their bids. Her father the king, more alert than he had been for years thanks to the gift she had given him that morning, was enjoying the attention he had never been sober enough to notice before. She had to endure the endless round of hopeful young faces asking her to dance, mindful that she should spurn no one important nor raise anyone's hopes too high by showing them undue consideration. The whole affair was a dance in itself, infinitely more intricate than any of the set pieces played out on the floor of the great hall. Better by far the simple enthusiastic revelling of the hill country villagers, their only concern who might bed who that night.

The music came to an end with a flourish and the young man who had been her partner for this dance released her, bowing extravagantly. Beulah smiled at him as sweetly as she could manage. She couldn't remember his name.

'Would Your Highness honour me with another dance,' the man said. Beulah revised her opinion: he was little more than a boy, though tall and well built. His face was smooth and unlined – she doubted it had ever seen a razor – and his shoulder-length hair was the colour of old straw, tinged with the ruddiness that marked him as a southerner. His face was a picture of earnest hope, as if his whole life had been building up to this day. And maybe it had been. She had been heir to the Obsidian Throne since she was seven, after all. Any sensible noble family would be grooming its eligible sons for the possibility of an alliance. Beulah shuddered at the thought of being married to this boy, of waking up in the same bed as him.

'I am tired of dancing,' Beulah said, aware that the boy was still waiting for an answer from her. 'Perhaps later. Now I would sit with my father.'

'May I take you to him?' The boy bowed once more and held out his arm to take hers.

Scowling, Beulah realized that it was going to be more difficult to rid herself of him than to purge a street stray of fleas. Perhaps it would be as well to show him some favour. After all, she had no intention of marrying any of the young men her father might think suitable. She had no intention of leaving any such decision up to him. If she seemed to have chosen this fey youth, at least the others would give her some peace for a while.

The young man was sweating nervously as he led Beulah by the arm across the hall and up the stone steps to the foot of the great Obsidian Throne where King Diseverin sat in his customary pose, slumped against one massive arm with a goblet of wine in his hand. Seneschal Padraig stood by the old king's side, whispering something in his ear. Diseverin seemed to be listening intently to the seneschal, his eyes unusually bright and focused. Beulah hoped that she had not overdone her earlier work. Her plan required her father to be more true to his normal self.

'Ah, Beulah,' the king said as she approached, now leading the obviously terrified boy, who clung desperately to her arm. She almost felt sorry for him. No quiet upbringing in sleepy coastal Abervenn could have possibly prepared him for this encounter. But one of his tutors must have succeeded somewhere, for just when it was beginning to look like he would be dragged away for insulting the monarch, he dropped to his knee, bowed his head and spoke.

'Your Majesty, may I return your daughter Princess Beulah to your safekeeping.'

'Eh? Oh yes, of course,' King Diseverin said, distractedly waving his goblet. A page hurried to refill it, another brought a single chair, setting it alongside the throne for Beulah to sit on. The young man released her hand and she settled herself down, feeling like a child beside the massive black stone seat. Her would-be suitor still knelt on one knee, his head bowed, unmoving save for a slight tremor that shuddered up and down his form.

'Who are you?' the king asked after a long uncomfortable pause.

'Merrl, eldest son of Duke Angor of Abervenn,' the youth said without raising his head.

'Angor, eh?' the king said, turning his attention to his daughter. 'What need have I of ships, boy? There's no enemy in the southern seas.' He took a deep swig from his goblet, wiping his mouth on the sleeve of his shirt. 'You may go now,' he said to Merrl. The youth scuttled backwards, still not looking up at his king, descending the steps before turning and fleeing into the crowd.

'He's not bad, I suppose' Diseverin said. 'And the House of Angor is nothing if not rich. Still, you might want to think a bit more strategically in your alliances, Beulah. Look to the north. Dina and beyond.'

The princess looked up at him, noting the lines on his face, the bloodshot cast to his eyes and the shaking of his hand as it clasped his goblet. Yet for all his death-wish alcoholism, King Diseverin had been tutored in statecraft from a very early age. Some of that wisdom learned still remained. Just a pity that he was too weak-willed to make anything of it.

'How can I possibly find a suitable partner if you insist on scaring them all away,' Beulah said, though she was glad to be rid of the simpering Merrl. After all, she had work to do. 'Dance with me, father,' she said, turning to face the king, looking up from her low seat into his unsteady eyes.

'Eh? What?'

'Dance with me. Just once,' Beulah said. 'It's my birthday after all.'

'I don't know,' the king said. 'I've not really done anything like that in a long while.'

'All the more reason why you should,' Beulah said, standing and holding out her hand. 'Perhaps if you danced some more, you wouldn't be so sad all the time.'

The king looked at her outstretched hand, then at her face. Beulah smiled at her father again, batting her eyelids in the coquettish manner she had seen some of the court ladies use on the young noblemen who came to Candlehall. It was as unnatural a mannerism to her as could be, yet it seemed to sway the king. Shuffling wheezily, he edged himself off the throne, taking her hand to steady himself. Seneschal Padraig was at his side in an instant, wringing his hands like a penitent.

'Your Majesty,' the seneschal said. 'Is this wise? In your state of health?'

'I've been feeling much better since this morning,' the king said, the faintest hint of the old commanding tone of his father edging into his voice. 'And besides, what will all my nobles think if their king has not the health to dance with his own daughter on her majority?'

'At least allow me to ask the players for a slow tune,' the seneschal said.

'By the Shepherd, man, no,' the king said, leaning heavily on Beulah now. As ever, his touch made her skin crawl, but she could feel the anger growing in him now, sense the strain on his heart as it pumped faster, reddening his face in a haze of tiny burst blood vessels.

'This is a formal occasion,' the king continued. 'From this day on, Princess Beulah has a measure in the responsibility for the state. I will honour her with the Processional. She is my heir, after all.'

Beulah allowed herself to be led down to the dance

floor by her father, lending her strength to him so that he did not falter on the steps. Looking over her shoulder, she could see Padraig standing beside the Obsidian Throne, still wringing his hands. He had always been ambitious, growing his power ever larger as the king slipped deeper into his drunkenness, but he couldn't bring himself to disobey his monarch. In a way Beulah was grateful to him. Without Padraig's warnings and nursemaid concerns to egg him on, her father might never have agreed to dance. As it was, he had played into her hands perfectly.

They reached the floor, now surprisingly clear, as the music came to a halt. Those few who had been dancing looked around nervously, unsure what to do now that they found their king in their midst. There was a moment of unease when the master of ceremonies announced the Processional. At least five other couples of high birth would be required for the dance, and yet all of a sudden no one wanted to join in. Finally Merrl, perhaps the last person Beulah would have expected, stepped on to the floor with a slight-looking young woman on his arm. Beulah eyed them suspiciously as they approached, unsure what to make of this potential rival. She was a head shorter than Beulah, her hair tied up in an intricate shape atop her head to make her seem taller, though it had the opposite effect.

'Your Majesty, Your Highness, may I present my sister, Anwyn,' Merrl said, again making an extravagant bow. If he had overcome some of his earlier terror it had been transferred to his sister. She stared goggle-eyed before remembering to curtsy. 'We would be honoured to be witness for your Processional.'

'What? Oh, yes. Of course,' the king said. 'It wouldn't be much of a Processional if there was just the two of us.'

Other couples, emboldened by Merrl's bravery, soon joined the party, and in short order four sets had assembled. The musicians played the introduction, everyone bowed, and then the dance began.

It was an old dance, formal and precise. Traditionally it was danced by a ruling monarch in recognition of his chosen heir, and so danced only seldom. Beulah could remember the endless hours of tedious training she had undergone as a child, the seemingly random steps and counter-steps, bows and curtsys. She had always been better taking the lead than following, but now she had to allow her father to guide her about the floor while trying to maintain delicate contact with him.

Safe in the constraints of the dance, the assembled guests soon forgot the courtesies of rank. On the dance floor they were equals. The Processional required that they each move from partner to partner within the set, always returning to the original as the music progressed. Each time Beulah was returned to her father, she renewed the contact, and each time she leached a little more of his life out of him. Never enough to make him stumble, but enough that he began to sweat, his bloodshot skin turning ever paler and greyer. Beulah knew her father: he was too stubborn to stop the dance. He would carry on until the music ended or he dropped.

The Processional reached a slower part, and Beulah once more linked arms with her father, stepping slowly up the dance floor towards the great empty bulk of the

Obsidian Throne. Her hand clasped his and through that touch she could feel his confusion, his fear.

'You'll not sit on it again,' she said, leaning close to whisper in his ear.

Startled, the king missed his step, staggering to try and get back into the rhythm of the music. Beulah could feel his heart racing, trying to pump sluggish blood through veins grown thick with decades of indolence. She reached out for it with a thought, slowing it until it matched the speed of the music.

'I should thank you, really,' she whispered. 'You gave me to Melyn because you didn't want to be reminded of mother. You sent us all away as if we were no more important to you than serfs. But I've learned so much from the inquisitor, the power of the warrior priests is mine to wield.'

The tempo of the music increased as the dance moved towards its end. Beulah once more released her father, leaving him just enough strength to keep going as she twirled around the set. She felt a curious surge of excitement as the seconds went past, building to an almost uncontrollable glee. She wanted to laugh and realized as she came face to face with young Merrl that she was grinning like a mad woman. It didn't take a genius to see that the boy was infatuated with her, nor that his sister looked at her with ill-concealed hostility. Had she not other plans for this evening, she might have risen to that challenge. Perhaps she would later on, if the opportunity presented itself. Merrl would be easy to seduce, easier to discard, but Anwyn was another matter.

The cycle of the music took her away from the pair,

past other less memorable faces and finally returned her to her father. He looked extremely unwell, the sweat stringing his lank yellow-grey hair, his eyes red and bleary, his face ashen. He seemed to be having difficulty breathing, and as Beulah once more took his hand she felt the trembling in his heart as it struggled to beat.

'Not long now, father,' she said, laughing. In her mind she took his heart in her hand, felt its warmth and the surge of blood that accompanied each pulse. The music swelled to a crescendo as they took the final spinning steps of the Processional, and then, as the last chord rang out, all the dancers back in their original positions, all the spectators looking on with awe and regret, Beulah squeezed.

King Diseverin did not cry out. In the end, Beulah knew, he didn't even feel any pain. He looked at her with a mixture of surprise and understanding on his face, and as the last echoes of the music were soaked up by the massive hall, he crumpled to the floor.

A smattering of applause began, congratulating the band on its performance, the dancers on their skill. It quickly died away as Beulah dropped to her knees, letting a low wail escape from her lips. She clung to her father's arm, feeling the last of his life ebb out of him, drinking the last of his being like the wine he had so enjoyed. Within moments others were kneeling beside her. She recognized Seneschal Padraig, bending towards the man who had been his king.

'My lady,' the old man said, 'please, let me near.'

Beulah clung to her father, making sure that his heart had stilled, that there was no chance of recovery.

'Please, Princess Beulah,' the seneschal said again. 'I must attend to the king.'

Beulah felt a familiar hand on her shoulder. Steady strength flowed from it into her, though she did not need the help.

'Come, Your Highness,' Inquisitor Melyn said. 'There's nothing more you can do here. Leave this to Padraig.'

Beulah held on to her contact with her father for a few seconds longer, until she was absolutely sure that he was dead. There was no spark in the body at all, the connection she had made now nothing more than a touch on cooling, clammy skin. Slowly she let go, allowing herself to be lifted from the floor and led past silent revellers towards the stone steps that climbed to the Obsidian Throne. Behind her she could hear the increasingly desperate sounds of Seneschal Padraig trying to revive her father's corpse. It really should have been a job for Archimandrite Cassters. The Rams were meant to be the healers, after all, but the old priest simply stood on the edge of the dance floor staring in disbelief.

'Well played, my lady,' Melyn said as he saw her settled on the small chair beside the throne. 'Now let us see how Padraig picks up the tune.'

Beulah watched and waited as the huddle of people around her father's body grew. She noticed the other members of her dance set hovering nearby, anxiety writ large across their faces. Merrl still clung to his sister's arm, and Beulah wondered whether he would be a tender lover or try to dominate her. She doubted he had any experience at all in that direction, but that could be an advantage.

The seneschal stood up, motioning everyone away from the body. His face was doom-laden as he walked away from the dance floor and climbed the steps to where she sat. When he was still several feet away from her, he fell to one knee, dropping his head in a defeated bow.

'The king is dead,' he said in a voice that was both quiet and carrying, seeming to echo around the silent hall like a whisper. 'Long live the queen!'

17

Many have remarked on how dragons copy human ways, and one of the most notable is in the adoption of honorific titles. Thus an elder dragon might refer to himself as Sir Ystrad. It is only males who do this; females however often append a descriptor to their name, such as 'the Fair'.

To the casual observer this may seem amusing or fanciful, but to dragons it is anything but. To be addressed as 'Sir' is to be acknowledged the head of one's family, and to be accorded a descriptor is to be recognized as a master of one's chosen skill or as possessing the most perfect form of a certain attribute. In this way dragons, who are essentially egalitarian in nature, show their respect for others of their kind.

Father Charmoise, *Dragons' Tales*

Errol had little time to reflect on his strange encounter with Inquisitor Melyn in the weeks that passed. Confined once more to his vast empty dormitory and the endless, lightless vaults of the library archives, the whole episode began to take on the same dreamlike quality of most of his existence.

Andro kept him busy in a room whose walls were lined

from ceiling to floor with racks containing rolled-up parchments. Each of these had to be taken out, carefully unrolled and scanned to see what its contents were. Errol would make a note in a large leather-bound volume, assign the parchment a temporary reference number and return it to its place on the rack. The room was not large in comparison to some of the great spaces down in the depths of the monastery, but even so Errol had estimated the number of parchments in the room at several thousand. On a good day he might manage a couple of hundred, if their subjects were not so dry as to be unintelligible or so interesting as to absorb him for hours.

There did not seem to be any pattern to the parchments save that they were unbound and all about the same size when rolled. There were sets of accounts for the royal household dating back several centuries, minutes of meetings of the inquisitors, seneschals and archimandrites of the three religious orders, ornately scribed deeds of title to obscure tracts of land, field reports of hunting parties. One series of ten parchments detailed an expedition carried out some five hundred years earlier in search of the fabled Cenobus, seat of Magog, Son of the Summer Moon. From what Errol could piece together, this great beast of a dragon had lived thousands of years earlier still, and was the scourge of men until brave King Diseverin, the first King Diseverin, had slain him in an epic battle that had lasted days and shaken the earth. Fable had long held that the dragon had lived in a vast castle in the depths of the forest of the Ffrydd, where great treasures were hoarded, lying undiscovered to this day.

Something about the tale struck a chord with Errol.

The theme was familiar, as if he had heard it before but told differently. The account given in the parchments didn't seem right but the details were slippery in his mind. Whatever the truth of the matter, the expedition had been an unmitigated disaster. Led by Prince Lonk, heir to the Obsidian Throne, it had been one misadventure after another, culminating in the party splitting into two, the prince heading on into the deep forest with most of the dwindling supplies and two warrior priests as guardians, leaving the rest to make their way back to Emmass Fawr. The writer of the report, one Father Keoldale, had been the only survivor of that band, discovered near death by a roving patrol as he tried to navigate the treacherous ridges of the Rim mountains. Of Prince Lonk and his companions there had never been any sign.

Errol knew from his history lessons that the disappearance of the only direct heir to the throne had plunged the Twin Kingdoms and the House of Balwen into the terrible events of the Brumal Wars. Had it not been for the bravery of Prince, later King, Torwen the Twin Kingdoms might still be at war, or worse under the control of the Llanwennogs. At least that was how the story had been told to him before. Now he could read the account of how that dark time had begun, first hand, from the quill of the only man to survive the expedition.

Errol was still reading the account of the fateful expedition when Andro came into the room some hours later. Guiltily he looked across at the clean, empty pages of the reckoning book and the pile of parchments gathered around the reading desk.

'Let me guess,' the old man said, smiling. 'Father Keoldale's account of Prince Lonk's search for Cenobus.'

'How did you . . . ?' Errol asked, but Andro merely waved him silent.

'It's no sin to be curious, Errol,' he said. 'And of all the fascinating tales waiting to be discovered in this room, that one at least holds some historical relevance. There are lessons to be learned from it. The folly of pursuing impossible dreams when there's much to recommend the life you already have, for instance.'

'I don't understand,' Errol said.

'Lonk was heir to the throne,' Andro said. 'The Twin Kingdoms were experiencing a period of peace and prosperity such as they never had before. We even had a sketchy peace with Llanwennog. Our merchants travelled the world, dealing in the most exotic of goods. It was the time when Candlehall grew from a small citadel around the Neuadd into the great metropolis that it is today. Prince Lonk stood to inherit that, but instead he chose to follow a madman's words on a fool's quest. And his father let him. It was perhaps no bad thing that Weddelm's line ended there. It was a weak-willed and idiot branch of the House of Balwen.

'But I didn't come here to give you a history lesson, Errol. It's late and you should be getting your rest.'

Was it late? Errol didn't feel tired. His head was filled with Father Keoldale's words: his account of the terrible journey through the great forest of the Ffrydd and the weird creatures they had encountered on their way. It seemed like only a few hours since he had begun the day's work. Still, if Andro told him it was time to go, he would have to go.

Scooping up the scrolls, Errol placed them in the rack on the side of his desk, ready for archiving the next day. He extinguished the covered lamps that had been his daylight and followed the old man out of the room.

'How did you know what I was reading?' he asked as they walked the long dark corridors of the library archive, the only light coming from Andro's covered lantern, its glow revealing row upon row of dark-spined books in black-oak shelves.

'I remember the first time I came across that parchment myself,' the old man said. 'Back when I was a novitiate, oh, too many years ago to even think about.'

'You've already archived that room?' Errol asked, astonished that he could have spent the uncounted days of his labour on a task already completed.

'Oh don't look so shocked, Errol,' Andro said. 'Archiving is not something done once and then finished with. It's endless. Many years have passed since I last sorted that room. Parchments have been taken out and returned to the wrong stacks or not returned at all. New scrolls have been added and some things just put there because whichever librarian was on duty that day couldn't be bothered walking any further. Time has a habit of making chaos from the most perfect order. You'd do well to remember that.'

They had reached the refectory and Errol noticed it was unusually empty. Was it really so late that all the other librarians had eaten already? It was so hard to keep track of time down in the depths of the great monastery, away from the sun and the true passing of the days.

'I have to leave you now,' Andro said. 'Inquisitor Melyn has need of my services. Don't tarry long, Errol. Tomorrow will be a long day and it will begin earlier than you're accustomed to.' Smiling as if at some inner joke, the old man hung his lantern on the hook by the door that led to Errol's lonely dormitory and then left the room.

Errol grabbed himself some bread and cheese from the store cupboard, wishing that there were some stew in the pot by the fire. Empty, the refectory was a depressing lightless place and he had no great desire to sit there eating on his own. Part of him was tempted to take the lantern and return to the room. There were still several parchments of Father Keoldale's account to read, but he knew that he would be in trouble if he were found out. Reluctantly he took up his meagre meal, lifted the lantern off the hook and made his way along the corridor towards his bed.

It felt different even before he reached the dormitory door. Over time he had grown used to the quiet presence of the other librarians, forgetting the sense he had previously relied on to tell him when others were nearby. The monastery was full of people, four thousand or more, he had heard tell. But there was something at once familiar and foreign that made Errol pause before stepping into the dark room.

It happened in a whirling instant. Someone snatched the lantern from his hands, knocking the food to the floor. Someone else grabbed his arms, pulling them up sharply behind his back. A heavy cloth sack dropped over his head. The smell of earth and raw potatoes filled his nose as a rope was swiftly wound around his middle, pinning his arms. Hands too numerous to count pushed and jabbed at him, spinning him round and round until he lost all sense of direction. He stumbled; something caught his foot and he fell headlong into darkness, but before he hit the stone floor, the hands caught him, lifting him up into the air as if he weighed nothing at all. However many people were tormenting him, they were silent, their purpose united. Errol was helpless, trapped and terrified as he was born along, out of his lonely dormitory and away to whatever fate awaited.

Flurries of winter rain lashed across the clearing, carried by the cold northerly wind that had been blowing for a week now. Benfro looked out of the window from his seat near the fire and shuddered. It wasn't that the cold and wet chilled him, just that they made the day seem so miserable. He had hoped for sunshine and even the first snowdrops of spring appearing under the still-leafless trees. Perhaps to be able to go outside without getting his feet covered in mud. This was, after all, his special day. Today he was fourteen years old.

'Come now, Benfro. It's time to leave. You don't want to be late for your own party.' Morgwm opened the door, an oiled-leather bag slung over one shoulder. Benfro stood up, placed the heavy grating in front of the banked-up coals and followed her outside.

A brief lull in the rain saw them across the clearing and up the track towards the village. Heads down against the wind, it was difficult to hold much of a conversation, but as they neared the spot where Errol had met Frecknock so many months before, where she had cast her terrible spell on him, he stopped in his tracks.

'What is it?' His mother asked.

'I . . . I can't say,' Benfro said, the compulsion as strong as ever. It was a constant niggle in the back of his mind now, a worry that made it increasingly hard for him to concentrate on his studies. At times he even found it hard to remember where certain herbs and potions were stored. Whenever he tried to conjure up his mental image of the storeroom, instead all he could see was those pink fleshy hands reaching for that silver goblet.

'Well don't dawdle now, Benfro,' Morgwm said. 'The others will all be waiting.'

'Frecknock won't,' Benfro said.

'What? Of course she will,' Morgwm said. 'Frecknock may not like you very much, but she would never miss a feast.'

'She won't be there,' Benfro said again. There was a lot more he wanted to say, about how he knew where Frecknock would be and what she would be doing, but it would not come out. Even saying her name gave him a dull ache at the back of his head.

'Well, never mind. It's rude to keep your guests waiting, even on your hatchday.'

They trudged on through the constant wind and occasional showers, reaching the village in companionable silence. There was no one about, the assorted houses appearing dead and empty. A shiver ran down Benfro's spine as if he were seeing a terrible portent – his home, his world stripped of life. For an instant, in his mind he saw the whole village blackened and charred, smoke lofting lazily from the wrecked homes and climbing into a hazy blue sky.

'What is it, Benfro? You look like you've seen a ghost.'

Morgwm's voice snapped him back into himself. Benfro looked at his mother's smiling face and felt the reassurance of her presence, her open unquestioning love for him. Despite the cold wet winter afternoon, the terrible premonition and the constant niggling hurt of what Frecknock had done to him, he was cheered by her presence and her strength.

'It's nothing,' he said. 'Just this moon-cursed rain and mud.'

'Come on then,' Morgwm said. 'Let's get inside. Ynys Môn will have built up the fire by now.'

They strode on and were soon crossing the wet grass of the green towards the great hall. A plume of smoke rose out of its chimney like a signal, and the gusting wind brought splendid aromas to Benfro's nose. His stomach rumbled in anticipation.

The doors were closed as they approached them, which surprised Benfro, though he supposed it was just to keep the rain and wind out. He stood in front of the great oak slabs, took hold of the heavy iron handles and pushed.

The doors were locked.

Confused, Benfro turned to ask his mother what was going on.

She wasn't there.

'Mother?' he asked the wind, looking from side to side. There was nowhere she could hide and there hadn't been time for her to have gone round the building. Besides, she had been at his side – he had felt her presence as surely as he knew his own wings. And then she had just gone.

A chilling sense of fear and loneliness gripped him as he stood in the cold staring at the barred doors and the blank-faced cottages clustered around the green. With only the wind's low moaning song for company it felt like the whole world had deserted him. He was truly alone, a tiny speck in the vastness of all. For a moment it overwhelmed him completely. He was as paralysed as if he were made of stone, helpless and terrified. Then the swirling wind changed direction once more, bringing the aroma of cooking to his nose. Faint sounds escaped from behind the great shuttered windows, and the spell was broken. This was some kind of test, he realized. Some strange ceremony that no doubt would give the villagers something to laugh about as the afternoon turned to evening and the party got into full swing.

He considered walking around the building to the back, where the kitchens were, and trying the small door there. He could imagine all the old dragons clustered around the front doors waiting for him. It would be a great jest to creep up behind them and give them a surprise. On the other hand, this did not seem like one of Meirionydd's jokes, and he couldn't remember a time when his mother had done such a thing to him. He knew that the dragons were inside the great hall – he could sense them. There was nothing to be gained from standing out in the cold and the rain. Benfro lifted his hand and rapped hard on the oak doors.

'Who goes without?' came Sir Frynwy's unmistakable voice in all its storytelling grandeur.

'It's Benfro,' Benfro said, tiring of the game before it had even started. 'Let me in, please. It's wet out here.'

'What brings you to our hall, Benfro?' Sir Frynwy asked, his tone still serious and filled with pomp.

'It's my hatchday. I'm fourteen today,' Benfro said, then added under his breath, 'There's supposed to be a feast.'

'Fourteen, you say,' Sir Frynwy said. 'And under what sign were you hatched, Benfro?'

'You know as well as I do, Sir Frynwy. I was born at the Confluence, when the Wolf Running was in the House of Northern Cross.'

'A hatchling of the Confluence?' Sir Frynwy said, his voice booming through the old wood. 'And what would you take from us, Benfro?'

'Take from you? Nothing. Well, some food, I suppose, and perhaps a story?'

'A story?' Sir Frynwy said. 'That is no small thing to ask. What would you give us in return?'

'I don't know.' Benfro was beginning to feel anxious. This exchange seemed like some kind of formal cere-mony, at least on Sir Frynwy's part, but Morgwm had not told him there would be anything like this. There never had been on his hatchday in the past.

'Would you give us your respect?' Sir Frynwy asked.

'Of course,' Benfro said. 'You already have that.'

'Indeed? Would you give us your trust?'

For a moment Benfro had to consider. There was one of the villagers that he would not trust as far as the end of his tail, but he was certain that she was not inside the hall.

'Yes, again. I have always trusted you,' he said.

'Hmm. Would you give us your loyalty?' Sir Frynwy asked.

Benfro could begin to see where this was going. 'Always.'

'And would you give us your love?' The old dragon asked, flinging open the doors. He stood there staring down at Benfro with a curious expression on his face. Behind him the others clustered round.

'I can't give you what you already have,' Benfro said. 'But I wouldn't seek to steal it from you, either.'

Sir Frynwy's solemn face broke into a wide grin. 'Spoken like a true dragon, Benfro,' he said. 'Welcome.'

As Benfro stepped into the familiar hall he felt almost as if he were a stranger newly arrived. Ynys Môn produced a basin of warm water for him to wash his feet in.

'Welcome to our village, Benfro. May your feet never forget its soil,' he said.

Sir Frynwy handed him a heavy leather-bound book.

Benfro opened it to reveal page after empty page of finest-quality vellum.

'Welcome to our family, Benfro. May your life with us fill this book and many more.'

Meirionydd placed a long scarf of fine material around his neck. It was soft to the touch and shimmered in the light from the candelabra. She wound it twice over his head so that the ends did not reach the floor, then she kissed him loudly on each cheek, twice, much to his embarrassment.

'Welcome to our hall, Benfro,' she said. 'May you find warmth and shelter in it whenever the need arises.'

One by one the others presented him with gifts, each with a tie to the village and the dragons who lived within it. Finally his mother stood before him, empty-handed.

'Welcome to Gwlad, Sir Benfro,' she said, and Benfro couldn't help noticing the stir of surprise that murmured around the room. 'May it be a kinder world for you and your heirs.' Then she wrapped him in a fierce hug.

After that the formalities seemed to be over and everyone began to chat while plate after groaning plate of food was brought from the kitchens and laid out on the long table in the middle of the hall.

Sir Frynwy made his way across the room to where Benfro stood surrounded by a small mountain of gifts.

'Well, Sir Benfro,' the old dragon said. 'It looks like I have a rival.'

'What do you mean?' Benfro asked.

'Sir Benfro,' Sir Frynwy said, making a mock bow. 'It's not often a dragon so young is granted such a title.'

'But it's just a word, isn't it?' Benfro knew as soon as he spoke that he had made a mistake.

'Just a word? Indeed, I think not,' Sir Frynwy said. 'Do you think I insist upon my title out of some vanity?'

'No, of course not. But . . . well . . . I thought mother was just making a gesture.'

'Of course she was making a gesture, young dragon. She was giving you the greatest honour she could bestow. In front of our entire community she recognized you as the head of your family. It's not an easy thing for her to do, to accept that your father has truly gone.'

'My father? What's he got to do with it?' Benfro asked.

'Sir Trefaldwyn should be the head of your family,' Sir Frynwy said. 'In giving you his title, Morgwm has announced publicly that she no longer believes he will return.'

Benfro looked round at his mother, who was chatting

with Meirionydd at the head of the table. She didn't look any different to the dragon who had woken him early that morning and set him to his chores. He doubted that he would have any more say in how the house was run than ever he had. And yet she had given him something beyond price, he realized. She had given him a measure of responsibility that only an adult should have. It made him feel twice as tall as the cold wet dragon who had stepped through the doorway only minutes beforehand.

'Now, if my hearing's not playing tricks on me,' Sir Frynwy said, a mischievous twinkle in his old eyes, 'you mentioned something about a feast?'

Benfro let himself be led through the waiting dragons to the head of the table. For a moment he had been about to take his customary seat on the floor near the fire, but Sir Frynwy steered him towards the large chair that the old bard normally took for himself.

'Today is your fourteenth hatchday, Sir Benfro,' he said, a gentle mocking in his voice. 'The head of the table is yours. And from this day onwards you'll join us as an equal. It's to be hoped we don't have to wait so long until there's another kitling underfoot.'

Benfro sat in the great carved chair gingerly, as if some elaborate joke might be played on him. But no explosions or other loud noises accompanied his rest and gradually he relaxed into the unusual place. The rest of the villagers had taken their normal places along the benches, with Sir Frynwy squeezing on the end to Benfro's right, and his mother, who rarely attended the village feasts, sitting to his left. The whole table was laid with food, but nobody was eating. Instead all eyes were on him. Then he remembered that Sir Frynwy always said something before each meal. He tried to remember the words.

'Great Rasalene, whose spirit watches over us in the night. Pure Arhelion, who lights our path through the days. Encourage us in our loyalty. Honour us in our truth. Upbraid us in our arrogance. Deflate us in our pride. You have left Gwlad for your children, may we keep it a place fit and ready for your return.'

The murmur of assent that went round the table was perhaps not as fulsome as it might have been. Benfro was painfully aware that he did not have Sir Frynwy's bard's voice, nor could he command a fraction of his gravitas.

Nevertheless, the old dragon leaned towards him and spoke in a conspiratorial whisper that still managed to carry to all in the room: 'I really am going to have to watch my back, Sir Benfro.'

Ynys Môn let out a great barking laugh and he was soon joined by the others. The ceremony was over and now it was time to eat.

Terror gripped Errol as he was bundled along corridors and up stairs. Shrouded in the potato sack he could see nothing, but he could feel the many hands that held him up, hear the hushed breathing of his captors. He wasn't sure, but he thought that there were at least twelve of them, and something he couldn't quite pin down gave him the impression that they were young, novitiates perhaps. It could have been the barely controlled excitement that ran between them, or maybe the inexpert way they carried him, banging his arms, legs and occasionally his head against walls, doors and anything else that got in the way.

Despite the clammy fear that made his heart race and his breath come in ragged gasps, a part of him remained detached, observing almost as if he floated above the scene. He could see a band of youthful novitiates in their dark brown cassocks carrying a smaller figure draped in an old cloth sack and bound with a short length of cord doubtless borrowed from a curtain somewhere. He noticed that their route was tortuous, twisting first one way then another, but always heading up and roughly in the same direction. Errol did not know which way his dormitory faced, since it had no windows, but he was fairly sure that he was heading north.

The journey seemed to go on for hours, and with time the feeling of being disconnected from himself grew, diminishing the fear. It seemed unlikely that these novitiates meant him any great harm or they would have done it already. This was surely some prank, some initiation ceremony for one of their number. He tried to remember what Father Castlemilk's book had said about the first years of being a novitiate, but it had touched only lightly on the day-to-day reality of the great monastery, focusing instead on the various stages of learning that needed to be mastered before one could become a warrior priest.

From his detached vantage point Errol watched as the group came out into the open, stepping into a courtyard walled in on three sides by tall buildings but open on the fourth. It was dark, but the first hint of dawn was making flat patterns out of the mountains, tingeing their edges with the merest hint of pink. The sight sent a thrill through him that nearly snapped him back into his body. If he could just stay this way a moment longer he would see the sunlight for the first time in ... how long? He couldn't tell.

The group of novitiates carried him across the court-yard towards where it opened on to the mountain vista. With each second the light grew, showing more of the view east towards the rising sun. For a moment true terror ran through him as Errol thought he might be cast over the edge and into a black void, but as the group came closer to the edge, they slowed down, then stopped some ten feet short. Still curiously outside his body, Errol watched as he was carelessly dropped to the ground, not-ing almost as an afterthought that he was winded by the fall. Then rough hands once more grasped him by the arms and hauled him to his feet.

One of the group stepped away, closer to the edge. His hood was up over his head, but something about the way he moved was familiar to Errol. He seemed to be watch-ing the horizon, though his eyes darted back and forth between the three great buildings that overlooked them as if he feared being seen. No longer held aloft by many hands, Errol could feel the weight of the earth supporting him, smell the dirt in the potato sack. The bruises of his many bumps against corridor walls and door jambs began to drag him away from his flying freedom and back into his body, so that as the light gradually grew, he slipped more and more into the semi-darkness of his rough hes-sian hood.

'Is it time yet?' one of the novitiates asked, and Errol found that he was once more completely himself.

'Nearly.' The voice was hauntingly familiar. A rush of memories burst through the dull drudgery of Errol's existence in the library archives. He saw trees in the day-light, fields of newly cut corn stacked into castles for small boys to battle over, a great rock jutting out over a river, a cottage in a small clearing in the woods, a young woman, scarcely more than a girl, dressed in a long green riding cloak, its hood pulled up to obscure her face.

'Now,' the voice said, and Errol recognized his step-brother Clun. An instant later the ropes were untied from his middle, the sack pulled off his head, and he stood blinking and staring into the rising sun.

It was magnificent. The sun painted an orange strip on the snow-capped ridge of mountains so distant he could not focus properly on them. To a boy who had never seen anything more than a mile or so away, it was an impos-sible, dreamlike thing, but more so was the great expanse that spread out from where he stood, reaching across that vastness from a dark point so far below him it made his stomach clench just to look at it. Errol had read about the forest of the Ffrydd in countless books, had even seen maps of it drawn on old parchment. He had lived all his short life on its southernmost fringes, where the trees burst through the Graith Fawr, that cataclysmic rift in the Rim mountains, like a wave crashing through a mud dam. Yet nothing could have prepared him for that first glimpse of its enormous, splendid beauty.

'Happy birthday, Errol,' Clun said. 'Andro said you might enjoy this. Now let's get out of here before one of the quaisters sees us.'

18

King Brynceri settled his capital on the hill overlooking the middle reaches of the River Abheinn at the centre of the Twin Kingdoms. In his lifetime he built the great hall of the Neuadd and began work on the surrounding palace and fortifications. He also built his personal chapel, away from the hubbub of palace life, and it was to here that he increasingly retreated in his latter years, the better to converse with his lord, the Shepherd. Nestling against the great wall that surrounds the citadel, the chapel is small in comparison to the splendour of the Neuadd, but it is a masterpiece of the mason's art, exquisitely carved with reliefs depicting the first times, when the Shepherd walked among his flock and gave the gift of magic to King Balwen.

When Brynceri finally died, it was his wish that he be interred within the defensive wall that towered over his chapel. Since then, all rulers of the Twin Kingdoms have been placed in alcoves within this, the Wall of Kings.

Barrod Sheepshead,
A History of the House of Balwen

After his mother's solemn gift and Sir Frynwy's ceding of the top seat, all the other dragons of the village treated Benfro like a hero of the old times. One by one they addressed him with kind words and predictions of a long and prosperous life, rounding off each declaration with a toast to Sir Benfro. The only disappointment was that while the villagers all drank wine from a large wooden cask that sat at in the far corner of the hall, he was allowed only one goblet of the thick red liquor, heavily diluted. Once that was finished there was only water. He had complained of course, but Sir Benfro or no, his mother's all-too-familiar look of reproach soon silenced his protests.

Sir Benfro. The name sounded so important and yet so insignificant. For a while, as they ate and talked and laughed, Benfro considered why he felt no different. Then he remembered the old man, Gideon, with his strangely formal speech. Gideon had called him Sir Benfro, and at the time he had thought it no more than a simple error on his part, a result of his poor grasp of dragon speech. But it hadn't been his mother who had first addressed him as Sir Benfro, and for some inexplicable reason that mattered to him. Even the enthusiastic recognition of the villagers didn't make it seem real.

Perhaps it was because he had never known his father, never known very much about him even. It was difficult to consider himself head of the family when his mother had hardly acknowledged the existence of Sir Trefaldwyn in fourteen years.

'Why the long face?' Meirionydd asked, her quiet voice breaking through Benfro's thoughts.

'Oh, nothing,' Benfro said, then remembered that there was little point lying to Meirionydd. 'I was just thinking about my father.'

'He would have liked to be here,' Meirionydd said. 'He'd have done everything in his power to be at his son's fourteenth hatchday. I suspect his absence is as much a reason as any why your mother gave you the gift she did.'

'Why did he leave us?' Benfro asked. 'Didn't he love my mother?'

'Ah, Benfro, don't ever say that. Don't even think it.' Meirionydd moved closer to his seat. 'Your mother and father loved each other so completely it was impossible to tell where one ended and the other began. They were soulmates, destined to be together for ever. Sir Trefaldwyn's decision to leave, to set out on his mad quest, was not taken on his own. It was a thing they did together.'

'Mad quest?' Benfro asked.

'Dear me, this Fo Afron wine loosens even the tightest of tongues,' Meirionydd said. 'It's not my place to tell you such things.'

Benfro felt his anger beginning to rise. Once more he was to be treated as a kit, despite all the gifts and toasts. Meirionydd, ever insightful, saw his mood changing and spoke quickly to head it off.

'Don't be angry Benfro,' she said. 'It's true you should be told about your father, but it's not for me to do that. You must ask your mother. I'm sure she'll tell you now. Won't you, Morgwm?'

Meirionydd turned to face Benfro's mother, but she was looking the other way, scanning the crowd of faces.

When finally she turned at Meirionydd's nudge, Benfro could see concern writ large across her face.

'Where is she?' Morgwm asked, not waiting to see what it was Meirionydd wanted. 'Where's Frecknock?'

'She was here earlier. Why?' Meirionydd said.

'I couldn't remember seeing her. Did she present you with anything, Benfro?'

Benfro racked his memory, seeing all the faces of the villagers as they had given him their presents. He couldn't remember seeing Frecknock among them. Nor could he imagine her giving him anything he would want to keep.

'No,' he said. 'I don't think so. I told you she wouldn't be here.'

'You did?' Meirionydd asked. 'Why?'

Benfro couldn't say why. He knew the reason perfectly well – she had used the celebration as a cover for her actions – but he found it impossible to voice the thought.

'She doesn't like me much,' he said.

'She doesn't like you at all, Benfro,' Meirionydd said. 'But that's no reason to miss an important gathering. At least she should have had the courtesy to tell someone. Did she, Sir Frynwy?'

'Eh? What?' The old dragon had been deep in conversation with Ynys Byr, but now he turned to face Morgwm and Meirionydd across the platter-strewn table. Benfro watched on, hopeful that someone might notice his plight.

'Did Frecknock tell you she would not be here?' Meirionydd repeated the question.

'She was here first thing this morning,' Sir Frynwy said. 'Then she asked if she might be excused. I thought she meant to come back before the party started. I haven't seen her since. Is she not here?'

'No,' Morgwm said. 'And she wasn't here when we arrived either.'

'Well, she's young. And we all know how she feels about Benfro,' the old dragon said, turning to face Benfro in his seat. 'I'm afraid you stole Frecknock's place as the kitling of the village. Before you hatched she was rather spoiled by us all. She'll get over it in time. I suspect she's sitting at home. Perhaps I'll just head over there and try to persuade her to join us.' And so saying, Sir Frynwy slid off the end of the bench, bowed politely to Benfro at the head of the table and left the hall.

'How did you know she wouldn't be here?' Morgwm said to Benfro after the heavy door had swung shut on the clearing afternoon sky.

'I . . . I just knew she wouldn't,' Benfro said, his thoughts battering against the barrier that prevented him from telling the truth.

'Does it matter that she's not here?' Meirionydd asked, the expression on her face not unlike the one she wore when daring him to do something that would probably get him into trouble. As far as his hatchday celebrations were concerned, Benfro couldn't have cared less whether or not Frecknock was there, though if pressed for an answer he would have said he preferred her absence. But he also knew what that absence meant and what terrible danger it could bring down on them all.

'I can't say,' he said, knowing it sounded odd and hoping Meirionydd would pick up on that.

'You can't say or won't say?' she asked, staring deeply into his eyes.

'I can't say,' Benfro said, holding that stare without blinking.

'Do you know why she's not here?' Meirionydd asked. There were many reasons, Benfro knew, but only one that he couldn't talk about.

'I can't say,' he said again, trying to emphasize the negative. Meirionydd looked at him more closely still, those piercing gold-flecked eyes seeming to grow around him.

'Benfro dear, are you all right?' Her voice was in his head, enveloping him, banishing the sounds of the party so that he felt like he stood in a sun-filled clearing in the woods with nothing but the wind for company. Even as he thought about it, the scene materialized around him. He didn't recognize the clearing, but it was a peaceful place and he was content to just sit and gaze at the blue sky, the soaring birds and the gently swaying treetops.

'She's put a glamour on you, Benfro,' Meirionydd said. Benfro looked round to see her standing beside him. Only she was different somehow. The Meirionydd he knew was old, her scales chipped and dulled with the years, her face lined from centuries of smiling. She carried herself as if her joints ached continually, stooping like the weight of the entire world pressed down upon her shoulders. The dragon who stood beside him was undoubtedly Meirionydd, but she was young and beautiful.

'Meirionydd?' Benfro said, trying not to stare.

'Ah, dear me, yes,' Meirionydd said, seeming as surprised as Benfro. 'This is not quite how I intended to appear to you. How strange that you should see me like this, and in this place. But never mind. It's something we can talk about another time. Now you must tell me all about Frecknock.'

'But I can't speak about it,' Benfro said. 'She did something to me so that I couldn't say it.' Only after he had finished speaking did he realize that he had voiced the words and she had heard.

'It's a crude working, really,' Meirionydd said. 'Otherwise you wouldn't even be able to think about it. I'll undo the damage when I can, but for now I think time is of the essence. So tell me what dreadful secret Frecknock would have you keep.'

'She took the *Llyfr Draconius*,' Benfro said, and as he told his story, the terrible sense of frustration burst out like water from a makeshift dam kicked over at the end of a day's play. When he had finished he felt as if a great burden had been lifted from him, almost as if he floated in the air.

'We've been blind and stupid, all of us,' Meirionydd said. 'Frecknock's young and headstrong. We thought to teach her about the world around her and the subtle arts so that she might come to appreciate the life we live, to share it with us. We never thought she might want more, but it's only natural that she should seek a mate.'

'But this Sir Felyn, I think he's a man,' Benfro said. 'I saw his hands. He reached for a goblet of wine. They were just like Gideon's.'

'Slow down, Benfro,' Meirionydd said, frowning. 'What do you mean you saw his hands?'

Benfro wanted to gabble. It was such a relief to be able to speak his mind that the words jumbled in their eagerness to spill out. Taking a deep breath, he tried to calm himself and explain fully what he had seen. Meirionydd's beautiful young face grew longer as he neared the end of his telling, and when finally he fell silent she too remained quiet for long moments. Then she seemed to come to some decision.

'There's much you've told me that shouldn't be possible, Benfro,' she said. 'Even I've never managed to travel the lines and see through another's eyes without their knowledge. Still, Morgwm's told me about your flying dreams, so I have to accept that you've unique talents.

'No, don't get full of yourself, young dragonling,' she added. 'There'll be time to look into your unusual skills later. Right now Frecknock must be our priority. I don't doubt that your assumptions are correct about this stranger. The only Sir Felyn I ever knew was a weak-willed dragon who died at the hands of the warrior priests over five hundred years ago. There aren't many of our kind out in the world beyond this forest. It's not been safe for dragons for millennia. Far more likely that a skilled adept of the High Ffrydd has duped her.'

'Gideon mentioned an Inquisitor Melyn,' Benfro said. 'Could it be him?'

'If it is we're in grave danger indeed,' Meirionydd said. 'Melyn is the worst kind of man there is. Pray to the moon that you never meet him. Do everything you can to avoid him. Now come. We must return to the party before anyone notices.'

Benfro was about to ask how he could get back to the party when he had never left, but Meirionydd turned back to him as if she had suddenly thought of something.

'Benfro,' she said. 'I would never put a compulsion on you, that's a bad thing that can only rebound on whoever practises it, but I'd be grateful if you didn't tell your mother about this place. She might not like knowing that I still carry it around with me.'

'What do you mean?' Benfro asked.

'This is where I first met your father,' Meirionydd said with something like melancholy in her voice. 'He was magnificent, Sir Trefaldwyn. Did you know that he could fly? After a fashion, at least. Dragons could never truly fly – that's just a myth – but his wings were so large he used to leap from the tallest trees and glide to the ground. And he would tell me stories, like Sir Frynwy's only more vivid, more real, as if he had really been there. Sometimes when he spoke of Gog and Magog it was as if he had actually met them, as if they had truly existed.'

'But he was my father,' Benfro said, confused. 'Morgwm's my mother . . .'

'Trefaldwyn only ever had eyes for Morgwm,' Meirionydd said. 'That much was apparent from the moment they met. But I loved him in my own way, even though I knew it was hopeless.'

'Don't you hate her for it? My mother?' Benfro asked.

'Hate her? Quite the opposite, Benfro dear. Morgwm's my closest friend. She was before Trefaldwyn came along and she remained so even when they were joined. Ever since he left on his mad quest I've felt her sadness each day. But I wouldn't want her to think that I held this place special. It's my burden and I never meant for you to come here, but obviously there's more of your father in you than any of us realized. So let's keep it our little secret.'

'Of course,' Benfro said, trying to absorb all that he had seen and heard. But even as he committed the clearing to his memory and gazed once more on Meirionydd's youthful beauty, he could feel it slipping away. She seemed almost to age in front of his eyes. The wind in the trees became the murmuring of a dozen conversations and somewhere his mother was calling his name.

'Benfro? Benfro? Are you all right, Benfro?' He snapped awake, if he had truly been asleep, to find himself still staring at Meirionydd. The old dragon turned to his mother.

'Benfro's fine, Morgwm,' she said. 'But we have to find Frecknock. I need to speak to her before she endangers us all.'

As if in response, the doors opened and Sir Frynwy stepped back inside. He hurried to the table and slid himself back on to the bench.

'She's not at home,' he said, a look of terrible worry frowning across his old face, 'and someone's taken the *Llyfr Draconius* from my study.'

Beulah sat impatiently in her chair as maidservants adjusted her gown and did unnecessary things with her hair. She hated all the pampering and preening, the need for ridiculous costumes, the whole ceremony. She would much rather be out in the field, planning her next move or stamping her authority on the Twin Kingdoms. But she needed the people behind her, and the people loved all the pomp and show.

Candlehall was at a virtual standstill. There wasn't a bed or floor to be begged. Even the staff in the palace of the

Neuadd were having to double up, their rooms given over to the minor nobles who suddenly appeared like flies around the decaying body of the old king.

It had been building for weeks now: first the preparation of the king's body and the lying in state, the black of mourning and tiresome rituals that had kept her locked up in the palace. Then the presentation of the noble houses, in order of precedence, each pledging their allegiance to the Obsidian Throne while trying to garner favour and reduce their tithes at the same time. Beulah had been grateful for the help of Seneschal Padraig during that time. The old man might have been working desperately to retain his power base within the palace, but Beulah was wise enough to know that she needed him, at least in the short term. Now there was just this day to get out of the way – the funeral followed by her coronation. Then she could throw off the fripperies of court convention and set about building the Twin Kingdoms into the power it should be.

'Ow! Enough. Get out, all of you. Leave me alone.' Beulah winced as a comb caught in her hair. The maids rushed to finish off her dress before scuttling out of the room like frightened crabs, bobbing and curtsying to her back. She watched them go in the tall mirror, then studied her reflection.

Give them their due, they had done a good job. Beulah almost didn't recognize herself. Her face had been dusted white, though close up her band of freckles still showed through the chalk. Her hair, normally tied in a single ponytail, had been washed in exotic oils, the tangles teased out and then styled in the current vogue. It felt wonderfully clean if impractical, bunched up on either side of her head like two great buns. The oils had softened its normal dark brown colour into a deep red, matching the gown she would wear to the funeral. Any clothes that required the help of two or three people to get on were a complete nonsense, as far as she was concerned. This gown was even worse, using wire in places to make her seem busty where she was not, and to hide her musculature. It was not how she liked to be seen, nor how she liked to see herself, but Beulah understood the need for the show. For the time being at least she was a figurehead, and pressure was already mounting for her to choose a consort. To produce an heir. Well, she would let old Padraig think he was in control for now, and she wasn't above having the odd dalliance with some of the sons of the noble houses. They would learn soon enough that she was made of stronger stuff than her father.

'Your Majesty, you look ridiculous.' Inquisitor Melyn stepped into the room, dressed in his usual dark brown robes. Beulah cursed him silently for the privilege of his order. The warrior priests of the High Ffrydd only ever wore simple garments, unlike Seneschal Padraig and Archimandrite Cassters, who would no doubt be trying to outdo each other with their raiments today.

'I quite agree, Melyn,' Beulah said, turning to talk to the man rather than his reflection. 'But it's something I will bear. Just for this day. Is it time yet?'

'I came to fetch you, my lady,' Melyn said. 'Your carriage awaits.'

'Carriage! I haven't ridden in a carriage since I was three. Why can't I ride?'

'In that gown?' Melyn asked as Beulah struggled across the floor cursing the high-heeled slippers some genius had designed for her. She longed for her soft leather trousers and well-fitting boots. Even the outfit she had worn to her birthday party would have been better than this, if a little inappropriate.

'This won't be over a moment too soon,' Beulah said, allowing the inquisitor to take her arm and leaning on it perhaps more heavily than she would have liked as she fought for balance.

'Patience, my lady,' Melyn said. 'Your time will come soon.'

The carriage took them across the palace complex to the Neuadd, where the king lay in state in front of the Obsidian Throne. Beulah was secretly grateful for the coach, though it would normally have been no more than a ten-minute walk.

King Diseverin looked healthier in death than ever he had in life, a testament to the undertaker's art. His face was pale pink rather then bloodshot, his eyes closed. Washed and prepared with the arcane skill of the preservers, ironically he no longer smelled like a rotting carcass in the middle of a vineyard. The funeral robes in which he had been dressed were new, expensively cut and bore no stains of food and drink that had missed their target.

Beulah sat on a small throne alongside the empty black chair as each of the leaders of the three orders gave his eulogy. Then she followed the bier as it was carried out of the Neuadd and loaded on to a magnificent hearse pulled by six white chargers. The cortège proceeded at a snail's pace through the main streets of Candlehall in an ever widening spiral. To each side the crowd stood silent, most heads bowed. Everyone wore the deep red of mourning so that it looked as if someone had sliced the throat of the city and now it bled thick venous blood.

After what seemed like hours they reached the chapel of Brynceri, nestling by the city walls. The bier was carried inside and Beulah followed her father on his last journey. The chapel was small, with barely enough room for the most senior members of the orders and a few of the oldest nobles. More eulogies were said, the same old trite half-truths and exaggerations. Beulah wanted to shout at them to get on with it, or at least to tell the truth – that her father had been a weak and useless king, that he had allowed his own wife to die and had sent his youngest daughter to the castle of his sworn enemy when she was only six. Instead she bit her lip and held her peace. Time was on her side. She could afford to wait.

Finally the king was placed in an alcove in the city wall alongside the hundreds of other kings and queens of the House of Balwen. Beulah watched as the masons bricked up the hole, wondering why her mother's body had been laid in a simple grave in the chapel grounds. She had been queen and surely ought to have had a place in the wall. Earlier kings had made arrangements for their dead wives to be buried with them, but Diseverin had somehow forgotten. Yet another notch on the tally of why she hated him. Perhaps it was tactless, maybe it even shocked a few of the elder statesmen present, but she lingered only long enough to see the last stone in place before turning her back and returning to her carriage.

The journey back to the Neuadd was quicker, taking

the direct route. People still lined the streets, their red cloaks and dresses gleaming in the midday sun. This time no heads were bowed and some even cheered. Beulah smiled and waved though in truth the common people irked her. They were so simple-minded and petty, so easily aroused and more easily pleased.

Back in the Neuadd the small chair beside the Obsidian Throne had been removed and Archimandrite Cassters stood on the steps in front of her. Seneschal Padraig stood to one side, holding the crown of state on a cushion. She suspected there had been much wrangling as to who would have which job in this coronation.

'King Diseverin is dead,' the archimandrite said in a loud pompous voice. 'Who dares to take his place on the Obsidian Throne?'

'I bring you Beulah of the Speckled Face, Princess of the House of Balwen.' Inquisitor Melyn stood beside her like the father of the bride at a wedding. He sounded bored.

'Come forward, Beulah,' Cassters said. She glanced sideways at the inquisitor and rolled her eyes then tottered forward on her uncomfortable heels towards the archimandrite. At least the flowing skirts of her gown hid the small frantic steps she took, maintaining the semblance of an air of dignified competence and majesty. She reached the steps and knelt on the soft red cushion that had been placed there for her, bowing her head to the old priest for what she vowed would be the last time in her life.

'By what right do you make your claim to the Twin Kingdoms?' Cassters said, his voice quavering with the importance of his task. 'By what right do you seek to take the Obsidian Throne for your own?'

'By right of my birth,' Beulah said, trying to disguise her impatience with the whole ceremony. Behind her, standing in carefully arranged rows of seniority and influence, the great merchants and noblemen of her realm waited in silent anticipation. This was something that they expected to witness, a shared experience that tied them to her power base. Yet another one of the tiresome and seemingly endless round of ceremonies and functions that were supposed to stamp the mark of her authority. She would rather have sent her loyal warrior priests into the houses of any who dared to gainsay her. Fear was a much more potent motivator than mindless adulation.

'And is there anyone among us who would deny this claim?' The archimandrite said, raising his voice for the whole hall to hear. Beulah waited, counting the seconds, daring anyone to speak. She could sense the tension in the air, the massed thoughts hesitant and expectant. Close to the great throne and its focus of the power of the Grym she could hear some of those thoughts, though she couldn't identify who was thinking them. They were all caught up in the excitement, some simply empty and waiting, some wondering how best they might manoeuvre themselves into positions of favour, one or two even lovesick at the thought of her. One thought jarred against the sea of approval and she focused on it as she might a lone poppy in a field of golden wheat.

There is one with a better claim. He will come forward and take what is rightfully his.

Then, as if it knew it was being heard, the thought

vanished, the presence that had hovered behind it closed to her more totally than even Inquisitor Melyn could manage.

'The Twin Kingdoms have no leader, the Obsidian Throne sits empty,' Archimandrite Cassters said, his voice bringing Beulah back to her senses. 'Beulah of the Speckled Face, Princess of the House of Balwen, has claimed the right to rule and none has sought to gainsay her. Do you, Beulah, swear by the Shepherd to maintain the rule of law, to hold the scales of justice, to protect your citizens from harm?'

'I do so swear,' Beulah said, projecting her words as a thought to all the gathered witnesses. 'I will maintain the rule of law. I will hold the scales of justice. I will protect my people from those who would do them harm.'

'Then by the power of the Shepherd, our most mighty lord and master, I crown you Queen Beulah. May your reign be long and glorious.'

Beulah felt the crown being placed on her head and for an instant all she could do was hope that it had been well washed since her father had worn it. The last thing she wanted was to catch his lice. Then she realized that all around her voices were shouting, 'Long live the queen.' She looked up into the round smiling face of Archimandrite Cassters.

'You must take the throne now, my queen,' he said, kneeling before her. Slowly, she rose to her feet, cursing once more the awkward uncomfortable slippers. Then she remembered the crown on her head. She could do what she liked now and hang the consequences. She kicked off the slippers, losing three inches of height in the process, then reached up for the strap that held the red gown of mourning around her neck, unclasping it and throwing the garment to the floor. Beneath it she wore a plain but elegant dress of royal blue. As she strode past the kneeling archimandrite and up the stone steps to the throne, she could hear a murmuring among the crowd as if some thought it too early by far to be casting off her mourning. Yet she knew that even more would be impressed by her willingness to put the past behind her and begin her reign on a positive note. It was all about symbolism, and though it bored her to distraction she would play the game of state to the best of her ability.

The throne towered over her, magnificent almost to the point of absurdity, its true seat the height of her head and wider than the largest bed in the palace. Legend had it that King Brynceri had carved it himself after defeating the last great dragon, Gog, though Beulah had never understood why he had made the thing so large. Its legs were now hidden by the stone steps that climbed up to it and a smaller seat, more suitable for a man, had been inserted into the original. It was obvious that this was from a later age than the original. The stone was lighter and coarser, painted to match the smooth polished black of the original, and its carvings were not in the same league as those that adorned the original arms and that massive towering back.

There were many mysteries about the throne, but its power was undeniable. All her life Beulah had felt it whenever she came into the great hall of the Neuadd. She had longed for it as an alcoholic yearns for the oblivion of drink, and yet she had been forced to wait by the constant vigilance of Seneschal Padraig and his countless Candle spies. She glanced sideways at the old priest, who had backed away from the spot where she had been crowned and now resumed his habitual place. That would change soon, she thought as she turned to face the congregation, feeling the power of the throne behind her and savouring the moment.

A thousand faces looked at her across the great expanse of the Neuadd. The cries of 'Long live the queen' had ceased and everyone waited for her to take the throne. This was the moment she had worked for, and yet as she felt their expectant gaze she hesitated. She could see mapped out for her a long hard life. No more would she be able to take a horse and ride out into the countryside alone. Nor could she visit the monastery at Emmass Fawr unannounced. She would have to deal with daily requests for money, help, advice, justice. Soon she would have to choose a halfwit noble as a consort and, worse, bear him children. Her own childhood had been miserable, why would she want to inflict that on anyone else? Yet the state needed an heir, and most likely a spare as well, to avoid the inevitable civil strife that would occur should she not reproduce. Her life was no longer her own.

For a long moment Beulah wavered. Was this really what she wanted? Then she remembered the look on her little sister's face as she was taken away from the palace. She saw her mother lying dead in a pool of her own blood, the king sprawled in a drunken stupor in a chair nearby. She saw perfect Lleyn kissing the enemy in a bower up at Ystumtuen, giving herself and the Twin Kingdoms away to the House of Ballah like some cheap whore. All the things that had driven her to learn and grow strong came back to her in that instant. And ahead of her, standing in the place where he had left her, Inquisitor Melyn fixed her with his calm penetrating gaze and nodded.

Beulah took a deep breath, grasped the cold stone arm of the throne and hoisted herself into the seat.

Cheers rang out in the great hall. Some people even threw their hats into the air. Beulah drank in their adulation, feeling herself at the nexus of everything. She let them continue for long minutes, focusing on individuals nearby and marvelling at how open they were to her probing mind. It was as if the throne amplified the power of the Grym, concentrating it into her and filling her with energy. How could her father have been so dead to this that he had to drink himself insensible? Or maybe it had been just too much for him; maybe that had been the cause of his affliction. Well, it was hers now and she was going to make the most of it. With a single thought she reached out to all the assembled gentry, projecting her words along the lines so that they all heard her voice boom out like a giant's.

'My people, I thank you for your support on this most special of days. You will see that I have thrown off my gown of mourning. I would ask you all to do the same. King Diseverin is gone. Not even the power of the House of Balwen can bring him back. Let us remember his best moments and move on.'

Beulah had them spellbound, and their rapt attention fed power into her that almost made her dizzy. There was nothing she could not accomplish with the combined might of the Twin Kingdoms behind her. Now was the time to begin the tasks she had set herself.

'I sit here on Brynceri's throne and see our kingdoms grown soft and weak,' she said. 'We have grown used to the comforts that our wealth brings us, but we have forgotten what brought us this wealth in the first place. We were once a powerful nation that stood up to all who would do us ill. Now we make poor treaties with our enemies and send them our children to be slaves. That will end. No more will we bow to their belligerence.'

A murmur ran around the great hall as the assembly digested this. To her left, Beulah could see Seneschal Padraig turning pale. She silenced everyone with a mental command.

'Even now King Ballah's people spread through the Caenant plains. Where once they were wanderers, now they build towns and cities. Will we wait for them to mass their armies? Will we sit here in idle luxury while the enemy builds its strength on our doorstep? And by what right does Ballah claim these lands anyway? Caenant was Brynceri's birthplace and is the cradle of our people. We should not be so willing to cede it to distant Tynhelyg.

'I say, enough of appeasement,' Beulah said, standing. On the dais above the crowd, with the Obsidian Throne towering behind her, she felt like she was flying. 'It's time to take the true word to the unbelievers,' she said. 'It's time for us to move against Llanwennog.'

19

Seneschal Tegwin, head of the Order of the Candle in Divitie XXIII's reign, was the first to propose a census of all the dragons in the Twin Kingdoms. Since they were no longer to be persecuted, and indeed enjoyed a certain degree of protection from the king, it was only right that they should contribute to the revenues of the state in the form of tithes. Recording dragon numbers, their ages and status was the obvious first step in this bureaucratic process.

It was to be a mammoth undertaking. The work was shared between the three orders and took almost fifty years to complete. This is not because the Hafod and Hendry were awash with dragons; quite the opposite. So few remained, and they had grown so adept at hiding, that finding them proved almost impossible.

Father Charmoise, *Dragons' Tales*

The sun hung low in the afternoon sky, pale and cold. The ground was wet with recent rain and the trees dripped heavy spots from their bare branches, filling the forest with a quiet roar. Overhead, the last few clouds were drifting away on a lightening breeze. The earlier storm had blown itself out and now the world felt fresh and clean and new.

Benfro pushed his way past evergreen shrubs, their leaves slick with water, heedless of the damp on his scales and the loam sticking to his feet. Behind him, Meirionydd and Sir Frynwy moved more cautiously along the narrow animal track. Both of them were breathing heavily with the exertion though Benfro would hardly have considered the pace fast.

'Are you sure this is the quickest way, Benfro?' Meirionydd asked, wheezing slightly. Benfro stopped and turned, agitated at their slow progress.

'I've come this way a dozen times,' he said. 'It takes at least an hour off the journey. If you don't keep stopping, that is,' he added.

'We're not all as young and fit as you,' Sir Frynwy said. 'Some of us haven't walked much further than the distance between our houses and the great hall in decades. Are you sure this is where she'll be?'

'She'll be there, I'm sure of it,' Benfro said, glancing up at the afternoon sky. It was lighter now than it had been in the morning, thanks to the clouds clearing, but it wouldn't stay light for long. They needed to hurry. In the dark they would not be able to approach quietly. He wasn't really sure that they would be able to approach quietly anyway. Old Sir Frynwy made as much noise as a rutting boar as he plodded through the undergrowth. At least Meirionydd seemed to know how to tread without snapping dead branches.

'We must hurry,' Benfro said, turning once more to clamber up the slope. 'It's not far to the proper track now. We can be there in under an hour.'

Their sluggish pace continued, and with each passing moment Benfro's anxiety grew. Even when they left the animal track and started along the wider path that ran parallel with the river, Benfro felt each additional second as a terrible disaster. Right now, further upstream, Frecknock was calling out in search of a mate, unaware that she was bringing herself and the villagers the attention of men. Worse, the attention of their sworn enemy, the Inquisitor of the Order of the High Ffrydd.

Finally, when he was beginning to think they might never arrive, Benfro heard the noise of the river playing over the rocks and falls not far distant.

'Quiet, now,' Meirionydd said. 'It's important she doesn't know we're coming.'

'Go and have a scout, Benfro,' Sir Frynwy said softly. 'Tell us what you can see.'

Benfro crept forward to the end of the path and looked out across the clearing to the flat-topped rock. There, sitting just as she had been the last time, eyes tightly closed, was Frecknock. The thick leather-bound book lay beside her and the firepot glowed with its tiny flame in front of her.

'She's there,' Benfro said when he had pulled himself back through the heavy shrubs that clustered around the river's edge. He described the scene. Meirionydd closed her eyes as if concentrating on something.

'She hasn't started yet,' she said. 'But it can't be long now. I suspect it is only vanity that has held her up this long.'

'Vanity?' Benfro asked.

'Some other time, Benfro dear,' Meirionydd said. 'For

now, we've got to get down there, and fast. It's critical she doesn't make contact with anyone.'

Benfro led them along the path a bit further and then down the steep slope to the first of the river pools. It had been late autumn when last he had seen Frecknock up here, and the river had been at its lowest. Now, in the holding of breath between winter and spring and after weeks of endless rain, the water was high, rushing between the larger rocks and over the smaller ones in a torrent that threatened to carry anyone who tried to wade through it over the nearby cliff edge. How Frecknock had made it to the flat-topped rock he couldn't begin to guess. There was no way he would be able to get any closer.

The light was failing now as the sun dropped behind the western flank of the valley. The flickering glow from Frecknock's firepot danced across her features, and Benfro could see her lips moving as she mouthed silent words of power and longing. With her eyes closed and the roar of the river, he realized that they could have marched up the path singing at the tops of their lungs and not disturbed her. He was wondering how they were going to get across the deluge and break her spell when Meirionydd stepped away from him along the bank a few paces. Something about her posture caught his attention, and he watched her. She was clearly looking for something but he couldn't see what it could be. There was nothing along there but tangling shrubs, the muddy bank and the rushing water at their feet.

'What are you looking for?' he asked, but Sir Frynwy put a gnarled hand on his shoulder and hushed him. Meirionydd scrambled further along the bank, clambering over rocks and tree roots worn smooth by the passing water. She stopped at last, sniffing the air like Ynys Môn after the scent of a boar, then made complicated motions with her hands. The air seemed to shimmer like a summer heatwave; something made Benfro blink, and then his mouth fell open with an audible clunk. She had the *Llyfr Draconius* clasped in her hands.

Benfro looked across at the flat-topped rock, twenty paces or more distant. Frecknock still sat there, her eyes screwed shut, but now a look of confusion was spreading across her features. She reached out with her hand, feeling for the spot where the book had been. Benfro couldn't begin to understand how Meirionydd had retrieved it. Then he remembered what his mother had told him about how the villagers acquired most of their food. Had Meirionydd done the same with the *Llyfr Draconius*?

'It's over, Frecknock,' Meirionydd said, and Benfro was startled by the closeness of her voice. It filled his head in the same way that Sir Felyn's had, but hers was a kind, gentle voice with none of the sense of otherness that he had heard in the alleged wandering dragon's speech.

Frecknock's eyes snapped open in surprise and alarm. For an instant Benfro was confused. He could see the young dragon from two slightly different perspectives and he could feel her embarrassment mixed with fury. And then he could see three dragons standing on the riverbank looking at him. He recognized Meirionydd and Sir Frynwy, but who was that scrawny-looking small creature by the old bard's side?

'Get out of my head, you horrible little squirt.' Benfro felt Frecknock's words as a slap in the face magnified a thousandfold. His senses reverberated and for a moment he thought he might lose his balance and topple into the swift-moving water. But Sir Frynwy's hand on his shoulder gripped him tight. It was an anchor and a strength that helped him find the way back to where he was supposed to be. Even so, his knees sagged under him as his vision began to clear. At least now he only saw the world from his own eyes.

'Steady there, Benfro,' Sir Frynwy said. 'Are you all right?'

Benfro was about to reply, but then became aware that Meirionydd and Frecknock were deep in conversation. He couldn't hear the words clearly over the roar of the river, but by Frecknock's dropped head and submissive posture he could see that she was being berated and, it seemed, accepting that what she had done was wrong. Then Meirionydd beckoned to her, and Benfro nearly fell over again. Frecknock stood, blew out the flame in her firepot and stepped off the rock. But instead of dropping the few inches into the roiling water, she seemed to flow across the space and appear at Meirionydd's side on the bank. Together they made their way back, clambering silently up to where Benfro and Sir Frynwy stood. Only when they were far enough from the river to speak comfortably above its noise did Meirionydd turn to Frecknock.

'I think you owe Benfro an apology,' she said. Frecknock looked completely defeated. Certainly the two older dragons seemed convinced by her posture and silence. But Benfro could still feel the taste of her fury, the sting of her anger as she had . . . what? What had she done? What had he done? Had he really been inside her head, seeing the world through her eyes and feeling, for that briefest of instances, the world as she felt it? And if so, how?

'I'm sorry, Benfro,' Frecknock said, finally looking up and staring straight at him. 'I had no right to do what I did to you. And I know now that it was both foolish and selfish. I hope you'll be able to forgive me some day.'

Benfro was almost taken in. If nothing else, Frecknock could be very persuasive. But he knew her too well. He could see beyond the downcast eyes and hunched wings to the dragon who had gloated over him when he was powerless to do anything. He remembered the months of agony when he had not been able to speak of what he had seen. And most of all he remembered her arrogance. Frecknock knew that she was better than all the other villagers. She had not long been studying the subtle arts and yet she was more skilled than all of them, save possibly Meirionydd. And she longed for something more exciting than the daily boredom of village life. She wanted a champion to come and free her, to take her away to exotic places. Benfro could understand that desire. He too yearned to see the world. But he knew the danger that existed should he be captured. No doubt Frecknock thought that she could overcome any man who might attack her, but what she didn't see in her arrogance and ignorance was that the danger was not just to herself.

Benfro nodded an acceptance of her apology, not trusting himself to speak. Silently in the gathering gloom of evening they began the journey back to the village. He doubted that his hatchday party would resume once they arrived, and he wasn't really sure that he was in the mood for it any more. At least they had succeeded in stopping Frecknock before she made her calling this time. But Benfro knew for sure that this would not stop her from trying again.

'Dig, you fools, dig! I haven't got time to stand around waiting.'

Queen Beulah sat on her horse, hood up to protect her from the constant rain. Her cloak was heavy with water and the ground puddled with it, sleeking the grass and turning the dirt to sticky, soupy mud. The gathered workmen huddled around the two ornate headstones looking uncertainly at each other and shivering in the cold and wet.

'Dig, you imbeciles, or I'll have my men run you through,' Beulah said. Beside her the captain of the Royal Guard shifted nervously on his horse. Behind him a dozen warrior priests stood silent, motionless and uncomplaining in the rain. A flatbed wagon with a heavy canvas cover stood to one side.

'They're worried for their souls, Your Majesty,' the captain said quietly. 'It goes against the teachings of the Shepherd to disturb the last resting place of the dead.'

'I'm well aware of the teachings of mother church,' Beulah said, her voice loud enough to carry to the miserable labourers. 'But this act has been blessed by Inquisitor Melyn himself. Your souls are the least of your worries if you don't obey me.' She let the rein slip from her right hand, lifting it free of her cloak. With a single thought, a blade of pure white light sprang from her fist, crackling in the wet. The workmen stared, terrified, and beside her the captain let out an involuntary gasp. Behind her she could hear the troop of warrior priests shuffle their feet in the mud. Beulah smiled. It did no harm to challenge their preconceptions about women and magic from time to time.

'Now dig, because your lives depend on it,' she said.

The labourers set to with satisfying energy, though it was awful work. The soil was so wet that it slopped back into the hole when they piled it too close to the edge. Beulah could feel her patience slipping away with the minutes. She had taken a chance coming here. The Obsidian Throne might be hers now, but she knew better than to take it for granted. Her father's reign had been weak; what better time to foment revolt than in the first few days after her coronation? But she had heard the voice. Someone else had a better claim. And if that were true it could only be the offspring of her sister.

In the dull grey of the winter rain it was almost impossible to make out the buildings of Ystumtuen. Even so the feel of the place was unmistakable. Beulah had hated it here and she still did, cut off from the lights and excitement of Candlehall. Stuck out in the foothills, surrounded by endless miles of forest and hunting parkland, there was nothing to do here except kill mindless animals, eat them and drink large quantities of ale. Beulah preferred the endless politicking and the machinations of the court; that was where the real power was to be found. But Lleyn, perfect Lleyn, had loved the ruins with the same perversity of nature that had attracted her to the dark Llanwennog, Balch.

The clang of metal on stone woke Beulah from her musing. She still grasped the blade of light in her right hand, its warmth and power reassuring, filled with the

319

surging energy of the earth. Even in this dead winter place there was more than enough life to light it. But it had served its purpose so she let it shimmer away to nothing, turning her full attention to the hole in front of her.

'Haul them out of there and on to the wagon,' Beulah shouted over the rain. 'And make it quick. I have to be gone from here within the hour.'

The workmen were covered in mud from head to toe, their clothes slicked to them like wet sacks. The hole was deep and its sides treacherous as they struggled to lift the heavy stone coffins up and over the edge. The first safely on the back of the wagon, they returned for the second and almost had it clear of the pit when one man's foot slipped in the dirt. For a moment Beulah thought they had it. Then the weight, shifting suddenly to the other men, overbalanced them all. Slithering to get out of the way of the falling casket, two workmen screamed as they fell under its weight, their cries abruptly silenced by the crunch of stone crushing skulls. There was a dull thud as the casket finally came to a halt on its side. The lid slid off and a skeletal bundle fell out into the rain-filled hole.

Fourteen years had desiccated the corpse, but the stone had prevented it from rotting. Beulah recognized the clothes it wore and the dark hair that hung in long ringlets from the shrivelled head. His skin had darkened in death, but there was no mistaking those features. A silver amulet hung around his neck on a long chain.

'Hello there, Prince Balch,' she said. 'The years haven't been kind.'

The men in the hole had backed away from the corpse as if it might suddenly spring up and attack them. One of them made the sign of the crook around his face and down the centre of his chest. It was a stupid, superstitious gesture that annoyed her far more than it should. This was an enemy who had no reverence for the Shepherd and no loyalty to the Obsidian Throne. It was bad enough that he should have been given such an honourable burial without these men making like he was some kind of saint.

'You there,' Beulah shouted at the man, 'fetch me his amulet.' The man looked up at her with terror on his face but she lifted her right hand slightly and he hurried to obey, kneeling in the mud and trembling as he reached for the silver necklace.

'Your Majesty, his throat's been cut,' the man said, his fear seeming to abate slightly as the corpse remained still and did not try to steal his soul from him. Beulah laughed at the superstitions of the peasants who lived and worked in these backwoods.

'Of course it has,' she said. 'You don't think he wanted to jump, do you?'

Such was the man's surprise at her words that he jerked away from the body, forgetting the amulet clasped in his grip. The silver chain jerked once, lifting the body, then time and old wounds took their toll as the prince's head lolled back, the neck snapped, and the head fell off into the mud. Stumbling backwards, the labourer scrambled out of the pit along with those of his colleagues still alive. His terror was almost total now, Beulah noticed. The whites of his eyes gleamed large from the mud-streaked blackness of his face.

'Give it to me,' she said, holding out her left hand. 'Then you'll be paid.'

The mention of money was enough to give the men the courage to line up. There were five of them and the man with the amulet seemed to have been promoted to the position of leader.

'Thank you,' Beulah said as she took the amulet from the sodden peasant. He looked at her expectantly, not casting his eyes down now as he had done earlier. His face was thin and drawn, his eyes piggy and stupid. Alongside him, their backs to the pit, his fellow workmen were no better.

Beulah swung her arm in a single effortless arc. Like a bolt of lightning in the gloom, the blade of light was there for an instant, then gone. One by one, like a child's game of falling stones, the workmen crumpled, toppling backwards into the pit, their heads neatly severed.

The amulet was heavy in her hand as Beulah turned her horse away from the carnage. She looked at the family crest of the Llanwennogs intricately wrought and set with precious jewels, then slipped it into a pocket in her cloak.

'Fill in the hole,' she said to the captain. 'And see to it that the other coffin is delivered to Emmass Fawr. Melyn will know what's to be done with it. I must ride with all haste for the palace. I will take two guards and spare horses.'

'Of course, ma'am,' the captain said. If he felt anything about his orders or the person giving them, he didn't let it show. 'Hamer, Jone, you will go with the queen at once.'

The two guards broke away, heading back to the derelict tower where the horses were tethered. Beulah watched as other guards began to fill in the hole. In minutes her escort returned, mounted and leading the other horses.

'No one must know what's in this wagon, Captain,' Beulah said. 'The future of the Obsidian Throne depends on it.'

'I will guard it with my life, Your Majesty.' The captain bowed in the saddle and clasped his hand to his chest.

'Yes,' Beulah said. 'Yes, you will.' Without waiting for a response she spurred her horse to a gallop and sped away for the road to Candlehall.

Errol itched at the collar of his new cassock and surveyed the pile of parchments that awaited him. He was still in the same room, still working his way through the same wall, slowly cataloguing what he found in the same thick leather-bound book. It was weeks now since his birthday, and he was beginning to wonder if he would ever finish his monumental task.

At least he was able to go above ground on those rare occasions when Andro let him have some time off. He had classes to attend too, and when these were held in the higher towers he sometimes even caught a glimpse of those magnificent mountains, snow-covered in the early spring and brilliant against the clear blue sky.

It seemed that Errol's enforced stay in the library archives had marked him as more of a thinker than a fighter, or perhaps it was just that he was so much further advanced in his reading and writing than the other novitiates that he could proceed faster to the more cerebral aspects of the training. Whatever the reason, and no one would explain it to him, he was not required to undergo the arduous physical training that Clun and the other novitiates spent at least half of every day doing. Instead

he had to go back down into the library archives and continue with the tasks he had begun. Younger and
considerably smaller than the other boys, this suited Errol
fine. In any case, while he had always had a fascination for
the warrior priests and their magical powers, as he learned
more about the truth of warfare he came to realize that a
life of quiet study and scholarship need not be a bad thing
after all.

Besides, he doubted that he would have been able to
keep up with the other novitiates in their training, judging
by the change that several months' hard exercise had
wrought in Clun. His stepbrother had grown inches taller,
and his muscles, impressive back in Pwllpeiran, would
have given the old smith Tom Tydfil a run for his money.

Thinking of the burly smith brought a strange melancholy to Errol's heart. He had not realized how much he
missed the simple life of the village. Every so often simple things would trip a memory and he would find himself
back there, walking the woods or listening to ancient tales
of warring dragons and men. And always there was that
element of confusion, as if his memories were hazy with
age, not the fresh-minted things that they should have
been. Lately he had found that delving too deep into his
past life gave him nasty headaches, so Errol instead threw
himself into his work in an attempt to forget. At times it
was difficult though, particularly at night as he lay awake
while his mind whirled with the day's new discoveries.

Sighing, Errol tried once more to focus on the manuscript that was allowing his mind to wander so. It was a
tally of some form, columns of numbers and names
cross-referenced in some arcane fashion he could not

quite understand. It was a relatively new document, the parchment still supple and the ink fresh. The script was neat and well executed, written in the common tongue of the Twin Kingdoms, unlike some of the more obscure texts he had uncovered. But the names were all archaic and foreign-sounding, the numbers meaningless.

'Ah, there you are, Errol.' A voice broke through his mystified staring before his mind could begin to wander again. Errol looked around to see Andro standing at the door, his white hair almost glowing in the lantern light. The old man crossed the room to see what he was doing, leaning over the desk and peering closely at the manuscript as if his eyes were failing.

'The first survey of King Divitie,' he said, straightening up. 'Ah, I remember this well.'

'You know what it is?' Errol asked.

'Of course,' Andro said. 'I wrote it.'

'Well, what is it?'

'It's a census, of a sort,' Andro said. 'It lists all the known dragons within the Twin Kingdoms, their stated age at the time of the census, where they lived and what tithe they were expected to pay to the court.'

Errol looked back at the parchment. The names were certainly foreign, things like Sir Cadrigal, Ystrad Fflur and Ynys Môn. Yet they had a certain flowing elegance to them that tripped neatly off the tongue and made his own name seem ungainly. The claimed ages of the beasts amazed him, for there didn't seem to be any less than eight hundred years old. Some of them were more than fifteen hundred.

'How can this be?' Errol asked, pointing at the figures. 'Surely nothing can live that long.'

'Well, it may be that dragons aren't very good at counting, or it may be that they exaggerate their own age to make themselves feel important. It may even be that they truly do live that long. Certainly they live longer far than humans do.'

'And what of these red lines?' Errol asked, pointing to marks that had been scored through at least two thirds of the names.

'Dead,' Andro said. 'Most slain by our very own warrior priests.'

'But I thought King Divitie lifted the aurddraig,' Errol said.

'So he did, young novitiate. But not every warrior priest was happy at the king interfering with what they thought of as their sacred duty. Close by, where he could keep an eye on things, the dragons were more or less safe; especially if they kept out of the way. But in the Hendry boglands and further east out on the Gwastadded Wag, they were fair game as ever. And we only have scant intelligence as to the fate of dragons in the northern plains of Llanwennog. I've heard some tales of captured beasts being trained as circus animals, but most information that trickles in is about deaths.'

'Are there any left? Are they living out there in the forest?'

'I know of no dragons alive,' Andro said. 'This document's out of date and useless. You needn't add it to the archive.' He reached across the desk, rolling up the parchment and tucking it under his arm. 'Now I think you've done enough for today. Why don't you get along upside and take some exercise. You're looking a bit pale, and the fresh air will do you good.'

Errol was about to complain that he had only just started his work, but the chance of spending the afternoon outside rather than stuck in the bowels of the great monastery was too good to pass up. Hurrying so as not to be caught by any change of mind on the part of his mentor, he grabbed his small canvas bag and darted out the door.

20

The Order of the High Ffrydd was the first of the great religious orders to be commisioned by the House of Balwen. Its sacred charter was to track down the dragons, servants of the Wolf, and exterminate them, and this task they set about with great fervour.

In the early days of the order Gwlad teemed with dragons. Quite unlike the pathetic creatures that lurk in the depths of the Ffrydd to this day, these creatures were powerful and aggressive monsters. They did not die easily and many a warrior priest returned from his duties gravely injured, some not at all.

It was Inquisitor Moorit who first established a medical faculty in the great monastery at Emmass Fawr to treat those injured in the work of the order. Novitiates who had no aptitude for fighting were encouraged to pursue studies in medicine, and over time the skill of the medics of the order became known across the whole of the Twin Kingdoms. The sick would travel from afar, by whatever means they could, in the hope of finding relief. Many died on the cruel road to the mountain-top retreat.

In the reign of Diseverin IV a dreadful plague began to spread through the Hendry boglands.

Fearful that people would spread the disease crossing the Twin Kingdoms in search of treatment, the king ordered Moorit to release three dozen of his most able medics so that they might travel through the boglands and heal the sick.

So successful were these medics that Diseverin decreed they should continue to wander the Twin Kingdoms, giving freely what medical care was required to any who asked it. This was their charter, and those three dozen became the first coenobites of the Order of the Ram, with Aldwyn their first archimandrite.

Father Gideon, *The Order of the Ram*

'Concentrate harder, Benfro. See the life that flows through everything.'

Benfro squinted in the semi-darkness of Sir Frynwy's dusty book-lined study. He could see the motes dancing in the single shaft of light that shone through a split in the shutters. He could see the dark shapes of the shelves, weighed down with generations of knowledge. He could see the familiar shape of Meirionydd sitting across the room from him, her arms crossed and ears pulled back in concentration. As he screwed his eyes up even harder he could see spots and swirls of ghost light dancing across his vision. What he couldn't see was anything resembling a glowing line of power.

'I can't do it,' he said, slumping back into his chair. 'There's nothing there.'

'This room is aglow with the Grym, Benfro,' Meirionydd

said in her measured, patient tone. 'It's one of the best places in the village to seek the Llinellau. You're so certain that you can't do it. If only you could have that same trust in your ability you'd have no difficulty.'

'But I believe the Llinellau exist,' Benfro said. 'I'm sure that I saw them the first time Frecknock . . .' He trailed off, not wanting to talk about the incident. He had not seen anything of the young dragon since they had all walked down from the flat rock on his birthday, weeks ago. Meirionydd had come to see him the next morning and he had begun his training in the subtle arts the day after that. Since then all his attempts to see the Llinellau Grym had failed.

'It's not a question of belief, Benfro,' Meirionydd said. 'Men believe that an all-powerful god exists who looks over them and protects them from harm. They expend great amounts of energy doing his will, not least in their persecution of our kind. Yet in all my years I've never seen this Shepherd, nor met any man who has. He exists as nothing more than an idea.'

'Why do they believe in him then?' Benfro asked, grateful for the distraction from his failed attempts. He could feel a dull pain beginning to grow in his head from all that squinting.

'They believe because their priests tell them to. And because it's easier to believe than to know. They live very short lives, some not even fifty years. It's much easier for them to explain their fortune, good or bad, in terms of some all-powerful deity than to accept responsibility for their actions. And the priests wield the power. You've heard no doubt that the Order of the High Ffrydd can

conjure blades of light, but they have much more insidious ways of compelling people.'

'What do you mean?' Benfro asked.

'The priests have a very limited understanding of the
subtle arts,' Meirionydd said. 'But they know how to get
inside your head, to influence your thoughts. They spe-
cialize in fear and violence. That's how they see power, as
a means to keep others in line. Their Shepherd is just a
convenient story to justify their brutality.

'But enough about men,' Meirionydd said. 'Your
mother's the expert on them anyway. I'm here to teach
you about the subtle arts, so you can stop trying to distract
me and concentrate on the task I've set you.'

Benfro leaned forward once more, straining to see the
ghostly lines that he had been told criss-crossed the room.

'Don't try so hard, Benfro,' Meirionydd said. 'It's not
like a muscle that can be forced to grow with brute
strength. It's as its name implies, a subtle art. So relax,
close your eyes, imagine the room all around you.'

Benfro settled back into his chair and did as he was
told. He had not visited Sir Frynwy's study often, but he
could build up a picture of the room in his mind. The
walls, with their ceiling-high shelves stacked with books,
were an unfocused mass at first, but as he concentrated,
so he could recall individual spines, their colours and tex-
tures. He left the few gaps in his memory as hazy
book-impressions and moved on to the furniture. There
was his own chair with its back to the door and, across the
room, another identical chair obscured the empty fireplace. The shutters were drawn, just that one crack letting
in the early spring sun, shining in a sharp line on the desk

with its untidy overgrowth of parchments, papers and precariously piled books. Benfro imagined himself looking up and saw the ceiling, crusted with cobwebs in the corners, the plaster cracked and stained even in the poor light.

'Can you see it now?' Meirionydd asked, and the sound of her voice reminded him of what was missing from the room. In his mind he glanced back at her chair, but instead of the graceful old dragon he had known all his life, he now saw the beautiful young creature who had freed him from Frecknock's spell, and spreading out from her like the glow of the morning sun through the trees, an outline in vibrant shades of orange and purple and blue of something larger and more magnificent still, a dragon of such a stature and power that she had to be someone from one of Sir Frynwy's tales.

Then before he knew what was happening, he was flying again, soaring over treetops still brown but tinged in places with the first flush of spring green. For a moment he thought that he was heading back to the mountains, but the great mass of the forest was dropping away from him, spilling down the hills and folds, trees breaking up into small clumps, giving way to grass, short and blue-grey. He could see small settlements, the occasional house nestling in a copse betrayed only by a wisp of woodsmoke spiralling up on the windless air. They were small dwellings, too small for any dragon to live in. Some of them had small enclosures around them, where animals Benfro had never seen before grazed or slept in the morning sun. His shadow passed over one of the enclosures, a flash of darkness impossibly large. Frightened, the animals clustered together, looking up to see what hunted them. Blind panic took over and they careered around their pen, crashing through the rough wooden fence and galloping towards the trees. Amused but unconcerned, Benfro sped on.

The trees thinned further still, greening fast as spring brought their sap back up from the ground. Unnaturally straight hedgerows quartered the open land, grass filling some of the squares, most just dark bare earth. The hills here were smaller, gently undulating away on both sides so that the world looked like a vast patchwork blanket thrown down carelessly on the ground. Wide tracks of hard-packed earth criss-crossed the land, linking the settlements that seemed to get bigger and bigger as he flew further down the valley. The river that had been little more than a meandering stream grew steadily wider, its curves and bends straightening as it snaked its way gradually downwards. Benfro was entranced by the way the light flickered on its waters, sparkling like candlelit jewels over shallow rapids, reflecting a solid more powerful presence through the deeps. Still he flew on.

It appeared first as a dirty brown smudge in the air, far in the distance. With a few lazy flaps of his great wings, Benfro propelled himself forward, curious to see what lay ahead. Beneath the haze a hill rose sharply out of the flat plain, the river ribboning around it like a flash of light, almost completely encircling it before turning away once more. As he came closer, the hill seemed to be encrusted with small square boulders, arranged in neat lines as if some giant kitling had been at play. Closer still and he realized what it was he approached, though even then the scale of it took his breath away. They were not boulders but buildings.

They stretched around the hill in all directions for miles, seemingly endless variations on the theme of four walls and a roof. There were long lines of grimy-faced two-storey houses that followed the straight lines of roads spearing in towards the hill like killing blows. Larger buildings cropped up here and there, as if dropped from above. Tall towers spired into the sky, reaching up to challenge his flight. The acrid smell of burning wood reached his nostrils, the air stinging his eyes. Benfro swept over a massive wall that sought in vain to contain the flood of construction, great eruptions of new building pouring out where it had failed at several gates and along the lines of the roads that fed into this incredible place.

Benfro banked away from his course and followed the line of the wall as it rose and fell around the city, for that was what this place must surely be. And yet clear though the buildings and streets were from his height above them, he could see no men. Surely in a place this large there should have been hundreds of them, more even, though he had difficulty in conceiving of such a number. Someone had to have lit the fires that filled the air with their unpleasant smoke. And yet there was no one.

Dogs, he saw, padding the streets and scavenging in the piles of refuse heaped up against the wall. Other animals stood tethered to buildings, patiently waiting with loads strapped to their backs. Benfro had only ever seen such animals in books before, and it was only as his wings brushed a tower that he realized he had been slowly diving to get a better look. Panicked by his lack of caution, he climbed swiftly back into the air, the wind from his power-ful downstrokes spooking the animals. Several dogs looked up at him and began howling, their bays like the wolves that lurked on the edges of the forest. The noise raised his hackles, a faint prickling of fear seeping into the wonder that had been his only sense.

There seemed to be a centre for that fear. It wasn't within him so much as smothering him from outside. Looking up, Benfro saw the buildings of the city climbing the side of the hill, his gaze rising ever higher as he gained altitude until he could see the top. It was dominated by a massive structure like the great hall in the village only a hundred times its size, maybe more. It was made of dark stone, different to that of all the other buildings in the city, its surface strangely fuzzy and unfocused. Tall thin win-dows of coloured glass rose from the ground right up to its eaves. At one end of the hall huge black-oak doors, studded with great iron rivets, stood open. The entrance was a giant mouth, calling him in like the great palace atop the mountains. Only here the fear was less. It was discom-fiting, yes, but not paralysing. He could still control his wings, still fly away, though it caused him great anxiety to turn his back on the empty hall.

Suddenly Benfro realized the strangeness of his situ-ation. He was flying, and yet his wings were thin scraps of skin that couldn't possibly lift him off the ground. He was circling a great city of men somewhere far to the south of his village, and yet he was sitting in Sir Frynwy's study being taught the subtle arts by Meirionydd. Or at least that was where he should be. Caught between two incompat-ible worlds, he panicked and his mastery over the air vanished. With a sickening lurch in the pit of his stomach, he plummeted down towards the great stone hall.

'You, boy. What are you doing here?'

The voice cut through Errol's thoughts like a knife. He turned to see a lone man dressed in the pale robes of a medic striding along the corridor towards him.

'I'm on my way to the exercise courtyard, Quaister,' Errol said, bowing his head. 'I've come from the library archives, where Master Librarian Andro has discharged me of my duties for the day.' He kept his voice low and polite, aware that to be found wandering the corridors alone was excuse enough for some of the more irascible quaisters to hand out dreadful punishments.

'Never mind all that, boy,' the man said. 'Have you any medical knowledge?'

Startled by the direct manner of the question, it took Errol a while to gather his wits.

'Yes, sir,' he said. 'My mother's a herb woman. I've often helped her with the sick in our village.'

'Fine. Good,' the man said. 'I've need of assistance in a medical matter, though I doubt anything either of us can do will save my patient. Come.' He turned on his heels and Errol had to jog to keep up with him as they hurried along the corridor and then down a twisting flight of stairs hewn into the rock. Catching what glimpses he could, he saw that the medic was a young man, perhaps in his early thirties, with close-cropped dark brown hair and a clean-shaven chin. His robes were paler than those the novitiates wore and woven from a finer cloth. Repeated washings had only served to set the stains that marked their front and sides.

'You could be flogged for what you just said, you know,' the man said after they had been walking for several minutes. Errol had not been in this part of the monastery before and he was concentrating hard to remember salient details should he have to find his way back to the library archives alone.

'I could?'

'You said that your mother's a herb woman. Now I don't know if things have changed since I was a novitiate, but I was taught that the church was my mother, the Shepherd my father and the order the only other family I would ever have or need. It's a stupid convention, really. Why should we pretend we have no past before we come here? You, for instance,' he stopped mid-stride and turned to face Errol. 'What's your name, boy?'

'Errol,' Errol said. 'Errol Ramsbottom.'

'Well, Errol Ramsbottom. If you'd stuck to the teachings of mother church, I'd still be looking for someone to help me. That would've made me angry and wasted both of our precious time. In here.' He opened a door and they descended yet more steps, the permanent chill of the monastery deepening as they entered the lowest levels Errol had yet encountered. The walls here were carved from the rock, not built up. They were deep inside the mountain

'Where are we going?' Errol ventured to ask.

'To the mortuary,' the medic said. 'Like I said, I don't think our combined medical skills will save this patient, since she's been dead for quite a long time. Our good leader, the inquisitor, is keen to know more about the condition she was in at the time of her death. Such secrets are there to be uncovered, if you just know how to look. Still, I'd rather be helping the sick than disturbing the dead.'

Errol stared at the back of the medic's head as they twisted their way into the dark recesses of the mountain. He had never heard anyone, not even Andro, speak of the inquisitor in such a flippant manner.

'Umm, who are you?' Errol asked, not wanting to offend but not knowing how else to make sense of what was happening around him.

'Oh yes, names,' the man said, stopping. 'I keep forgetting. I'm Usel, the surgeon.' He held out a hand as if someone had once told him that was what you did on meeting a stranger but he couldn't quite understand why. Errol shook it briefly and they continued down the winding steps into the depths.

Eventually, when Errol was beginning to wonder if they would ever stop, the steps opened out into a large hall. Torches hung in sconces along the walls, their flickering light lending a slightly hellish air to the scene.

It was cold, fogging his exhaled breaths as he recovered from the long climb down. Instinctively, Errol reached out for the lines, trying to draw the warmth of nearby living things into him. It seemed to be more difficult than he recalled, as if he had forgotten how that most basic of novitiate's skills was performed. Concentrating, he tried to see the lines criss-crossing the room.

There were none.

'Ah, yes. I probably should've warned you about that,' Usel said. 'We're too deep within the bedrock of the mountain to use the Grym. I dare say even Melyn would have a hard time conjuring his blade of light down here. That's why we have to use the torches.'

An uneasiness crept over Errol. It had nothing to do with the cold or the rows of alcoves carved into the rock wall that could have only housed one thing. Neither was it the smell of bleach that filled the air, not quite hiding a more unpleasant aroma that reminded him of the mornings back in Pwllpeiran when someone had butchered a wild boar in the yard behind the school. It was more a feeling of total isolation, of being cut off from the whole world, and it sent shivers running up his spine.

'Here, put this on,' Usel said, handing Errol a robe similar to his own only less stained. For the first time since being accosted in the corridor somewhere high above, Errol had the chance to see the man's face properly and revised his age upwards by twenty years. Usel's skin was pale and smooth, his mouth twisted into a permanent quizzical grin that made him look like a mischievous schoolboy. His hair was flecked with tiny flashes of white, his eyes pale grey and creased around the edges. They held Errol in a penetrating stare for a long moment before releasing him.

'Your father was a Llanwennog,' he said. 'From the north-east of the country if I'm not mistaken.'

'I never knew my father,' Errol said.

'Of course not,' Usel said. 'Otherwise you wouldn't be here. No doubt you were chosen to be a spy. It's not a job I'd like. Who was at your choosing, Lentin? Old Father Crassock?'

'Inquisitor Melyn came to my village, with Princess Beulah,' Errol said. Usel raised an eyebrow.

'Old Melyn actually got out there among the masses? And you've met the queen. Well, well. You're an important fellow, Errol Ramsbottom. I can remember when Beulah was younger even than you. She used to wander the corridors like she owned this place. I guess now she does.'

'What was Princess . . . Queen Beulah doing here as a child?' Errol asked, pulling the robe over his head.

'She was sent here by her father, just after her mother died. Melyn was her tutor.'

'But I thought the secrets of the order were forbidden to women,' Errol said, recalling the words of Father Castlemilk in his *An Introduction to the Order of the High Ffrydd*.

'Here's a lesson for you then, Errol,' Usel said. 'It's true that the order doesn't let women into its ranks. But Queen Beulah, well. She's royalty, one of only two descendants of the House of Balwen left. Gender's not an issue when you're royal. She can do whatever she pleases. Often does, from what I've heard.'

'Two?' Errol asked. 'Who's the other?'

'Princess Iolwen, Beulah's little sister,' Usel said. 'She was sent to Llanwennog as a hostage to continued peace. As far as I know she's still alive. She'd be nineteen now, if memory serves. King Diseverin gave her over to the tender ministrations of Seneschal Padraig and his order. He was probably trying to appease King Ballah after Prince Balch died.'

'Prince Balch?' Errol asked, feeling like he was an echo.

'Ah, now there's a story,' Usel said. 'And it's part of why we're here. After all, Beulah wasn't always first in line to the Obsidian Throne. It's this poor girl should've been crowned last month, not lying down here unlamented on the fourteenth anniversary of her death.' He turned, sweeping his arm across the room to where a wheeled trolley stood beside a narrow table lit by a candelabrum hanging on a chain from the dark recesses of the ceiling. On the trolley, no doubt placed there by a troop of strong men, lay a stone coffin, ornately carved and with dried earth still clinging to it.

Benfro could see the ground getting clearer, closer, with every passing moment. Confusion addled his thinking more than fear. He couldn't remember how to fly – but then he couldn't fly, so that was hardly surprising. Except that he was airborne and had got here, wherever here was, using his wings. His magnificent powerful wings. The pathetic thin scraps of leather that hung awkwardly by his side.

It all seemed unreal, yet at the same time he was certain that hitting the ground at the speed he was falling would hurt, albeit very briefly. He doubted he'd be alive long enough to feel pain for more than a few seconds.

Get a grip on yourself. Fly.

The words were deep within his head, though Benfro was sure that they were not his. With them came a sudden impulse to flex his wings so powerful he could only watch in amazement as he righted himself, stopped his plummet and came to a hovering stop just yards above the flag-stones. Once more he seemed to be in complete control, perhaps even greater control than before for he'd never felt so confident and strong. The ground was not far away, but he had denied it.

'Who are you?' The voice startled him out of his daydreaming so suddenly that he almost tumbled the last few feet to the barren stony ground that surrounded the hall. Scrabbling for purchase against the slippery air, Benfro turned and looked at the open mouth of those two great doors. A figure stood there, like a man only somehow different. But then the only man he had ever met was Gideon. Who was to say they all looked alike? This one was as tall as the wandering priest, but thinner. Something about it reminded him of his mother or Meirionydd, even Frecknock. He had never thought much about it before, but it made sense that there would be female men as well. This then must be one of them, but who was she and how could she see him when he wasn't really there?

'Who are you?' the figure asked again, and Benfro was gripped with a compulsion to tell her everything. He began to descend towards the doorway and the long wide flagstone path that led from it to the surrounding buildings. But he really didn't want to do that. Like in his earlier dream, something told him that to land was to surrender, that if his feet touched the ground they would never again leave it. Struggling, he rose once more into the air, feeling the fear that had gripped him turn into a hot rage. He was reminded of Frecknock during one of her more petulant outbursts, and the memory of the young dragon gave him added strength. He had learned to live with her inexplicable hatred of him. He had even survived her latest attempt to make his life a misery.

'You will come to me,' the figure said. 'You will tell me who you are, where you came from.'

'I . . . will not,' Benfro said, not without difficulty. The sound of his voice was almost an echo, as if it were far distant, but the familiar sound anchored him. Somewhere away from here he was safe. He just had to get back there.

'Your time is over, dragon,' the voice shouted. Benfro ignored it, wheeling and scanning the horizon to try and find the way he had come. The sky, which had been clear, was now clouding over, great rolls of blackness speeding towards him like frightened animals, obscuring the distance and blotting out the hills.

'You can't escape me,' the figure said. 'I control this land. It is mine.'

Benfro tried to remember his first view of the city. The hill rising up to the river had been the other way round, so he must have circled it. Then he realized: the river came down from the hills. He had followed it all the way here. All he needed to do was to retrace its course.

'I'll track you down,' the figure cried, its voice carrying despite the distance between them. 'I'll kill you. All of you. I am the only power here.'

Benfro tried his best to ignore her, but he could feel the waves of fear, anger and frustration boiling out from her. He beat his great wings hard, pushing the air from him as he tried to flee the city. Beneath him the river had turned a dull grey, reflecting the clouds overhead. Fat drops of rain began to splatter against his face, stinging his eyes and slicking his scales.

'You can't escape me,' the voice said, too close to be still on the ground. Benfro didn't turn, didn't look. He shut his eyes against the storm and thrust himself onward. It was no longer the wonderful feeling of freedom, the simple twist and flick of his tail, the flexing of his shoulders that effortlessly steered him through the air. Now it was like wading through sticky mud, swimming against a winter storm flood.

'I am your master and you will bow to me,' the voice said. Benfro was finding it hard to breathe now. It felt like someone had tied his legs and was pulling him back towards that menacing black hall. Still he fought against it. This was not real. It was just a dream.

'I . . . will . . . not,' he said and put all of his strength into a last mighty downstroke.

Everything happened very quickly. He felt a pain in his back as if something had sunk sharp talons into it, then he heard a wail of surprise. With a deafening roar, he rushed forward at impossible speed. For an instant he opened his eyes and saw the darkened countryside flickering past him. He no longer had any control over his flight, no longer seemed to have wings at all. He just crashed head over tail, convinced he was falling to the stone road, knowing that any minute now he would smash into the ground, his bones popping and cracking. He clenched his eyes tight shut and waited for the end.

21

There exists above the mortal plane another place that mirrors it closely: the aethereal. Animals, plants, and even buildings occupy this space with a mindless certainty, but thinking creatures cannot easily enter it. To do so requires not so much a manipulation of the Grym as the realization of a perfect state of consciousness. It is a skill few will ever master, though all should strive so to do, for within the aethereal the adept may communicate over vast distances with others so skilled.

As with all magic, there is a downside to this skill, for when an adept enters the aethereal, his mind leaves his body behind. The aethereal is a place of many wonders and distractions, of traps and unexpected dangers. And it is a place where time flows differently to the norm. Many a skilled warrior priest has entered the aethereal never to return.

Father Andro, *Magic and the Mind*

'Captain Derrin of the Royal Guard left this here this morning,' Usel said. 'I'm sure they have their reasons for digging the poor woman up, but it seems a bit barbaric to me.'

'Why are you showing this to me?' Errol asked.

'Well, I can't possibly do a proper post-mortem on my

345

own; I can't get the lid off for one thing, and I need some-one to takes notes for me as I go along. It's much neater that way. I was on my way to the library to ask Andro if I could borrow one of his novitiates when along you popped. Couldn't have been better, really.'

Errol thought that it could have been. He could have been out in the exercise yards enjoying the afternoon sun and practising his archery, not down in the bowels of the monastery, shivering and discomfited, with a slightly mad doctor and a royal corpse for company. On the other hand, Usel was a friendly enough person, quite unlike any of the other quaisters he had met. He also seemed to know a great deal and was happy to share his knowledge. He reminded Errol somewhat of old Father Drebble, who had always encouraged healthy curiosity and was happy to spend time with the genuinely interested.

'What should I do?' he asked and received a broad smile from the medic as a reward for his enthusiasm.

'First we need to get the lid off. You take the bottom, where it's lighter.'

Errol grasped the stone as well as he could and together they managed to half-lift, half-slide it off. It fell with a crash that echoed in the empty hall, coming to rest on the floor alongside the trolley. A waft of foul air filled his nose and he stepped back, coughing before inching close again to get a better look.

The corpse was withered and shrivelled, its skin turned black and leathery with the years but not decayed. The princess had been buried in a long white gown of thin material, no more than a bed dress, really. Her bare feet were twisted around as if she were in terrible pain and the tightening of her skin had opened her mouth in a silent scream.

'That's strange,' Usel said, peering into the coffin at the body and sniffing. 'She's better preserved than I'd have expected.'

'The coffin was well sealed,' Errol said.

'Even so, her skin looks like it's been tanned. If she'd just dried up I'd've expected her to be more grey. Here, help me lift her out.'

Errol stared, aghast for a moment, then thought about what he was being asked to do. It was no worse than dealing with some of the infected wounds and growths that his mother's patients had brought to their little cottage in the woods. Better, in many ways, since Princess Lleyn had been dead for fourteen years. Something Usel had said suddenly registered in his mind.

'When did she die?' Errol asked. 'You said it was fourteen years ago.'

'Indeed I did. I guess you were too young to remember, but most people will tell you the story. Tragic, it was. She died on her sister's birthday.'

'Queen Beulah's birthday?'

'Of course, Queen Beulah's birthday. Why?'

'That was the day I was born,' Errol said, looking at the corpse with a strange feeling of connection. 'I was born the day she died.'

'Well don't worry yourself about it – I'm sure a great many people died the day you were born. Now let's have a quick look at the body. It's amazing what you can discover after even this long in the ground. I can tell she was poisoned, for one thing.'

'Poisoned?'

'Yes, and a very nasty potion too. I haven't seen it used in a long while. It grows in Fo Afron on the other side of the Sea of Tegid. It's called gallweed and it kills slowly, leaching all the life out of a person over time. They grow steadily thinner and weaker until they just don't have the strength to live any more.'

'But how can you tell?' Errol asked.

'Well, there's a distinctive aroma to the corpse. You wouldn't notice it when she was buried, but now her body's dried out, you can smell it.'

Errol lowered his nose once more to the coffin and sniffed. There was surprisingly little odour now that the initial stale air had been expelled, but the body did smell very faintly.

'It's like spices. Ginger . . . no, cinnamon and cloves. No, that's not right either.'

'You're in the right area though, Errol,' Usel said. 'Now let's lift her out.'

Errol reached inside and put his hands under the thin calves. With that first touch he shuddered involuntarily as if someone were walking on his grave. A flurry of images flashed through his mind: a grey-haired man wiping his brow with a damp cloth; a woman dressed as a serving maid helping him out of bed; a lantern swinging with the rhythmic motion of a horse-drawn wagon; a cottage in a clearing in the forest, curiously large; a fully grown dragon peering down at him with a look of infinite sadness in her eyes. And then a terrible pain ripped through him. He felt his legs give out, and as he plunged into blackness, the clash of falling knives echoed in the stone-vaulted hall.

'Where's Inquisitor Melyn? Have him report to me immediately.'

'Your Majesty, the inquisitor left for Emmass Fawr at first light this morning.'

Beulah cursed herself for forgetting. There was so much to remember that even a conversation held just hours ago had slipped her mind. The servant who had come running at her call knelt before the Obsidian Throne gently shaking. His fear filled the great hall with an odious stench.

'Leave me,' Beulah said, then turned to the guards who stood either side of the dais, supposedly there to protect her from assassins, though any who made it this far would find her far from helpless.

'All of you, leave,' she said. 'I wish to be alone.'

For a moment she thought one of the warriors was going to protest. No doubt if the inquisitor found out that they had deserted their posts, even on a direct order from the queen, they would be publicly flogged. She didn't care. If Melyn was on his way back to Emmass Fawr that meant he would most likely be on the Calling Road. And that meant that she could contact him, with difficulty. She didn't want soldiers and servants clogging up the calm of the Neuadd with their petty fears and worries, their endless thoughts about gambling, drinking and whoring.

'You may remain at the doors,' Beulah said to the officer of the guard as he marched his men from the hall. She had no doubt he would have done it anyway, supplementing the soldiers who already patrolled outside. It didn't matter to her as long as they were on the other side of the walls.

'Your Majesty need only call and we will be here,' the officer said, bowing deeply. Beulah scowled at him as he left, then pulled herself together, gathered her wits about her and sank once more into the power that was the throne.

It felt like a warm bath, soothing away the aches and worries of her new reign. As she slipped from the physical world, so the discomfort of the cold stone seat evaporated, leaving her relaxed, poised, ready to embark on her journey.

She paused a moment to consider the Neuadd from this altered perspective. It was still the same hall, magnificent to the point of overkill. Its great pillars soared up into the carved arches of the ceiling; the mirror-smooth floor reflected the morning sun, filtered into a thousand different colours as it passed through the great windows to either side; the Obsidian Throne towered over her, black and threatening as a nightmare, yet alive somehow with the power of the world. And still there was something different about the hall that she couldn't put her finger on.

Beulah came to this other place often. It was the starting point for her forays into the minds of her nobles and the rich merchants of Candlehall. She understood now why the House of Balwen had allowed the great city to swamp the hills surrounding the palace. From here she could eavesdrop on the thoughts and conversations of any of the city's inhabitants. But it required skill and a mental discipline she doubted her father had ever mastered. Nor her grandfather before him. Beulah wondered what they had felt when sitting on this great throne. Both of them were of the House of Balwen. Both of them would have had some natural ability with the Grym and the powers of magic. Yet both had been weak-willed. Sitting on the throne must have been a kind of torture, hearing the constant chattering thoughts and anxieties of a hundred thousand subjects all around them. No wonder then that her grandfather had spent much of his reign hunting at Ystumtuen, like his father before him. And perhaps it explained why her father had resorted to drink. What had happened to the once-noble line of warriors that it had produced three generations of such weak-willed men? False kings who would make peace with dragons and Llanwennog, would even barter their own flesh and blood for a quiet life and a soft bed? She would restore the pride of the Balwen name and make the Twin Kingdoms great once more.

Concentrating, Beulah coalesced her thoughts into an image of herself. On the edge of her senses she could hear the clamour of the city, feel the presence of sweating, toiling peasants, avaricious merchants and effete gentry. Even the mindless existence of the pack animals could be a distraction that had to be pushed to one side. Dogs were particularly hard to ignore with their simple single-minded drives: eat, sleep, breed. Focusing away from them, she cast her mind out across the hall, out the door, through the palace and along the northern road.

She went quickly, not lingering to be sidetracked by the endless possibilities of the city's mindscape. Past the old wall and the Warrior Gate, it became easier as the distractions lessened. She sped up, covering the ground at a speed no horseman could hope to match. Faster she went, faster still until it felt like she flew just a few feet above the road.

Even here, in the dream, she could feel the draw of the Calling Road, insidious and compelling. The ancient spell that had imbued it with power was as potent as the day Inquisitor Hardy cast it. Life seemed so much more complicated now than it had back then. Beulah longed for the days of strong kings and iron rule. What would Brynceri have done about the endless rounds of diplomacy and bureaucracy? What would he have done about upstart dragons? She couldn't help but think it would have involved fire and the sword. In both instances.

Up ahead, far in the distance, Beulah could make out the mind shape of a troop of men riding at a trot. In an instant she was with them, moving silent and unseen through the ranks of their thoughts. They were pale ill-defined beings in this realm, although some, where the skill burned more brightly, were more substantial than others. A few were no more than wisps flickering above the solid forms of their horses. Only their leader appeared as fully formed in the aethereal as in the physical. Melyn rode at the head of the column, bolt upright in the saddle. He appeared younger than his years, as if his mind harboured a vanity that even his prodigious strength of will had not been able to dampen.

'Queen Beulah, it's good to see you,' he said without turning. It was a small show of his superiority in the ways of magic, and Beulah hated him for it as much as she cursed herself for not trying harder. Occasionally she managed to catch him unawares, but obviously not today.

'I'm sorry, my queen,' Melyn said, turning to face her. 'Forgive an old man his little games. What brings you to the ghost road?'

'This morning, not an hour ago, I saw a dragon flying over the city,' Beulah said. Melyn flinched at the words as he always did when this subject was brought up.

'I assume this wasn't a physical dragon,' the inquisitor said. 'No one else saw it.'

'I was as I am now,' Beulah said. 'There are few in the Twin Kingdoms who have this skill, and only I can sit on the Obsidian Throne. But if any others were watching, they'd have seen it. It flew, Melyn. It had wings the size of a house. It circled the citadel as if it were looking for a nest.'

'You tried to ensnare it?'

'Of course,' Beulah said. 'I thought I had it too, but it escaped. One moment it was there, the next it was gone. I might believe I'd killed it, but I can't be sure. It must have escaped me.'

Melyn sat silently on his horse for a while. Beulah floated along the road beside him, fighting back the anger that retelling of the intruder had kindled in her. At the time she had been so furious she had crashed out of her dream state and almost fallen from the throne. She needed to retain control of her emotions.

'You're fading, Beulah. Get a grip on yourself,' Melyn said. The rebuke stung her, but years of training kept her focused.

'What are we to do about this?' she asked. 'I can't have these creatures infiltrating the aethereal. You know as well as I do that I must have total control over it to succeed with our plans.'

'My warrior priests will seek it out,' Melyn said. 'There are few enough of them left and we've archives accounting where all of them live. Your intruder will be captured and brought before you. It's up to you what you decide to do with it.'

'I wish I had your confidence,' Beulah said, 'both in the skill of your warriors and in the accuracy of your lists.'

'My lady is too harsh,' Melyn said. 'Even if our archives weren't accurate, the intruder would have come from nearby. Dragons have only a rudimentary ability to exist in the upper sphere, as well you know.'

'Nevertheless it came to Candlehall, to the Neuadd. It was drawn here,' Beulah said. 'And it was strong enough to fight me. This was no accident. Do what you have to at Emmass Fawr. Consult your archives and deploy your warriors, but I think this creature will be back before long. I expect you to lead the hunt for it yourself.'

'Of course, Your Majesty,' Melyn said, bowing his head to her image. Beulah stopped and let the troop pass her by. She waited for a few minutes, watching as they dwindled into the distance along the arrow-straight track. Overhead the sky was grey-blue and flat, as it always looked in this place. She scanned it for signs of movement but could see only birds. On a whim she reached out for one of them, grasping it with an invisible hand and squeezing the life out of it. She was reminded of her father on the dance floor at her birthday ball. This tiny feathered creature was no different, really. It had a simple life force and rudimentary intelligence. Without remorse, she relieved it of both. There was a faint, startled flash of anxiety and then the bird disappeared. Beulah imagined that anyone actually there that morning would have seen a sparrow flying across the sky and then suddenly drop to the ground for no reason. It amused her to have such a power over even the most insignificant of her subjects. But at the same time it angered her to know that other creatures walked the upper sphere, flew in its skies in defiance of her. It would not be for much longer.

Turning, she sped back along the road in a whirling blur. Returning to her physical self was always much easier than reaching out into the aethereal, and in moments she was back at the Neuadd, looking down on herself seated on the Obsidian Throne. A flick of her imaginary head changed the perspective and once more she could feel the hard stone, cold and uncomfortable even through the thick cushions. As she came back to herself she looked once more around the vast hall and realized what it was that was different. The Neuadd she saw now had windows of coloured glass which was jumbled and patternless. She knew the tale of how Brynceri's great masterpieces had been smashed by the armies of Llanwennog at the time of the Brumal Wars. When the invaders had finally been driven out of the Twin Kingdoms the great hall had been repaired. Only the damage to the windows was too great for the pictures that had graced them to be re-created. In the upper sphere she saw the windows as they must have been before, depicting wild scenes from early history and legend.

It was too late to study them more closely now, Beulah knew. Once she had begun the return to the physical, there was no turning back. Still, it would be interesting to study them at greater length some other time.

'Guards,' Beulah shouted as soon as she had centred herself. The doors opened and the officer of the guard came running across the hall, two of his men slightly behind him. All three dropped to their knees as soon as they reached the dais.

'Fetch me Seneschal Padraig, I've a proclamation to make,' Beulah said. The officer sent one of his guards and there followed a tense few minutes' silence as they waited. Beulah tried to refocus her mind, to see the windows as they had originally been, but she was too excited at the prospect of what she was about to do. She felt like a giddy schoolgirl contemplating breaking one of the rules, then laughed out loud. She was queen. She made the rules now.

Finally Padraig appeared. He came wheezing through the doors and limped as quickly as he could across the floor. He didn't kneel, only bowing his head. Beulah considered rebuking him for his impoliteness but realized that if she forced him to kneel it would take him hours to get back up again.

'Your Majesty,' the seneschal said. 'I am at your service.'

'Of course,' Beulah said. 'Now make a note of this. As of noon today it's my intention to reinstate King Brynceri's original charter of the Order of the High Ffrydd. The order will continue its current military activities, but it will also be charged with hunting down and exterminating all dragons within the Twin Kingdoms. In addition, the payment of aurddraig will be resumed. Ten gold flocks for every head delivered either to me here at Candlehall or to the order at Emmass Fawr.'

'Majesty, is that wise?' Padraig asked, his eyes wide with shock. 'We've had no quarrel with what few dragons still live for almost two centuries. Their tithes are a welcome addition to the treasury each year.'

Beulah looked down on the slight figure of the priest. His flesh was pale around his jowls and he looked deeply unhappy at this news. Was it simply that he was being denied the few slads that trickled in each year from the remote parts of the Twin Kingdoms, the tribute paid by each dragon to the throne? Knowing how closely the seneschal monitored the treasury, it probably was.

'I don't want their gold, Padraig,' she said, fixing him with her stare. 'I want their jewels.'

'This is what you've been hiding all these years? Why didn't you tell me?'

'It was important that as few people as possible knew.'

'Does he know?'

'Of course not. And he never should.'

Errol came slowly to his senses, wondering where he was and why he was so cold. He could hear the voices of two men, and it took a while to register that he knew who they were. The careful, measured tones were those of his tutor, Master Librarian Andro. The other voice, questioning and incredulous, was the surgeon he had met, Usel.

Usel. He remembered now. He had gone down to the mortuary to help the medic examine a dead body. A princess.

'What about Melyn? He wants a report by the end of the day.'

'He must never learn the truth of this. I'm sorry, my friend, but you must do everything in your power to stop him finding out.'

Errol opened his eyes to a view of a stone-vaulted ceiling flickering gently in the light of numerous torches. He tried to sit up, but his head ached like someone had hit him with a rock, and his body felt impossibly weak. Instead, he rolled sideways until he could make out the blurry image of the two men in heated conversation.

'Oh, I can keep this from the inquisitor, don't you worry about that,' Usel said.

'Well, be careful, Usel. And don't underestimate our leader. He didn't get to be inquisitor just by being old, you know. Ah, it looks like our young patient has woken.'

Errol groaned as Usel came over and knelt beside him.

'How are you feeling?' the surgeon asked.

'Tired,' Errol said. His voice came out as a whisper.

'Well, I guess you would be. You gave me quite a turn fainting like that.'

'I fainted?'

'Dead away. I've seen it happen before with trainee surgeons. Fine one minute, the next . . . bang.' Usel made a falling motion with his hand, then helped Errol up into a sitting position.

'The post-mortem?' Errol asked, glancing across the room to the narrow table, its burden now covered with a white sheet.

'Oh, I did that. Don't you worry about it.'

'Come, Errol,' Andro said, helping him up. 'Let's get

you out of this cold cave and back upstairs. Get some sun on your face and the Grym in your bones, you'll be right as rain.'

Bemused, it was all Errol could do to be led out of the mortuary and up the stairs. His strength seemed to return to him the further he left behind the stone coffin and its tragic occupant, so that by the time he reached the ground floor of the monastery he was hard pushed to remember what all the fuss had been about.

'Feeling better?' Andro asked.

Errol nodded.

'Good. Well, you'd better go off and get some exercise. Then I want you back in the library after evening prayers to help me with the archiving. Trainee surgeon indeed. If Usel wants to poach my best novitiates he'll have to try a lot harder than that.'

Benfro swam up from the darkness in a panic of thrashing limbs. He was flexing his wings desperately to stay aloft, but the ground was close beneath him. He had to roll when he landed, take the momentum out of his fall or it would snap his bones. At least if he could still walk he stood a chance of getting away. Acting as much out of the instinct honed from years of climbing cliffs and trees as from any conscious thought, he threw himself forward blindly.

There was a terrible crash, the sound of splintering wood and heavy objects hitting the ground, but the impact was far less than he had been expecting. Barely winded, he lay still, eyes clenched tight shut, breathing heavily.

'My dear Benfro, are you all right?'

Lying on his back, Benfro thought for a moment he

must be dreaming. He knew that voice well, but it was a world away, surely. Then, as the rush of sensation began to subside, he remembered a time before he had been flying over the land, before he had seen the great city, before he had been caught by the tall thin figure. It seemed days ago, but the more he thought about it the more he realized it had been only moments since he had begun to re-create the room in his mind. Slowly, he opened his eyes.

It was still dark, lit only by the single sliver of light that pierced the crack in the shutters. He was staring up at the ceiling and couldn't help noticing the mottled patterns on the plasterwork, the heavy cobwebs that lurked in the corners and around the simple chandelier with its stubs of candle ribboned by melted wax. The details held his attention completely as he tried to remember where he was, who he was and what he was doing. All these things he knew, he realized, but the understanding of them was elusive, as if the memories were greased.

The patterns of light and dark shifted in the room and a face loomed overhead. It peered down at him and blocked his view of the chandelier, forcing him to reconnect with reality.

'You fell out of your chair,' the face said, and Benfro remembered that it had a name. Meirionydd.

'Actually, to be more accurate, you threw yourself out of your chair,' she said. 'It was very impressive.'

'I . . . What just happened?' Benfro asked, looking around the room and then down at his own body as if unsure that it was real. He was sprawled on the floor in a quite undignified pose, a rug rucked up against him like a heavy blanket.

'You tell me,' Meirionydd said. 'I only asked you to look for the Llinellau, not go off for a little jaunt.'

'I went . . . away?' Benfro asked, rolling over and sitting himself up on the floor.

'Not physically, no,' Meirionydd said. 'But for a moment your spirit was gone. I take it you were flying again?'

Benfro told her what he had seen, the memories slowly settling themselves into a more or less logical order as he tried to recall them. Meirionydd listened quietly, asking questions only when he muddled up the details or jumped ahead too far. When he had finished she sat for a long time silent. Benfro watched her, waiting, confused and frightened. This was not what he had expected the subtle arts to be all about.

'You saw only one woman?' Meirionydd asked after long moments had passed.

'Woman?' Benfro asked.

'Men and women, male and female. Like Palisander and Angharad, Rasalene and Arhelion. I'm sorry, Benfro, I sometimes forget how young you are. And what little you know of the world of men. We've kept it so deliberately. They're not something that a kitling needs to be curious about. But maybe that decision was wrong. Still, this woman you saw must have been a very powerful mage. And you too have a natural talent that is stronger than anything I've ever seen. You must be very careful, Benfro. You understand so little of what you are doing, and that's dangerous, for you and for us.'

'What do you mean?' Benfro asked, worried by Meiri-onydd's serious words.

'You are a dreamwalker, Benfro. You walk with ease in

places that a trained mage might take years to reach. But you don't know how it is that you do these things; they just happen. And the places you go are dangerous places. Emmass Fawr and the Neuadd are both seats of power for men, though they belonged to us long ago. You're attracted to them like a bee to a flower. It's a miracle you haven't come to any harm so far.'

'I don't understand,' Benfro said. 'What are these places? How do I get to them?'

'That's the problem,' Meirionydd said. 'You don't know how you do it. You need to learn, and I'll do everything I can to teach you. But it's difficult. You'll have no control until you've learned how to see the Llinellau Grym. Yet something seems to be stopping you from mastering the most simple of the subtle arts.'

'Could what Frecknock did to me have, I don't know . . . affected my ability to see the Llinellau?'

'I doubt it,' the old dragon said. 'She merely put a suggestion in your mind that made it impossible for you to talk about that incident. No, it's something in your nature, Benfro. But don't worry. We'll overcome it. I've had worse students than you. Why do you think Ynys Môn spends all his time hunting and fishing?'

'He can't see the lines either?' Benfro asked, feeling a lot better in himself.

'Oh, he can see them,' Meirionydd said, 'if he tries. But it took him long enough. And he's never had much of a talent for it. Now enough chattering. You have to practise until it comes. And if that takes ten years, so be it.'

22

For all great workings of magic, be they spells that affect thousands or simple conjurings that are personal in nature, for every enchantment there is a vulnerable spot. Most obviously this is the conjuror himself, for he is the fulcrum directing the Grym to his will. But there are spells which persist even after the mage who has performed them has gone, spells which are anchored not in the body of a man but in the world itself. No spell can be sealed entirely, for were such a thing done then that spell would wither and die. The skilled mage will see the point where Grym ends and conjuring begins, and there he will find the key to unravelling the spell.

Father Andro, *Magic and the Mind*

Melyn studied the boy who sat across the desk from him. He had changed in the months since the choosing. The round-cheeked puppy fat of youth had melted from his face, hardening those features that had so worried the princess. Queen now, he corrected himself. So much had happened since that night when they had ridden into the village with low expectations. It was undeniable that the boy had the features of Prince Balch, but that in itself didn't mean he was related. It did mean that he would make an excellent spy, just as soon as his unswerving loyalty to the order could be ensured.

'Andro tells me that you're a quick student,' Melyn said, pouring two goblets of wine and pushing one across the desk towards his charge. It was a heavy sweet wine from the Caldy peninsula, not something he had much of a taste for himself, but it would quickly intoxicate the boy and break down his barriers.

'Master Andro is very kind,' Errol said, 'but most of what we learn in class I've already learned back home. Father . . . Kewick was a good teacher.'

Melyn looked deep into the boy's eyes, fixing them with his own gaze. He felt the link between them, easier now that he had done it a few times, though there was still that initial resistance to his suggestion. As if discomfited by his stare, Errol took up the goblet and swallowed a mouthful. Almost immediately Melyn could feel the barriers begin to dissolve. He worked on the boy's mind, suggesting that he drink more and reinforcing the idea that he had learned all his young wisdom from the fat predicant.

'Your reading and writing are impressive for a boy of your age. Especially one from your background,' Melyn said, letting his flattery work on Errol's ego, building up a vision of trust in himself and the order. 'I've asked Andro to begin tutoring in the language of the Llanwennogs,' he added, pushing the desire to learn towards the boy as he said the words. He needn't have bothered; Errol's passion for knowledge was vast.

'Don't they speak like us?' he asked.

'It's similar,' Melyn said, 'but different enough in its way. A man from the Hendry could make himself understood in Tynhelyg, but they'd know him for a foreigner whatever he looked like.'

'Why would I want to go to Tynhelyg?' Errol asked.

'Think, boy,' Melyn said. 'You've the looks of them and the brains to learn to be like them. Who better to send into our enemy's camp to discover what he plans?'

'You want me to be a spy?'

'Of course I do,' Melyn said, and along with the words he pushed the idea of a life of excitement, travel to far lands, adventure and danger into the boy's thoughts. There was already a seed of acceptance in his mind – the inquisitor simply sought to feed it, nurture it into the same sort of powerful driving force that was Errol's natural curiosity.

'But you won't be going any time soon,' the inquisitor added. 'It takes years of training, and even then most don't make the grade. Do you think you have what it takes?'

'I . . . I don't know,' Errol said.

'Good,' Melyn said. 'I'd think less of you if you were certain you could do it. But I knew you had promise as soon as I saw you. I reckon you'll do well.'

'Thank you, sir,' the boy said, lifting his goblet once more as the inquisitor willed him to do so. It was definitely getting easier to manipulate him, Melyn realized. It saddened him in some ways. Far better that the boy had come to him willingly. Modifying large chunks of his memory was a crude way of ensuring his trust and loyalty to the order, and one which could very easily backfire. Time would set the suggestions solid so that the boy would know no other truth, but time was always in short supply. Yet, handled properly, Errol Ramsbottom could become a powerful weapon in his hands. The risk was certainly worth it.

'Sir Felyn? Are you there?'

The voice was quiet, almost an echo on the wind rather than something spoken.

'It is I, Frecknock, calling out to you for help.'

Melyn glanced at the boy sitting across from him. If he too had heard then he made no sign of it. Damn her timing, he thought. He had planned to spend at least another half-hour working on Errol. Now he would have to begin all over again. But then the secrets the stupid and wilful young dragon could reveal were far more important than the boy right now. She might even be able to shed some light on the queen's recent encounter.

'I'm afraid I'm going to have to ask you to leave now, Errol,' Melyn said gently, planting a notion of discomfort in the boy's mind. 'We'll continue this conversation later. Tell Andro I want you to learn the language of the Llanwennogs. I expect you to be able to answer me in their tongue next time we meet.'

Melyn watched as the boy hastily drained his wine, stood, bowed and darted from the room. Once the door had latched shut, he settled back in his chair and collected his thoughts, willing himself once more into the role of Sir Felyn, wandering dragon in search of a mate.

'Sweet Frecknock,' he thought, sending the words in the Draigiaith, that terrible, difficult language that made his skin crawl whenever he heard it.

'Ah, Sir Felyn,' came the reply. 'I thought I'd lost you for ever.'

'And I too,' he thought back. 'What has kept you from

me for so long? I would have come to your side but you never told me where I could find you.'

Melyn sent his mind out along the lines, trying to locate the source of the voice. It didn't take him long to touch the alien mind, so small and self-centred, filled with its own petty worries and anxieties, frustrations and rage.

'It was the kitling, the little squirt. He told them what I was doing. They came and stopped me. They took away the book. But I don't need it now. I can do the calling without it.'

Melyn choked back the rage swelling up in him. No licence to breed had been sought in his lifetime. There should be no kitlings among the dragons.

'I'm sorry to hear of your woes, sweet Frecknock,' he thought, struggling to send a soothing calm out with his words. 'But your skill in the subtle arts is plainly far superior to those who would thwart you. Your beauty is matched by an inner strength I've not seen for many centuries.'

'You flatter me, Sir Felyn,' the thought came back. Not angry or mistrustful – he could sense that she liked his attentions.

'I speak only the truth as I see it. But I would see you with my eyes as well as touch the fair brilliance of your mind. Tell me how I might find you, and though I be at the far end of Gwlad, I'll not stop until I can be by your side.'

'The far end of Gwlad?' came the reply, and Melyn cursed himself for underestimating the stupidity of his quarry. He had meant it as a simple figure of speech, and she had taken it to mean he was months if not years of travel away from her. The sad disappointment in her tiny little mind was a sickly taste in his mouth like bile from a gut punch.

'Sweet Frecknock, don't be so sad,' he thought. 'I'm not so far away, surely, that I can't reach you in a week, maybe two. Tell me where to come and not even the Inquisitor of the Order of the High Ffrydd will keep me from reaching you.' It was true, he realized with a wry chuckle. He would positively speed himself to her.

'I can't tell you exactly where I am.' Frecknock's thought came to him peppered with anxiety.

He sent soothing, formless thoughts back to her, gently encouraging disclosure, assuring her that she was doing the right thing.

'The others rely on her protection,' she thought. 'They may be small-minded and mean-spirited but they're the only family I have, and I wouldn't want to see them suffer the same fate as my parents. They were killed, you see. By a mob of men. My mother, who would never hurt a fly, was hacked to death. My father was trapped and burned when he tried to take his revenge. I was lucky to escape with my life. It was only after months of wandering in the forest that Morgwm found me and brought me here.'

'You've suffered more terribly than any should have to,' Melyn thought, suppressing the urge to cut the link with this simpering halfwit. He needed more information to confirm the suspicion that was growing inside him, more than just a name. 'It's fortunate indeed that you were found, that even now you live with others of . . . our kind. Tell me, sweet Frecknock, how can you all live together without attracting the same attention that claimed your poor parents?'

'We're protected here,' Frecknock's thoughts were a mixture of emotions, some cautious and sad, others excited and hopeful. Melyn could only assume that years of skulking and hiding had beaten down her spirit. Now the excitement of her success in finding him again was chipping away at her long-learned reticence. Silently he pushed a feeling of encouragement at her, building on the sense that he could be trusted. It was not dissimilar from what he had done to the boy Errol. The inquisitor smiled to himself as he realized how alike they were, and yet so different.

'I don't fully understand it yet,' Frecknock continued. 'It's an ancient spell, very powerful. Any who come to this part of the forest will only find the path to the cottage in the clearing. Only Morgwm can take them to the village, unless they have been there before. So you see, good Sir Felyn, I can't tell you how to get here. You must first find Morgwm herself and persuade her of your good intentions.'

Melyn racked his brain for the memory. He had read a list, somewhere, that detailed all the dragons known to still live in the Twin Kingdoms. Andro would be able to find it for him, but he needed it now. And he had heard the name before, he was sure. He had ridden with Padraig, decades earlier when they were both young men, when warrior priests had accompanied predicants as they travelled the Twin Kingdoms collecting tithes. Had she not been one of the first dragons to awaken his suspicions? Yes, the more he thought about it, the more he remembered her. A healer, peddling quackery to the nearby villagers, she had shown him little deference, no respect. And she had paid her tithes with newly minted coin she could only have acquired by theft.

'Morgwm the Green,' he thought, remembering finally. He could feel the rush of excitement channelling back along the lines into him.

'You know her?' Frecknock's giddy anticipation almost made him laugh out loud. She was so simple, so stupid.

'It's been many a year since last I saw Morgwm the Green,' Melyn thought, 'but I know where she lives. I'll come to her cottage in two weeks' time. Wait for me, sweet Frecknock, but tell no one. I'd like to surprise my old friend.'

'Of course, Sir Felyn. It will be our secret,' Frecknock thought. 'Oh, I cannot wait to meet you. You must have such stories to tell of the long road, such adventures as would turn even Benfro's head.'

'Benfro?' Melyn queried.

'Morgwm's kitling,' Frecknock thought. 'He's a pest who gets far more attention than he deserves. He's the one who stopped my last calling. He was spying on us. He's only fourteen and they're already teaching him the subtle arts.'

Melyn almost exploded with rage. Only a lifetime's mental discipline stopped him from channelling it all into Frecknock, revealing his true self even to her love-blinded senses.

'A kitling, and a boy dragon at that,' Melyn thought in a tight-closed series of words with no emotion attached. 'I look forward to meeting him. Though not as much as I look forward to meeting you, sweet Frecknock. But now I must go. There is much that needs to be prepared for my journey. You should go too, lest someone once more interrupt our private thoughts. Two weeks, sweet Frecknock, and I will stand at your side. But remember, tell no one.'

Melyn thought he heard her voice faintly echo, 'No one,' but he had already cut his mind off from hers. He was cold with rage, calm in a way he had never been. The Shepherd moves his flock to a plan only he can know, he thought. And this was surely the work of his god. Now was the time to purge the world of the evil that was dragons. He stood up and crossed to the door. Outside his rooms the corridor was dark, the flickering torches on the walls making the shadows between them impenetrable.

'Osgal,' he shouted.

The tall man emerged from the shadows, buckling his belt. He had a slightly green look about him. 'Inquisitor,' Osgal said, dropping to one knee and bowing his head, 'please forgive me.'

'Whatever for?' Melyn asked. 'Get up, man.' He was in too much of a hurry to worry about whatever it was ailed the captain of his personal guard. There were many preparations to be made for his journey. He would need a troop of warrior priests for one thing. It wouldn't hurt to take some of the novitiates along with him either. This was the sort of training they needed, not endless bookwork and sword practice.

'Gather your men and select ten of the novitiates,' Melyn said. 'We ride at dawn.'

'My lord, might I ask where we are going?' Osgal asked.

'Ystumtuen and the edge of the great forest,' Melyn said. 'We're going dragon hunting, Captain.'

23

When attempting to influence your enemy's thoughts, it is important to keep your manipulations as simple as possible. Far better to work with what is already there than to try and build a completely new reality. As in all magic, observation and preparation are the keys. Know your enemy better than you know yourself. Know his friends and family, his past experiences and his future ambitions. Then you can plant your suggestions so that he will think them his own.

Father Andro, *Magic and the Mind*

Errol was puzzled as he left the meeting with the inquisitor. Had he done something wrong to be so suddenly dismissed? He couldn't think of anything. In fact the details of the whole encounter were slipping away from him as if they were unimportant. And yet he knew that something had happened, something that jarred with the confident, stern but avuncular feelings the inquisitor seemed to have towards him.

'What is it about old men and young boys?'

Errol nearly jumped out of his skin. The corridor outside Melyn's quarters was gloomy, lit only by occasional torches hanging in iron sconces from the rough stone wall. A face leered out of the darkness, promising violence and pain. Without thinking, he took a step back and the menace faded, replaced by a deep-throated chuckle. Captain Osgal stepped out of the shadows.

'Don't panic, boy,' he said. 'I know that you're here on the inquisitor's business. You won't get a thrashing, this time.'

'I . . . I've finished for this evening. I was just heading to the chapel for candle lighting.' Errol was nervous of the captain. There was something about the man that filled him with a deep unease, as if Osgal had done him a great disservice at some time but he could not remember what, or when. It didn't help that the head of the inquisitor's personal troop had a reputation worse by far than any of the quaisters in the monastery.

'Not so fast, young Ramsbottom. The inquisitor has a guard in this corridor at all times. This is my shift right now but I have to go . . . somewhere for ten minutes. You'll stay here and guard the corridor until I get back.'

'But I'm not armed,' Errol said.

'Don't be stupid, boy.' Errol could see the discomfort on the captain's face. By the way he was holding his hands across his belly and the faint sheen of sweat on his face, it wasn't hard to imagine what he wanted ten minutes for. Errol wondered what they had been serving in the officers' mess that evening that could disagree so fundamentally with a constitution as robust as that of Captain Osgal.

'There's a full troop of warrior priests on the lower floors of this building,' the captain said. 'Any intruder would have to get through the main gates undetected and across the monastery complex unchallenged before they even came close to here. And if they made it as far as the inquisitor's study then they would have him to contend with. You won't be needed to fight off hordes of Llanwennog spies, but if His Grace comes out of there and doesn't see a guard in this corridor, it'll be my head on the block. So just stand there in the shadows and try not to fall asleep. Ten minutes, that's all I need.'

Errol watched as Captain Osgal hurried away, unsure whether he was going to be thanked for being helpful or reviled for being party to the soldier's moment of weakness. On balance, he favoured his chances of the latter, and the thought of yet more humiliation and punishment at the hands of the man filled him with a deepening sense of gloom.

Settling back into the shadows as instructed, Errol considered his life since he had come to Emmass Fawr. It wasn't the great adventure he had expected, though neither could he deny that the opportunities for learning were far greater than anything he might have found back home. Home. The word seemed almost alien to him. This was his home now, or so he was told every day. The order was his family, not Hennas and Godric. There was no room, nor any need, for Maggs Clusster in his life.

The thought brought Errol up short. He hadn't considered his past for a while, and neither had he thought about Maggs. Now that he did, he realized that she was the wrong person. He knew her well enough, but what he knew about her was not what sat at the front of his mind. He had never walked hand in hand with her through the trees, nor had he sat on warm summer evenings by her side as they gazed over the forest from the rock at Jagged Leap. Maggs was the sad-faced thin young woman who had appeared at the cottage door late one night with a terrible tale. The girl whose own father had got her pregnant. The girl whose bully of a brother, Trell, had pushed Errol into the pool where old Ben Coulter had drowned. Pushed Errol and . . . someone else.

It was the first time Errol had thought of her in months. The green girl, he liked to call her. Sometimes she was in his dreams, sad and silently calling his name. Always he had thought of her as Maggs, but now it was as if a barrier in his brain had been pulled down. He knew that she wasn't Maggs. So who was she?

The familiar dull ache spread across the front of his head. It always seemed to come when he thought hard about his past. Errol tried his best to ignore it, massaging his temples and concentrating on the floor as he racked his memory for a name, even a face. Without summoning, the lines appeared to his eyes, criss-crossing the floor and walls in a pattern far more intricate than any he had seen before. They were thinner than usual, almost invisible like the lightest of morning dews evaporating from leaves. The corridor pulsed with the power of the Grym as if it were alive. Instinctively, Errol reached out and connected with it, looking for relief.

In an instant his perspective changed. It was as if he no longer stood in the darkness looking at the flickering torchlight that lit the door to the inquisitor's study. Instead he was the walls and ceiling. He was the floor and the heavy wooden door. He was the heat of the flame, fluttering as it consumed the thick grease. The ache in his head was gone simply because he could no longer feel his head. He was far greater than that, spreading out along the lines, becoming the building, the monastery, the mountain, the whole of Gwlad.

Errol bit his tongue, a reflex action that pulled him back into himself with a sharp tang of pain. His heart hammered in his chest and cold sweat prickled the back of his neck. He had been drawn out so quickly it was breathtaking. There would have been nothing of him left. He would have spread himself too thinly and dissipated into the colossal emptiness of the Grym. Somewhere in the back of his mind he remembered the words of Father Castlemilk about the perils of losing oneself in the web of power. Down in the classroom, when they had practised the application of magic, it had been controlled and they had been closely watched by the quaisters. Here the whole world was open to him, and he had almost lost himself to it.

On the other hand, his headache was gone and he could think more clearly than ever. He buzzed with an energy that knew no restraint. Only the realization of where he was stopped him from laughing out loud. Deep down, he knew that it would be foolish even to think about going back into the Grym, but like an alcoholic faced with a bottle of wine, he could no more help himself than he could deny his true nature.

This time when he gave himself up to the lines he was ready for their terrible dissipating pull. Errol held tight to an image of himself and was pleased to see that image coalesce into existence in the corridor. It was slightly disorienting to see himself and see through his own eyes at the same time, but it felt oddly familiar, as if this were something he had done many times before. Even the pull of the Grym all around him was a reassurance, as if it was there merely to remind him that he existed. And he had known instinctively how to cope with it.

Curious, Errol looked around. He knew that he was in the corridor outside Melyn's study, and yet it was subtly different. The walls were still the same rough stone; the sconces and torches were there; even the floorboards, polished by age and uncounted thousands of feet were unchanged from the many times he had stared at them before, waiting to be summoned into the inquisitor's rooms. Only the doorway was different.

It glowed with an unnatural red light, a sickly emanation that clashed with the peace and quiet surrounding him. It was obvious to Errol that it was a ward of some form, meant to keep him out. It pushed him away in much the same way as the Grym pulled him, an insistence that was not physical but nonetheless hard to deny. As he inspected the door more closely, he could feel the pain once more at his temples, as if his head were being squeezed by a vast hand of cold stone. Whatever lay beyond that door, the inquisitor did not want anyone seeing it.

Errol didn't know how he had done it. One moment he was around the corridor, the next he was back inside the inquisitor's study, staring at the old man as he sat at his desk, eyes closed as if asleep. Maybe it was the voices that had called him, or maybe it was the thought of the door as an impenetrable barrier that had piqued his curiosity. Either way, he felt a surge of guilt and fear. What if he were caught here? He wasn't even really sure where here was. It looked like the inquisitor's study but it felt very different, somehow colder and even more uninviting than it usually was.

The voices came to him again. He couldn't quite make out what they were saying, as if the two speakers were standing in an adjacent room. Yet one of the voices he recognized as that of the inquisitor. As he recognized the speaker, so the words became clearer, but Melyn was not using his usual tone, nor was he speaking Saesneg. Instead the words were in a language so foreign to him it could have been from another world, guttural and sibilant, with odd glottal stops and strange clicking sounds. Yet for all the effort speaking such a bizarre tongue must have been costing the inquisitor, he was not moving a muscle.

The other speaker was female. Errol didn't know how he knew this, but as he focused on her voice, so he began to see the link that joined her to the inquisitor. Without knowing what he was doing, he followed that link. It was as if he had stepped across an enormous chasm. He knew that he had covered a vast distance, and yet in the blink of an eye he was no longer in the inquisitor's study but standing on the edge of a clearing in a deep forest.

It was dark, a few stars overhead twinkling through gaps in the cloud. Around him Errol could see that the trees were putting on their first spring growth of leaves. The scent of blossom hung heavy in the warm air and the night was full of the sounds of animals waking from their long winter sleep. All of these things registered only lightly on his consciousness, for what grabbed his attention and held it as strongly as any cord sat still and stiff in the middle of the clearing.

It was a dragon.

She was a dragon. Again Errol did not know how he

knew, but he was certain that the creature in front of him was female. She had her eyes tightly shut and sat in a very similar pose to the inquisitor. With a start Errol realized that they were communicating. But what possible reason could a dragon have for wanting to speak to Melyn? The inquisitor hated their kind with every fibre of his being. His mission in life was to hunt them all down and exterminate them. Only King Divitie's edict had thwarted his ambition, but it was months since Queen Beulah had lifted that. All the talk in the dormitories and refectory had been about the preparations for the hunt.

Errol was deeply troubled by the promise of slaughter. He knew that he felt no antipathy towards dragons. Quite the opposite. Seeing this one now, seated and calm in the dark, he was filled with a strange melancholy, an inexplicable feeling that he wanted to be friends with her and all her kind. The creature should have filled him with fear and disgust, but instead he felt safe and loved. He knew so much about dragons, about their history, their legends and their teachings. But how could he have learned all that if he had never even met one before?

Father Kewick taught you, the voice of his memory told him. But it wasn't right. It didn't sound like him. It sounded like Inquisitor Melyn. And Errol knew Father Kewick. The fat old priest from the Order of the Candle was interested only in his books on administration, accounting, clerical work. Errol could distinctly recall the dull lessons in which his teacher had told him that dragons did not actually exist, that they had been invented by King Brynceri as an excuse to form his military order.

There was no way the predicant would ever have taught him about dragon lore. So how did Errol know about Palisander? Gog and Magog? Rasalene and Arhelion?

A name – Sir Radnor – appeared in Errol's mind like a bubble of marsh gas erupting from a muddy pool. With it came an image of a familiar place, Jagged Leap, the rock standing proud above the river, and sitting on its flat top much the way this small thin dragon sat in her clearing, a massive, magnificent beast fully three times her size, with huge wings outstretched to reveal the intricate patterns of his multicoloured scales. A warm happiness filled Errol. He remembered the endless hours he had spent listening to the spirit of the mage as it told him its stories. But alongside the happiness was a growing rage. He had been tricked.

As the memories came back, Errol began to see what had happened to him. At his mother's wedding the inquisitor had tried to get into his mind and failed. A sudden terror gripped him as he realized that he had not wanted to join the order. Quite the reverse – he had been planning on running away from them. Not alone, with somebody else. But who? He was so close, but still that memory was locked away from him.

He remembered the princess staring at him as if he had personally insulted her whole family. He remembered going outside, being cold. What had he done with his jacket? He'd given it to someone. Then . . .

The floodgates opened. Then he had been kidnapped by the troop of warrior priests who had accompanied the princess and the inquisitor to the village. He had been tied up and Captain Osgal had forced a skinful of wine down his throat. Errol could taste the sour liquid, feel it burning as it went down. He had never drunk alcohol before, and it had hit his stomach with unfamiliar harshness. He had brought it straight back up again, he remembered, peppering Osgal's tunic with bits of the wedding feast and a dark red stain like blood. The captain had just laughed and then forced another skinful down. This one had stayed put, as had the third, by which time Errol's senses had almost entirely gone. Yet he watched from this strange dreamscape as if he recalled it all perfectly.

About an hour had passed. He must have slept a bit and then been woken. His head had whirled sickeningly and someone had held him up so that the inquisitor could stare straight into his eyes. Errol had tried to fight, but she was not holding his hand and lending him her strength. Who was she? He knew, but he couldn't remember. Green. The girl in green.

What had passed next was a nightmare of embarrassment. Melyn had taken control of him as if he were no more than a puppet at the Lammas fair. He had staggered back into the hall, reeking drunk and with wine and vomit staining his wedding shirt, and announced to all who were still awake to hear it that he was going to join the Order of the High Ffrydd. His mother had been proud, crying a lot but saying that she knew it was the best thing for him. The inquisitor must have cast his magic on her as well, for Errol knew that Hennas hated everything to do with the warrior priests who had hounded her around the Twin Kingdoms.

Some time after pledging to serve his princess as her personal protector, Errol had finally succumbed to the wine and passed out. Even so, he saw the events continue as if he had witnessed it all. He had been carried to a cart and thrown on to a bed of hay in the back. Clun had clung to his father for long moments before finally climbing in too. And then the whole troop had ridden out of Pwllpeiran, leaving the happy couple dazed, confused and childless. Errol could only assume that the inquisitor's glamour had been powerful enough to cloud the judgement of both bride and groom, for it was a most unusual wedding gift.

Outside the village the troop had moved at a slow pace along the track towards the old ruined palace at Ystumtuen, at least two days' ride away. Errol watched their progress in his mind, wondering how it was that he could see things he had not witnessed before. And then he saw her.

The girl in green.

She was wrapped in a long dark cloak that camouflaged her well. She was hiding in the trees at the side of the track, watching the caravan pass with a look of sadness and horror on her face. As he saw her, his heart was filled with such sorrow and yearning that he feared it might stop beating. She was his greatest love, the only thing in the whole of Gwlad that he cared for. They had planned to escape, to run away from the persecution of the religious orders. But he had been captured. He wondered where she had gone, what she had done, even as he struggled to remember her name.

'I said, wake up, boy. Can't you even stay awake for ten minutes?'

Errol felt a hand on his shoulder, shaking him hard. He was standing once more in the clearing watching the dragon mouth silent words in an alien tongue. He was standing in the inquisitor's study, watching his most hated enemy set a trap that would exterminate an entire race of noble creatures for no better reason than spite. He was standing in the shadows in the corridor and Captain Osgal was beside him.

'I . . . I wasn't asleep,' Errol said, shaking his head to try and bring some order to his maelstrom of thoughts as the three images faded back into just one.

'A likely story,' Osgal said, then shoved Errol away towards the end of the corridor and the stairs. 'Go on. Get out of here, you useless little shit.'

Errol bolted like a rabbit from a ferreted hole. He took the stairs two at a time and caused considerable mirth among the warriors on the ground floor as he burst through their guardroom and out into the courtyard. He sprinted across to the library building, and only once he was surrounded by its massive old stone blocks and unreasonably high ceilings did he slow down. There was so much to think about, so much to try and piece together. He had to find Clun and warn him. They had to try and escape. The whole of the Order of the High Ffrydd was founded on a lie, he knew now. He wanted no part of it.

And there was the small matter of the girl in green. He had promised to be with her for ever. He longed to see her again, to be with her. There was so much they had to do together, a whole world to explore and understand. He knew her name now. It had come back to him with Osgal's harsh touch.

Martha.

24

Sir Teifi teul Albarn, claimed age 1,035 – killed by rioting mob, fourteenth day of Ragger-month in the sixtieth year of King Divitie XXIII – 7 large jewels, 1 small.

Morwenna the Wise, claimed age 895 – killed by rioting mob, fourteenth day of Ragger-month in the sixtieth year of King Divitie XXIII – 4 large jewels, 3 small.

Unnamed female kitling, age 4 years – missing, assumed killed by rioting mob, fourteenth day of Ragger-month in the sixtieth year of King Divitie XXIII – no jewels.

From the *Dragon Register*
of the Order of the Candle

'Where are you going, squirt?'

Benfro froze in his tracks, feeling the warmth of spring leach out of the day as if a cloud had passed over the sun. The birds were trilling in the trees, new flowers had blossomed in the grass around the gnarled old trunks and the forest sang with life. He had spent the morning cooped up in Sir Frynwy's study with Meirionydd, still with no success in his quest to see the elusive Llinellau, and he had been looking forward to an afternoon's fishing with Ynys

Môn as a precursor to a planned week-long hunting trip into the deep forest. Despite his lack of magical success, Benfro felt upbeat and confident that in time he would crack the problem. The winter was over and he had been filled with a delicious optimism. Until now.

Turning in the road that ran up through the village towards the green and the great hall, Benfro saw his nemesis standing in the unkempt garden of one of the cottages. With a start he realized that it was Ystrad Fflur's house and that someone had thrown open the shutters, letting air into the empty rooms.

'What are you doing?' Benfro asked as Frecknock stared at him, an unusually indulgent look on her face.

'Oh, I just thought this old place could do with some attention,' she said. 'It's been well over a year since the old boy died and no one's been in here except the spiders.'

'Why should you care?' Benfro asked. 'You've got a perfectly good house. You weren't thinking of moving, were you?' he added, appalled at the thought of Frecknock taking over the cottage where he had spent so many happy hours. Better for it to sink into decay or even burn to the ground than to have that happen to it.

'Of course not, squirt,' Frecknock said. 'But you never know; someone might. So, what are you doing this afternoon?'

Benfro did a double take. He could see no malice in the question, no sneering condescension. Frecknock's tone was almost jovial, as if she were simply making polite conversation. He had seen her out and about a couple of times since the night of his hatchday party, but she had not uttered a single word to him. Until now.

'I'm going to find Ynys Môn,' he said. 'We thought we might see if the spring trout have started running.'

'Ah yes, fishing,' Frecknock said. 'Ynys Môn's very proud of his skills as a hunter. Personally I can't see the point when you can just reach out and help yourself.' As she spoke, she stretched out her hand and plucked something out of the air. Benfro couldn't help but stare. It was one thing to know how the villagers kept themselves fed, another to watch it in action. Frecknock's brazen display fascinated him, but it also appalled him in its lack of decorum.

'Here, squirt,' she said and threw the object at him. She wasn't very good at throwing, but Benfro was a good catch. He caught the object and stared down at a shiny red apple just beginning to show the wrinkling sign of long storage.

'It's all right, I haven't poisoned it,' Frecknock added. 'Can't promise whoever grew it in the first place hasn't though.'

'Why are you giving me this?' Benfro asked, eyeing both the apple and the dragon suspiciously.

'Because I can,' Frecknock said. The implication was obvious. And you can't. Benfro knew that there had to be something to her good humour. So that was it: someone had let her know that he was struggling with his studies. Well, he could cope with her crowing. She had been learning for almost a hundred years, after all. If it meant that she wouldn't be as spiteful as he had become used to then he could put up with her taunts.

'Thank you,' he said, holding up the apple and then

taking a bite. It was sweet and juicy, though the skin was a bit thick and tough.

'Any time,' Frecknock said, smiling. Benfro shuddered at the unnaturalness of it all, then turned to resume his journey, glad that he had come off unexpectedly well in this encounter.

'Hey, squirt.'

Benfro hesitated, then looked back. 'Yes?'

'Your mother. She had any visitors recently?'

'No,' Benfro said. 'At least not while I've been there. You know she's quite good at making sure I'm somewhere else when men are coming. Why?'

'None of your . . . Never mind,' Frecknock said, and for a minute Benfro saw his old foe behind this confusing new facade.

'Are you expecting someone?' Benfro asked, the seed of a nasty feeling forming at the back of his mind.

'No,' Frecknock said too quickly to be entirely convincing. The tip of her tail gave an involuntary twitch. 'Just curious. It can't be easy, having to deal with men. They can be so vicious and brutal. I was more wondering if any dragons might have dropped by.'

'Dragons?' Benfro asked. 'Are there really any others out there? I mean, I've never seen one.'

'There's hundreds of dragons in the whole of Gwlad,' Frecknock said, her tone at once annoyed at his obvious stupidity and pleased that she knew something he didn't. 'Some live all alone deep in the forest; there's dragons in the Hendry boglands and up in Llanwennog. Others travel the long road, never staying anywhere for more than a day or two. That's your father to a T, by the way. He never could stand to be cooped up for more than a week.'

'I wouldn't know,' Benfro said. He was used to Frecknock's taunting and knew better than to rise to it even if the barb hurt. 'I've never met him. But you must have. Maybe you could tell me something about him.'

'I never much cared for Sir Trefaldwyn,' Frecknock said. 'He was always too full of himself, preening around with his great leathery wings like some strutting cockerel, flirting with all the female dragons, even though he would no more leave your mother than he would cut off his own nose. He wasn't as good a bard as Sir Frynwy, nor as good a mage as Meirionydd. He couldn't heal like your mother can and he was too impatient to hunt. Quite honestly I don't know what he was good for. Siring you, I suppose, and look what a wonderful thing that turned out to be.'

Benfro could feel his blood warming at the string of taunts. But he knew that they were meaningless even if they annoyed him. So his father was not perfect. He knew that all too well. If it weren't so, he would have been around for the last fourteen years. Yet never in that time had he heard his mother say a bad word about him. She had been sad, at times desperately so. Benfro knew the anniversary of the day Sir Trefaldwyn had left the village only too well. A week either side of it Morgwm would be taciturn and short, but on the actual day she would take herself off into the forest, not returning until the sun began to rise on the next morning.

'Why did he leave?' Benfro asked. He didn't expect Frecknock to give him a true answer, but then no one else in the village had ever really spoken about his father, except to say that it was a subject only his mother could possibly discuss.

'Who knows? Cold feet at becoming a father?' Frecknock said. 'Maybe he wandered off and got killed by some men.'

'Would they do that?' Benfro asked. 'I thought dragons were protected by the king.'

'You really are quite stupid, you know that, squirt,' Frecknock said. 'Firstly King Divitie, whom Ynys Môn so nobly saved from his well-deserved death, spent most of his youth persecuting and killing us. Even after he graciously agreed to stop it, we were still hunted. And mostly the king didn't really care. He still got our jewels and he didn't have to pay out gold for them. Oh yes, occasionally if someone was a bit too blatant about it he'd string them up by the neck in the courtyard of the Neuadd, but we didn't stop dying just because he stopped killing us. And in order to maintain the pretence of protection we had to pay tribute to the crown. I was presented to him as a kitling – can you imagine anything more terrifying?'

'You?' Benfro asked, genuinely surprised. In truth he had never imagined Frecknock as anything other than as she was, but she must have been a kitling once, and she was young enough to have been hatched in Divitie's reign, if he remembered the history right.

'You've met, what, one man?' Frecknock asked. 'Well imagine what it feels like to be surrounded by hundreds of them, to be poked at and prodded by their clammy warm hands, to hear only their jabbering tongue and know that they're laughing at you, that you're completely at their mercy.'

For the first time in his life Benfro felt sorry for Frec-knock. Not enough sympathy to forgive her for the lifetime of torment she had visited upon him, but know-ing she too had suffered at the hands of others went some small way towards explaining why she did to him what she did. He had not been presented to the royal court. His mother had flouted the laws of the king. No wonder Frec-knock was jealous of him.

'What changed then?' Benfro asked. 'Why'd we hide ourselves away from men?'

'Because they can't be trusted to keep their word,' Frec-knock said. 'Hasn't your mother taught you anything about them? They killed my parents for nothing. We weren't doing anything to harm them – we weren't even living close to any of their settlements – but still they came, in the night. My parents died so that I could escape. I wandered through the forest for months before Meiri-onydd found me. She brought me here and I've been here ever since.'

Benfro stood silent, aware that he was staring at Frec-knock and yet unable to look away. He hadn't known. He'd never even thought to ask where her parents might be. None of the other dragons in the village had parents, but then they were all many hundreds of years old. Frec-knock was not much older than him, really. Not on the scale of the lives they might hope to live. How self-centred was he to have never even asked about her? But then he had asked very little about the lives of any of the villagers. It wasn't right to pry, surely. If they wanted to tell him, they would. Just as Frecknock was doing now, though he couldn't for the life of him think why.

'Clear off, squirt,' Frecknock said, her mood changing as if she suddenly realized who she was talking to. 'I've got to get on with dusting out this house. Just because it's empty doesn't mean we can let it fall into ruin.' She turned away from him and walked towards Ystrad Fflur's front door. Bemused, Benfro watched her back as she went, wondering whether he should say something. He looked down at the half-eaten apple in his hand and then remembered himself. This was Frecknock, after all. She could have made the whole thing up as some elaborate plot to get him into trouble. If he knew one thing about her, it was that he was better off where she wasn't. Taking another bite of the sweet fruit, he hurried off in search of Ynys Môn.

25

The almshouses of the mindless are a potent reminder of the dangers inherent in magic. These low stone buildings were begun in the time of Inquisitor Hardy, and are separated from the main monastery complex by Meddwyn's Arch. Every novitiate must take his turn caring for the lost souls who inhabit these houses. They are the victims of magic gone wrong, of spells miscast. Some have brought their woes upon themselves, others have been unlucky enough to be in the way of another's mistakes. All are beyond healing, condemned to live out their lives with no more self-awareness than sheep.

Some say that it would be a kindness to deliver a swift death to the mindless, but in truth they do not suffer as we might imagine they should, for they have no imagination with which to suffer. Keeping them close to the monastery serves as a constant reminder of the terrible responsibility that allegiance to the order brings.

Father Castlemilk,
An Introduction to the Order of the High Ffrydd

Errol sat in the library archives staring blankly at the parchment laid out on the table in front of him. It was written in tiny curling letters and the text was obscure. The words of whatever language it was written in sounded vaguely familiar, but he could make no sense of them.

Not that he would have been able to concentrate on it even if it had been clearly printed in modern Saesneg. His mind was too much of a turmoil for that, too full of worries and a burning sense of anger. Ten days had passed since his last encounter with the inquisitor and over those long hours memories, true memories, of his childhood had slowly reformed from the mess of contradictions and lies that Melyn had put in their place.

He had spoken to Clun that first evening, but his stepbrother had just laughed, caught up in the excitement of being picked for his first proper mission. Ten of the new intake of novitiates were accompanying the inquisitor and his personal guard on an important mission. Errol knew exactly what they were going to do, but when he tried to explain it to Clun, the older boy had asked him what he thought he had joined the order for if it wasn't to rid the world of dragons. Errol could see the inquisitor's teachings patterned on to his stepbrother's mind, but he could also see how easily they fitted the boy who had once been his friend.

The troop had ridden out the next morning, and with each passing day since Errol had grown more and more uneasy at the prospect of their return. He wanted them to fail, but he didn't want any blame for that failure falling on Clun. Neither did he particularly wish for the inquisitor to return, successful or not. He couldn't imagine what would happen the next time they had one of their meetings.

In his wilder fantasies Errol saw a ragged troop returning with the dead body of the inquisitor, slain as he fought
a great army of dragons. When he allowed his mind to
wander, he saw Clun as the hero, rescuing the body of his
leader at great personal risk. But the image soon dissolved
under the remorseless logic of his own situation. The
inquisitor was powerful enough to rewrite a person's
memories. A few dragons would be no match for him at
all. And those dragons that remained in the forest of the
Ffrydd were sad and pathetic things, pale shadows of the
great monsters of legend. He had seen one, after all, so
vain and stupid she couldn't see she was condemning herself to death. It was far more likely they would return
soon in bloody triumph. Errol didn't want to be around to
see that.

'Not sleeping at your desk, are you, Errol?' Andro
asked. Errol looked round, startled. He had been so
wrapped up in his thoughts that he hadn't heard the old
man coming.

'I keep staring at this parchment, but it only makes
half-sense,' he said, hoping that he might be able to find
some distraction from the endless circle of thoughts that
kept dragging him down into despair.

'Let's see,' Andro said, leaning over the desk and peering so closely at the tiny letters that his hooked nose
almost touched the parchment. 'Ah yes. Father Charmoise's attempt at writing Draigiaith in a phonetic
variation of Saesneg script. Fascinating. Brilliant mind,
Father Charmoise. A pity he went mad in the end.'

'Draigiaith?' Errol asked.

'The language of the dragons,' Andro said. 'Oh, I know,

most of them speak Saesneg now, those that are still around to speak it. Us poor humans find it quite hard to get our mouths around some of the sounds. Still, I expect when they chat among themselves it sounds pretty much like this.'

'You've met dragons?' Errol asked.

'Oh, of course. Many, many times,' the old man said.

'But you're part of the Order of the High Ffrydd. Our charter's to hunt down and kill dragons. Have you . . . ?'

'Killed dragons?' Andro's face changed from its cheerful welcoming smile to a more sombre visage, thoughtful and sad. 'Regrettably, yes. In my youth I once killed a dragon. It's not something I'm especially proud of, but it happened. I've done my best ever since to make amends.'

'That's why you took the scroll, wasn't it?' Errol said.

'When I compiled that list, it was to be a simple census. I spent years travelling around the Twin Kingdoms seeking out those dragons that were still alive. There weren't many, even then. Most people just thought they were a myth. A few old folk would speak of a great beast that lived not far from their village, or they'd tell tales of buried hoards of treasure guarded by monstrous creatures that breathed fire. But mostly they thought of them as stories. They used them to keep children in line. No one actually believed that they existed.'

'I know,' Errol said. 'It was like that in my village.'

'But you knew better,' Andro said. 'What made you so certain that they existed?'

'I'm not sure,' he said. 'It just seemed right that they did. Then Martha introduced me to Sir Radnor.'

'Martha? Sir Radnor?' Andro asked. Errol explained, as

best he could, about his childhood and the spirit of the old mage that lived under the rock at Jagged Leap. He told him about his mother's wedding and the arrival of the inquisitor and the princess, about waking up in the back of the wagon with confused memories. And he told him about his meetings with Melyn, particularly the last one where everything had come back to him. Andro listened patiently, without interrupting, and when Errol finally lapsed into silence the old man sank on to the bench beside him.

'Melyn wants you as a spy because of your Llanwennog looks,' Andro said. 'But he won't trust you until he's certain he has you completely under his control. That's why he invites you to his study, so he can bring you round to his way of thinking.'

'But I don't want to be a spy. I don't want to kill dragons. I just want to learn about them, and about the rest of Gwlad.'

'Then maybe you should have been a Ram.' Andro sighed. 'Ah, Errol, fate dealt you a cruel hand when it sent Melyn to your village. Crueller even than you realize. And now that he has you, he'll use you to further his own ends without a care for what happens to you, whether you live or die. The inquisitor lives only to rid the world of his two worst enemies, Llanwennogs and dragons.'

'What is it about dragons?' Errol asked. 'Why does he want to kill them?'

'I don't really know. Because they exist, and because he believes they're an affront to his god? He wasn't always that way. Before he became inquisitor he was merely fascinated by them. He used to spend days down here going through the archives. I believe he may even have taught himself their language from this very document.'

Errol glanced back down at the parchment. He had to fight the urge to recoil from it as something touched by the inquisitor, as if somehow he might catch whatever contagion it was that Melyn had.

'But something changed his mind about them. For years now he's argued that the dragons are a threat to the natural order of things. That they should all be exterminated,' Andro continued. 'But until now his words have fallen on deaf ears at court.'

'Until now?' Errol said. 'Oh. Queen Beulah.'

'The queen's Melyn's puppet,' Andro said. 'He more or less raised her. She was given to him to tutor when she was only six. It's hardly surprising that one of her first declarations as queen has been to reinstate the aurddraig and Brynceri's original charter of the order.'

'Is that why you took the parchment?' Errol asked. 'You wanted to protect them?'

'Oh, I doubt there's much I can do that they can't do for themselves, Errol,' Andro said. 'Dragons are far wiser and far more skilled in magic . . . How does it translate? Oh yes, the subtle arts. They can do things we can't even conceive of. But yes, I took the census from you and destroyed it. I see no point in giving Melyn a head start.'

'But if they're so strong, why do they let us kill them?'

'I truly don't know, Errol,' Andro said. 'They're complicated creatures, quite unlike us. Who can tell how their minds work. Still, they're not stupid. They built this place, after all.'

'But they're . . . They did what?' Errol asked, his brain catching up with his ears.

'Emmass Fawr,' Andro said, lofting his hand around the archive room as if to indicate the whole of the vast edifice around them. 'At least the central core of it. Generations of warrior priests have added to the complex, but the original building, including this library archive, was once the palace of Maddau the Wise.'

'Maddau,' Errol said, trying to recall the name. 'I've heard of her. Some of Sir Radnor's stories about Palisander of the Spreading Span mention her. But how could a dragon, even lots of dragons, build such a vast place? And why build it so big?'

'Why would men do the same thing?' Andro asked. 'Have you never wondered why the ceilings are thirty feet high, why the doors are tall enough and wide enough to drive a wagon through? Haven't you noticed how the quality of building materials and the skill of the builders change between these old halls and the inquisitor's lodgings?'

Errol had, ever since his first day in the place. 'But that still doesn't explain why they built so big,' he said. 'I've seen a dragon – she wasn't much bigger than a pony.'

'You've seen what dragons have allowed themselves to become,' Andro said. 'But the creatures who used to inspire fear and awe in our ancestors were huge and powerful beasts. They had wings that could carry them high into the sky and they could breathe flames that devoured only what they wanted them to devour. These were the great dragons of legend, Palisander, Gog, Magog, Maddau. You've heard their tales and how they warred among themselves. Back then, when the Twin Kingdoms were no more than a collection of tribes brought together by the wise leadership of King Balwen, dragons barely noticed us. And that was the problem.'

'How so?' Errol asked, fascinated.

'Because they destroyed the land with their warring. People were killed simply because they were in the way. Crops were burned and livestock slaughtered. Famine and pestilence followed. For hundreds, maybe thousands, of years men lived in caves along the coast or up in the mountains, scarcely daring to travel to the plains. Then Brynceri came along and showed that dragons could be killed, that men could master the same magic, tap the power of Gwlad and use it against the enemy. That's when we began to take the land back from them and it's the reason we've persecuted them ever since. We keep them down so that they don't become the great power that they once were. Melyn, on the other hand, would go a step further and eliminate them entirely from existence. I don't agree with him on that and many other points, but he's by far the most powerful magician on the planet, and for my sins I taught him most of what he knows.'

The old man fell silent and Errol sat beside him wondering at his words. The parchment lay in front of them, the tiny letters spelling out words in a language utterly alien yet hauntingly familiar. But still it was a language, rich and complex like the species that spoke it. Dragons might have killed men indiscriminately thousands of years ago, but now they were a race on the brink of extinction. And they had so much knowledge, such grace and dignity. He couldn't feel indifference towards them even if he tried, let alone enmity. If nothing else, the fact that Inquisitor Melyn sought their destruction was enough to put him firmly on the side of the dragons.

'I have to help them,' Errol said. 'I don't want them all to die. There must be something I can do. Some way of warning them.'

'Errol, the inquisitor's been gone ten days,' Andro said. 'Even if I'd been able to dispatch a messenger right after him it would have done no good. No, there are far more important things that we must do, you and I.'

'Like what?' Errol asked, angry at his tutor's dismissal of the dragons as if they were no more important than sheep.

'Like teaching you a great deal of magic,' Andro said. 'Inquisitor Melyn will be back. It may be a week, it may be a month. Either way he's going to want to see you again, to reinforce what he's already put in place. You're going to have to learn how to fool him into thinking he's succeeded.'

'I could run away,' Errol said. 'If I left now, I could get a good head start.'

'And where would you go?' Andro asked. 'Back home? Candlehall? Llanwennog? You've no experience, Errol. Right now your only hope is to stay with the order. Learn everything you can from it, but be aware that it's not your friend. I'm sorry to have to say it, but you've no choice anyway. No novitiate can leave the monastery without the express permission of the inquisitor. I can't see him giving it to you and neither can I undo the spell that holds you here. You must at least graduate before you can go beyond the great arch.'

'Can I really learn enough to fool Melyn?' Errol asked. The situation seemed hopeless to him.

'It's possible,' Andro said. 'Otherwise I wouldn't suggest it. But you'll have to work very hard indeed to trick Melyn. He is the best.'

Errol looked at the man sitting beside him and realized that he was old. Impossibly old. His skin was translucent, showing the withered muscles and spidery blue veins underneath. His fingers were bent and claw-like, each knuckle a swollen ball of pain. His arms were sticks, no strength in them to lift more than a parchment. Yet his eyes sparkled with intelligence; his speech was measured but not slow. He carried himself like a man in no hurry to die. He had hope, if not for the dragons then at least for Errol. And he was prepared to help him.

'When do we start?' Errol asked.

26

Perhaps the most potent symbol of the power and skill of the mage is the conjuring of the blade of light. Inquisitor Ruthin is said to have been the first man to master the art when he came to Brynceri's aid against the monstrous Maddau. He passed the knowledge on to his first followers, who became the warrior priests of the Order of the High Ffrydd. To this day it is the final requirement before elevation to the rank of warrior priest that a novitiate show his ability to conjure the blade. Many a quaister bears the scars of where he has tried and failed, and the hall of the dead in Emmass Fawr bears witness to those who have died in the attempt.

> Father Castlemilk, *An Introduction to the Order of the High Ffrydd*

It was the uneasy quiet that gave them away. Normally the forest would have been a riot of noise: birds chittering in the treetops, leaves rustling in the endless thermal currents, somewhere the bark of fox cubs playing their games. Life was a continuous cacophony, a swirl of sounds that sometimes grew so intense you couldn't think straight.

Yet now it was silence.

Benfro looked up at the distant sky. Here on the track you could see a strip of blue above the canopy, pale as a stolen egg. There were no buzzards turning on the air currents, not even a sparrow. A shiver ran across his shoulders, itching in the pit of his back where his wings met. He crept to the forest verge, instinctively hugging the shadows. Then he caught the odour on the breeze. Something unnatural had come this way, something which struck a chord in his memory though the smell was as different as boar from deer. He recalled the old man, Gideon, with his halting speech and polite manner. There had been an aroma about him that was not unpleasant so much as alien. A harsher, heavier version of that stench hung on the air now. Men.

Benfro slid through the thick foliage at the side of the path and into the interior of the forest. It was cooler here and dark, which suited him just fine. The stench of the men was noticeably fainter, the gentlest of breezes pulling it away from his senses. Slowly, quietly, he picked his way through the tangled undergrowth, past the massive trunks and arched roots of the ancient trees, heading for home the back way.

As he neared the clearing and the house, Benfro heard voices wafting on a gentle breeze. Their accent was guttural, harsh and unfamiliar to him. This was not Gideon come back to pay a friendly visit. Too far away to make out the words, he could understand all too easily the contempt in the tone. Once more he felt the itching between his wings and a sharp anger that anyone could be so offhand with his mother. Still he was not so stupid as to go barging into the clearing. With practice born of playing on his own all his childhood, he crept on silent feet into the thick brush that edged the clearing and settled down to watch.

His first glimpse of the man was a shock. He seemed so small, shorter even than Gideon. Or perhaps it was the way the cottage towered over him that made him look childlike. He paced around on spindly legs that surely couldn't hold his weight, and his back was swathed in a cloak of coarse grey material that tumbled from his shoulders to the ground, dulled with mud splatters as if it had not been washed in many weeks. He stared around the clearing, two tiny dark eyes filled with a malevolent strength, taking in all around, searching. His gaze caught Benfro's attention, held it with a grip that nearly stopped his hearts. For long seconds the man held his gaze so that Benfro was sure he had been spotted. He drew in on himself, as Ynys Môn had taught him, trying to disappear even though the thick leaves of the bushes hid him from view. He froze, not even daring to breathe until those eyes reluctantly turned away.

Before he could do anything, a band of a dozen or more men, smaller still than the one he had locked eyes with, came trotting around the corner of the cottage, mounted on horses that were nervous and skittery. They dismounted in perfect synchrony, moving with a singularity of purpose, as if linked by one terrible mind, and they surrounded the familiar form of his mother.

Benfro gasped when he saw her. This was not the proud dragon he knew and loved and feared as only a son can. This was some timid beast, like Frecknock cowering under Sir Frynwy's wrath. She was staring at the ground, shuffling, wings pulled so tight against her back they looked no more than a second, loose skin. With horror he watched as she allowed the troop to push and prod her into a place in front of their leader.

'Kneel,' the man said, that guttural voice oozing disgust. Benfro understood enough of the language to feel his contempt. Worse yet, it was a voice that Benfro had heard before.

'Kneel before your masters, like the wyrm you are,' the man said. To Benfro's surprise his mother didn't bite the creature's head off – it would easily have fitted into her mouth. Instead, she sank slowly to the ground, first her belly grinding in the dirt, then her long neck and head. Prostrated like that, her gaze was finally lower than that of her persecutor.

'You try to fight us,' the man said, a note of wry amusement in his voice. 'Do you really think that a lowly creature such as yourself could hope to master me? No, Morgwm, you can't help but bow to my will.'

'You know my name,' Benfro's mother said. 'Might I have the honour of knowing yours?'

'Ha!' the man spat. 'Novitiates, observe.' He addressed the words to his band, ignoring Morgwm. 'Your average forest dragon pretends to be a cowardly creature, pathetic and harmless. Don't be fooled by this exterior; don't fall for its lies.'

'I mean no harm to you,' Benfro's mother said. 'If I've offended you in some way, please accept my humblest apologies, good sir.'

'Offended, Morgwm? Oh yes, you've offended mightily. I see you're still peddling your quackery.'

'My medicines? I only seek to alleviate suffering.'

'Silence, cow!' the man shouted. His eyes were blazing with a fierce red light now and Benfro could feel his anger as a force in the clearing. No, it was more than anger. It was a hatred so pure and visceral that he could taste it. What could his mother possibly have done to warrant such treatment?

'Roots and berries, tree bark, mud. You seriously expect such things to cure illness? You think you know more than the palace apothecaries? Your base witchcraft is an affront to their wisdom.'

'Ah, I know you now,' Morgwm said, and Benfro could hear the sadness in her voice. 'You must be from Queen Beulah's court. Warrior priests of the High Ffrydd. Am I addressing Inquisitor Melyn, perchance? You've aged since last I saw you.'

Benfro was almost knocked out by the wave of pure fury that pulsed from the man. Some of the band shuddered where they stood. Morgwm flinched but held his gaze, and in that moment Benfro realized what was coming next, knew all too well why his mother had prayed he would never have to deal with men.

'Your disrespect for the queen is but the least of your crimes, cow. Your kind have been an affront to humanity for too long. Well, that's about to change. You don't have Divitie's protection any more.'

'I never thought it would last this long,' Morgwm said, and now Benfro could see something of his mother's true nature. It was a subtle thing. She didn't appear to move, but her posture changed to one of calm defiance. Whatever the inquisitor might do to her, she wouldn't fear him.

'Your Grace, I've searched the area as you instructed.

There's nothing here but forest and the track we came in on.' The warrior priest who walked up to the inquisitor was tall and well muscled. His cloak was cleaner than most, probably because the horse he led was bigger than the others. It looked at the prostrate form of the dragon without any outward sign of disquiet. Benfro had not seen many horses in his life, but he recognized this animal as something special.

'Of course there isn't, Osgal,' the inquisitor said. 'An illegal village of dragons would be very well hidden indeed. Even I can't sense the magic that hides them. Such a spell would have to be tied to a life. There'd need to be a gatekeeper. Would there not, Morgwm?'

Benfro watched in growing horror as his mother simply stared at the inquisitor, her great eyes unblinking. He could sense the growing anger in the man as a wall of heat spreading out across the clearing to where he hid.

'Yes, I know all about you, Morgwm the Green,' the inquisitor said, and Benfro suddenly realized he was speaking Draigiaith, the harsh tones of the Saesneg gone, replaced by a softer, gentler voice that nevertheless held far more menace. Benfro knew exactly where he had heard it before. Without the righteous fury and indignation, it was plainly Sir Felyn who spoke. And when the inquisitor unfolded his arms from across his chest, raising them into the air above Morgwm's head, he could see those terrible pudgy pink fingers.

'I know that you think yourself better than me, that you consider your kind above our laws,' the inquisitor continued. 'And I know all about your little band of renegades hiding out here in the forest.'

'Oh, I doubt that very much,' Morgwm said. 'Your mind is far too small to understand even my simplest thoughts. I, on the other hand, know exactly what you intend to do. I have prepared for it for a long time.'

'Is that so?' Benfro felt a wave of the man's hatred boil across the clearing. 'And yet you do nothing to protect yourself. I guess it's true then what they say about dragons. You really are base, timid creatures at heart. The world will be better off without you.'

'So be it,' Morgwm said, blinking her long eyelids once. 'But don't think that this is the end. This is the beginning.'

She turned, briefly taking in the bush where Benfro hid. If she knew he was there, she made no more sign than to close her eyes one last time, then she turned back.

Benfro wanted to scream, wanted to run through the band of warriors and flatten them, yet something in his mother's demeanour stopped him. That and the palpable sense of fear and foreboding that swamped his senses. Before he could do anything, the inquisitor had conjured a blade of pure white light from nowhere. He raised it high above his head, the air singing as it was rent asunder. Then, with almost contemptuous ease, he brought it down in a silent arc, meeting no resistance whatsoever as it severed Morgwm's head from her neck.

Acknowledgements

It has taken a very long time to get my little dragon into print, and a lot of people have helped me along the way. It was my long-suffering partner, Barbara, who first looked at the Welsh for Pembrokeshire and suggested that it was the perfect name for a dragon. My brother, Duncan, was an early supporter of the books, giving me much useful feedback over the years, and reading them to his children, Fingal, Hector and Magnus. I am also hugely indebted to Stuart MacBride, not least for his sage advice regarding sheep and their lack of credibility as evil villains.

Dreamwalker, like several other of my books, was first published as an ebook under my own imprint, DevilDog Publishing. Thank you to everyone who bought that edition, and double thanks to those considerate readers who alerted me to errors in the text.

Unlike that first edition, this printed book is very much a team effort. My agent, the effervescent Juliet Mushens, took on the challenge of finding a publisher. Alex, Sophie and all the team at Michael Joseph have honed my prose and polished the book until it gleams – if any errors remain then they're down to me. A big thanks to you all for making real this story that has been a part of my life for over a decade now.

And finally, I have taken monstrous liberties with the language, place names and mythology of Wales in creating this book. To the people of that wonderful country, my apologies. It was too good an opportunity to pass up. Diolch yn fawr i chi pawb!